HARD FALLS

HARD FALLS

DEPUTY RICOS TALE #5

BY

ELIZABETH A. GARCIA

IRON MOUNTAIN PRESS

HOUSTON, TEXAS

_____

Hard Falls
A Deputy Ricos Tale, #5

First Printing
10 9 8 7 6 5 4 3 2 1

ISBN-13: 978-1517727208
ISBN-10: 1517727200

Edited by Lee Porche

Illustrations by
Judy Singleton Probst

Cover Photo By Tim McKenna

Iron Mountain Press
Houston Texas

Dedicated to Joyce Pattishall,
a remarkable woman and my beloved aunt.

About Deputy Margarita Ricos

Margarita Ricos is a 25 year old sheriff's deputy in Brewster county West Texas. She's smart. She's courageous. She has a lot of heart. She's a *Chicana* with attitude who grew up on the edge of the United States. There, the peoples and cultures of two countries are blended, more than separated, by the once-fierce Rio Grande.

Terlingua is an unincorporated settlement built around a mercury mining ghost town of the same name. It lies in the southern part of Brewster County, the largest county in the largest state in the lower forty-eight. It has more square miles than inhabitants and more mountains than you can count: tall, short, wide, narrow, jagged, rounded, naked, stunning mountains.

Margarita and her partner, Deputy Barney George, are entrusted with preserving the peace and upholding the law in a land where the flowers and people grow wild.

Because Margarita was raised on the edge of the United States, she has a broad perspective of "the border," its people, and its issues. In spite of its problems, she chooses to remain in the vast land of mountains and desert, a muddy, winding river, fiery sunsets, unique dangers, and indescribable beauty.

Margarita is an advocate of justice and fairness in a world that is neither. She takes comfort in the steadfastness of the scenery she adores and her love for and commitment to her community.

Other Deputy Ricos Tales

"One Bloody Shirt at a Time", Deputy Ricos Tale #1 - won "Best Crime Novel of the Year" Texas Authors Association 2014.

The Beautiful Bones, Tale #2

Darker Than Black, Tale #3

Border Ghosts, Deputy Ricos Tale #4, won "Best Crime Novel of the Year", Texas Authors Association 2015.

Other Titles from Beth Garcia

"The Reluctant Cowboy "

"The Trail of a Rattler"

Acknowledgments

One of the riches brought to me by writing is new friends. Two of these are Tim and Julie McKenna. They began as loyal readers and quickly moved into the category of true friends. The stunning photograph on the cover of this novel is Tim's and is used through his generosity.

Thank you to all the people who encourage me with your calls, letters, Facebook comments, and emails. Some days you are what keep me going in spite of "writer's block" and other frustrations. You make me smile, grin, laugh, and even cry. You make me feel like I can fly.

I'm indebted to my first readers, who see my work before it's ready and "roadworthy." Thank you for helping me to get it right and for bugging me to "keep writing."

Ralph Waldo Emerson wrote, "Nothing can bring you peace but yourself." Writing is my way of doing that. It also brings me joy, lots of it, in act of "making things up" and in the finished story. If you enjoy what I write, my joy increases until there is not enough laughter, happy dancing, or singing to express it. In other words, readers put the icing on my cake.

Thank you to Iron Mountain Press for taking another chance on me. In truth, I think it's Deputy Ricos they believe in. Or else she's holding them at gunpoint.

Dino Price created the cover of this novel and did a great job. Thank you, Dino.

The beautiful artwork on these pages is the work of Judy S. Probst. It was a gift to me, and to all of us.

Lee Porche is my hard-working editor. Thank you for editing my work with such diligence and good humor. It helps so much that you enjoy reading what I write.

There is one more person to whom I am grateful, Tony Franco. He created my website and keeps it fresh and informative. He thinks of important things that never occur to me. He even likes my books! Tony, what would I do without you?

This is a work of fiction. No character is somebody you know. I even move the scenery when it suits me, so please don't take things literally. Also, I feel I must say that there is no "McFarley Ranch." Like Cimarron Mountain, McFarley Ranch is in my head. I'm not pointing fingers at anyone. I simply entertain myself and hope that in the process, I also entertain you.

Peace and love,

Elizabeth A. (Beth) Garcia

In the Big Bend Country, 2015

Ways to reach me:

By email: beth@elizabethagarciaauthor.com

Facebook: https://www.facebook.com/ElizabethAGarciaAuthor

My website: http://www.elizabethagarciaauthor.com/

Pinterest: https://www.pinterest.com/garciabeth/

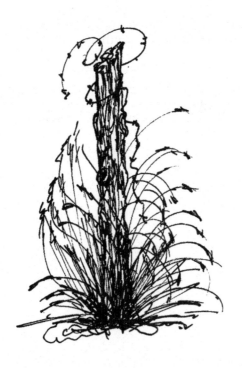

Chapter 1

I don't want to.

Oh, grow up. It's your job. You have to.

I knelt beside him and stroked his head, then ran my hand over it once more and down his smooth gray neck. His bright eyes followed every move I made as if he knew what I had to do.

A vehicle had hit a burro and sped away from the scene, leaving him to die. A passing motorist with a kind heart and a satellite phone called 911, and that had brought me to the scene. The poor little fellow was injured past any hope of putting him back together. A person didn't need a degree in veterinary medicine to see that, although we were fortunate to have Dr. Dave in Terlingua. I called him because he is a kind, gentle man and can put an animal down with a painless injection.

The doc was my first choice, but when a recording answered my call, my heart sank. Our vet retired from a full-time practice a few years ago and is in his office when he wants to be. Most likely he and his wife were out riding motorcycles. It was a perfect March day for it. The sunshine was bright and warm but not yet hot. The jagged mountains that poked up in all directions were sharply defined against the deep blue of a cloudless sky. Bluebonnets carpeted the sides of roads, hills, patches of desert, and any other place they found to their liking.

I sat on the side of highway 118 in my Sheriff's Office Ford truck. Since I wanted to be alone, passersby stopped to see what was going on. Wasn't it obvious? To top it off, my satellite phone bleeped. I didn't want to talk to my boss, either.

"Did you do it?" asked Sheriff Ben Duncan.

"Yes."

"Are you okay?"

"Yes."

"Margarita, you don't sound so great."

"It had to be done and I did it."

"His owner just called me."

"His owner?"

That he had an owner was a surprise. There is a herd of wild burros, tough escapees from Big Bend Ranch State Park, and I thought he was one of them. The state had decided to remove the animals because they're not indigenous to the area. I didn't know all the reasoning behind it, but they had started shooting their burro population. A few had evaded that fate and were now hanging out on and around the Terlingua Ranch Resort and Highway 118. They caused various problems and now lost their lives in other ways.

"Vidalia Holder says he belongs to her," said the sheriff. "She wants to take him to a vet."

I groaned. Ms. Holder could be a problem; she took pride in being a problem. She loved animals but was not as fond of humans. I got that, but she took it too far.

"If he's hers, why is he out here on the highway?"

"Who knows?"

"Sheriff, not even Dr. Dave could've saved him."

"I'm sure that's true, but this is Vidalia Holder we're talking about."

"He had two shattered legs and probably internal injuries. He was suffering. If she'd seen him, she'd have begged me to shoot him."

"The problem is that she 'wasn't given a chance to see him.' She demands to have a say in things affecting her animals."

"How could she know about this so soon?"

"How does anyone in Terlingua find out things the way they do?" The sheriff's voice was strained, as though someone was standing on his last nerve. For once I didn't think it was me. "It beats the hell out of me, Margarita."

"I hope she's not coming here."

"She is, so please wait for her."

"I have to wait anyway until the crew comes to remove the body."

"Right." He took a long breath. "I thought you said there was no brand on him."

"I didn't find one, but I couldn't turn him over. Even if I could've lifted him, there's no way I would have. He was in too much pain."

"She's threatening to sue me over this."

"I'm sorry, Sheriff Ben, but she doesn't have a leg to stand on." Just like her poor little busted-up burro.

"That won't stop her, Margarita."

I knew that was true.

Fifteen minutes later Ms. High and Mighty Vidalia Holder arrived on the scene. Her truck careened to the body of her burro and screeched to a halt that left marks along the highway. She jumped down and left the door open in her haste.

I took a deep breath and went to face the squall.

She stomped towards me, anxious for battle. "What in hell were you thinking?"

"Ms. Holder, please move your truck off the highway."

"You weren't thinking; that's your problem. You're so excited to use that shiny new pistol of yours you can't see straight. You shot my Buddy!"

"Ms. Holder, look at his injuries and you will see that—"

"Shut up, you hateful little girl! He was an innocent animal."

"But look at him! He's injured past—"

"I knew you'd be this way if you got into law enforcement. What is wrong with that stupid, stupid sheriff?"

"Please be reasonable, Ms. Holder. I—"

"Shut up! I'm going to sue you and that ignorant old man, too." She was on a roll and didn't want to hear facts. Reality is whatever she chooses it to be. Forget the facts. Who needs 'em?

After she chewed my ass, she pulled out her satellite phone, dialed the sheriff, and chewed his. She tried to tell him the burro had not been injured in the way I claimed. Also, she accused me of acting out of ignorance and worse, malice.

My boss knew better than that. He called me when the snarling rampage was over. "Is she still there?"

"She left in a cloud of burning rubber and hot air."

"What an unpleasant woman. I guess you heard her say you were lying about his injuries and love to shoot anything that moves."

"I heard her, Sheriff. I have photos showing the extent of his injuries, and I have witnesses."

"Yes, but regardless of any of that, she's going to sue us."

"Why is she suing you?"

"Didn't you hear her yell that I'm an incompetent old man who needs to get his head out of his ass?"

"I think she's sweet on you, Sheriff."

He laughed, but his final words on the subject were, "You shot him, Margarita. I want you to talk her into withdrawing the lawsuit."

That's so unfair! "How will I do that?"

"I know you can. Just put your mind to it."

I was as likely to talk the stars down out of the sky.

* * *

My reward for a hard day's work and a long run is the fiery adiós of a Big Bend sunset. I lingered on top of the sandstone bluffs near my house. They jut up out of the desert and tilt towards the sky, but back on earth they form one side of the small but impressive Tres Outlaws Canyon.

While up there gawking, I noticed a man across from me on the other side of the chasm. I rarely see other humans when I run, and never there. He appeared to be a lawman and reminded me, in dress and bearing, of my Texas Ranger father, Zeke Pacheco. But this man had a camera and it was pointed at me. When the stranger realized I'd busted him, he waved and yelled something. It might have been friendly, but the wind yanked his voice away and it disappeared somewhere out in the desert. I waved back and smiled.

He walked out of sight and I turned my attention to Cimarron Mountain, a mountain among mountains. In this land of layer upon layer of astounding mountains, that's putting it up there, I know. You can have your favorite mountain and I'll have mine. Cimarron is like a friend who knows me and loves me anyway. I can lean on its strength and it never asks anything in return. Its natural beauty and quiet peacefulness are there for me, always.

High on the bluffs, I'm face-to-face with it, so to speak, so we're more equal. Well no, "equal" we are not. The mountain is huge, jagged, multi-layered, and littered with broken-off boulders, rockslides, wildflowers, and cacti. It has scar-like canyons cut into its sides from coursing water during torrential rainstorms. In contrast, I'm small and have one small scar from a bullet wound on my shoulder. I'm not impressive or imposing, and I can't be seen from a long distance. Nobody will ever stand in the Chisos Mountains of Big Bend National Park and think, "Oh look, I can still see Margarita!" but they will still be able to see Cimarron.

When I ran back home, lengthy shadows were falling across the dirt road. I half-expected a stranger to grab me, but I made myself put one foot in front of the other and tried to take control of my criminal mind. By the time I reached my house the mountains had become dark splotches against a fading sky and the golden glow had faded to gone.

Running makes me feel powerful, unstoppable in a way nothing else does. It also makes me feel happy for no particular reason. I shouted, "Woot!" and turned a couple of cartwheels in the road in front of my house. I was upside down with my shirt over my face when I realized I'd seen something that was wrong.

Someone was standing on my porch.

My knees went weak, but then my friend Craig Summers called, "It's me, Margarita."

I sucked in a relieved breath. "Craig!" I ran up to him and gave him a hug. He was clean-shaven and smelled of Zest, but his jacket carried the scent of campfire smoke. Craig is an outdoorsman, an observer and lover of the natural world. Enclosed rooms, heating, air-conditioning, and houses with roofs are fine if you want them, but they're not for him.

He looked concerned. "Did I frighten you?"

"I couldn't tell it was you at first."

"Wouldn't it help to leave the light on?"

I stepped inside and clicked on a living room lamp. It spread a muted glow to the porch that didn't interfere with night-watching. "Sure," I said, "but I never think to turn it on because it's not dark when I leave."

He gave me an exasperated look and sat in one of the rockers.

His bearing tempted me to say, "At ease, soldier," but I kept it to myself. Other than black combat boots, he was dressed more like a civilian than usual, in blue jeans, a red flannel shirt, and blue wool jacket.

"Should I put on a pot of coffee, Craig?"

He grinned. "Sure. Thanks."

"I guess you want it so strong the smell of it will keep me awake all night."

He chuckled and nodded. That's the way he likes it.

"Hey, you want to come in? I'm going to change into warmer clothes."

"I'll wait here," he said. "Look at the sky."

Once night overtakes day in Terlingua, it is seriously dark. We have no light pollution so the stars are a wonder: bright, twinkly, and they seem close enough to reach up and touch. Whoever wrote "The stars at night are big and bright" must have been sitting on a hill in the middle of my desert.

I returned to the porch wearing leggings, a heavy sweater, and carrying two mugs. One held steaming coffee and the other tea.

"Thanks," Craig said when I handed him a mug.

I sat next to him. "So what brings you?"

Craig is not a person who "visits." He's a reclusive man in his sixties, whom I've known since I was eleven. He's had a hard life that includes being in Viet Nam as a Marine. He endured a POW camp, torture, a daring escape, and things I don't know. Craig is a layer of mysteries maintained by silence and secrets. Every year he reveals a bit more of himself to me. The process is too slow to suit my curious nature, but there is no point in pushing him. I love him like a relative although he's not related to me by blood.

His only answer to my question was to sigh and take a sip of coffee.

"Is everything all right, Craig?"

"Now that I'm here, I don't know what to do."

"What's going on? You're scaring me."

"You should see this." Craig handed me a photo.

It made me feel sick. In it, I was standing on my porch talking to the sheriff. He was wearing his uniform and had an engaged expression on his face, typical Sheriff Ben. I was wearing running shorts. Only. My shirt had been removed. At least my back was to the camera, but that didn't change the suggestive nature of the picture.

At first I couldn't speak. Then I exploded. "What in hell?"

Craig chuckled because I don't usually curse around him or curse at all. "I think that big guy is rubbing off on you." He was referring to my deputy partner, Barney George, and yes, he was.

"This has been Photoshopped," I said, making an attempt to be calm.

"What is that? Is it done with a computer?"

"Yes; it's done with a computer and a special program."

"It looks real."

"I would never take my shirt off in front of Sheriff Ben, Craig. Not ever. You know that, right?"

"Of course; that's what I thought."

"This was taken when he came by a few days ago. It was an innocent visit about Sheriff's Office business, and I was wearing a shirt."

"Who took it?"

"I have no idea. Someone was spying on us." I thought of the man on the other side of the canyon.

"Someone could be watching us right now for all we know."

"Please, Craig. I'm freaked out enough." I felt like I was in one of those dreams where you show up in class naked. "What is the point of this picture? How did you get it?"

"It was on the bulletin board at the Post Office. What I don't understand is why somebody would think to pair you up with a man older than your father. He's as old as me."

Sheriff Duncan is in his mid-sixties. He's tall with thick white hair and blue eyes. He's a good-looking man, but he could be my grandfather, and he's my boss. Also, he's married, happily, with children and grandchildren.

"Well, it's not unheard of," I pointed out.

"But he's your superior officer."

"Yes. That would make it even more inappropriate. Someone is trying to make trouble, either for him or me or both of us."

A dark look passed over Craig's face. "Who would do that?"

"I don't know."

"What should we do?"

"I don't know, Craig. I guess there's nothing to do until we see what happens."

"Do you think the sheriff knows about this?"

"I hope not." For me, a scandal would be just another aggravation in a long line of them. There was always something. The sheriff had more to lose.

"Should you warn him?"

"I don't know. I need to think about it."

We sipped from our mugs in silence while watching a night scene so perfect it defied anything bad ever happening.

* * *

When Craig left, I wanted to drink. Maybe I would have a shower first.

I went into my house and did a strip search of it. I found keys, change, CDs, and a tube of lipstick, but no liquor. I had long ago gotten all alcohol out of my home. I knew that, but I searched in case something had been overlooked. The more I looked and didn't find, the angrier I got.

I took a hot shower and dressed in leggings, lined boots, and an over-sized sweater. I ate whatever I found in my fridge that didn't require preparation: cottage cheese, yogurt, an apple, a slice of my mom's double-chocolate cake. Then I made a mug of tea, grabbed a warm jacket, and went onto my porch to drink it. As I rocked, I remembered how much I used to enjoy adding a splash of Jack Daniels to my tea. I would drink anything with Jack in it.

Okay. Take a deep breath.

After I calmed down, I started to call Barney but decided against it.

Cimarron Mountain had become a large, dark stain against a backdrop of winking lights. I calmed myself by savoring the tea—it was Raspberry Zinger—and studying the stars. For each exceptionally bright one, I named a reason not to go to a bar. There were many. An obstinate part of me wanted to name reasons to go, but I got in out of the cold and called Zeke instead.

It's aggravating, but I have two fathers. One is Miguel Ricos. He raised me and I call him Papi. The other is Zeke Pacheco and I call him "Zeke." Zeke is my biological father, but I've only known him a little over a year. Long story. Dad, Father, Papa, Daddy, Pa—all those terms belong to Papi. I need an affectionate name for my Other Father, but until I think of one he's "my Zeke."

"Hey Zeke," I said when he answered.

"Hey, sweetheart," he responded in a voice full of sleep and love.

"I'm sorry I woke you."

"I'd rather talk to you than sleep. What's up?"

I started to tell him about the awful photo and that some low-life was trying to stir up trouble. I wanted to tell him about the innocent creature a coward had left for dead by the road. And that his owner was threatening to sue me, and all I'd done was what I thought was the right thing, the humane thing. And she was suing the sheriff for not firing me on the spot. I wanted to whine to my Zeke that these things made me feel sick and made me want to drink to forget them.

My next thought was that instead of those things, I should describe the way the brilliance of the stars transforms the mountains and desert and how, in an inexplicable way, the stars transform me.

"I just wanted to hear your voice," I croaked past a lump in my throat.

"Are you all right?"

"Yes."

"You don't need to lie to me."

"I'm okay. Did you talk with Max tonight?"

"Oh yes. I speak to him every night."

Zeke and I had recently met my grandfather. For his entire life, Zeke thought he'd been abandoned and had no parents. His father, Maximiliano Pacheco, lives on a ranch in the foothills of the Sierra Madre near Ciudad Chihuahua in Mexico. It took effort to find him but we had. It was amazing to watch Zeke and Max together and to be a part of them.

After he told me about their conversation and that Max had sent me his love, my father said, "I think you need to get a sponsor." He was referring to AA, and it was eerie the way he heard things I didn't say.

"How did you know I was obsessing about drinking?"

"It's late and you sound…wrong…somehow. I know the signs." Then he added, "As your father, I can't be your sponsor."

"I don't trust anyone enough."

"Pick someone and give them a chance. I think it will help. Have you been going to meetings?"

"Yes."

"Does it help?"

Yes, amazing as that was. I always assumed an Alcoholics Anonymous meeting in Terlingua would be a gossip-fest, and that anything I said would be on the street the next day. And not just "out there" but morphed into a drama I'd no longer recognize as mine. The reality had been different. As far as I could tell, nothing I said ever left that room.

Zeke suggested I do something for me, anything I would enjoy that didn't include drinking or obsessing about drinking. So I went onto my porch with another mug of hot tea. It was March and a cold breeze blew from the north, enough to force a normal person inside. I needed my time out there, cold, hot, or in-between. The wind could howl and snow could blow on me for all I cared. Bring it on.

The desperate need to drink eased its grip. I dismissed the topless photo as just more yada, yada from local troublemakers. The night sounds of the desert were more interesting. There was peaceful quiet except for the occasional call of a night bird, the yip of a coyote, or the soft sigh of the wind.

Cimarron was standing firm. For now, so would I. I went to bed.

Chapter 2

I never got along with the former school superintendent, Dena Jablonski. She believed girls should behave like "ladies." I knew, even then, that there are as many kinds of girls as there are stars in the night sky.

Long pants make sense for playing and sitting on the floor and for just about everything, but Old Lady J expected dresses at school. She demanded demure behavior and for girls to be quiet. I proved over and over that girls can sing, shout, and curse just as loud as boys.

Ms. Jablonski resigned as superintendent when her older brother was arrested for stalking and murdering young women. For reasons only she knows, she never questioned his penchant for "following girls." She didn't think that was stalking, and she didn't believe he would harm anyone.

The D.A. chose not to prosecute her. He thought it was a question of bad judgment more than criminal behavior. "If being stupid was a crime, a shitload of people would be in jail right now."

I don't know if the school board would have kept her on. We'd never know now.

"Margarita." She seemed surprised and not pleased to find me at her door, even though she had called the Sheriff's Office that morning.

"Yes Ma' am."

"Come on in."

We followed the gray-haired, wide load into her living room. It had been ten years since I graduated from Dena Jablonski's high school, but I still felt guilty in her presence. *It wasn't me!*

"Sit," she barked.

Before we sat, I introduced her to Buster, a deputy trainee along for the lesson, except I told her his name was Richard Mayhew because it was. Even though Buster was twenty-one, he looked younger. He was a big mess of freckles and unruly red hair flecked with gold. His eyes were bright green, but it was his hair that was really somethin', not that I studied it or anything.

Barney, our fellow deputy, claimed Buster was so young he didn't shave yet and maybe he didn't, but who cared? He seemed anxious to learn the job and that was the bottom line, not how he looked.

Jablonski examined him up and down with her watery blue, judgmental eyes. She saw a law enforcement officer who looked sharp in his uniform. When her eyes moved to me, I think she saw a girl wearing an identical uniform, but misbehaving.

I sat. "What can we do for you, Mrs. Jablonski?"

"One of the teachers, Bradley Jennings, is missing."

"Why didn't Ms. Petrie call?" Lilly Petrie is the new superintendent. She's Ms. J's longtime buddy and clone.

She glared at me. "I told her I was going to call."

"What makes you think he's missing?"

"He didn't come to a mandatory workshop on Saturday and he always calls in if he's going to miss. Nobody seems to know where he is. They've been calling him and never get an answer."

"Has anyone checked at his home?"

"Of course not!" She waved her hand, dismissing the idea. "That's your job."

I reminded myself to breathe. "Is Bradley Jennings married?"

"No. His wife died a long time ago."

"So he lives alone as far as you know?"

"Yes, as far as I know. Don't you know him?"

"No, I don't believe so. How long has he been here?"

"He's had a place out at Terlingua Ranch Resort for a few years, but he's taught here for only two. I hired him."

"What does he teach?"

"English Literature and also a couple of composition courses. What does that have to do with his disappearance?"

"That's hard to say. If we're going to look for him, we'd like to know something about him. Do you have a photograph of him?"

"Yes." She left in a huff and shut the door on her way out.

"I guess she's getting us a picture of him," Buster commented.

"Or she's giving us a time-out."

"What?"

"Oh, nothing."

"You went to school in Terlingua, didn't you?"

"Yes, all twelve years plus kindergarten."

"So you know her?"

"Yes."

"And you don't like her?"

"No, I don't. She's mean and hates kids."

"I don't think she likes you, either."

"You're right; our dislike is mutual. In my senior year I voted her 'Most Likely to Star in a Recurring Nightmare.'"

Buster chuckled at that.

"She hates me more than ever because her brother is in prison for murder. She believes I put him there to get back at her. The law and a judge put him there, not me."

"But you arrested him."

"Do you think I should've let him keep on stalking and murdering women?"

"Of course I don't think that." Buster took an audible breath and changed the subject. "Were you a bad student?"

"No. I was a good student. She thought my behavior was unbecoming a girl."

He snickered but in the interest of peace, I ignored it.

Soon Jablonski was back with a photograph of Bradley Jennings. He was a nice-looking man with light brown hair and gray-blue eyes and he wore glasses.

"How old is he?" I asked.

"He's forty-eight. This is the photo he submitted with his C.V., and I think it was taken a few years ago. He looks a little older now but basically the same."

"The kids are probably giving him gray hair," commented Buster. It was just an attempt at levity, and he didn't deserve the look Jablonski gave him. He would learn. That was why he was with me on a call that only needed one deputy.

"What does he drive?" Buster asked.

"He drives a blue Volvo station wagon, an older model."

"Who are his friends?" I asked.

"How would I know that?"

Because you know everything that goes on at the school, you old bat.

"If he's not at school," said Buster with calm professionalism, "and not at his house, we need to know where to start looking."

"I have no idea where to look. Isn't that something you should figure out?"

"Yes ma'am," Buster agreed, "but it's a big world. Anything you can tell us will help us narrow our search."

The old battleaxe sighed as if we had showed up unannounced to waste her precious time.

"You called us, Ms. Jablonski," I reminded her. "Do you want us to find him or not?"

"Of course I want you to find him."

"How tall is Mr. Jennings?" I asked when she didn't volunteer anything else.

"I don't see what his size has to do with anything."

"If we see him somewhere, we want to recognize him," Buster explained with sweet patience I wished I possessed. "It helps to know what we're looking for."

"He's a small man. He's a little taller than you, Margarita. To you youngsters he would probably seem old."

I stood. "We'll take a ride out to his house to see what we find." I felt sure he would be there ignoring Jablonski's calls. It's what I would do. Maybe he was drinking. When I was in first grade our teacher drank vodka out of his coffee cup until he got fired. But in fairness to Jablonski, she wasn't the superintendent then. In fairness to Mr. Sorenson, he was a good teacher in spite of his vodka habit.

"Please let me know what you find," Jablonski said.

"I'll give you a call after we check out his place."

She dismissed us without standing, offering her hand, or thanking us. It was a relief to get out of there.

"What is a C.V.?" Buster asked first thing.

"It stands for curriculum vitae, which is another way to say résumé."

"Oh. Wouldn't it be easier to just say résumé?"

"Yes, but then you wouldn't be impressed by the old girl's vocabulary, would you, Buster?"

"I'm not impressed now," he grumbled. "People should say what they mean."

I called the dispatcher in Alpine, our county seat. It's eighty miles away and where the Sheriff's Office is located. Our office in Terlingua, Texas is an extension of that one. I explained to him where we were going in case we were needed. Barney had the day off, so no one was at the office. In an emergency, people could call 911 or they could wait.

Terlingua Ranch Resort, referred to locally as Terlingua Ranch, was once a working cattle ranch. During the 1960s, it was sold in parcels of five acres to whole sections. It was promoted as a peaceful get-away and a great place to hunt; but that was before hunters decimated the population of nearly every wild animal on its more than two hundred thousand wild, rugged acres.

The ranch can be entered in various places, but we were headed to the main ranch road. It's about twenty miles from our office to the Terlingua Ranch turn-off on Highway 118. I asked Buster to drive so he would remember the way in the future.

Some parts of the ranch are so remote they can't even be reached by four-wheel-drive vehicles during some parts of the year. Dirt roads cross arroyos and go up and down mountainsides, and are difficult to maintain even in the best weather. Often our rains come in torrents that wash out roads, bridges, and anything else that gets in the way of the flooding.

The area we serve is so spread out and parts of it so remote that a deputy's day can be eaten up by the travel to and from a call. Today wouldn't be too bad because the Jennings home was only a few miles off the main road. Still, it took about forty minutes to get there.

It was a crisp, bright day, cool enough to need a sweater or light jacket, but not cold. It was one of those typical early spring/ late winter days when everything stands out, and the long-distance vistas make you think you could see into next week.

The teacher's Volvo was sitting under the carport, but nobody came to the door when we knocked. We tried that entrance, another one in back, and all the windows. Everything was locked. When I made a second trip to the rear of the house, I noticed something I hadn't noticed on my first time around. There was a burn barrel about forty yards from the back door and it had recently been moved from a spot more or less fifty yards away; shoved and tugged there, judging by the marks on the ground.

"That was recently moved here from over there," I said.

"How do you know that?"

"Do you see how the weeds are blackened around it but still there?"

"Yeah."

"Come over here and look at its original position."

Buster walked over. "I see. This spot has been cleared off by repeated burnings. Also, I can see where the barrel must have sat for a long time, since there's a round circle with nothing growing in it." He scratched his head. "But what does this tell us about the missing man?"

"It might tell us nothing, but look at this." I had already returned to the barrel. On the ground beside it was a piece of white cotton material that was stained with something that looked like blood. I put on gloves and lifted it while Buster watched.

"How can you tell if it's blood?" he asked. "It could be paint."

"I'll show you if you'll bring the evidence kit from the Explorer."

He went to get it while I poked through the barrel with a stick. I had no reason to dig through it, yet a nagging feeling said I should. With my improvised tool, I fished out a scrap of gold lame. Which meant what? A fancy evening dress? An Elvis suit? Or it could mean nothing at all.

When Buster returned we went to the darkest spot we could find, which was in the carport. I sprayed luminal onto the material and then held it under a small black light. It showed the stain was most likely blood. That could also mean nothing, but it gave us a defensible reason to break into Bradley Jennings' house. I put the material into an evidence bag, laid the bag and other items in the kit, shut it, and headed for the back door.

"I'm going to break out a pane," I said, even though I dreaded going in.

"We could kick in the door."

"Yes, and if we had to get in fast that would okay, but for all we know Jennings is simply away and not in trouble. Why destroy his door?"

Buster shrugged. "It looks cool when they do it on TV."

"Right, I agree, but here in the real world we don't have a reason to bust in like the house is on fire."

When we entered, the smell was overwhelming and one I recognized: death.

"Is anyone home?" I yelled, though I expected no answer. "Put on gloves, Buster." I handed him some. "Don't touch anything."

"I know that."

"I know you do, but it's easy to forget at a real scene. We don't touch or move anything."

"What is that smell?"

It was more an expression of revulsion than a question, but I answered him anyway. "It's blood in a large quantity that has been here a couple of days."

We crept through the house with our pistols drawn and found Bradley Jennings naked, lying face down on the floor of his bedroom. Drying blood that was blackening fanned out around his bashed-in head and lower body, and spatter was everywhere. It was a sickening sight that made my stomach roll. The back of his head was not just bashed in, it had been obliterated. Tears filled my eyes at the horror and sadness of the scene.

I glanced over at Buster. He seemed to be fighting the urge to vomit, so I said, "If you're going to be sick, go outside."

He ran and made it as far as the kitchen.

After a few minutes I went to check on him. He was hunched over the sink.

"I didn't mean to sound callous, Buster. It's that we don't need to have your DNA mixed in with any other that might be here."

He nodded in understanding but didn't speak.

"Try washing off your face. That always helps me. Just take your time and come in when you're ready. You know where I'll be."

I walked around the body in a wide circle. Somebody had caved in the teacher's head with a weighted silver candleholder, or that's what it looked like. It was lying beside him on the floor. There was also blood below the waist, though less than what had come from his head. It made me think his lower abdomen had been stabbed, or his genitals. It was just one more upsetting thought at a scene rife with things to be upset about.

I took out my cell phone to call the sheriff, but there was only one bar. There are too many mountains between Terlingua Ranch and the tower, so cell phones work seldom to never.

I passed back through the kitchen, where Buster was at the sink splashing water on his face.

"I'm going to call the sheriff on the radio, Buster. How are you?"

"I'm okay."

"Why don't you sit at the table until I come back?"

Instead, he followed me out and sat on the stoop while I went to the truck. I used the satellite phone instead of the radio for privacy's sake. We can't give important details on the radio because of people who listen in and want to help, or worse, offer opinions. With only three deputies working we don't have the staff to manage lookie-loos, and the last thing we need is a bunch of people arguing about who did what to whom and when and why.

"Deputy Ricos for SBD," I said when the dispatcher answered. 'SBD' is Sheriff Ben Duncan.

"Call back in five," he responded.

Before I could call the sheriff, he called me. "Did you find Bradley Jennings?"

"Yes sir, but we found him dead. He's been murdered, Sheriff."

A murder in Terlingua is shocking, and it took him a moment to respond. "You found him at his home?"

"Yes. It looks like he was bludgeoned to death with a weighted candleholder."

"Good grief. It must be a gruesome scene. Is Buster with you?"

"Yes sir."

"I'm on my way, and I'm going to notify the Texas Rangers and Barney."

If I had a choice, I would pick Barney, but I kept my mouth shut except to say, "Barney's off today."

"I realize that, but he'll help if he's around. He can lift prints while we look for other evidence."

"Sheriff, if you're busy, Buster and I can do it."

"Buster has never witnessed a true-life murder scene. Are you sure?"

"Yes sir. He'll do fine. I'll show him what to do."

"He knows what to do. It's doing it at a real scene that's hard."

"Right, I know."

"I'll call Barney. You and Buster go ahead and start. I'll be there after a while."

"Okay, Sheriff. Should I call Mitch?" Mitch Dalton is the head paramedic at Terlingua Fire and Emergency Medical Services. He sometimes did the transporting of the dead to the morgue.

"No. The Rangers will want the body taken to El Paso. The hearse will come from there, I imagine. Sit tight for a minute and I'll call you back about Barney."

I took the phone to where Buster sat on the stoop. "Are you feeling better?"

"I'm okay."

"Sheriff Ben is calling Barney to come help us."

"I wish you wouldn't tell him I threw up."

"I won't."

"Really?"

"Why would he need to know that? Besides, I've thrown up. When we go back in there, I still might. There's no need to mention it to Barney either way."

"He already has enough things to hassle me about."

"Listen; he hassles me, too. You just have to stand up to him."

"But he treats you pretty well."

"He does now. But at first he was put out to have to work with a woman, and he let me know it a thousand ways. At least you're a man."

He laughed and started to say something, but the phone blipped.

"Barney will be there," Sheriff Ben said when I answered. "I'm coming too."

"Okay, Sheriff."

"Carry on."

I sat on the stoop a few minutes more, admiring the Christmas Mountains. The man inside was dead, so it was difficult to make myself hurry back to work. Buster wasn't rushing in, either.

Parts of Terlingua Ranch border Big Bend National Park and the scenery is just as awe-inspiring. I guess when the park was laid out they had to stop somewhere, and they stopped just short of the Christmas Mountains. As it is, Big Bend National Park is about the same size as the state of Connecticut, so it wasn't cheated when it comes to acreage. But in this land of wide open spaces, deep canyons, and mountains as far as the eye can see, the area protected by the national park seems like a drop in the ocean.

Buster brought me back from my mini-vacation. "You were saying that Barney hassles you because you're a woman."

"It's not because I'm a woman. It's because I'm a woman in law enforcement." I stood and brushed off my pants. "If you have qualms about working with a woman, I hope you keep them to yourself."

"Well I—"

"Let's get to work."

Buster followed me inside. "I don't have problems working with a woman, as long as she's good at the job."

"And I don't have a problem working with a man, as long as he's good at the job."

He gave me a look that was surprise more than anything.

"It all remains to be seen, doesn't it, Buster?"

"I guess so."

Before we got to work, we opened every window in the house. That helped a little.

"The first thing we do at a scene is take photographs," I said, "because things will get moved or taken for evidence. It's good to have a record of how everything was in case we need it to refer to later. While I'm photographing the body and the bedroom, why don't you go through the house and see what looks out of place or odd for any reason. Don't touch anything, just observe and make copious notes. I know it seems tedious but you'll understand the importance later."

He went to do that while I tried to convince myself that I was only watching a TV crime show, not living in one. I photographed the body from every angle. We didn't turn it over because the sheriff and Barney were coming, and I thought they'd want to see the scene the way we found it. Besides, I didn't want to see his face. The face makes things personal. Once a body has a face, law enforcement is more engaged in finding justice for the deceased. It can also make us throw up. Or cry.

Somebody had been out-of-control angry with Bradley Jennings. Surely the first blow had killed or at least stunned him. But his killer had kept at it until the skull was mush in places.

I left the candleholder on the floor. Then I looked around on the dresser because things there had been disturbed. It was confusing since some expensive jewelry was there in plain sight: a gold watch, some diamond cufflinks, a silver I.D. bracelet, and a gold one. Leaving behind expensive things was wrong for robbery, so what was someone searching for? Also, every drawer in the dresser had been ransacked, but again, it wasn't possible to tell what, if anything, was missing.

After a while I went into the bathroom that adjoined the bedroom. I sucked in a sharp breath when I saw what waited there. Scrawled on the mirror in blood was one word: SORRY. It was a chilling addition to a murder scene that was awful enough as it was. Blood had dripped down the mirror onto the sink. It looked like something out of a horror flick. Did the murderer write "sorry" out of remorse or was he mocking the deceased? Or was it the living he mocked...or law enforcement?

The killer had cleaned up in the bathroom. Bleach was used and the empty container was still there. It appeared to have been wiped down. The entire room had been cleaned except for the mirror. There were several washcloths and towels faintly stained with blood. They smelled of bleach and were now dry. I photographed them but left them where they were hanging.

The medicine cabinet held nothing remarkable: aspirin, bandages, toothpaste, dental floss, condoms, and a prescription sleep aid. There were also a couple of tubes of lipstick, indicative of a woman's presence. Other than that, I found no other female paraphernalia, so it was possible they'd been there a long time. They might tell us something, so I bagged each of them for the crime lab.

Buster ventured to stand in the doorway of the bedroom with his eyes on the wall. "Do you want to hear my impressions, Margarita?"

"Yes, but let's go out and sit on the stoop again." I was no fonder of looking at blood and brain matter than he was…and that smell. Ay, Dios.

Chapter 3

Barney arrived in a mood. Given a choice, I wouldn't have disturbed him on his day off, but that was the sheriff's decision.

"What is the point of having a day off if I'm just gonna be called out anyway?" he grumped.

At six and one-half feet, Barney towers over me and most other people. He no longer intimidates me because I know him well, so the look that stops others in their tracks quit working on me a few years ago.

"Don't blame us," I said. "It was the sheriff's idea."

"You and Buster could handle this."

"I know."

"The sheriff is coming too, do you know that?"

"That's what he said."

"Why did there have to be a murder today of all days?"

"I'm sure Mr. Jennings regrets that his brutal murder inconveniences you."

He gave me a scathing look I ignored.

"Why is the sheriff coming?" Barney wanted to know.

"I guess it's because he's the sheriff and can do what he wants. Stop whining. At least you get to wear comfortable clothes."

Barney was dressed in blue jeans and a polo shirt of a blue shade that couldn't compete with his bluer-than-blue eyes. Also, he wore canvass loafers without socks.

"I was planning to go fishing and drink a lot of beer," he explained when he saw me looking at him.

"I could sure go for a cold one," Buster said.

"How are you holding up at a real murder scene?" Barney asked him.

"Fine." Buster looked over at me to see if I'd contradict him.

"Ricos, did you throw up?"

"Not yet."

"It must not be too bad, then."

"Oh, it's *bad*," Buster said with feeling.

"Come on, Beer Boy," I said to Barney. "We have a lot of work to do, unless you want to wait for the sheriff."

"No. Let's get a move on, Ricos."

Inside, the scene had not improved. I managed to keep my stomach settled and so did Buster, but for a moment, I thought Barney was going to lose it.

"Oh man," he said under his breath, "this is some kind of hell."

Nobody was going to argue with him.

"The sheriff wants you to lift prints," I said to Barney, "but I don't think you're going to find any. Surfaces have been wiped clean."

"What about that candleholder?"

"We haven't moved it, so that remains to be seen."

"Don't you want me to try to get something off it?"

"Yes, but let's wait on Sheriff Ben. I think he would want to see this scene as it is before we move things around. You should take a look in the bathroom."

"Sorry?" he bellowed when he saw it. "What the hell is this, Ricos?"

"I don't know what to think. It could be remorse, but using the victim's blood? That's horror movie stuff."

"Isn't 'sorry' supposed to be the hardest word?"

"Don't you think it is?"

"Well, yeah," Barney agreed. "I sure don't like to say it." He added, "Of course I'm so seldom in the wrong—"

"Spare us," I was quick to say.

"The killer is a fucking freak."

"Thanks, Barn. That narrows it down."

He set down his evidence kit in the bedroom and took a deep breath. "What do you know so far?"

"We know Bradley Jennings was a teacher. He failed to show for a seminar on Saturday and nobody could reach him. Ms. Jablonski notified the sheriff and he called us. Things have been disturbed, but that's mostly in the bedroom. Valuables are still here, including the sterling silver candleholder used to kill him. I don't think this was about robbery, except his laptop is missing."

"How do you know there was a laptop?"

"Because there's an empty space on his desk," Buster explained, "and a power cord to a laptop. The cord is still plugged in."

"I don't guess you found a cell phone or anything like that?"

"No. We found nothing electronic."

"So those things were most likely taken," Barney said.

"Assuming he had them."

"Other than the computer, the rest of the house is undisturbed," Buster said, "except a photo was removed from the living room wall. It was in the middle of a group of other photographs."

"What kind of photos?" Barney asked.

"People. Family, I would guess."

Barney took me aside. "Did you notice the blood below the beltline?"

"Yes."

"Are you thinking what I'm thinking?"

"If you're thinking he was stabbed down there or his penis is gone, then yes."

"Jeez, Ricos, tone down your imagination. I was only thinking he was stabbed. If his dick is gone, there would be a lot more blood."

"Not if he was dead first."

"Ho...ly...sh...it." He drew the words out. "Should we turn him over?"

"I think we should wait on the sheriff since he'll be here soon. If the man's penis *is* gone, he doesn't need it now anyway."

Barney started to laugh then shook his head slowly, as if disgusted with me for not getting it. I did though. It was past horrifying.

Buster and I dug through the trash container in the kitchen. The only thing that was possibly relevant was a framed photograph of Bradley Jennings with another man. The glass had been cracked but was still intact. The subjects were on a boat and had their arms draped over each other's shoulders. Jennings was holding up fish they had presumably caught. The other man was holding two beers. They looked about the same age, maybe brothers.

"I think this solves the mystery of the bare place on the wall," I said.

Buster shrugged. "Maybe it just fell off."

"Maybe, or somebody took it off and smashed it in anger."

"But what's to be angry about in that picture?" Buster wondered.

"I don't know. We don't have enough information yet, but we need to bag this as evidence anyway. The frustrating thing about investigating is that you have to sift through a lot of stuff that will end up meaning nothing."

We didn't find anything else of interest in the trash, but we determined that the cracked photograph was from the wall. It appeared to have been wiped clean of fingerprints, so somehow it was significant. Or else it wasn't.

By the time our boss arrived fifteen minutes later, we didn't know much more than we had known when Barney got there.

Sheriff Ben was wearing a black Stetson and a black, western-style jacket. He looked sharp enough to cut through quartz. His shiny badge was pinned to the jacket and he was wearing his gun belt. Everything was black: hat, boots, vest, coat, pants, and shirt. He was the Man in Black, western style. All eyes watched him, and we stayed as silent as the man on the floor.

Our sheriff stepped up and offered his hand as he always did, and I took it as I always do, but that photograph crossed my mind and I felt myself blush hot. It was awful. The sheriff gave me a quizzical look and then grinned, which made it worse. My face was on fire by the time I got away from his hand.

Because I couldn't bear to look at him, there was a roomful of Sheriff Ben. At six feet tall, he's not an unusually large man, but he might as well have been Paul Bunyan. When blue-eyed Barney walked up next to him in that bright blue shirt he was wearing, I thought of Bunyan and his blue ox and nearly started laughing. Then, we three deputies followed our sheriff into Bradley Jennings' bedroom, but one of us was about to spontaneously combust.

After Sheriff Ben got a long look at the scene, Barney and Buster helped him turn the victim over. I gasped to see the extent of the damage: his genitals were not cut or stabbed. They were gone. We gaped in silence.

I busied myself taking photographs, but it was a wonder any of them turned out. I was pointing and shooting without looking through the viewfinder. I did not want to see that scene. It was so mortifying I felt paralyzed.

"The fact that he's naked and emasculated is significant," said the sheriff in a voice that can only be described as horrified. "Then there's the 'sorry' on the mirror." He cleared his throat. "All of these things implicate someone who had an intimate relationship with him."

"Or he'd just come out of the shower and a prowler attacked him from behind," Buster suggested with new-guy enthusiasm.

The sheriff turned to him. "Why would a prowler take the time to remove the man's genitals?"

"Oh. Well, someone went through all his things," Buster countered in defense of his theory. "Of course, we don't know if anything was taken."

"Someone took the family jewels," commented Barney, the Brewster County Sheriff's Office champ when it comes to gallows humor.

"We can't rule out anything yet," said the sheriff, "but I don't believe a stranger killed this man. I think things in the bedroom were disturbed in order to make it look like a random burglary, but my guess is it's personal in the extreme."

While Barney began trying to lift prints, Buster and I went over our observations with the sheriff. That didn't take long. Then we moved outside to the burn barrel. Sheriff Ben agreed that something significant might have been burned, so the three of us turned it over and sifted through it. We recovered bits of clothing, photographs, and a couple of belt buckles.

"His killer might have been a woman who burned her bloody clothes after she bludgeoned him," I said, even though there seemed to be more than one set of clothes, and even though it was hard to think a woman had committed that violence.

"Jennings could have been burning these things before he was murdered," said Sheriff Ben, "and it's even possible that this is unrelated to his murder."

"Maybe his girlfriend left him and he burned whatever she left behind," added Buster. "It's obvious someone angry killed him, so maybe he was angry with her, too. Then later, she came back and killed him."

"That's one possible scenario." The sheriff's expression was thoughtful. "We need to find out if he had a girlfriend, and if so, get her name and address." Of course our sheriff meant for Buster and me to do it; he uses the royal 'we.'

"It's also possible," I thought out loud, "that he had a boy-friend."

Buster slapped his palm against his head. "I never think of that aspect."

I wanted to laugh but chewed on my bottom lip instead. Then I told the sheriff about the lipstick I'd bagged, which I thought supported the theory of a girlfriend or some other woman involved.

Barney slammed out the backdoor. "No prints. Every hard surface has been wiped down. It's also significant that there are no defensive wounds. Somebody surprised him."

"Nothing from the candleholder?" asked the sheriff.

"No sir. The crime lab might find something, but I think it was wiped clean."

Sheriff Ben ran his big hand through his all-white hair and took a deep breath. "We have a teacher murdered brutally by someone who was furious with him. It was overkill if I ever saw it. But whoever did it had the presence of mind to clean up afterward. Because of the nature of the items in the burn barrel, and because the victim was naked and emasculated, we're leaning towards someone who had an intimate relationship with him, such as a wife or girlfriend or other lover. But keep in mind that the burned items may have nothing to do with the murder. Who else could Jennings have made so angry?"

"A student," Buster suggested. "Teachers make kids angry sometimes, but no, a kid probably wouldn't remove a man's equipment. I hope." His hand automatically crept to his own equipment, but I think it was unconscious.

"It could have been an angry neighbor," I added, "but that seems unlikely too."

"Any family member," said Barney.

"The thing that makes those suggestions feel like they don't fit is the hack job," I said. "Neighbors, students, and family might kill someone, but to remove the private parts? I don't think so. I think it was someone he had offended with those parts."

"I believe you're right, Margarita." Then the sheriff asked our trainee, "So what should the next move be, Buster?"

"We need to know a lot more about the dead man."

"That's right. I'm going to call the school and see if Mr. Jennings had next of kin we need to notify. While I do that, I want the three of you to make a list of all the people we need to interview. And Buster, the other deputies know this, but in case you don't, there is to be no mention of the missing genitals or the writing on the mirror. Understand? We have to keep certain details to ourselves. Sometimes guilty people slip up and give themselves away. If someone mentions either of those details, we have them."

"Yes sir; I understand."

By the time the sheriff returned from making his call, we had a pretty good list going. He perused it and seemed to approve, but he added one name: Iva Cooper. "Her house sits up on the side of that mountain back there." He indicated where. "She watches with binoculars. I bet she can tell you some things, but you'll have to go at her gently."

I always marvel at how much our sheriff knows about the people he serves, even when they live in out-of-the-way places. Barney explains it by saying he's everywhere and knows everything, like God.

"She's reported a few things to me," the sheriff said as if he knew I was wondering about it. "She can be a bit difficult, so tread carefully."

"Should we call her before we go?" Buster asked.

"I would, yes. As to the others on your list, there's no need to warn them. Just pop in and see what they say."

"What did you find out from the school?" I asked.

"As far as they know Mr. Jennings has no close kin. They don't know of a girlfriend, but they wouldn't necessarily know anything about that."

I thought they sure as heck would, but I kept that opinion to myself.

"The funeral home is sending the hearse," Sheriff Ben said. "They'll take the body to the crime lab in El Paso. Barney, I want you to supervise the loading of the body, and then you can resume your day off. Thank you for coming. Margarita and Buster can begin interviewing the people on the list. I'll be in touch later."

"Okay, sir," Barney said and went back inside.

I took a deep breath. "May I speak with you a moment, Sheriff?"

"Sure. You want to come over here by my truck?"

I followed him to it and we leaned against it. I wanted to ask him about his new look, but it was none of my business and I sensed he wouldn't like the question.

For a few seconds we watched the sun shining on the mountains. An occasional cloud passed overhead, plunging a brilliantly illuminated spire into shadow. Then, as if by magic, the sun was back and some new thing would catch its fancy. All day long the sun and clouds play these games on our scenery.

"Is this about the lawsuit?" he wondered. "I knew you'd think of something."

"No sir. I don't have any idea what to do about that." Now that I faced him I didn't want to tell him. "Last night this photo was brought to me by a friend who removed it from the Post Office bulletin board in Terlingua." I handed it to him, but I had to force myself.

The sheriff looked at it. "Goddamn it!" I'd never heard our sheriff use that expression. He glared at it. "Goddamn it to hell."

I sucked in a breath. "Also, Sheriff, when I was out running yesterday, I saw a man who appeared to be photographing me."

"Did you speak to him?"

"No sir. He was too far away."

"What happened?"

"Nothing. He was across a canyon from me and he walked off. I ran home."

He waved the photo at the mountains in an angry gesture. "This is from the other day when I was at your house. As I recall, you were wearing a purple t-shirt with some kind of logo on it."

"Yes. Bat wings."

"I beg your pardon?"

"It has gold bat wings…a Batman shirt."

"Right." He ran a hand through his hair. "What the hell?"

"I don't know what to think. Maybe it's a joke or something."

"Is that what your gut tells you?"

"No sir. My gut says something is up and it's not good."

"Mine says the same thing."

"What's the point," I asked, "other than to stir up gossip?" That wasn't even a new thing. When I was first hired, some people couldn't understand that a man can hire a woman because he thinks she can do the job and not because he wants to sleep with her. In my experience, men who get passed over tend to use that "rumor" to make themselves feel better about losing a job to a woman.

"Gossip is the point." The sheriff sighed. "I thought we were past all this."

"I did too. Do you have any idea what's going on?"

"Well, I have an idea, but I don't know for sure."

"Can you tell me?"

The sheriff looked so sad I felt terrible for him. "Yes, I can tell you, but not here and not now. Can I catch up to you later? I'll be in Terlingua a while. Will you call me when you get back in cell phone range?"

"Yes. I'll do that."

"For right now, please don't mention this to Barney or Buster or anyone else."

He didn't need to worry about that. "No sir, of course I won't."

If Barney got hold of something this scandalous, he'd make me wish I lived on a different planet, and Buster, well, I can't mention sex around him because he badly needs a woman to teach him a thing or ten. He wants it to be me, but oh, hell no.

"Josh is coming and he'll take the evidence bags to the lab. I want you to stay here until he gets through with the scene." Josh Middleton is a Texas Ranger stationed in Alpine.

"Yes sir."

"Don't forget to lock up the house and put up the crime scene tape."

"We won't."

"I know you won't, Margarita." He looked forlorn and I didn't know what to say. Then he cleared his throat. "Thank you for having the good sense to keep this to yourself. I'm sorry to see you treated this way. It's so disrespectful."

That's our sheriff. He's a real gentleman in a world where they seem to be in short supply.

"It's okay, Sheriff. No harm has been done."

"No," he said, "not yet."

He drove away and left me standing in the driveway to wonder.

* * *

Buster and I showed Josh around the Jennings home and yard. He spent a long time looking at the body and then made his way through the house.

He called me over to the refrigerator. "What do you think this is about?"

"What do you mean?"

He indicated dishes stacked to the side. There were casseroles, a couple of pies, and three small cakes. All of it was covered but was growing mold. The freezer held more of the same, minus the mold. "Somebody tagged this food 'from Honey' and put a tiny heart next to her name. A few bites are missing from each dish, but other than that, nobody was eating it."

"Maybe Honey is a bad cook," I suggested.

"But why bring him food? Did he have a recent death in his family?"

"Yeah," Barney yelled from where he was working in the next room, "but he's the one who died." He waited a beat and added, "And somebody cut off his junk."

Josh laughed. "I don't know how you put up with him."

"I don't know either."

"I heard that, Ricos!"

We decided that someone named Honey had a crush on Bradley Jennings and brought him food that he didn't eat for some reason.

"Maybe Honey was trying to poison him," Buster suggested, "and he got suspicious. When he wouldn't eat her cooking, she offed him with a candlestick."

Josh's eyebrows rose. "There's a theory, Buster. If you wanted to kill a lover, would you leave your name on poisoned food?"

"Well, no. That would be stupid."

Josh took a sample from each dish for the crime lab to check because, "People do stupid things or we might not ever catch them."

Except for the food, Josh was noncommittal, but he asked for our thoughts. They were mostly along the lines of being horrified that we'd had such a brutal murder in our community.

After that, he looked over the evidence we'd gathered. We had the scraps of cloth from the burn barrel, along with pieces of photographs, and belt buckles. There was also the bloody scrap of material I'd lifted from the ground.

Barney had put a comb, a hairbrush, and two toothbrushes into separate evidence bags. He took them with the hope that a lover, and possible killer, might have used one of those things.

The towels and wash clothes had been bagged as well. There was the smashed framed photo and the bag containing the two lipsticks. The last of the bags contained swabs of blood, a few hairs, and lint that Barney had taken from the deceased's hair.

Sheriff Ben had summoned our Justice of the Peace, and when he arrived he knocked once and came through the back door. He's the closest thing we have to a coroner, and the only function he serves regarding the dead is to pronounce them as such. His happier duties include marrying people and serving as a local judge for small claims and misdemeanors, such as traffic tickets.

Chuck is a short, wide man with a pot belly and a pleasant disposition. Barney refers to him as "Chunky Chucky," but not to his face, of course.

"Can we get this over with?" Chuck asked after he greeted us.

Barney led him to the bedroom and handed him a handkerchief to put over his mouth and nose, not that it would help much.

Only a few minutes had passed when Chuck flew out of the house as if Bradley Jennings' ghost was chasing him. "Adiós, y'all," was his breathless good-bye, along with a wave of his puffy hand. When the door slammed, Buster and I cracked up.

Barney came out of the bedroom shaking his head. "Chuck has a worse aversion to dead bodies than you do, Ricos."

"I doubt that."

The hearse came to transport the body to the crime lab in El Paso. Barney and Buster made sure the dead man was respectfully loaded into it while I helped Josh put the evidence bags into his truck.

After the hearse left, we sat around in the yard talking about the things we were supposed to be doing instead of sitting around talking.

Buster and I had interviews to do, so we told Barney we had to get going. He claimed he was going home to "fish in the river and drink beer" or, as he would later admit, just to drink beer.

Chapter 4

When I called ahead, as the sheriff instructed, I thought Iva Cooper relished the prospect of a visit from law enforcement. I didn't tell her the particulars on the phone, only that we needed her help regarding a neighbor. I think that appealed to her nosy nature because more than likely, she had already seen the Sheriff's Office vehicles at Jennings' home.

Before we had a chance to knock on her door, a spindly woman with a nose like a beak opened it. Her hair was short, straight, and blue-gray in color. She brought to mind the great blue herons that poke along the banks of the Rio Grande.

"Mrs. Cooper?"

She frowned. "I'm *Miss* Cooper, but come in, please."

I introduced us and we followed her into a living room that was old-fashioned in the extreme. The velvety, dark purple furniture was at least as old as she was. What wasn't covered in plastic was adorned with white, lacy doilies on the arms and headrests. I took a look around, trying to be casual, but the old woman busted me.

"Sit," she commanded sternly.

"I was admiring all these photographs." I had never seen so many in one room. They covered the walls, sat in front of the books on bookshelves, and were prominent on every table. They seemed to be mostly of one boy, with all ages represented except adult. If there were some of him as a grown man, I missed them because Miss Cooper was rushing me.

"That's my brother Bailey. He died."

"I'm sorry."

She didn't want me looking at her memories and herded me towards a sofa the way a determined cow dog would.

"He was very handsome and smart, my Bailey. He was fifteen years younger, so I helped raise him. We adored each other." She repeated her command to sit, except she added, "please."

I sat.

"I guess you work with that tall, handsome Sheriff Duncan?"

"Yes ma'am."

She sighed. "Too bad he's married."

Buster looked over at me, but I wasn't touching that comment.

"How can I help?" she asked.

"Sheriff Duncan said you might've seen people coming and going from Bradley Jennings' home. Do you know Mr. Jennings?"

"I don't know him well, but I've looked after his house for him."

"So the two of you are on friendly terms?"

"Yes, he's a good neighbor, a very quiet man. Sometimes we talk about birds. I'm a birdwatcher, you see. That's why I look around with binoculars."

Okay, we'd buy that for now. Buster glanced at me; he was suppressing a grin.

"He's not in trouble, is he?" she asked, breathless.

"I wonder if you've noticed anyone at his home in the last few days."

"Can I get you something to drink? I have sweet iced tea, and of course, hot tea. I could make coffee, or perhaps you'd enjoy a cold pop?"

"No, thank you," Buster said.

"We're fine," I said, "but feel free to get something for yourself."

"You were asking if I've seen anybody with Brad recently, and the truth is, I have. A few days ago, Dena Jablonski visited him and not for the first time."

"The former school superintendant?" I blurted.

"Do you know another Dena Jablonski?"

"No. I apologize. It was just a surprise."

Miss Cooper leaned closer to us, as if to impart a secret. "She was a frequent visitor of late. I believe she's quite sweet on our Mr. Jennings. She brought him a chocolate layer cake, and the time before that, oatmeal cookies, I think."

"Did Mr. Jennings ever indicate to you that he's romantically involved with Ms. Jablonski?"

"Oh, no, I don't think he's interested in her in that way. She had been his boss, for one thing. Besides, he has several other women pursuing him." Ms. Cooper was enjoying our undivided attention. "I don't think he's very taken with any of them, either."

"Do you know someone named Honey?"

She gave a snorting laugh. "Oh yes. Honey pursues Brad like a bird dog after a quail. She doesn't have a prayer, but that hasn't stopped her."

"What is her last name, Miss Cooper?"

"Pugh."

I almost blurted, "For real?"

"She lives a few miles from Brad, but driving over never bothered her. She would do anything for 'her' Brad."

"When was the last time you saw him to talk to?" I asked.

"I saw him a week ago Saturday at the potluck supper at ranch headquarters. That floozy, Flora Smith, was throwing herself at him as always. He's polite, bless his heart, but I don't think he has any interest in her, either."

"Where does Flora Smith live?"

"She lives across the road from Brad. Hers is the white house with turquoise trim." Miss Cooper leaned even closer and spoke in a whisper. "Truth is I saw her go over there a couple of nights ago. She thinks she's clever, sneaking around in the dark, but she carries a flashlight so she won't step in a hole."

"How do you know it was her?" Buster asked.

"Because the light came from her house and bobbed over to his."

"I see," he said, and his eyes flicked to me and back.

"She was looking in the windows."

"So you don't know if she went inside or not?" I asked.

"No, I can't honestly say. I've seen her over there, day and night, looking in the windows. What do you make of that?"

"I don't know, ma'am," Buster said, "but we're going to speak with her."

"I think she's a sex pervert," the old woman hissed. She sat back in her chair with a satisfied expression. It gave the impression she'd wanted to tell somebody that for a long time. "I can say with one hundred percent surety that she is."

"Do you know if Mr. Jennings had any enemies?" I asked, trying hard not to lose it.

"I can't answer that because I don't know. Why do you ask?"

"I'm sorry to tell you this, Miss Cooper, but Mr. Jennings has been murdered."

"Murdered?" Her hand flew to her mouth. Then she jumped up. "It was Flora!"

"Why do you say that?"

"He didn't want to have sex with that hussy, so she killed him." Her hand went to her heart. "Or maybe he did have sex with her and… Oh no, he wouldn't have."

"We'll be speaking with Ms. Smith," I assured her. "Can you think of anything else to tell us about Mr. Jennings that might lead us to his murderer, assuming it's not Flora Smith. Do you know if he had family?"

"He had a brother in San Antonio. He spoke of him once or twice. I don't think they were close, but I imagine Brad left him everything."

"So his parents are deceased?"

"Yes, they died quite a few years back."

"Do you know anything about his wife?"

"He never had a wife."

"Oh, I was under the impression he did."

"He told me he'd never been married, because I asked, you see."

"I see. Is there anything else?"

"I believe that on a matter of this import, Sheriff Duncan should have come himself. You tell him I said that."

"I will, Miss Cooper, but he's busy. I'm sure that's why he sent us."

"Tell him I saw him down there at Brad's, and I made sweet tea for him. He loves my tea. If he comes by later I'll make fresh."

"I'll tell him. Please call us if you think of anything else."

She took my arm on the way to the door. "Be sure you tell him, all right?"

"Yes ma'am, I won't forget."

"You'd better talk to Honey. She's clueless, but she might know something."

"Yes. We will."

Once we were back in the Explorer, Buster sighed. "That ol' broad needs to get laid. Do you think she's ever had sex? I bet she never has."

"Your point being?"

"Maybe she'd mind her own business if she had a sex life."

"Sex is not the answer to every problem."

"Name one it wouldn't help," he challenged.

Naturally, I couldn't think of one, so I put the ball back in his court. "Maybe you could help an old lady out."

"Very funny, Margarita."

"It was just a thought."

"I can't stop thinking about that crime scene. Why would someone take a guy's dick and stuff? Wasn't that the grossest thing you've ever seen?"

"Yes, it was."

"We're not just looking for a murderer. Somebody in this community ripped out a man's business and took the whole package with them!" Buster was riled.

"Yes. It's sickening."

"So what do you think they're doing with it?"

"Nothing, I hope. Could we stop talking about it?"

"What if we walk in somewhere and see genitals in a jar?"

"We make an arrest."

"What about that former superintendent? Would she be the type to keep a man's dick in a jar on her desk?"

Totally.

"Maybe that sex pervert Flora Smith has them," he continued without taking a breath.

"Slow down, Buster. Don't jump to conclusions based on what one person says about another. But we'll go see her and also Honey Pugh."

"What kind of name is Honey Pugh, anyway?"

"It's weird. We should also see the other closest neighbor, Roger Feldman."

"What about getting something to eat?"

"After seeing that scene, you still want to eat?"

"I always want to eat. I'm starving."

"We could stop at that little snack place by the highway."

"Don't let me die," he whined and fell back against the seat as if faint from hunger. Great; I was working with another joker.

* * *

It was getting close to sunset when Buster and I arrived at Ms. Jablonski's house. She wasn't happy about it.

"Sheriff Duncan already told me you found him dead," she said with a show of the attitude that makes her so unpopular.

"We're aware of that," I said, "but it's our job to follow up."

She sighed with woeful impatience. "Come on in."

Buster and I sat without being invited because it didn't appear she was going to invite us, and we weren't going to stand around like her loyal subjects. Without realizing it at first, I found myself glancing around for a jar with Bradley Jennings' genitals floating in it.

"Mrs. Jablonski, why didn't you tell us you were a frequent visitor at Bradley Jennings' home?" I asked.

"What difference does that make?"

"Don't you think it's relevant to tell the whole story and not just pieces when you report a person missing?"

"How do I know what's relevant? That's your job. You didn't ask me if I'd ever been over there."

Ay-yi-yi...

"Did you know he was dead when you sent us out there?" I asked on a hunch.

"I might have."

"Might have? You either did or didn't!"

"All right, yes, I knew he was dead."

"Why didn't you call in his death instead of pretending he was missing?"

"I thought you'd think I killed him."

"Why would we think that?"

"Don't you always suspect the person who reports a murder?"

"We interview them, but reporting a murder doesn't make a person guilty. We look at a lot of other factors too. Do you know if anyone was angry with Mr. Jennings? Had he had words with someone?"

"No. He was a kind man. I can't imagine how he would've made someone angry enough to kill him."

"What about a fellow teacher or a student?"

"A student?" That got her going. "I can't imagine a child being so brutal."

"I don't like to think that either, but it's a possibility," I said. Several seconds passed. "Were you aware that you weren't the only woman bringing Mr. Jennings gifts of food?"

I had never seen Old Lady J blush. Then she sniffed. "Yes, I was aware of it."

"Did it make you jealous?"

"What are you implying?"

"I'm not implying anything. It was a simple question."

"I felt jealous at first, but I soon figured out he wasn't interested in any of us except as friends. His heart had been broken and he wasn't ready to let anyone else in. He made it clear."

"What were you doing two nights ago, Ms. Jablonski?" Buster asked.

She gave him a scowl that makes little kids wet their pants, but when he didn't recoil or wet his pants, she answered. "I was at home."

"Can anyone verify that?"

She glanced at me, wide-eyed. "No. I was alone."

"When did you discover his body?" I asked.

"Yesterday evening. I was worried he might be sick."

"How did you get into the house?"

"The back door was unlocked."

"Did you lock it when you left?"

"Yes."

"Did you touch the body or move anything?"

"Are you kidding? It was almost dark. When I saw that body on the floor, I couldn't get out of there fast enough."

"I still don't understand why you didn't tell us the truth to start with."

"It's suspicious to know about a murder and not report it," Buster added in an accusing voice.

"I didn't think of that." She touched her hand to her hair in a nervous gesture. "I thought you'd jump to conclusions." She was looking right at me when she said it.

"We don't do that," I said. *Off with her head!*

* * *

Buster and I took our conclusion-jumping bones back to our office. Ms. J. didn't tell us anything we didn't know, and claimed she had no idea who had been burning clothes out back or why. Nor did she admit to knowing what was missing from her friend's home. As much as I wanted the guilty party to be her, I didn't think she did it. It was clear the old biddy had been in love with him, or at least fond of him. In spite of my dislike of her, I felt her sadness

"Yes. I'm sorry to tell you this Manny, but they'll tell you at school tomorrow. Mr. Jennings was murdered."

He sucked in a breath. "Murdered?"

"Did you ever have him as a teacher?"

"Sure, I had him last year and this year. He's a great guy—was a great guy."

"Have you ever heard anyone speak angrily about him?"

"Sure, kids get angry with teachers. He was a good one, so he gave us a lot of homework and writing assignments and junk. But I never heard a kid speak about killing him. You don't really think it was a student, do you?"

"I'm just asking questions. Did Mr. Jennings ever speak of his personal life?"

"No, I never heard him say anything about it. All I know is that someone he loved died a few years ago. I think it was his wife, but he doesn't talk about it."

"Then how do you know that?"

"I overheard Mrs. Jablonski tell another teacher."

"Can you remember what she said?"

"She said Brad wasn't ready to date anyone because he had lost a great love, or it was something like that."

"What teacher was she speaking with?"

"It was Ms. Warrington. Ms. Warrington kinda liked him, I think."

"If you hear anything or think of anything that might help our investigation, will you please call me, Manny?"

"Sure. Of course I will." He paused. "Margarita, it seems unreal that somebody would've murdered Mr. Jennings. It makes me so sad."

"I know, Manny, and I'm sorry to have to tell you such bad news."

I collapsed into the overstuffed chair in my office, put my boots up on the desk, and stared out the window at Cactus Hill. In the Big Bend Country, darkness doesn't fall as much as ease itself in. After the flaming sunsets, a golden glow lingers, daylight making its last stand. That was the scene I witnessed on my hill. It never ceases to amaze me how things out there stay so perfect, so orderly, or how quickly the study of that world brings peace into mine.

I don't know how long he'd been standing there when I became aware of a tall lawman in a full-length duster blocking my doorway. His tooled leather holster and service pistol were eyelevel with me. He was holding his black hat and looked like a sheriff from an old western movie. All he needed was a horse and a swagger.

I jumped to my feet. "Sheriff! I was sitting here thinking." At least it was true.

"And what were you thinking?"

"It seems as though the more I understand the more I realize how little I understand and will probably never understand. And then I wonder if, when I'm really old, absolutely nothing will make sense."

He laughed and pointed a finger at me. "You're on to something."

There was a short, awkward pause.

"Would you like to have a seat, Sheriff?"

"No. Yes. I guess so." He sat.

I looked at him. He looked at me. I expected him to say something. He didn't.

"Sheriff?"

"Yes." He seemed miles away.

"You said you might know what's going on."

"Somebody sent the photo to Marianne." Marianne is his wife.

"Oh Sheriff, I'm sorry. So this is going to be a thing."

"Yes. It'll be a shit-storm, I imagine.

"Marianne doesn't think that photo is real, does she?"

"No. She knows better." He hesitated then said, "I need to go home. We'll talk later. Can you trust me until then?"

"Yes, of course I trust you."

"I trust you too," he said. "I'll be in touch soon."

"I'll be here, sir."

He repositioned his hat and tapped the brim. "Carry on."

I resumed my position in the chair-with-a-view. The moon had already risen and looked pinkish in the fading light.

The only motive I could think of for causing scandal where none existed would be to wreck Sheriff Ben's marriage or his career. But why in the world do either thing to a small-town sheriff? And why use me to do it?

Chapter 5

The following day Buster and I continued our interviews with Bradley Jennings' closest neighbors. When I say "neighbors," don't think of the suburbs. The houses on Terlingua Ranch are widely spread, but in some areas they're visible from each other. That was true of where Brad Jennings lived. Flora Smith's house was at least the equivalent of three city blocks from his house; Miss Cooper's was much farther.

I know you can't tell about a person by their looks, but Flora Smith hardly seemed a sex pervert type. Nor would I have pegged her as a likely murderer. She was a plumpish, blondish, fortyish woman with a pleasant round face. She came to the door dressed in tan slacks and a green pullover, and with a friendly smile on her face. At least she hadn't been watching through binoculars, because she seemed surprised to have deputies at her door.

I introduced Buster and myself and she invited us in. My partner's eyes wandered the room, looking for jarred genitals, I presumed.

Once we were settled, I started the interview. "Ms. Smith, when was the last time you saw Bradley Jennings?"

She gasped with the surprise of it and blushed. "Why are you asking me that?"

"Please answer the question," I said gently.

"I saw him three or four days ago."

"Were you at his house or was he here, or was it some other place?"

"I went to his house to say hello. We often dropped in on each other."

"You haven't seen him since?"

"A few nights ago I baked lasagna and my recipe makes so

if you'd be willing to go there with us and take a look to see if you can tell what's missing."

"Do you mean right now?"

"Well, yes, if that's convenient. It would be a big help."

"Will I have to see his body?"

"No, ma'am, his body has been taken away."

"I just don't think I could bear to see him dead."

"I understand."

"Was he shot?"

"No, it appears he was hit in the back of the head."

"Who on earth would do such a ghastly thing to sweet Brad?"

"That's what we're trying to figure out."

I thought Buster was daydreaming, but he surprised me by asking a question. "Is it true that you looked into Mr. Jennings' windows day and night?"

"Well no, who told you that? Of course I didn't!" She calmed down after that outburst. "I used to look in to see if he was home, or busy. Also when he wasn't there, I'd look in to see that everything was all right." She took a breath and spoke again. "Iva Cooper told you that, I bet. She's so jealous of my relationship with Brad. She tries to monopolize him at ranch functions, such as the potluck supper we have once a month, and card games. You wouldn't think such an old woman would be so hot to land a man, would you?"

I didn't dare look at Buster or I would've lost it.

"She mentioned that she house sits for him, yet you've said you did that."

"I did. She never has. Brad didn't trust her."

"Why is that?"

"He felt she'd go through his personal things. She's a nosy old bat who needs a psychiatrist." She stopped speaking abruptly but seemed to have more to say.

"Please speak freely," I said.

"You probably think that's mean, but she has an abnormal love for her brother. Didn't she go on about him while you were there?"

"No, but she did mention him."

"Well, that's unusual. She goes on about him until I started to wonder if they had a sexual relationship. She says he took her everywhere and thought she was pretty. He believed she was brilliant. He died a few years ago, and I think it put her over the edge, if you know what I mean. She has his photographs on every available space in her house. It's creepy. She even has some of his clothes in her bedroom."

"How is that relevant to Mr. Jennings' murder?"

She blushed deeply. "It's not. I apologize. I get frustrated with her." She sighed.

"Did students ever come to Mr. Jennings' house?" Buster asked.

"No. He tried to keep his professional life separate from his home life. He said that was the only way to keep his sanity."

"Were you aware that the former school superintendent visited him several times?"

"Brad mentioned that Dena had brought him baked goods a few times. He said she was interested in him, and it made him uncomfortable. It was wrong, her being in a superior position as his boss. That changed to where she's not his boss now, but he still thought it was inappropriate."

"So they weren't having a sexual relationship, as far as you know?" I asked.

"No. I'm sure they weren't."

"Do you know if he was having a sexual relationship with anyone else?"

"I don't think he was. As I said before, he was still getting over an earlier love. He didn't talk about it, but it was a feeling I got from what little he did say."

"Do you know anything about his background?"

"He came from San Antonio and was a teacher there, too. He bought his place here ten years ago, but only came a few times to check on it. After we met, I offered to watch it for him and he accepted. When I asked, he said he planned to retire here someday. When he moved in two years ago but wasn't retired, I was sure it was because he was grieving and wanted to be alone. That's all I know."

* * *

We entered the kitchen through the rear door of the Jennings house. Flora immediately noticed something missing.

"There was a photograph in a beautiful frame on the counter by the canisters. It was of Brad, his brother, and another man."

"Do you know who the other man was?"

"No, and I never asked. I thought maybe it was a brother who died."

"What made you think that?" I asked.

"I guess it was because there had been so much sadness in Brad's life."

"I see."

In the living room, photographs were missing, according to Flora. "The side tables used to have a few photos," she said. "I never paid much attention to what was in them, but I can't imagine why they'd be gone. Why would someone break in, kill Brad, and take photos that have no value?"

Yeah, I was wondering that too.

Flora opened a closet door in the living room. "All his nice suitcases are missing. Of all the..."

"Maybe they were used to take away his things," Buster suggested.

"He had a set of expensive leather suitcases, and he kept them right here."

We could see the empty space where they had been.

"People don't get murdered over suitcases and photographs," Buster declared, "or not usually anyway."

I agreed with a nod of my head. It was weird.

I had second thoughts about taking Ms. Smith into the bedroom, but she said she could do it. I went ahead to shut the bathroom door. Then I tried to stay between her and the pool of blood on the floor.

She thought two significant photographs were missing from the bedroom. She couldn't decide if anything had been taken from the bureau but gasped when she opened a beautiful walnut wardrobe. "Half of this has been emptied!"

"What was there?"

"I'm not one hundred percent sure, but I believe his wife's clothes were here. At any rate, a woman's clothes and shoes were here and now they're gone."

Buster and I exchanged a look. I believe "burn barrel" was the thought that passed between us. Chances were high that those were the clothes that had been destroyed. What, if anything, did that have to do with the murder?

Buster and I wanted to look around a bit longer, so Flora Smith decided to walk home. We thanked her for her help and asked her to call if she thought of anything else we needed to know.

"What did we learn from her?" I asked Buster after she'd gone.

He thought about it for ten seconds. "We should make sure our drapes are closed all the way."

I laughed. "No kidding. That was a little freaky but at the same time, she seems harmless."

"She needs to get laid just as bad as her horny friend, Miss Cooper."

"I bet they can't resist a redheaded, green-eyed man in uniform," I said to shut him up.

"Stop it with the old lady jokes, Margarita."

"I'm just sayin'."

We searched extensively and could not find one thing that seemed to be a clue to the murder of Bradley Jennings.

* * *

Honey Pugh lived eleven miles from Jennings in a small but attractive house made from a prefab storage building shaped like a barn. It was even painted like a barn. A white planter at the end of her drive held a metal sign that read "Home of Honey Sue Pugh."

Buster laughed. "Honey Sue Pugh sounds like someone Dr. Seuss made up."

I agreed but reminded him that we needed to keep it together and be respectful no matter what Ms. Pugh was like.

"I guess we can't be criticizing names," he continued. "You're the girl named after a salty tequila drink. And I'm stuck with the name of a dog. Barney is named after that goofy deputy on Andy Griffith. What the hell is happening here?"

I laughed. "I wasn't named after the drink, and Barney was named after his grandfather. If you want to be happy, don't mention Barney Fife to our Barney unless he brings it up."

"I'll remember that."

Ms. Pugh came to the door and smiled at us. "Hello."

"Hello, Ms. Pugh," I said and then introduced us.

The woman was dressed in fading blue sweatpants, a Texas A&M

t-shirt, and leather hiking boots. Her hair was the only Dr. Seuss-ish thing about her. It was a light purple shade of gray and some of it stuck out from a short ponytail, but that was all. She seemed as normal and not-a-murderer as everyone else we'd interviewed.

"Do come in." She held the door open.

"It smells great in here," Buster commented as we entered.

"That's my freshly-baked coffee cake." She seemed proud that Buster had noticed. "Would you like a piece?" She addressed both of us.

Buster indicated "yes" and I said "no, thank you" at the same time. He had let the mouth-watering fragrance seduce him while I had remembered the uneaten food in Mr. Jennings' fridge.

Honey brought mugs of coffee and two slices of what she called her "special recipe" caramel-pecan coffee cake. It looked gooey and delicious but I noticed that Buster only took one bite, washed it down with coffee, and then cleared his throat. He gave me a look of distress, so I took the lead in the questioning.

"Ms. Pugh, we're here about the murder of Bradley Jennings."

"Murder? Brad?" She looked wounded. "Brad is dead?"

"Yes ma'am. I'm sorry. I thought you'd know."

She dabbed at her eyes with the corner of her t-shirt. "I was a close friend of Brad's. Why hasn't anyone told me?" She began to cry.

"I'm sorry for your loss. We're here because we found your name on some dishes at Brad's house. We were hoping you could tell us if Brad had any enemies."

"Brad was the kindest man I've ever met. I can't imagine who would kill him. Was he shot?"

"No; he was hit in the back of the head."

She grimaced and then buried her face in her hands and began to sob. "Did he suffer?"

I moved closer and put my arms around her. "I don't think he suffered. It appears he was hit with a heavy object. I think the first blow probably knocked him unconscious."

"Who would do that to a man like Brad?"

"That's what we're trying to find out," Buster said, making a comeback. He made a knife-across-the throat gesture and pointed at the cake.

I grinned and nodded.

The interview with Honey Pugh took longer than the others but we didn't learn anything new. She cried and continued to wonder out loud who would've done such an awful thing. She didn't even know how awful.

Ms. Pugh, like Ms. Jablonski and Ms. Smith, had been in love with "sweet Brad Jennings." She, too, understood that he'd lost a great love and wasn't ready for a new one. That hadn't stopped her from hoping.

On the way to the next interview Buster said, "I wonder what his secret was that made all the single women so crazy about him. Do you think he had a giant—?"

"Haven't you been listening?" I interrupted. "Brad was kind to them. That's a seductive trait in a man."

Buster looked incredulous. "You're saying his secret weapon was to be *kind?*"

"What a concept, huh?"

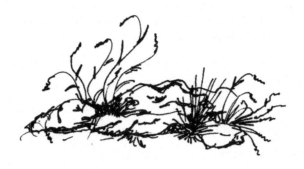

Chapter 6

"I bet Mr. Jennings never told Honey she can't cook worth a dime," Buster mused a few minutes later.

"Was the coffee cake that bad?"

"Let me put it this way. Cooking is not that lady's strong point. Poor Brad."

I laughed at that.

We pulled up at the home of Roger Feldman. When he saw the yard, Buster whistled low. "Like rodeo much?" was his single comment.

Sun-ravaged saddles were slung over the porch railing, and various styles of leather chaps, dried and cracking, were stapled to the wall of the house, along with lariats, bridles, and reins. Rusting spurs hung from the porch ceiling. There were two weatherworn mechanical bulls in the yard. Both of them had seen better days, long ago better days. Feldman's place was so aggressively cowboy in style it caused me to doubt that he was one. He had a rifle though, and met us at the door brandishing it.

I held up my badge. "Please put the weapon down, Mr. Feldman. We're Brewster County deputies Ricos and Mayhew, and we're only here to ask you a few questions."

He poked the rifle at us. "Get the hell off my property!"

"Are you Roger Feldman?"

"Who wants to know?"

"I just explained who wants to know. Now put the weapon down."

"Get the hell out of here! I own this ranch, free and clear."

"Nobody is disputing that," I said, "but you have to put that rifle down *now!*"

"This is still America! No little Messican girl is gonna come 'round telling me what to do in my own home."

Buster started towards him. "Now you listen here, you old—"

I grabbed Buster's arm but addressed the old man. "Mr. Feldman, we can do an interview here or take you to our office. Either way, we are going to interview you."

"On whose authority?"

"Sheriff Ben Duncan. We're his deputies."

He looked me over. "We took Texas away from the Messicans."

"Yes sir; I'm aware of that, and we're not here to take it back."

A snorting laugh escaped Buster and then he coughed hard.

"What are you here for?" he asked me. Then he addressed Buster. "Who the hell are you?"

"I'm Deputy Richard Mayhew."

"You ain't old enough to be no deputy."

"We're both deputies," I said before Buster hurt him. "Put the rifle down."

"Kiss my ass!"

"Please be reasonable. If we take you to the office, it'll be in cuffs, and you'll have to stay there until tomorrow, which means you'll be in a cell overnight. It's not comfortable and you won't like it."

"I'd like to know what army is going to take me out of my own damn house. You ain't big enough to move me." He waved his weapon around. "Get off my land!"

Buster had slowly backed away from the door and was starting around the side of the house. He glanced over his shoulder at me; I gave a slight nod. Then I held the old rifleman's attention until there was smashing of wood at the rear of the house. Buster finally had just cause for kicking in a door.

When Feldman heard the racket, his instinct turned him in that direction and I grabbed the rifle. In the struggle it fired into the doorjamb, causing splintered wood and sawdust to rain down on us.

My partner flew down the hall holding his Beretta in front of him. "Drop the weapon!" he yelled.

By then Feldman had lost his weapon to a little Messican girl. Chaos reigned for a few minutes, and then all was quiet except for the muttered cursing of a bitter old man.

We cuffed him and sat him down in his living room. I didn't want to take him in because we'd have to deal with him and then bring him back—all of it wasted effort.

"Should we go ahead and arrest you for the murder of Bradley Jennings?" I asked. "It would be smart on your part to answer a few questions."

"We should arrest him," Buster grumbled. "He refuses to cooperate."

"Give him a minute, Deputy Mayhew. Wouldn't you rather help us, Mr. Feldman?"

"I wouldn't have shot you," he said in a soft voice. That was as close to an apology as we were going to get.

"Threatening an officer on duty after he has identified himself to you is against the law," Buster pointed out with attitude.

"Lots of things are against the law."

"Murder is one of them," I said, even though I didn't think he had done it.

"I ain't murdered nobody!"

"It makes us suspicious when someone refuses to cooperate. You're impeding a homicide investigation."

He scratched his nearly-bald head. "Brad Jennings, you say?"

"Yes. What we want to know is if you've seen anything unusual at his house in the last few days—visitors, cars you didn't recognize, things like that."

"No. I hardly ever look in the direction of his house, so I prob'ly wouldn't notice somethin' odd. Women were always taking him food, but I guess you know that."

"Do you know if Mr. Jennings had one girlfriend in particular?"

"Naw, I never pay no attention to the he and she crap 'round here."

"Were you on friendly terms with him?"

"Not particularly, but we weren't enemies. I didn't know him."

"If you see somebody messing around over there, will you notify us?"

"I guess it wouldn't do no harm."

"Thank you, Mr. Feldman." I handed him my card.

He stopped us as we were leaving. "Say, I wish women would bring *me* food."

"Maybe you shouldn't answer your door with a goddamn rifle shoved in a person's face," was Buster's advice.

* * *

Late that afternoon I was again sitting on my porch after a run. As long shadows stretched across my desert and everything else, I heard an ATV motor coming my way. I sucked in a relieved breath to see that the unknown visitor was my friend Craig Summers instead of somebody looking for trouble.

"Hey Craig," I called as he strode up the path to my house. "Should I put on a pot of coffee?"

He grinned and plopped into the chair next to mine. "Sure. Thanks." His cat Marine stuck his head out of Craig's jacket, looked around, and disappeared again.

"Hi Marine," I said, but he had a good thing going and nothing to say to me. "Was it strong enough last time?" I asked Craig.

"It was perfect."

After I started the coffee, I came back to the porch. "Craig, it's going to get cold tonight. I want you to come here and stay with me a few days." Because of his age and the hard life he's had, I worry about my friend. I can't say much to him about it, but I try to look out for him.

"I'm right as rain where I am."

"You don't have heat and it's supposed to be icy before it warms again."

Craig lives in an unfinished house on a large piece of land I own. It's on a high bluff and gets freeze-your-bones cold and windy.

"You nag me worse than a wife," he complained, but it was in a good-natured way.

I started to rev it up a notch, but Craig asked, "What about Marine?" That question meant he would come.

"Of course I want him, too."

"We'll see what he says about it," he said in his dry way and made me laugh.

When I brought him a cup of coffee, he asked, "Have you found out who took that photo of you and the sheriff?"

"No, Craig. Have you heard anything?"

"Nothing."

"After you finish the coffee, let's go get your things."

"If I have to put up with you, I might as well marry some pushy old gal."

"Once this cold front passes I'll take you to look for one," was my retort.

Chapter 7

"It's cold as a witch's tit." Buster was shivering and complaining as I entered the office the next morning. He and Barney were huddled over the coffee station and didn't seem to notice my entrance. I was in no mood for their crap.

"I wonder why witches don't have two tits like other women," mused Barney. "People always say 'witch's tit,' like there's only one."

"Maybe only one of them is cold," was Buster's take, "and the other one is hot." He touched his chest with a finger and made a sizzling sound.

It's a wonder I didn't groan and charge out of there.

Although I didn't make a sound, they became aware of my presence and put an inordinate amount of attention on getting their coffee right. I happen to know Barney drinks his black. "Cream and sugar are for sissies," was his macho opinion.

"Good morning," was all I had to say about it. I passed them, ducked into my office, removed my jacket, gloves, and scarf, and collapsed into the overstuffed chair. I didn't care whose tits they went on about as long as they weren't discussing mine.

During the night the wind had howled as it dragged a cold front down from the north, kicking and screaming. By morning, heavy gray clouds lolled on mountaintops and oozed over the edges like icing melting off a cake. It was great weather: cold, damp, dark, and mysterious in a way, a welcome change in a land that is beaten down by the sun most of the year.

"I don't guess you got in a run this morning," Buster said, making conversation from the doorway to my office.

"I'd planned to go this evening, but when I woke up and saw the weather, I couldn't wait to get out in it."

His mouth opened. "But why? It's dark and freezing and looks like snow."

"She's weird," was Barney's explanation.

"I love this weather," I countered. "And it's not snowing or raining."

"She'd go even if it was," Barney added.

"Aren't you off today, Buster?" I asked.

"I was thinking I should come in and help with the murder interviews so I could get some experience," he explained. "I'm doing it on my own time."

"That's very conscientious."

"He's doing it to impress the sheriff," Barney said, "and you, prob'ly."

Buster colored a deep red and started to speak, but the phone rang. That took my colleagues away from my office long enough for me to check Cactus Hill. It wasn't high enough to capture a cloud, but a ghostly mist swirled about wetting things. Watching it slink around the trees and boulders felt like looking through hangover eyes: now you see it, now it's fuzzy, oh…now it's back.

I called Bradley Jennings' brother in San Antonio and got an answering machine, so I asked him to return my call as soon as possible. We had expected him to call when he got word of his brother's murder but he hadn't.

"Ricos!"

"Yeah?"

"Want to come out here?"

"Not really."

"Well, come out here anyway."

I sat in a visitor chair next to Buster, who occupied the other one.

"What is it, Barney?"

"There's no need for three of us to go, so why don't you and Buster finish up your interviews on the ranch? I'll canvass the high school teachers to see what they know. I'm also going to get into one of Jennings' former classes and speak with the students, once I get permission from Mrs. Petrie."

"What if she won't give it?" Buster asked.

"Then I'll get a court order."

"She'll cooperate with you, you being so big and blue-eyed and all," I said. "Plus, you were never one of her students."

"You gave her hell, didn't you, Ricos?"

"She would probably say that."

"What would you say?"

"I was just a normal kid."

"Huh. Why am I suspicious of that?"

I grinned, left his desk, and gathered my things. "Let's go, Buster."

"I'll radio you if I find out anything useful," said Barney. "You can call me back on the sat phone when you have a chance."

"10-4, Good Buddy," chirped Buster.

Barney's look was hilarious.

* * *

On the way to the ranch, Buster complained about the weather. "It's not supposed to be this cold here." "It's so gloomy." "Why doesn't it go ahead and rain and get it over with for cryin' out loud?"

He was making conversation or trying to get a rise out of me. I had my own thoughts, quiet ones, and wanted to soak up the weather so I could bring it out and play with it when the sun was hot and pitiless. There's something deeply sensual about the clouds-on-the-mountains days. They make me want to crawl into bed with a good man.

Before long, thunder began growling like the first warnings of a wary dog. Then it boomed and rumbled, and threatened to bring down the already low-slung sky. The day grew even darker, and big drops splashed the windshield.

Buster flipped on the wipers. "Oh, hell, here it comes." I could barely hear him over the crashing thunder.

"You haven't lived here long enough, Buster."

"What is that supposed to mean?"

"We never curse rain. Ever. 'Hot and dry' is our usual weather forecast and sometimes even in winter. Sunny weather gets old, that's all I'm sayin'."

"We shouldn't be having this kind of weather in March."

"The weather does what it wants, especially in March."

"I hate rain. I guess I spent too much time in Lake Jackson."

"Is that where you grew up?"

"Yeah. It rains a lot. Buckets. It's nearly in Louisiana, in case you don't know."

"How did you end up in West Texas?"

"I got a deputy job in San Antonio, but I really wanted to live in a place more laid-back. About that time, I met Sheriff Ben. He came by the Bexar County Sheriff's Office to speak with our sheriff and mentioned he was looking for help in Brewster County, so I spoke up. Did you know that the Bexar County sheriff is his son?"

"No, I didn't know that."

"Yeah, there are two sheriffs named Ben Duncan in Texas."

"What is his son like?"

"He looks a lot like his father except younger, and his hair is still blond. They don't call him Sheriff Ben. He seems like a good guy, but I wasn't there long enough to get to know him well."

I thought having a son become a lawman must make our sheriff proud.   * * *

Buster and I interviewed an elderly couple, George and Jane Pendleton. The Jennings house was visible from theirs, barely. Mrs. Pendleton met us at the door of her expensive home, apologizing for the storm as if it had been her idea. We hung our wet coats on a hall tree and took off our soaked, muddy boots, and left them by the door.

"Why is it that young people refuse to wear rubbers?" she wondered aloud.

We took the wrong meaning and blinked at her in surprise. Then I made the mistake of glancing at Buster. His mouth was open; then he had a coughing fit that doubled him over. I nearly choked myself from trying not to laugh. We were cold, wet, and hysterical at a murder interview—off to a great start.

Mrs. Pendleton seemed oblivious to our breakdown and showed the way into a spacious living room where her husband waited in a wheelchair. We introduced ourselves to him and sat together on a sofa.

When I asked if they had seen any out-of-the-norm activity at the Jennings home, Mrs. Pendleton explained why they hadn't. "George had a heart attack and we haven't been here in the last month, until yesterday. We can barely believe anyone would murder such a kindhearted man."

They told us what everyone else had: everybody liked Bradley Jennings. They were shocked he had been murdered and couldn't imagine who had done it. They would call us if they heard anything or thought of something we should know.

When we left their home the rain had stopped, but we still had to slog through muddy puddles to get back to the Explorer.

"Cold water is seeping through these boots," Buster complained. "My feet are soaked and my toes are frozen."

"Mine, too. It's like Mrs. Pendleton said, Buster. We should've used rubbers."

After that, we went to the only other house in the area adjacent to the Jennings place, owned by young retirees. Fran and Lewis Woods had sold a successful bar and restaurant business in Dallas and were able to retire in their forties. Like others, they had known Bradley Jennings, but they had a different take on him.

"You're asking us about wives and girlfriends," said Lewis Woods, "but we think Brad was gay, or at least I do."

"What makes you think that?" I asked.

"The women around here chased him non-stop and he never took an interest in any of them."

"From what we've heard, he was heartbroken," I said. "That might explain his lack of interest in women."

"Maybe he didn't like pushy old ladies," suggested Buster.

"Well, yes, that's true," Lewis said. "It was humorous watching them compete for him, but heartbroken or not, I think Brad Jennings was gay. It was a strong feeling I had, but maybe I'm wrong."

After a little more 'going nowhere' talk, Lewis added another tidbit. "I never told you this, honey," he said, addressing his wife, "but Brad made a pass at me once."

She stared at her husband with her mouth open.

"It was that time I attended a potluck without you, about three weeks ago. Brad and I were going for the potato salad spoon at the same time. I had my hand around it and he put his hand on mine and gave it a bit of a squeeze. He didn't say 'let's get together,' but the invitation was there—in his touch."

"Why wouldn't you have mentioned it?" Fran was incredulous.

"I didn't give it much thought. Maybe I misunderstood."

"Did Brad's approach upset you?" I asked, even though it didn't seem like it had. A gay man making a pass at a non-gay man could lead to murder. But on Terlingua Ranch, where it's easy to ignore your neighbors? That was a stretch.

"Oh, no," Lewis said. "I wasn't upset. In fact, I thought it was kind of funny, given that all those single women were throwing themselves at him."

"Did Brad ever contact you about getting together?" asked Buster.

"No, and later he saw me with Fran, which would have removed all doubt about the possibility."

Not necessarily.

"I hope that's true," Fran said.

"Oh Frannie, don't give it another thought."

The look that passed between the two made it impossible to believe that either one was capable of bashing a man's head in or hacking off his genitals.

* * *

Buster and I went by the ranch headquarters to the management office of the Property Owners Association of Terlingua Ranch, Inc. They operate a restaurant, motel, campground, showers, and a swimming pool. They also have the daunting responsibility of maintaining the more than two thousand miles of dirt roads that crawl all over the ranch.

Nobody there could think of anyone who would want Brad Jennings dead. Two names were mentioned that we didn't realize were connected to our victim: Tamara Hagan, a relative newcomer to the area, and Vidalia Holder, the owner of Buddy the now-deceased burro, not that either was accused by anyone. Because Vidalia was known and disliked, her name caused the most speculation. She'd been another persistent suitor of our man Brad until they got into it over a horse. An animated discussion among the staff kept us entertained. The consensus was that Vidalia could kill a man over anything, a disagreement about a horse included. I didn't disagree, but it was hard to image she had committed a murder so brutal.

As far as the ranch staff was concerned, Jennings was well-liked and easy to get along with. They knew nothing of his love life except to say that the older, unmarried women of the area chased him, which we knew. He had a great singing voice, which we didn't know or need to know. We left there no closer to solving the murder than when we had arrived, except that we now had other people to see.

We had three more murder interviews to do, but we ate lunch first. When we came out of the Bad Rabbit Café, which is known locally as "The Lodge," big, fat snowflakes were falling. They weren't sticking because of the wet ground, but the temperature had dropped.

"Look at this, Buster! Doesn't it make you want to sing and dance?"

"No, and I hope you aren't going to start."

I laughed. "Where's your sense of fun?"

"We're supposed to be conducting a murder investigation."

"This will probably be the only snow we'll see until next winter."

Buster hunched his shoulders against the cold. "Could we get going? I want to change my socks and shoes."

"By the time we get back they'll be dry."

"Yeah, that's what I figure."

The heater in the truck warmed Buster's mood. He quit complaining and admitted that the scenery was spectacular, even though the sharp peaks of the mountains were playing peek-a-boo in the snow-filled fog.

* * *

By the time we reached the office, the snow had stopped. Not much stuck, but it had been magical to watch.

Buster and I were mulling over the murder when Barney

crashed into the office and dropped his things onto his desk with the usual slap and bang.

"Did you get anything useful?" I asked.

"Not much. How about you?"

"Jennings might be gay," Buster blurted.

Barney collapsed into his chair. "And what brought you to that?"

Buster recounted the interview with the Woods couple.

"Well, it would make sense from the point of view that a male lover would've had the strength to bludgeon someone the way he was bludgeoned. It's hard to imagine a woman being so brutal."

"True," I said, "but a very angry woman could have done it."

"You want to watch yourself around her, Buster," Barney said.

An exaggerated look of knowing passed between the jokers.

"All I'm saying is not to get set on any one theory. We need a lot more information."

"Yes, as in *anything*," Barney said.

"Vidalia Holder was one of the deceased's admirers," I told Barn. He knew her because of past problems.

He groaned. "That figures."

"None of the people we interviewed knew Bradley Jennings well. All people could really say about him was that 'he was nice.' We heard him described as sweet, mild-mannered, shy, kind, friendly, heartbroken, and reclusive. Yet he was killed and mutilated in an exceptionally brutal manner."

Things were not adding up.

"That's what I heard from the teachers I interviewed," said Barney. "I hope when I die I get more than a 'he was nice.'"

"Oh, don't worry," I assured him.

He rolled his eyes.

"We should put all the information we have on a murder board," Buster suggested, "like they do on crime dramas."

Barney gave him a look, but I thought it was a good idea.

"It would help us organize what we know. Maybe that would help point out what we still need to know."

"Yeah…like who did it," Barney grumped, but in the end he agreed.

We didn't have a "murder board," so we sent Buster to the hardware store to see what they had we could use. It's a tiny establishment, so we weren't sure he would have any luck.

While he was gone, a detective with the San Antonio Police Department called to confirm that Dr. Ted Jennings had been notified of the death of his brother.

"He claimed to know nothing of his brother's love life," Detective Sanchez said, "except that Brad had never married as far as he knew. He also claimed that he and his brother had been close. So saying he didn't know about his brother's love life is evasive, wouldn't you say?"

"Yes," Barney said, "I agree."

"That led me to wonder if the brother had killed the victim. I pressed him enough to discover an alibi."

"Which is?"

"He was in emergency surgery twice on Friday, and wasn't able to leave the hospital until around midnight. Since the death was on Friday evening, he doesn't appear to be a suspect."

"True," said Barney, "except that exact time of death has not been determined by the coroner, so the doc isn't entirely off the hook yet."

"Let me know if you want me to do anything else."

"We'll take it from here," Barney said, thanked him, and cut the call.

"If they were close, they would know about each other's love life." I stated the obvious.

Barney agreed. Then he said in an accusing voice, "We're close, but it seems I don't know about your love life."

"And you're referring to...?"

"You know damn well, Ricos—you and our boss."

"I know you haven't fallen for that tired, over-worked rumor."

"Tired? I saw a photo of you with him. Somebody put it in my face. Let's just say I've never had a conversation with you where you took your shirt off."

"Barney, get a grip. Somebody took my shirt out of that photo."

"Why haven't you told me about this already?"

"The sheriff asked me not to."

"Why? Is he feeling guilty?"

"He's trying to keep a lid on a jar that already exploded. I guess everybody's seen it?"

"Yep. The consensus is that it's a damn pity the photographer didn't get your front side."

"You mean the guys at the café."

"True."

"Buster saw it?"

"Buster is crushed. He thinks Sheriff Ben is too old for you and that what you need is a young stud like him."

I groaned.

When Buster returned, he had purchased a 12-pack of cork squares. Before we did anything with them, I said, "Buster, I'm not having an affair with the sheriff."

He held up his hands. "That is not my business."

"I want you to know the truth."

"I don't care what you do with that man." His facial expression and body language begged to differ.

"That's great, but you still need to know the truth. I'd appreciate it if my colleagues would defend me instead of shoving me into the fire." I explained about the Photoshopping.

Buster appeared be listening but I don't think he took in a word because he said, "I wish you'd take off your shirt when you work with us."

I threw up my hands.

Barney said, with a forced-serious face he could barely maintain, "Enough of that talk, Buster. That's sexual harassment and she'll—"

I didn't hear the rest of it because I went in my office and slammed the door so hard stuff fell off the wall.

I stood at my window where at least things made sense. Bluebonnets reigned in the higher reaches of my hill, resulting in patches of purplish blue around the boulders and sticking up out of prickly pear stands. Coming down the slope a few yards, yellow was the dominant color, along with glimpses of white and even a few more solitary bluebonnets. *Ay carajo,* I hate men sometimes.

Spring never lasts long enough to suit me. The moisture we'd had would help extend it, but in no time it would be hot and the bluebonnets would go to seed until next year. Men. Grrr.

Someone pounded on my door.

"I'm busy," I yelled.

Barney opened the door. "Like hell you are."

"Get out."

"We're sorry, Ricos."

"That's true."

"Ouch."

From behind Barney, Buster said, "In all seriousness, we're—"

"Save it, Buster."

"Keep your shirt on, Ricos."

I hate men.

* * *

We attached the corkboard squares to the wall in my office so our 'murder board' wouldn't be seen by visitors. Before we left that evening, this is what we had:

At the top we wrote: Bradley Jennings bludgeoned to death with a sterling silver weighted candleholder, genitals removed. We posted a photo of him from before his demise and the photo Jablonski had provided.

Below that was written: no fingerprints at scene. Computer is missing, along with female clothing, photographs; some expensive items were left behind and some items burned; is that relevant?

Sent to lab:

Two lipsticks, comb, hairbrush, two toothbrushes, various blood swabs, a scrap of cotton containing a bloody stain, ash and scraps of material from the burn barrel, framed photo from the wall, fingerprinting attempts, and food samples taken by Josh Middleton.

Closest Neighbors:

Iva Cooper: a spying busybody. She said Flora Smith and Dena Jablonski had been the most recent visitors bringing food; she claims she house sat for Brad once, but Flora Smith says not.

Flora Smith: in love with victim, regularly shared food, admitted to looking in his windows; house sat for him; seemed shaken and heartbroken over his death.

Roger Feldman: obnoxious old man; didn't know victim but

recognized him in passing. Buster added that "the grumpy old fart" was dangerous.

George and Jane Pendleton: weren't home at time of murder; liked Brad but didn't know him well

Fran and Lewis Woods: knew him from potluck dinners and games nights; Lewis thinks Brad made a pass at him but claims that was never repeated.

Teachers:

Dena Jablonski: reported Jennings missing; knew he was dead. She was pursuing him and taking him food. His death appeared to unnerve her to the point of tears. "She's the type to whack off a man's business." (Margarita's opinion)

Lana Warrington: 45 years old, single; lives in Terlingua, invited Jennings to lunch, dinner, and to help chaperone senior prom last year; brought brownies, pies, and cookies to work; claims she's never been to his home.

Darlene McNally: 32 years old, divorced: lives near Ghost Town; invited Jennings to meals, events, and took a casserole to his house once. Accepted that he was not interested; he was nursing a broken heart, and she quit pursuing him.

Connie Rodriguez: 45 years old, married but not living with husband; lives near the school; same as above except she became interested in someone else.

Lucinda Caminos: 55 years old, divorced; lives on Highway 170 between the Ghost Town and Lajitas; asked Jennings out once and gave up.

Others:

Students from Jennings' class: shocked reaction, say nobody hated him; general consensus is that he was a good teacher who was well-liked.

Dr. Ted Jennings: Brad's brother claims not to know anything about his love life. The doc was working Friday night. "Wouldn't a surgeon have done a better job of removing a man's equipment and not such a hack job?" (added by Buster)

Honey Sue Pugh was in love with Brad and took him food he didn't eat. She claimed not to know about his death until we interviewed her.

Vidalia Holder and Tamara Hagan interviews to follow

Random people at Ranch office and the Lodge: "He was a great guy. He was a real sweetheart." "He was a good singer." "Who would want to kill a quiet, sweet man like him?" "A lot of women were after him, but he seemed uninterested." "His wife died, I think." "He was cute."

Without doubt, Brad Jennings knew someone who wasn't on our murder board. Or else someone on our board was not who they appeared to be.

Chapter 8

The sheriff looked up from his desk and smiled when I walked in the following day.

"Good morning, Sheriff."

"I hope it will be. Sit. You want coffee?"

"No, thank you."

"I'll be right back." He took his mug, so I assumed he was bringing coffee for himself. Our sheriff likes it the way Craig does, strong enough to stand and salute.

When he returned he shut the door. "Will you to do something for me?"

"Of course." I knew he needed something because he'd called me to come.

"It's above and beyond the call."

"What do you need?"

"I want you to go to the county commissioners meeting this afternoon. Do you think you could get up some kind of disguise?"

I hesitated with the surprise of it, and he took it wrong. "I don't want to argue with you so if you'd rather not—"

"Of course I can do that. Your request is unusual, that's all. You don't want me to go as a deputy?"

"That's right." The sheriff dragged his hands through his mass of white hair, not a good sign. "I don't want you going as yourself, deputy or otherwise."

I tried to be quiet and patient. Both are a challenge for me.

He took a swig of coffee and sat back in his chair. His blue eyes were sad. "Everything is going wrong, Margarita."

"How can I help?"

"I don't see how you can." He studied me while one finger drummed the desk. "I've always had enemies. If a man in my position doesn't, then he isn't doing anything. But this is a new level of vicious. The talk is hurting my wife."

"I'm sure she doesn't believe it."

"She doesn't, but it pains her to have people talking behind her back about her cheating dog of a husband."

"It seems as though everyone in this county would know better." His reputation is sterling. He and Marianne have something good and everybody knows it. But there's the jealousy factor. Considering the grand nature of everything—our giant county, the go-on-forever vistas, the wide-open, mind-boggling spaces, the layer-on-top-of-layer of mountains, the unending sky, and even a river named Grande—the humans can act awfully small.

"People love to talk," the sheriff was saying, "and there's always something, but this...this is different. This rumor is being driven by someone."

I agreed.

"I want you to go to the commissioner meeting to look at the crowd and see if you recognize the man who was photographing you."

"I don't think I'd recognize him. I only saw him once and from a distance."

"It's still worth a try. There's something about that that bothers me."

"It bothers me too."

"To tell you the truth, Margarita, I don't know what you'll be looking for. Just look, please. You have an eye for things others miss and you have an instinct I'd bet money on. I don't want you to go as yourself because someone might see you and act differently. Do you understand what I'm saying?"

"I think so."

"I sound like a paranoid old man."

"No, Sheriff. You have a right to be paranoid."

"This year is an election year for me. Were you aware of that?"

"Yes sir, but nobody runs against you."

"Someone is going to. His name is William Jackson, but he's called Billy Jack for reasons you probably understand."

"No sir," I admitted, "I don't understand what you mean."

"I forget how young you are. In the early seventies, there was a popular movie about a hero named Billy Jack. He was touted as a 'half-breed' Vietnam War veteran, a half Navajo and half-white former Green Beret singlehandedly fighting injustices perpetrated against his Indian friends."

"The way Steven Seagal takes on five men?"

"Yes, like that. My point is that William Jackson uses the name Billy Jack in an affected way. Most voters over forty probably understand the Billy Jack reference, and many of the voters in Brewster County are over forty. It's ironic that Jackson is neither Native American nor a practitioner of the martial arts. Nor has he ever been in the Army, let alone Green Beret. But he wants to be seen as a hero who saves the county residents from a sheriff who is no longer up to the job."

"But—"

He held up his big hands. "I know what you're going to say, and I thank you, but facts confuse people. They don't care about facts. Billy Jack is already speaking of me in terms of a man who should have retired by now, as if I'm a feeble-minded has-been." He leaned back in his chair and frowned. "I'm not feeble-minded."

"I know that."

"Nor am I going to lie down and become a has-been on command."

"No sir. I'm sure of that."

"Margarita, I assume that by now Barney has seen the photo?"

"Yes. Buster has seen it too."

"Surely to God they didn't think that photo was real."

I wanted to ask why he makes me work with two jokers, but I was afraid he'd bring me to Alpine where things would be worse. "They know better, Sheriff." I didn't have the heart to tell him the truth.

"Good. I would hope so." He was silent a while then said, "I believe this so-called 'Billy Jack' is behind that photo. I know it sounds far-fetched, but an excellent way to discredit me would be for me to be caught in a sexual relationship with a young subordinate. And he does want to discredit me."

"Maybe that's true, but would it keep you from being reelected? There's always gossip in this county. Most people would take it with a grain."

"That's true, I guess, but there is a lot you don't know. To begin with, Jackson is an old family friend of Judge Mullen."

I groaned. He was speaking of our relatively new county judge, Amanda Mullen. I'd voted for her because I thought a woman would be an improvement, but it had turned out to be another lesson in making assumptions. In many ways, she was worse than the male judge we had before. In spite of her gender, she's another Texas good ol' boy. It's extra-disappointing because instead of being a shining example of a woman in a position of power, she's a puppet at best. And she's arrogant, even though her money came from her family and nothing she did personally.

"A month ago, Amanda made a pass at me."

My mouth dropped open.

"Of course I turned her down."

I was speechless and hoped he didn't expect me to say anything.

"I would feel better if you didn't look so shocked."

"I'm sorry, Sheriff. I…well…it's that…"

"Better stop talking."

I nodded mutely.

"Since the county government controls the Sheriff's Office budget, I'm in deep shit, even deeper than before. We need more deputies. They expect crime stats to go down and at the same time, want me to eliminate deputy positions. I don't need to tell you all the reasons their thinking is whacked."

"No sir."

"Judge Mullen wants her friend Jackson in the sheriff's position. She has a formidable amount of money, and I believe she and Jackson have hatched a scheme to discredit me. And it's only beginning."

"They underestimate you, Sheriff, and me as well."

"Yes and in more ways than one." He finished his coffee and changed subjects with the abruptness of Texas weather. "Do you think Buster will work out in the long run?"

"Yes, I do. He just needs experience and he's getting it."

"He didn't want to work down there, you know."

"He's never said that to me."

"Good." He changed direction again. "I think Amanda's offer was the first attempt to discredit me. Now they're trying this." He shrugged. "I adore my wife and she seems to adore me, and I'd like it to stay that way."

I nodded.

"Ever since we married, we've agreed to keep our attention on our love for each other and our marriage and that has made us strong. It helps that Marianne is a woman to die for." He winked and then stood. "Are you sure you don't want coffee?"

"Yes sir. I'm sure. I need to sleep sometime between now and next week."

He chuckled and left to get more of his evil brew.

I never realized this before, but I wanted a man like our sheriff—but younger.

He came back and sat. "Now you know what I know. I would appreciate it if you kept it to yourself about Amanda's pass."

"Of course I will."

"Have you thought about our Vidalia Holder problem?"

"Is she really going to sue us? Can't the D.A. just throw it out?"

"He might. It's hard to say."

"I think you'd be better at talking her out of it, Sheriff Ben." I was going to comment that he had a way with women, but it didn't seem funny now.

"She thinks I'm a poor excuse for a sheriff and not much of a man. I know I don't need to remind you that this is not a good time for a lawsuit."

"I'll think of something," I assured him, even though I doubted it.

"Red White wants to talk to you. He might have information relevant to the Jennings murder."

"I'll find him."

"It would help my reputation if we could solve that murder pronto."

Yes, and I could be working on that instead of going to a lame meeting. "We're working as hard as we can, Sheriff."

"I know you are." He took a breath and said, "We have a crazy woman suing us; an exceptionally brutal murder in an isolated place with no witnesses and no forensic clues; an arrogant, wealthy man with no scruples running against me; a county judge who wants me to have sex with her; an incriminating photo making the rounds; and a strange man following and photographing you. Oh, and my wife is hurt and angry. Did I forget anything?"

"No sir. I think that covers it."

"I've been in law enforcement a long time, Margarita."

"Yes sir."

"What I know for sure is this. Some days we wear the badge. Some days, the badge wears us."

* * *

Redmond "Red" White is a fellow deputy stationed in Alpine. Guessing, I'd say he's thirty-five. Not guessing, I can say he's prematurely bald or else shaves his head; I'm not sure which. Either way, he's not called Red because of his hair. His eyebrows say his hair is brown.

He caught me when I was getting into my Mustang. "We need to talk, Rita."

"Hi, Red. The sheriff says you have information about the murder in Terlingua."

"I do. Let's get some coffee."

"Hop in."

"I can't. I'm on duty, so I need to have my truck in case I'm called."

"I'll meet you if you say where."

"Let's go to the doughnut shop."

I almost groaned but followed him there without comment. We took a table on the far side of the place so we wouldn't be overheard.

"What do you have on our murder?" I asked after the coffee was served.

"It's not actually me that has it. It's Trooper Pierson."

"That's all I can tell you," Trooper Jupiter said. "I've gotta go." He stood, smoothed wrinkles from his tight pants, resituated his hat until it was just so, and shook Red's hand.

When he turned to me, I hugged him. "Thank you, Jupiter."

He gave me a tight squeeze. "You're welcome. Take care of yourself."

After he left, I plunked down with a big sigh of relief.

"That wasn't so bad, was it?" chirped Red. He was a man on thin ice.

I bit my tongue and drank the now-cold coffee. A waitress came by and splashed in more, but it didn't help.

"Margarita, may I ask you something?" Red whispered.

Oh, crap. "Go ahead."

"You're not sleeping with the sheriff, are you?"

"Of course I'm not."

"I didn't think so, but there's a lot of talk and somebody is passing a photo of you and him talking. You aren't wearing a shirt."

"Yes. I've seen it. We were talking on my porch, but it was about business. My shirt was removed in Photoshop by somebody trying to make trouble."

"I figure if you were going to sleep with him, you'd be more discreet."

"I've never even thought about sleeping with him, Red."

"He's old, but old guys are always getting younger women."

"Are you listening to me?

"Yeah, I heard you."

"I would never sleep with my boss. And I don't go after married men."

"He's been touchy as hell. You should be glad you work in Terlingua and not up here," Red said.

Amen. I gave thanks every day to wake up to our down-south mountains with their no two peaks alike and their pointy spires and sheer stone faces and our miles of gleaming desert and wide-open spaces, and a thousand other reasons besides.

Red looked around. "We think he's having an affair," he spoke in a voice so low it was difficult to hear him. "You say it's not you, so it must be somebody else."

"What? You can't be serious."

"I am."

"When you say 'we' do you mean the deputies?"

"Yes."

"Why do you think that?"

"He's tired all the time and disappears for long periods at a stretch, during which he doesn't answer his cell. We think he's having a mid-life crisis or something."

"But he's sixty-something," I blurted and immediately regretted it.

"You think old people don't have sex?"

"No, Red, I know they do. What I mean is he's past mid-life unless he's going to live to be one hundred and twenty-something."

"Mid-life is only an expression."

"Yes, I get it. What else makes you think he's having an affair?"

"He goes around dressed fit to kill."

True. Our sheriff had been looking sharper than usual, which is saying something, but I thought that was about his new political challenger and not about chasing women.

"I guess if he's having an affair, that's his business."

Red nodded in agreement. "Do you think he's attractive?"

"Are you setting me up?"

He laughed. "You're always so suspicious."

"I have trust issues."

"No shit."

"In answer to your question, I do think he's attractive. He's old for me, but I can imagine that women older than I am would be interested in him."

"So it's not out of the realm of possibilities that he's having an affair?"

"I guess not, but I don't think he is."

"Are you going to the commissioners' meeting this afternoon?"

"I hadn't planned to," I lied.

"I'm going because I want to see who this William Jackson is. You know about him, right?"

"I heard about him today."

"This is a perfect example of what I mean about the sheriff losing it. He should have told you already. William Jackson announced a few weeks ago that he's going to run against Sheriff Ben in the November election."

"How would anybody win against him? Sheriff Ben is such a good sheriff."

"Well," said Red, "maybe it's time for him to step down."

I disagreed, but I kept my opinion to myself.

Chapter 9

I was so well disguised that neither the sheriff nor Red had a clue I was there. The worst-dressed woman in the room was Margarita Ricos. I wore a moth-eaten red wool beret, lime green ski pants, and a bulky red jacket that made me look twenty pounds heavier. A long, black, curly-haired wig, huge glasses, and black hunting boots added to the effect. A trip to the resale shop had paid off big time. For less than twenty bucks, I changed my looks drastically and not for the better.

Eye shadow is not my thing, so I wore midnight blue and lots of it. It made me look cheap. Perfect. Also, I hate handbags and rarely carry one, so I bought an extra-large purse with tiger stripes that added to the crazy lady look. If the unknown photographer or anyone suspicious showed up I wanted to be able to observe them, but nobody was going to see Deputy Ricos. Why the sheriff thought I should hide my identity I wasn't sure, but I followed his request to the letter.

It wouldn't do to make a late entrance, so I went in early and took a seat towards the rear, the better to watch the proceedings and attendees at the same time. I saw a few brave souls from Terlingua and hoped they wouldn't recognize me.

The proceedings got underway in the retarded manner of small town meetings: *Hey there, Marge! Hi, howya been? Fine, fine. Hank, y'all got any rain at your place?* All the commissioners were involved in *howya been?* conversations from their table. Most of them weren't seated yet. A gavel banged, but it did no good.

I thought, *at least they won't yap on endlessly about rain,* since we'd just had some, but wrong I was. It's not enough to get rain; ranchers have to brag about how many inches they got, more or less the same as comparing dicks, only more polite.

Settle down, I told myself in the stern voice of old lady Jablonski.

Amanda Mullen is not a judge in the way you might think. A county judge is head of the county commission, the entity which runs the county's business. The position doesn't require a law degree. Amanda Mullen has one, however.

She is tiny, late forties, with dyed brown hair cut in a stylish do…if we were living in the 70s. Her mouth forms a grim line. She barely has lips. Amanda always looks well groomed, as in just out of the beauty parlor, so she has that going for her.

Judge Mullen called the meeting to order and might have said some interesting things, but I was busy watching for Jackson and wondering about the people coming in and milling around. My mind wandered all over until they brought up the Sheriff's Office budget. I snapped to attention at the word "sheriff."

I tried to keep a blank face but it took concentration. The long and short of it was that the county commissioners wanted crime statistics to go down while at the same time removing at least one deputy position from the payroll. How could that make sense to anyone older than seven?

My heart went out to Sheriff Ben. If he was a man on the edge, this could be part of the reason.

The sheriff scanned the room so often I wondered if he expected me not to show. That mystery was solved when Marianne Duncan came in and sat a few seats over from me. She is what you'd expect our sheriff's wife to be: educated, articulate, fit, and attractive. I wanted to speak to her but remembered just in time that I was there as someone else. Her eyes were on her man, and I realized she'd come to give him moral support. When he spotted her, his face lit up.

Sheriff Ben stood and addressed the commission using a firm voice. He was dressed in a uniform that looked so crisp I was afraid it would shatter. He gave the month's crime stats with a heavy emphasis on the fact that most Brewster County crime is not violent in nature, and most criminals, no matter how large or small, are caught. He had the stats to prove it in his hand, and he waved them around in indignation that the county wanted to cut his budget by even one deputy. His plan was to add another.

"But Sheriff," Judge Mullen crooned, "you've recently added a new position in Terlingua." She said *Terlingua* as though it was a smutty word. "Before, you managed fine with just two deputies."

If she was going to trash Terlingua, I was bound to blurt something.

"Judge Mullen, it's imperative for the safety of the people of the Terlingua area that we have more than two deputies trained to work there. The area is growing and at times, my deputies are completely covered up."

That was no lie.

"The area they cover is more than half the county," the sheriff pointed out.

A man stood, cleared his throat, and spoke loudly. "It is my understanding that a vicious murder in South Brewster County has not yet been solved, Sheriff Duncan."

Ah, a troublemaker. Without needing to ask, I knew I was looking at William Jackson. "Billy Jack" was wearing creased blue jeans, a white business shirt of the kind you have to iron, and an expensive-looking sheepskin vest. He looked both properly western and prosperous. And he was completely bald. In his hands he held a black hat with a beadwork band which didn't make him any more Native American than a red beret and ski pants made me a crazy lady.

"I believe you're speaking out of turn, Mr. Jackson," Sheriff Ben said.

I almost laughed and clapped, but I had my hands over my mouth.

"To address your statement," the sheriff continued, "the murder was discovered on Monday. It is now only Thursday. This is not an episode of CSI. Murders are not solved overnight in the real world."

There was a titter from the gathering. I couldn't keep myself from clapping, and I wasn't the only one.

"I believe you sanction an unsavory amount of lawlessness in Terlingua, sir," asserted Jackson with a sarcastic edge to his tone.

There was a righteous uproar from the Terlingua delegation, small as it was. I was too angry to respond. I thought the sheriff would turn red and yell, maybe have a stroke, but he maintained his calm demeanor while I had lost mine.

"Your beliefs are your own, Mr. Jackson. My belief is that you're talking out your ear. You know nothing about Terlingua."

"Yeah!" and other expressions of agreement came from the Terlingua camp.

It was aggravating that Amanda Mullen made no move to take control. I had seen more professional meetings at the Girl Scouts. I started to stand but grabbed hold of myself just in time.

"The other thing you're not considering, Judge Mullen," said the sheriff, moving on, "is that I can and do call my south county deputies up here when they're needed. If it's not busy there and I need them here, they come."

"But that's costing the county more money," whined a mousy, gray-haired man who sat at the table, a commissioner, I presumed. "You have your deputies running up and down the county like a bunch of damn coyotes." He pronounced it "kye-oats."

The sheriff looked skyward briefly, as in *Beam me up, Scotty.* "That is because I don't have enough deputies, Mr. Trimble," he stated with a lot of "losing it" in his voice. "That's the point."

Touché.

"Also, you have a quick-draw deputy in Terlingua who killed a woman's pet burro." Jackson pronounced it boo-roe. "I don't believe she's been disciplined."

It's a wonder I didn't fly out of the chair. I swallowed down such angry words my stomach began to ache.

"Mr. Jackson, you're speaking of things you don't understand. That burro had been hit by a vehicle and had two broken legs and other injuries. The deputy had to put him down. She will not be disciplined because she did nothing wrong."

"I understand she's being sued over the incident."

"Anybody can sue for any reason. Being sued doesn't constitute guilt. I believe you should have a seat and stop speculating about things you don't know."

Jackson did not sit or shut up. "Your budget is not used efficiently, Sheriff Duncan. I believe that's what this commission is saying to you."

It was all I could do not to groan out loud.

"Mr. Jackson, you are grandstanding," stated the sheriff. A few people clapped and there was some laughter; a cheer rose from the Terlingua folks.

On it went. The sheriff's weapon sat on his hip. I knew it would be on safety, but I also knew it was ready to fire. I began to make up scenarios in which he took it out and used it. Sheriff Wyatt Earp would never have put up with this crap.

Eventually the commission moved on to other subjects they could argue endlessly, but they never decided anything about the Sheriff's Office budget.

I searched the onlookers for the photographer but it seemed hopeless. Distance had blurred his features and I wasn't even sure of his size.

The youngest commissioner was an acquaintance, the only commissioner I knew personally. His name is Conway Twitty Bradford, but he can't be blamed for that. I knew him from the law enforcement academy. In his early thirties at that time, he'd decided to change professions. He bragged that he had a deputy sheriff position in mind, but only for as long as it would take to make sheriff. Conway, or C.T., was born and raised in Alpine and had no intention of leaving, so that meant he would have to run against Sheriff Ben. I don't think our sheriff ever lost any sleep over that.

As things worked out, C.T. never finished the academy. He went to work with a plumbing company instead. A long attention span is not his forte. Also, he couldn't understand that just because a student is older than the teacher doesn't make the teacher unqualified.

Watching mediocre Conway puff and strut and attempt to look competent as a county commissioner made me laugh. It also gave me an idea. Maybe I knew a way to help Sheriff Ben.

At last, the meeting of the whacked minds ended. I let others stream out ahead of me to be sure I didn't miss anything.

Marianne met her husband halfway across the room. He put his arm around her shoulders and drew her close. She hooked a finger in his belt and gazed up at him as if they had just been married yesterday.

Three thoughts:

Sheriff Ben was not having an affair.

Something else was wrong and Jackson was behind it.

Who elected those people?

* * *

Ten minutes later the sheriff called on my cell phone. "I didn't see you at the commissioners meeting," he barked without saying hello.

"Didn't you tell me to go in a disguise?"

"Oh. Right; I did. Sorry. Did you see the guy who was taking photos?"

"If he was there, I didn't recognize him."

"Did you see anything that hit you wrong?"

"Sir, that entire meeting was wrong."

"Indeed it was, Deputy Ricos. Carry on." He cut the call.

Yes sir. You're welcome.

* * *

I made a quick change from "crazy lady" back to deputy and caught him as he was locking up his commissioner office in the courthouse.

"How's it going, C.T.?"

He jumped as if caught with his hands in the till—or in the case of Conway Twitty Bradford, caught with his hands on a woman not his wife. "My God, Margarita! You scared the hell out of me."

"I need to speak with you about an urgent matter, C.T."

"It can't wait?"

I stood as tall as my height allowed and tried to look intimidating. "No. It can't."

He sighed in a resigned way, unlocked the office door, and invited me inside.

"Thank you," I chirped and stepped into a dim room that smelled of stale cigars, yellowed papers, and a useless public servant.

"Have a seat." He moved behind his desk but didn't sit. Instead he leaned with his hands on it and watched me. C.T. was a man of medium height and build. At one time he was fine-looking and in good shape, but he was going to seed.

"You disappointed me today, Conway."

He blushed. "How's that?"

"You're just like those other nitwits. You go along with whatever the others say, even though I know you must have ideas of your own."

"What are you talking about?" He stared at me openmouthed. With C.T. it was hard to say if he was acting or if he seriously didn't know.

"I'm referring to the county commissioners meeting."

"How can you have a complaint? You weren't there."

"Oh, but I was."

"I didn't see you."

"That doesn't matter. I saw you and you disappointed me."

"What the hell are you talking in circles about?"

"Sheriff Duncan wants to add another deputy. We need one and he has the stats to prove it. Why do you guys fight him on a reasonable request?"

He didn't have an answer to that because he was a guy who went along with the crowd on things. I doubted he'd thought about it.

I got to the point. "Remember the conversation we had a month ago?"

"Of course I do. How would I forget it?"

"I'm here to collect the favor you promised."

"I figured that. What do you want?"

"I want you to point out to the dim bulbs on the commission that Sheriff Duncan should get respect instead of hassle. He doesn't deserve to be raked over the coals every time he needs something. I want you to vote for the budget increase he's requesting. It's not unreasonable, C.T."

"Shit. I can't tell those other guys what to do."

"I realize you can't make them do anything, but you can lead by example. Make a motion to increase his budget."

"Are you looking for a raise out of it or what?"

"I want my boss to get fair treatment in a county where he has proven himself capable and honest and true over and over."

"There are some that say he's getting too old to do his job effectively."

"Maybe so, but you don't need to be one of them."

When he didn't say anything, I added, "I work with him, C.T. He's not getting senile or forgetful or weak. If that were the case, I'd want him replaced too. He's just as capable as he's ever been. He's strong and sharp and has all his faculties."

"I don't see why this is such a big deal. He's retirement age."

"He's young for his age and you know it. It's wrong for him to be forced to retire. He should be the one to say when."

"Amanda says we need a man like William Jackson."

"Has she explained why?"

"He's younger and…I don't really know why."

"So you'd go along with her just because she says so? Leaders don't act like that, Conway. In your position, you're supposed to represent the voters of this county, not Amanda Mullen. The people of Brewster County adore Sheriff Ben. He has a few enemies, of course, but the majority of citizens know he works hard and does his job."

"You would say that."

"It's true and you know it."

"You're fucking him."

I held up my hands. "Stop right there."

"You can't say that's not true."

"That's in your head."

"Hell no, it's not."

"That's old, dead gossip from long ago."

"You wish it would die. Have you seen today's newspaper? There're letters to the editor calling for your dismissal."

"You can't believe everything you see in print. A letter to the editor is just someone's opinion."

"They sounded pretty heated up."

"I work with Sheriff Duncan; I don't sleep with him."

"I'm just repeatin' what I hear."

"Well, you should have better sense. Just because you hear something doesn't make it true. Nor should you repeat it."

"You know what they say. Where there's smoke…"

"In this county, the smoke is most likely coming from the burning gears in the overworked mouths of diehard gossipers and not from anything like a fire."

He chuckled. "You do have a point."

"Regardless of smoke or fire or whatever, this is not about me."

"Yeah…it's about you trying to ruin me."

"Not at all; it's about asking for a favor. Are you going to help me or not?"

"You wouldn't really tell Susie Ann, would you?"

"No. I have no reason to hurt her."

"Then what in God's name are you doing?"

"I would tell the people who could damage your so-called political career."

"I don't know if you'd really do that, or if you're just tryin' to scare me."

"Is that a risk you're willing to take?"

"I guess not."

Conway, married to a sweet, clueless woman named Susie Ann Scout, was having an affair with an acquaintance of mine, Judy Perkins. How I discovered this is not important. What she could've been thinking is not important. The important thing is that Conway had blurted that if I'd keep his indiscretion to myself, he'd owe me a favor. That was the wrong thing to say to a woman in my line of work. We need favors all the time. And if what I knew could help Sheriff Ben, I was willing to use it as leverage in battle.

The truth is I wasn't going to tell anyone what I knew because I hate that kind of talk, but C.T. didn't know that. People who enjoy spreading juicy tales about others tend to think everyone does. I had to hope Conway would believe I'd blab it. Since he would have done it, I thought he'd fall for my con and he did.

"I'll do you the favor this time." He sighed. "I think it's shitty to threaten a man's marriage."

"If you cared about your marriage, you'd be spending your spare time with Susie Ann instead of Judy."

"That's none of your damn business."

"True enough, but you flaunted it in my face."

"I was drunk."

"That's not an excuse."

"Fuck you, Margarita."

"Oh, C.T., you disappoint me. What kind of argument is *fuck you?*"

He turned red and jerked his arms around. "Just get out of here before I lose it and do something I'll regret."

"Have a great day, C.T."

I went on my merry way, spreading happiness.

Chapter 10

The following day was Friday. It was cold and wet, with intermittent snow, rain, and sleet, as if the weather gods were battling it out for control of the sky. Folks of the Big Bend area don't care how moisture comes as long as it does.

Buster and I left for Odessa before dawn to check out Slim Jimmie's, the gay nightclub that had provided Jennings with a parking sticker. Buster had already made arrangements to meet the owner at the location, along with the bartender and the bouncer who had been on duty Friday night.

The latter's name was Jessie Williams, a powerfully-built man who looked like a young Sylvester Stallone but spoke with a soft Texas twang. When handed a photo of Brad Jennings, he remembered him.

"He's been here twice recently," Jessie said as he studied the photo. "Both times he came up to the door but went back to his car. He acted like he wanted to go in, and then he didn't."

"Excuse me, sir, but you must know him well to recognize him in a photo," Buster said. "He was dressed as a woman, and in the photo he's not." He looked over at me with an "ah hah" expression.

"It's not that hard, Deputy. I know faces. I'm paid to."

"I see. I apologize for interrupting."

"On Friday night a man spoke with him."

"What did he say?" Buster asked.

"I couldn't hear everything, but your man said, 'I guess I'm not ready yet.' The other customer made a comment about coming out of the closet. I thought it was inappropriate and told him to shut up and move on or else leave."

"What did he do?" I asked.

"He shrugged and moved on. The only people who argue with me are usually drunk or too stupid to live."

No kidding. Buster and I exchanged a look.

"Do you know the name of the man who spoke to Jennings?" Buster asked.

"No. He's a customer I recognize, but there's nothing outstanding about him. Why? Is there a problem?"

"Did Mr. Jennings say anything else?" I asked.

"He went back to his car and sat there a long time, and he was sobbing. The reason I remember this so well is because I went to the car. It wasn't far from where I was standing at the door. The guy knew I saw him, so he wasn't surprised when I walked over and asked if I could help in any way."

"What did he say?"

"He said the love of his life had died a couple of years ago and he was trying to move on, but that it was hard."

A stab of pain pricked my heart.

"How long did he stick around after that?" Buster asked.

"Maybe ten minutes after I spoke with him."

"Did anyone else speak to him?"

"Not that I noticed."

"When Jennings left, you saw him pull away?"

"Well yes, I happened to."

"And you didn't see anyone follow him?" Buster asked.

"No. Did something happen to him?"

"Yes," I said. "He was murdered later that night."

"Oh. That's awful."

"We're trying to figure out who killed him," Buster said needlessly.

"Well, I sure hope you do."

"Can you get me the name of the man who spoke with Mr. Jennings?"

"Yes. I can do that next time he comes in."

"Thank you." I handed him my card.

"If you think of anything that might help us, will you call?" Buster asked. He handed him his card and Jessie promised he would.

The owner, who was neither slim nor named Jimmie, had nothing of interest to add, and ditto the bartender. We thanked them for coming in to help us. All of them expressed dismay over Bradley Jennings' murder.

Before we left we looked around in the bar but we didn't have a clue what we were looking for. Nothing looked strange or out of place. It was clean and it had a dance floor, stage, and both booths and tables.

We were disappointed to have gotten nowhere and complained to each other on the road home.

"Maybe he went somewhere else and met someone there," Buster suggested.

"Yes, but how likely is that? If he wasn't ready to go in the gay bar, can you see him going into a regular bar? And he was dressed as a woman."

"Maybe not; he could have changed his clothes."

"That's true, but somehow that doesn't fit."

"Yeah, you're right."

"I was sure the bar would be the key," I said with a sigh.

"Maybe it still is," Buster said. "That bouncer could've found out where he lived and gone over there and they got into it or something."

"That's remotely possible, but we don't have a shred of evidence to indicate that. We can't get a warrant for his DNA without reasonable cause. And even if we could get a warrant, what do we have to compare to his DNA profile?"

Damn, it was aggravating.

* * *

We were entering the Alpine city limits when Barney called on the satellite phone to relay a message. Bradley Jennings' illusive brother was at our victim's home. Would Buster and I stop there and interview him?

"Did you tell him he's not supposed to be there? It hasn't been released yet."

"You can tell him when you get there."

Dr. Ted Jennings looked a lot like his brother, but a few years older and a little taller. He came to the door looking glum, but that wasn't unusual since he was in his dead brother's home, and we were a nuisance he had avoided as long as he could.

"Come in and get it over with," he said when he opened the door.

"Sir, you're not supposed to be in this house," I said. "It's a crime scene, and hasn't been released by the sheriff or the Texas Rangers."

"Well, the tape was down and I just thought..." He made a vague gesture.

"The tape was down when you got here?"

"That's what I said."

"Why haven't you returned our calls? We would've told you not to enter."

"If you want to talk to me, come inside." He turned back into the house.

Buster and I looked at each other. He shrugged and pointed to my weapon. Yeah, it was tempting.

"I didn't go in the bedroom. Isn't that the crime scene?"

"The entire house is a crime scene," I said.

"Why is that?"

"Whoever killed your brother was all over this house. It's a crime scene until we're finished with it."

"It seems like you'd have finished with it by now."

I opened my mouth to let him have it when Ted Jennings collapsed onto a chair at the kitchen table, and his attitude changed. "I'm sorry. I adored my brother, and I feel so much sadness I think my chest is going to cave in."

"Dr. Jennings, we're sorry for your loss. I know you can't believe this now, but that awful feeling will get better with time."

"How would you know?"

"I lost a husband."

"Oh…you're so young…I apologize."

"It's all right."

"Do you have any leads?"

We sat down with him.

"We need your help," I said, and then explained the lack of physical evidence and gave a brief rundown of finding his brother naked and dead in his bedroom. I eliminated the worst details of the brutality that had been levied on Bradley.

"How can I help you?"

"Have you noticed anything missing?"

"His computer is gone and some photographs. Isn't that weird?"

"Yes, it is," Buster agreed. "We don't think he was robbed because of the easy-to-carry valuables left behind, but someone did take those other things."

"We suspect that a lover or would-be lover killed him," I said, "but we're having a difficult time coming up with names."

"Why would you jump to that conclusion?"

"He was naked in his bedroom, and his murder appears to have been a crime of passion. We can find no other motive. That might be wrong, but it's all we have right now."

"I don't want to talk about my brother's love life. It's none of your business."

"Do you have any idea who could've wanted Bradley dead?" I asked.

"No. He was the kindest man you'd ever hope to know."

"That's what everyone says, but he made someone angry enough to kill him. I'm sorry to have to ask about his love life, but this is a murder investigation. Was he married? His C.V. at the school states he was."

Ted Jennings hesitated a long time before he answered. "He was never married, or not in the traditional sense."

"So he had a serious relationship?"

"Yes, and it lasted a long time. They couldn't get married."

"Is that because he was gay?"

Ted wouldn't have looked as hurt if I'd struck him. "Why do you think that?"

"We have one lead that suggests it," I admitted without giving away anything.

"I spent my whole life protecting him," the brother said with tears in his voice. "I don't want to betray him now."

"Dr. Jennings, Buster and I want to bring his murderer to justice. Except as it relates to his murder, we don't care about his sex life."

I looked over at Buster, who confirmed that by nodding his head and saying, "Not at all. What Deputy Ricos says is true."

"We aren't here to make judgments or cause scandal," I continued.

"Please trust us with what you know because you're our only hope. We can't find anyone here who knew your brother well. Obviously, someone did and he made them angry."

"I don't know who he made angry. Maybe someone discovered his secret and killed him over it. That happens."

"Yes, and that's an angle we're working."

"Brad was still getting over the death of his life partner, John. He and John were deeply in love and had been for most of Brad's adult life. The last time I spoke to him he said he wasn't ready for a new man."

"Quite a few women were pursuing him, and that's what they all say, that he wasn't ready for a new love in his life."

"Maybe one of them killed him when they found out he was gay."

"That's possible and we haven't ruled it out," I said, "but nobody here appears to have known he was gay."

"Someone might have known who hasn't come forward for obvious reasons."

"That's true, and we're aware of it."

"I wanted him to return to San Antonio, where there is a better chance of meeting people. But he wanted to hole up and mend his heart. I understood that, and I was trying to respect his wishes and give him some space. I should've made him come home." His voice broke and he quit speaking.

"You shouldn't blame yourself," I said. "You probably couldn't have 'made' him do anything he didn't want to do."

He nodded in agreement and wiped his eyes.

"I find it odd that all the pictures of John are gone," Ted said when he recovered his composure. "That doesn't fit. I spoke to Brad a few days before he died and he wasn't in the emotional state to remove them. So someone else removed them, but why? Was it jealousy? Wasn't it enough to kill him? Why take his photos?"

"Those are our questions, too."

"I don't want to tell you this, but I know I should, so I'm going to. Brad used to dress as a woman sometimes. He had dresses, a couple of nice wigs, shoes, and jewelry. None of that is here."

"His neighbor thought they were his dead wife's things, and she noticed they were gone too," I said. "Some of them were burned in a barrel out back and we didn't know if Brad burned them, or an angry lover, or what."

"Brad wouldn't have burned them. He would've given away things he didn't want. I'm sure. I can't imagine him destroying things that someone else could use."

As our interview was winding down, Buster asked for John's last name.

"He used Brad's last name for the last twelve years, and I can't remember what his name was before. I'll look it up when I get home and call you."

"Thank you. I'd appreciate that."

Then we went through our usual routine of business card exchange and asking him to call if he thought of one tiny thing that might help us. He said he would. Then we told him he had to leave the house, and we promised to notify him as soon as the sheriff released it. He left agreeably and we replaced the crime scene tape.

Once we were on the highway again Buster asked, "Do you think that's weird, wearing women's clothing?"

"People are weird, Buster. Everyone is. It makes life interesting that we're all weird in our own ways."

"I just don't get that."

"You don't have to understand it. But it sure helps to know it. It's one more thing we didn't know about our victim."

"When are things going to start adding up?"

"It's already starting to. Maybe some macho man discovered Brad's secret and killed him over it."

Buster got excited then. "Yes! What if Brad was dressed as a woman and somebody made a pass at him? It could make a man furious to find out that a woman he liked was a man."

"Yes. We've got a few more pieces of the puzzle."

Because Buster was driving, I answered the beeping sat phone. It was Barney.

"Bring your teenager back to the office, Ricos. You have a visitor."

"Who is it?"

"A friend has come to accompany you to a nice church social and help you find yourself a soft-spoken, sensitive man."

"I don't know why I even talk to you."

"The sheriff pays you to."

"In that case, I need a huge raise."

"Ricos, your visitor is your pal Victoria."

"Oh. That's great!"

"I wasn't kidding about going to the church social."

"You don't know Vic very well, do you? Tell her we'll be back at the office within fifteen minutes." I hung up. "Step on it, Buster, lights and siren."

He perked up. "Oh, cool."

＊ ＊ ＊

After hugging and exclaiming over how fabulous we looked and some kidding around with Barney, I introduced Vic to Buster. Then we settled in my office with the door shut. I told her I was happy to see her and I was, but I wondered why she'd come. She never came to see me at work.

"Vic, did you come about the topless photo of me with the sheriff?"

Her mouth opened in surprise and she batted at one of her ears. "I would've sworn you said you made a topless photo with the sheriff. I must be going deaf."

It was a relief she hadn't heard the rumor, but of course then I had to tell her myself. When I finished, she said, "It would help if you had a boyfriend. That's the reason I'm here."

I was speechless.

"We're having a cook-out Saturday night," my lifelong friend announced, "and I came to invite you."

"And?"

"And what?"

"What else?"

"Why do you think there's something else?"

"Seriously, Vic? How long have we been friends?"

"All right. I want to introduce you to someone."

"I know you did not come here to tell me about a man."

"Well I sure as heck didn't come here to tell you about a woman." Her dark eyes twinkled with mischief.

Victoria and I have been friends since we were five and started kindergarten. Our parents are friends and like me, she is of mixed race, Hispanic and Anglo. We have so much in common it's easier to list how we're different. Here it is: As I grew I was sexually attracted to men, and as Vic grew up she was attracted to women.

"I know you'll like this man if you give him a chance."

It was not like her to push a man at me. Vic likes men, but understanding why anyone would have sex with one was beyond her grasp.

"I can't believe this." I glared at her. "Really, Vic? You know how I feel about my friends picking men for me."

"Who knows you better than I do?"

She had me there.

"Listen, I do want you to meet a friend, but that isn't why I came."

"I knew it."

"How're you coming along with the Brad Jennings murder?"

"I can't talk about it, Vic. We're investigating, but that's all I can say."

"I know something about Brad that you might not. Morgan and I were his friends." Morgan is the love of Vic's life, and she's a woman. They've been together ten years. Victoria shifted in the chair. "He was gay. I thought you needed to know that."

"I do know that, but thank you for coming to me."

"I was afraid nobody would tell you because no one here knew it except a few other gay people. How do you know?"

"Truly stellar detective work," I claimed with a straight face.

"Oh, hell." She shook her head with a tsk-tsk. "Always with the bragging."

"Okay. It was just regular detective work, but that's how I know."

"Nothin' gets past Super-Deputy Ricos."

"Don't be a lunatic, Vic."

She grinned but then got serious. "Do you know that Brad sometimes dressed in women's things?"

"Yes."

She threw up her hands. "Why the hell did I come here?"

"You came because you want to help me and I appreciate it."

"You're welcome."

"Do you have any idea who would've been burning clothes and things in Brad's burn barrel?"

"No. I can't imagine he would do it. He loved beautiful things and he took care of them. If there was something he didn't want he would've left it at the resale shop or given it away."

"That's what his brother said. Do you know if he was seeing anybody?"

"No. He wanted to and didn't. His love died a few years ago and he was still in mourning. They were together a long time."

"Is there anything else you know about Brad's life that might lead us to his killer—any little thing?"

"Brad was a dichotomy in that he was masculine and yet he liked to dress in women's clothes. He adored women but didn't want to sleep with them. He attracted them and, because he liked being around them and was so masculine, they never got it that he was gay. Do you understand what I'm saying?"

"Yes. Do you know the last name of his lover?"

"Brad said he used 'Jennings' for many years, so no, I don't."

"Did you know him?"

"No. He died before Brad moved here. His death is the reason he came, I think. The other thing you should know about Brad is that he adored his students. He loved to teach and was good at it. One reason he stayed in the closet was because he didn't want any trouble. You know how Old Jablonski was. Ms. Petrie is no better."

Jablonski had made Vic's life miserable all through our school years because she was different. By association I was guilty too, and she disliked me even more than she did Vic because I stood up to her.

"Do you know that Jablonski was pursuing Brad hot and heavy?"

"Yes, Vic, I know."

"Maybe she murdered him because he wouldn't get it on with her."

I laughed. "I thought about that, but in spite of how I feel about her, I don't think she did it. Of course, what I think isn't relevant and she's still on our list."

"Do you have a long list?"

"Vic, Brad was attacked from behind and beaten to death. Do you have any idea—no matter how remote it might seem—who would have done that? Did he have any enemies?"

"If he did, I don't know who that would be. He was laid back and easy-going. Everyone liked him."

"Not everyone liked him. He made someone furious."

"I hate to think his death has to do with being gay."

"I do, too. I want to think it's something else."

"It's probably not something else." Victoria sighed. "My friends in other places say, 'oh how great that you grew up there,' as if this is a great place to grow up gay."

"Vic, I grew up here too, remember? Horrible people are everywhere and, as small as it is, Terlingua is proof. Humans are humans no matter where they are."

"People on the outside looking in on Terlingua think we dance around with flowers in our hair and are always hugging each other."

"Vic, you're thinking of San Francisco."

She laughed. "Yeah, but you know what I mean."

"I do."

"Do you realize the school will stay just as messed up as when Jablonski ran it? Wouldn't it be peachy to have a superintendent who actually liked kids, and I mean all kids."

"I agree. Maybe you should apply for the job."

"That's about as likely as me being voted President of the U.S."

"I'd vote for you."

"Thanks. I'll hold you to that when I run."

"I feel sorry for anyone who doesn't know you, Vic."

"Yeah, I do, too."

That made me laugh.

"I had to talk myself into coming here," Vic said.

"Why?"

"It's because sometimes we know things about our friends that not everyone knows or needs to know. I have trouble betraying those things, even after a person is dead. But if there's anyone I trust with information like this, it's you."

"Thank you, Vic."

"You're welcome. I just don't want Brad to become a lame joke. People wouldn't understand. Shit. I don't understand the dress-up part, but I try to let people be."

"That's one of the ten million things I love about you, Vic."

"If you love me, you'll come to my cook-out, right?"

"No."

"But Rita, this man is a doll."

"Is that you calling a man a doll?"

"I like men. I know when they're smart and good-looking. I don't want to have sex with them but if you do, great. Say you'll come or I'll put Morgan on your case."

I groaned at that. Morgan can talk anybody into anything because she won't give up. It occurred to me that I should send her to speak to Vidalia Holder about dropping her lawsuit.

"The reason I can't come is this murder. I don't know what will happen between now and Saturday night."

"It's tomorrow, Rita. We're talking about tomorrow."

"Yes. You don't understand that I have to keep working this until I figure out who killed your friend."

"I don't mind if you take a night off. He wouldn't mind either."

"Vic, you misunderstand me. I work for the sheriff. He expects this murder to be solved already if not sooner."

"You have two strapping boys out there with nothing to do. Why don't you leave it with them for one night?"

I stared at her.

"Oh, r…right," she said, drawing it out, "The boys."

"Yes."

"Okay, what if we make it Sunday?"

"Vic, read my lips. When the murder has been solved, I can have time off. Until then, my time is not my own."

"So you're the sheriff's little bitch now."

I laughed. "You've got that right."

"Hurry up and solve the murder, 'cause this guy might meet somebody else."

"Que sera, sera," I said to annoy her. Besides, I didn't have any intention of meeting him.

She gave me her stern Victoria look.

"Vic, what is this mystery man's name?"

"If I tell you then you'll look him up and start talking to people and make a snap judgment about him."

"Is there something wrong with him?"

"If there is, I'm not aware of it."

"You swear?"

"I swear."

"I'll meet him after we solve this murder."

"I like it that you're trying so hard to find Brad's killer. Thank you for that."

"It's my job, Vic, but thank you for appreciating what I do."

"Well, I guess I'll leave you to work your magic."

"Vic, if I die, will you promise to keep my secrets to your-self?"

"Yes, of course, unless they'll help solve your murder."

"I hope I won't be murdered."

"No kidding, sunshine. You'd better pray on that."

* * *

"So your friend is a lesbian?" Buster inquired after Victoria left.

Barney headed him off. "Don't jump to conclusions, Buster."

"Yeah, you've told me that about ten thousand times."

"Well," Barney spoke slowly and with exaggerated patience, "that was number ten thousand and one."

Buster laughed and forgot about his question, so I didn't have to tell him that my friends are none of his business.

"How did it go at the school?" I asked Barney.

"The kids are stunned to know what happened to him, and they don't even know the gory details. They can't imagine who hated him enough to kill him."

We told him about our visit to the club in Odessa and then our interview with Bradley Jennings' brother at the scene of the crime.

We jotted our newest info and thoughts on our murder board. Then I took the opportunity to tell Barney and Buster about Sheriff Ben's opponent. It was the first chance I had to catch both of them together. Their response, minus the inventive curses, was similar to mine: oh hell no.

After that we went home. It had been a long day, and we still had no clue who killed Bradley Jennings.

Chapter 11

Marine was sitting in the window that looks out onto my porch, staring blissfully at the view.

"You're as bad as I am," I told the cat. He ignored me.

Craig was out and about, so I picked up around the house and carried on a one-sided conversation with Marine while I did.

"You could make yourself useful and help me, you know."

No comment.

I stared into the fridge for dinner inspiration and didn't get any. "What sounds good for dinner, Marine?"

No comment.

"It's your turn to make it."

No comment, plus a look of utter disdain.

I gave up on the kitty communication and dressed for a run.

When I took off, my muscles were tense and my mind was worried about Photo-shopped lies, murder, and Sheriff Ben losing the election—but worse, losing his wife. I had a jumble of heebie-jeebies. As my legs moved and my lungs sucked in delicious desert air and my eyes sucked in the timeless grandeur of what lay before me, I forgot my problems. What problems? I can run! The sky is so blue! Cimarron!

Instead of going up on the sandstone bluffs, I ran past them. The dirt road goes off to the left and I ducked into an arroyo that winds right. If someone was following me, they'd give up unless they were a serious runner. Or Batman.

* * *

Craig left me a note explaining that he missed his house and his billion-dollar view. He thanked me for everything and signed it, *With love, your Two Marines*. I did my usual shower, dress warmly, and eat routine and was ready for the porch.

As much as I love to watch night descend on my desert, it was too cold to sit outside long. I hadn't been in ten minutes when there was a knock on the door. I peeked out the front window. It was the lawman who had been across the canyon from me a few days ago. According to his shiny badge, he was a Texas Ranger. He was dressed the way my father Zeke dresses when he works: stylish Western with dark pants, a button-down shirt, a tie, leather boots, a brown felt Resistol hat and a pistol. I couldn't see what kind it was, but it was probably a Sig Sauer .357. Because it was cold, this guy also wore an insulated vest and a scarf.

He reminded me of Zeke. He was about his height with dark eyes and hair, a sturdy build, and a handsome face. Wait a minute. Was he Zeke's son? Had Zeke lied to me? Maybe Zeke didn't know he had a son. My brother! Yeah, this is the way my imagination hijacks my intelligence and we go for a little ride.

I took a deep breath and opened the door to stare at my brother.

"Hello." He greeted me in a mellow voice and with a smile that revealed a dimple in his left cheek.

"Hello."

"Are you Margarita?"

"Yes."

He held out his hand. Even his hand reminded me of Zeke's hands—bronzed skin, neatly trimmed nails, gold watch—large, attractive man-hands. *Ay Diosito.*

I took his hand and it was warm and strong. He'd make a fine brother.

He smiled. "I guess you're wondering why I'm here."

"Yes."

"Do you think I could come in?"

"Are you Zeke Pacheco's son?"

His mouth opened and he blinked. Then he laughed—so hard he wrapped his arms around himself.

"Ah." He collapsed against the wall and then into one of the chairs on the porch. "Oh, man." More laughing. "Oh my god." He caught his breath. "Whew," and then he started again. As he got it together, finally, all he managed was, "Wow."

I wanted to shut the door and forget this. Instead, I sat in the other chair because what the heck? You only live once.

"I'm glad you got that out of your system," I said.

That started him again, but then he said breathlessly, "I know Zeke." His voice sounded wheezy.

I liked this hysterical man.

"He's not my father." He laid a hand on his chest and tried to catch his breath. "Why would you think that? ¡Carajo! I'm sorry. I used to work with Zeke. That was before he was promoted." He turned to face me. "But you're his daughter, right?"

Oh crap, I wanted to tell him no; he had the wrong house in the wrong town, but I'd already admitted to being Margarita and besides, I wanted him to stay.

"Yes; I'm Zeke's daughter, but please don't hold that against him."

He touched my arm—well it was only the arm of my jacket. "Please forgive me for laughing. You surprised me with that…" His voice trailed away.

"It's my fault." What else was there to say?

He took an audible breath. "Let's go back to why I'm here."

"Yes."

"I'm working a murder and Zeke asked me to stop by and say hello if I made it to Terlingua."

"Why don't I know about this murder?"

"It could be because the body was found in Presidio County."

"Oh."

I looked over at Cimarron. How disappointing I must be to my mountain.

"It's beautiful here." He, also, was watching the long-playing show, *Nighttime on Cimarron*. He sighed. "It's so gorgeous it's hard to take it in."

I agreed and we were silent a few minutes. Things started to feel normal. My heart rate revved down a few notches, along with my imagination.

"I don't know why I blurted that to you the way I did. I think I'm exhausted. We had this murder and everything is going wrong... You do look a little like Zeke."

He was trying not to laugh again, but his dimple was fully engaged. "I've been told that before, but my mom swears my dad is David Camacho. And Zeke swears he's never met my mom."

"Well then, you're not my brother."

"That's true."

"Why were you taking pictures of me?"

"I wasn't. I was checking you out through the scope on my camera." He smacked the heel of his right hand against his forehead. "Good grief. That was an unfortunate choice of words. What I mean is I was trying to decide if you were Zeke's daughter. He said you had longish dark hair in a French braid and that you like to run. I was admiring the scenery from the top of that rise and didn't expect to see his daughter or anyone else across the way."

That was one hundred percent bull, but I didn't call him on it. Let him hang himself. Where he'd been standing was not a scenic overlook. Tourists and people not familiar with the area don't know how to get there or even that it exists.

"I assume you have a name." I thought that was a place to start.

"I apologize for not giving it already. My name is Len. Lennon Camacho. I'm a Texas Ranger, but you know that." He sighed. "Geez, we're off to a rocky start."

"I think we should go inside where it's warm."

"Do you think that'll help?"

"I don't know."

He seemed dejected, but he followed me inside. I took off my jacket and hung it in the little closet by the door instead of slinging it somewhere as I normally would. I offered to take his vest and scarf, but he looked nervous about giving them up.

I took a deep breath. "Would you like something to drink?" My normal self was finally starting to kick in.

He grinned. "I'd love bourbon, neat."

"Same here, but I don't have any alcohol in my house. I have coffee, hot tea, water, lemonade, soda—"

"Listen. You know what? I should get going."

"Okay, but you just got here."

He stood. "It was great to meet you."

"But…"

Len Camacho got out of my house as if the place was in flames.

After the door shut, I slumped against it. "This is why you're home alone on a Friday night." I really, really wanted to drink. I cried instead.

Chapter 12

The next morning I dressed, made tea, and sat on the porch to drink it. The sun was barely up, but it was casting a golden glow on everything. That, and the pink-tinged clouds lingering over the Chisos Mountains, announced it would be a gorgeous day.

My cell phone rang to the tune of Buddy Holly's *I Fought the Law* which meant it was Barney. He hates that I use that tune and would prefer *Too Sexy for My Shirt*, but it's my phone. I haven't decided about Buster's ringtone yet.

"Good morning, Barney."

"Are you awake?"

"No. This is my answering service. Deputy Ricos is in Cancun and cannot be disturbed until next week."

"You wish. I called to tell you that the guys at the café think—"

"Stop right there. Unless they know who killed Brad Jennings or who took my photo with Sheriff Ben, I don't want to hear what they think."

"Well aren't you in a cheery mood?"

"I'm in a fine mood, but I don't want to hear their slobbery views unless it solves a mystery."

"Oh, my picky, picky, little pard." He paused. "They think Wynne did it."

"The murder or the photo?"

"The photo."

If that was true, it was a bitter disappointment. Wynne was an adversary I thought I'd turned into a friend. Since the time I kicked his ass, things had gone more smoothly. He still thinks "girls" shouldn't be allowed in law enforcement, but he stopped harassing me about it. I thought he was coming around.

"I can't believe he'd do that," I said.

"They think he did."

"Did they say why?"

"Making trouble, trying to get your attention, who knows? It's Wynne. Do you want me to pick him up, rough him up, or both?"

"I don't want you to do anything. I'll handle this."

"That's a bad idea. You'll be giving him the attention he craves."

"Okay. Why don't you and Buster go and talk to him?"

"Do I have to take Buster?"

"He needs to see how to handle these kinds of problems."

"All right; I'll see what Wynne says and decide if I believe it before I dent his head in."

"I'm not convinced he did it, but if he did I think he should be taken to the sheriff for further questioning and accidental bruising and head denting."

Barney laughed. "Good idea, Ricos. The sheriff will launch his ass into outer space."

* * *

Barney and Buster came into the office at 9:30. I was waiting for them because we had more interviews to do and we needed to decide who was doing what. Buster's shirt was hanging out of his pants and his overall look was disheveled. One of his eyes was swollen and turning black, and he had a cut on his bottom lip.

"What happened?"

Barney gave me a look. Buster was silent.

"Did you guys go deaf? What's going on?"

"I don't think Wynne did it, but he and Buster got into it and our guy lost."

"You should've brought Wynne in for assaulting an officer."

"I assaulted him," Buster admitted.

Barney handed him an ice pack from the freezer to put on his eye.

"Why did you do that, Buster?" I asked.

"You don't need to lecture me. Barney already ragged my ass all the way back here. I'm sorry. That Wynne asshole punches all my buttons. I know we can't go around beating people up. I got it, okay?"

"I hope you do because you won't last in this job if you let people get to you."

"Does the sheriff have to know about this?"

"Yes," Barney answered. "He does. You've opened up his office to criticism and a lawsuit if Wynne decides to do it. And this is the worst possible time for it."

"Will I lose my job?"

"I don't know," I said. "At the least you'll have to endure an angry, endless lecture from an old man. You'd better show mucho remorse."

Barney addressed Buster. "Go home and get cleaned up and get back here pronto. We have a lot to do today. If we can solve this murder, Sheriff Ben will be so pleased he might skip the long tirade."

After Buster was gone, I sat down across from my partner. "What in the world happened? Weren't you with him at Wynne's?"

"Of course I was with him. He blew it."

"You're supposed to keep him from blowing it. Tell me how it happened."

"It'll just make you angry."

"Fine. It's not like I've never been angry before."

"I don't like that melts-cold-steel look you get."

"Too bad."

"Wynne admitted he said something to the guys about taking your picture, but it was ages ago, he claims. He said he wanted to catch you with your shirt off and was wondering—just thinking out loud—if you ever walk around naked in your yard. One of the others said, *maybe she comes onto her porch naked.* That's the incident those guys remember."

"What a bunch of sex-crazed old perverts."

"Ricos, men don't get any better just because they get older."

"You haven't explained why Buster attacked him."

"I'm getting to that. Wynne couldn't leave it alone. You know Wynne. He kept on about what a sweet little Latina gumdrop you are and—"

"Hold on. That sounds like you talking, not Wynne."

"I'm putting it into my words because Wynne's words will make you go over there and shoot him in the face. That's when Buster jumped him to defend your honor. Buster is sweet on you, Ricos, but no matter what he thinks about your attributes and stuff, he would never talk like that."

"My *attributes and stuff*? You'd better be talkin' about my intelligence and my sparkling personality."

He blushed. "We appreciate those things, too."

"*We?* So you were all talking about me?"

"It was just man-talk, Ricos."

I shoved back in the chair so hard it screeched. "I'll be back."

"Where are you going?"

I slammed out the door. Barney was either too lazy or too afraid to follow. My first thought was to go lie on a boulder on Cactus Hill, but instead I got into the truck and drove into Big Bend National

Park. My partner called, but I ignored him while Buddy Holly sang about fighting the law. It was ironic.

I slowed at the entrance station but was waved through by somebody new I didn't know. My Brewster County Sheriff's Office vehicle gets me in, no questions. I didn't go far, stopped in a pullout, and got out. The day was warming up to be a typical March day, if there is such a thing. The mountains…what can I say about the Chisos Mountains that I haven't said a hundred times? They are so steady and sure of themselves, shimmering in the sunlight as though nothing could ever bother them.

Within the range there's an anthill of activity: tourists arriving and leaving; rangers on patrol; animals going about their daily lives; plants growing, flowering, dying, and being born; trees getting new leaves or clinging to old ones; people hiking, talking, taking pictures, eating in the restaurant, or meditating on the awesomeness. The point is that the Chisos don't care about any of that. They stand still and appear untroubled by a single thing. That was the mindset I needed. If I could've spent all day there, I might have had a chance of feeling at peace, but I had ten minutes.

I borrowed the mindset of the Chisos Mountains and headed for Wynne's. Thanks to them, I wasn't going to shoot him, but I wanted some straight answers.

Wynne's door and mouth opened at the same time. I guess he didn't look out first to see who was knocking.

"Oh hell," he grumbled. "I know why you're here."

Chisos Mountains: cool and calm. "I swear Wynne, I thought we'd patched things up and you were starting to respect me as a human being."

"Look. I don't know what that asshole told you, but—"

"All I want from you is the truth about the photo that's circulating. It requires a yes or no answer. Are you responsible for it?"

"Hell fucking no."

"I'm taking your word on it. If I find out you're lying, there will be so much hell to pay you can't even imagine it." *Chisos, Margarita, Chisos.*

"I can damn sure imagine it. I hate this, Margarita. I hate that you think I'd take a photo like that."

"Spare me, Wynne. People think it was you because you were whining about needing a photo of me without my shirt. Or totally naked, whichever you could get. So spare me all the blah, blah, and yada, yada."

Wynne was a blazing sunset kind of red either from anger or embarrassment. I doubted it was the latter. "That little shit you work with attacked me. I'm going to sue the crap outta your sheriff and him and your whole damn office."

"No you're not."

"Why shouldn't I?"

"Think about it. If you sue, you and Buster and Barney will have to testify to what was said this morning. Is that something you'd want to repeat in front of the sheriff, me, and ol' Judge Grump?"

"No, I wouldn't…not really."

"Listen Wynne; Buster is young. He deserves another chance. He's sorry he reacted the way he did. Whether you sue him or not, the sheriff is going to hear about what he did because it's unaccept-able. However, you're not lily-white in this either."

"Do you have somethin' going on with that boy?"

"No."

"Do you want to?"

"No."

"He wants to."

"That's neither here nor there. I'll get to the bottom of the photo business and when I do, you had better not be there."

"Are you gonna whoop my ass again?"

"No. I'll take you to the sheriff and let him do it. If you're thinking he's *just an old man,* take a good long look at him sometime. This scandal is hurting him and his wife and he's pissed, way more pissed than I am. He could work you over until you wish you were dead, and every deputy he has would swear it was an unfortunate accident."

"Christ. Okay, I get it."

Damn. I'd totally forgotten my Chisos mantra. I didn't shoot him in the face though, did I?

Chapter 13

I preferred not to go anywhere with Barney or Buster until they grew up, but we still had a murder to solve. The sheriff said if we didn't move closer to that end today, he wanted two of us to go back to Slim Jimmie's in Odessa and observe the place for an evening. I didn't think that would help, and it would mean going with one of my fellow deputies, not people I chose to spend time with. However, it would be more entertaining than Terlingua Ranch interviews. Gay bars are full of interesting hunky types, but of course the downside of that is that they're gay.

Buster and I headed out to Terlingua Ranch to interview my newest nemesis, Miss Vidalia Holder. He tried to apologize to me about "the incident" but I didn't want to hear it.

"Save it for the sheriff. Barney is talking to him right now."

He groaned.

"If it makes you feel any better, I think the big ol' lug will sugarcoat the whole thing because he said some juicy things too. Am I right?"

Buster nodded slowly. He suspected it was a trick question.

Papi says to get to the truth you just have to stay quiet and people will blab to fill the void. That's when useful info has a chance to pop out. I used that method on Buster but he stayed quiet, so maybe he was smarter than I thought.

On my cell phone, Buddy Holly sang *I Fought the Law* until I answered it. "We're about to enter the no cell phone zone," I snapped, "so talk fast."

"Tell Buster the sheriff wants to talk to him in Alpine after this interview. He's off the rest of the day. And he's to go in his own car."

"Why didn't you call Buster's phone?"

"I called yours because I want to apologize to you."

"I'm listening."

That was where service ended and we were cut off. It was just as well. I didn't want to hear *I didn't mean anything by it, and yada, yada, bullcrap.*

I watched the Christmas Mountains and pretended I was hiking in them instead of sitting next to poor ol' busted-up Buster. He was young and had a lot to learn, but Barney? Shouldn't he have acted more professional?

Speaking of mountains, some of my out-of-town friends whine, "Your mountains are not very tall" as if that's somethin'.

I say, "Come and stand next to one and see how it makes you feel." I believe this vast land is more about feelings than anything more tangible than that. So what if there are taller mountains in the world? There will always be something higher or wider or heavier or deeper or more beautiful than something else.

"You aren't listening to me, are you?"

"No, Buster. I'm thinking."

"Are you going to hate me the rest of your life?"

"I don't hate you at all. But I want you to leave me alone right now. When you can name ten positive things about me that don't include my physical *attributes,* then you may interrupt me."

He rolled his eyes.

My mountains are perfect. If they were taller, we'd have more snow. I love snow, but I want it to be gone after a few days. I prefer mountains that are accessible when I want to climb them. I love their ancientness and the crumbling, tumbling-back-to-earth nature of them. Also, if my mountains were too tall, we'd have more rain. Too much rain would cause the desert to go away and that would be too sad to contemplate.

"I've got ten things," Buster announced.

"Let's hear them."

He enumerated on his fingers. "One, you're smart. Two, you're a wicked smart-ass. Three, you have the most amazing smile I ever saw. Four, you're dedicated to this place and your job. Five, you keep your cool when people are ugly to you and that's awesome. Six, you know how to handle a firearm better than anybody I know. Seven, you're a kick-ass dancer. Eight, you like to speed as much as I do. Nine, you speak Spanish like a person from Mexico. Ten, I feel safe training with you." He looked over at me. "Do you accept my ten things?"

"Yes. Thank you."

"Will you talk to me now?"

"What do you want to talk about?"

"I don't care. I just don't want you to be _not talking_ to me."

I laughed. "You're right. It's not professional, but it's also not professional to go see a suspect and talk about another deputy's ass and stuff."

"Okay. I know. I'm sorry I said a word to anybody about you."

"Do you understand how it undermines my authority when my partners treat me with disrespect?"

"We do respect you; that's the thing. I don't know what happened. It got out of hand too fast."

"Let's talk about something else."

"Do you think we'll solve this murder?"

"Yes. I know we will."

"How can you be so sure?"

"I'm sure because we're going to keep at it until we do. We haven't interviewed everyone yet. Also, we need to go back to Brad Jennings' home and go through every scrap of paper. We need to find out more about his past and the man he loved who died. Do you see where I'm going?"

"Yes, but we don't even know that man's name."

"We're going to find out. We might have to go to San Antonio, but we'll find his name. I think it's possible Brad's death is related to his relationship with his lover. It could be that someone was jealous of them or didn't like it that they were gay."

"It could still be someone here who didn't like it that he was gay."

"That's true but I hate to think it."

"What do you think about gay people?" he asked.

"In what way?"

"In any way."

"They're people with the same wants and needs as the rest of us. They're all as unique and individual as straight people are."

"Yeah, but I just don't get why a man would dress in women's clothes."

"Some straight men do that, too. You know that, right?"

"Yes, but I don't understand it."

"Maybe it's because our roles in society are too rigid. Brad had a side that liked pretty things. What is wrong with that?"

"Nothing."

"I'm a woman, but I have a side that likes guns and some other things that are considered 'boy things.' That doesn't make me a man, does it?"

"No, of course it doesn't."

"You don't have to understand everything. Just let people be who they are unless they're hurting somebody."

"I know." A few seconds passed and he asked, "Who is this woman we're going to see?"

"Vidalia Holder is not too bad in increments of five minutes or less. She loves animals but has no use for people. I get that, to a point, but she takes it too far. I want you to take the lead in this interview because she doesn't know you."

"But she'll think I'm too young to know anything."

"Prove her wrong."

"How do I do that?"

"Have confidence in yourself and remember that you know more than she does about law enforcement. You know the questions to ask. You have the fact that you're a young man going for you, too."

"Is this going to be another runaround with a horny old woman?"

"I don't know, but you'll get more out of her than I will. She's suing me for shooting her burro, so I'm shit on her shoe right now."

He laughed. "So is Sheriff Ben."

"Yep. She never gets the sheriff scraped off before she steps in him again."

We laughed about that, and then got serious and worked on a game plan for the cantankerous Miss Holder.

Before we approached her house, we spent some time speaking to Vidalia's animals. Horses, goats, two donkeys, and one cow occupied a large fenced area adjacent to a pasture. Dogs tore out from somewhere, barking, yipping, and whining, depending on which dog. She seemed to have every size. It didn't take long before she came out to stand on her porch and scream at us to get off her property.

"God knows, we want to," Buster said under his breath to me as he smiled and waved at her. "Hello, Ms. Holder."

Buster's masculinity, youth, and friendliness warmed the old gal a degree or two. "Come on to the house," she yelled, "but don't bring *her*."

Chisos Mountains, Margarita.

I walked along beside Buster even though Miss Holder made it clear I was unwelcome. At the rate I was going, I would soon be able to count all my Terlingua friends on three fingers.

Vidalia Holder is about ten years younger than Sheriff Ben. Her hair is dark with gray highlights that would be beautiful on a woman with a better personality. She's of medium height and is straight and in good shape from riding and taking care of her large place and many critters. It's difficult to think of her as attractive because of her grating temperament. The sheriff swears she sharpens her tongue on a whetstone.

"I'm suing her, you know," Vidalia confided in Buster as we climbed the steps onto her porch. "I don't understand why you brought her."

I hate it when people talk as though I'm not there, but I stayed quiet.

"Yes ma'am. I know about the lawsuit, but this is not about that."

That surprised her. "I suppose you'll want to come in." She held the door.

Before we stepped in, Buster shook hands with her. "I'm Deputy Mayhew, ma'am." He gave her his card. Poor Buster; now she had a new deputy to bug. He would have hell to pay for being young and for having green eyes.

She looked up at him with an innocent look that I didn't buy. "I'm Vidalia Holder. It's a pleasure to meet you." She whipped out her nice act for new guy. The rest of us were dead to her and also wise to her.

Ms. Holder gave me a stern look and jerked her head towards the door. I accepted her grudging invitation and entered.

Buster wasted no time in getting to the business at hand. "Ms.

Holder, we're here regarding the murder of Bradley Jennings."

"Oh!"

"You're aware that Mr. Jennings was murdered?"

"Yes, of course. Everyone knows about it."

"It's our understanding that you were frequently a visitor at his home. Is that correct?"

She threw a furtive glance in my direction. "It was never frequent, but I have been in his home a few times, and he's been here. Of course, I'd appreciate it if that didn't get around."

"Why is that?"

"It's nobody's business. The last thing I need is a scandal. This place is a hotbed of gossip and lies."

"Ms. Holder, what was the nature of your relationship to Mr. Jennings?"

"What is that supposed to mean?"

"Were you having sex with him?" I clarified.

"That is none of your business!"

Buster and I exchanged a glance. I was ready to zoom in for the kill, but I tried to be patient and work the plan. I noticed that Vidalia was wearing a man's flannel shirt over a t-shirt and it gave me an idea.

"Ms. Holder, we're conducting a murder investigation," explained Buster with incredible patience. "The nature of your relationship is important to that."

She examined her hands. "We were friends. I took him food. He rode horses with me a few times and ate dinner here. We weren't sleeping together."

I gave her the most doubtful look I could muster.

"What? You don't believe me?" She went from zero to super-heated in two seconds.

"It doesn't matter what we believe," I said. "We look at the evidence."

"You don't have any evidence about me." She turned to Buster with a pleading look. "Do you?"

"I can't talk about that, ma'am."

"You're wearing a piece of evidence," I stated, taking a guess.

"What?"

"You're wearing Brad Jennings' shirt."

Her reaction was pure guilt. She flushed beet red and jumped up. "So what? She looked from me to Buster with the panicked expression of a cornered animal. "So what if I am wearing it? I didn't kill him for it! He loaned it to me."

"We can't ask him if that's true, can we?"

She slumped back into the chair. "No."

"Women like to wear the clothes of the men they love." One more jab by Ricos.

"I wasn't in love with him and didn't sleep with him!"

"So you were just one of his admirers?" Buster clarified.

"This isn't going to be made public, is it?"

"You'll go on a list of females who had a relationship with the deceased."

Vidalia was so red I thought her heart would give out from pumping so much blood to her face in such a short time. "But that suggests I was sleeping with him!"

Buster didn't respond and pretended to look through his notes.

I dropped down with my talons out. "There is a way I could keep you off that public list of Brad's admirers."

"How? Please. If there's any way, I want you to do it."

"If I do you this favor, you have to agree to drop your lawsuit against Sheriff Duncan and me."

"That's blackmail!"

"No ma'am."

"It's dirty politics!"

"It's a reasonable request, a favor for a favor."

"You're exactly like the mafia."

Buster looked dangerously close to losing it and I wanted to, but I persisted. "I'm an innocent woman, a public servant who was doing a job no one else wanted to do. Your little burro was in terrible pain and would've died before a veterinarian could be located. You saw his body, Ms. Holder. It would've been cruel to move him."

I rested my case. I didn't see how she could have an argument, but she didn't keep that tongue of hers sharp for nothing. "You hateful little bitch! That sly fox Ben Duncan put you up to this, didn't he?"

Fox? It hit me then. Ms. Holder harbored unrequited desire for our sheriff. That wasn't even an unusual thing in South Brewster County. He was the most lusted-after older lawman I knew, not counting the fictional Sheriff Longmire.

"No," I said in answer to her question. "The sheriff doesn't know anything about it." And if he found out, I wasn't sure what he'd do. Better to do what I needed to and beg forgiveness later.

"I'll have to speak with my attorney."

"No ma'am. You need to call the D.A. right now and withdraw your suit. I need to witness it or your name goes on the list today."

"You bitch." Sigh. "You're such a bitch." She was about to pull out her hair. "You're a little bitch." She was also redundant.

I managed to keep my mouth shut. It must have been the magical power of the uniform. In regular clothes, I might've kicked her ass. In my uniform, I was a different woman. Sometimes I didn't even know her.

Vidalia Holder caved to the little bitch's demands. She made the call.

* * *

Buster and I high-fived each other in the truck. "I can't believe you pulled that off," he said.

"I can't believe it either; it was risky."

"How did you know about the shirt?"

"Men's shirts have buttons on the right side, not the left. And it looked about the right size for Brad Jennings. I followed a hunch."

"The sheriff will be impressed."

"I hope. He might yell at me."

"Are you crazy? The old witch is dropping her suit."

"Was that extortion?"

"I think it was."

I guess the stunt I pulled on Conway Twitty Bradford was extortion also. What was becoming of me? I didn't have time to dwell on it because our radio broadcasted "assistance needed" at a home where we were scheduled to do an interview.

"We're on the way," I assured the dispatcher. Buster had already turned on the lights and increased speed.

Dispatch responded with, "Sat phone."

I called him for the details. People from the Social Security Administration were in trouble at the Hagan residence. When they knocked on the door, Tamara Hagan had pulled a pistol on them and was verbally abusive.

"What does she have against people from the SSA? Did they stop sending her monthly checks, or what?" Buster quipped.

It seemed comical until Sheriff Ben called one minute later. "I'm going to try to make this the short version," he said. "Did you know that when you turn ninety, the folks from the Social Security Administration pay you a visit?"

"No sir, I didn't know that."

"Well they do and when they went to see this fellow, his daughter came to the door and said he'd gone sailing to the Bahamas. That didn't sit right and they began nosing around. It's a long story, but eventually they found his mummified body in a storage unit in Phoenix, Arizona. She's been collecting his social security payment for going on twenty years."

"His body had been there that long?"

"Yep; he was rolled into a series of sheets and then into a heavy rug and laid to rest as is."

"Did she kill him?"

"The sheriff there says not. It appears he died a natural death."

"Sheriff, how do all these odd people end up here?"

He laughed. "I don't know. I guess Terlingua is at the end of the road and they have nowhere else to go. You need to bring Ms. Hagan in since the SSA folks can't. They have her for fraud, but she won't listen to them. I coulda told them that, but I wasn't consulted. I want you to see if you can talk her into cooperating. She needs to give you the firearm first thing. You and Buster need to wear your vests."

"I'm on this, Sheriff."

"Also, the woman's sister is missing. It seems Terlingua is unraveling."

"No kidding."

"Keep me posted, Margarita."

"Yes sir."

All hell broke loose when we got to the residence. The arrival of "the law" made Tamara Hagan crazy. Well, I think she was already crazy, but the sight of us put her over the edge before any words were spoken.

We didn't even have a chance to meet the Social Security people before she came to the screen door screeching that she hadn't called the law. Her overall look was fearsome, totally Ma Barker on steroids. She hadn't bathed in who knew how long or changed her clothes or combed her wild gray hair. She smelled like…it isn't even describable how she smelled.

I won't repeat what she called me, but it made my blood pressure rise. I had to grab Buster's arm to keep him from doing something reckless on my behalf. If anybody was going to whoop her ass, I would do it.

Ms. Hagan spit, "You ain't gettin' my pistol and I got a rifle and two shotguns ready to fire. It don't make me no difference if I kill fuckin' deputies or Social Security assholes. You're all the same waste of space. Now back off!"

We backed off and called the sheriff.

"Well, for the love of Pete," he said with so much feeling it made me laugh in spite of my blood pressure crisis.

"There's no love here, Sheriff, only a truckload of crazy."

That caused him to laugh, but it was short-lived.

"I think her sister is dead inside the house," I continued. "Let me put it this way. The smell coming from there is putrefaction. Who or what it is I have no idea, but the place reeks of death." Not only did I have high blood pressure, my stomach was doing back flips.

"Let me call her," Sheriff Ben said in his confident way. "I bet I can talk her into letting you in to search the place."

I knew he possessed magic, but I didn't think he could talk that demented ol' woman into anything. Not to mention that we didn't want to go in her house. It could be booby-trapped, full of rotting dead things, or trip-wired for all we knew.

Get a grip, I ordered my imagination as we waited for the sheriff to call. I tried my new Chisos Mountains Mantra, but my brain laughed at me. Calming down might happen, but it wouldn't be anytime soon.

We went to speak with the Social Security people about staying back. It was wasted effort because the man and woman were already waiting it out across the road from the house, standing behind their government vehicle.

After ten minutes, Sheriff Ben called to say that Tamara Hagan had agreed to stand down. She was willing to turn her weapons over to "that red-headed boy with the gorgeous green eyes."

On hearing that, I think Buster considered quitting his job.

The sheriff said he would keep Ms. Hagan on the line in order to constantly reassure her that we'd do the right thing by her. I didn't know if his usual charm would work on a lunatic, but all we had was that and hope.

During the time we were speaking with the sheriff, Barney arrived with Mitch in the ambulance. We had a fast huddle about what was going on.

"Do you think she'll shoot me?" Buster was scared and nobody could blame him. It was a terrifying scene that could play out all kinds of ways.

"You're wearing your vest. I'll be next to you on one side," Barney said, "and Ricos will be on the other. We'll have you covered."

"What good will that do if she shoots me in the head?" Buster asked with good reason. "So you'll kill her for killing me? So freaking what?" Before anyone could say anything, he added, "Let's just do this."

I headed for one side of him and Barney the other. Before Buster made it to the door, the woman scooted the pistol outside. It clattered along the walkway and came to rest near Buster's boot.

That was followed by a rifle and two shotguns that made a loud clanking noise but didn't fire.

"That's all I got," she yelled. "I'm gonna want them back."

Buster cleared his throat. "Thank you ma'am, I appreciate your cooperation. May we come in?"

She turned away from us, talking in a low voice to Sheriff Ben. I don't know what he told her, but she motioned for us to enter.

Mitch ran up and handed us surgical masks that weren't going to help. We put them on, along with gloves, and entered what looked like a war zone. A dog, a cat, and numerous mice lay wherever they had died and were in various stages of decomposition.

"He was a good dog," the old lady said when she saw me looking at him.

"How did he die?"

She shrugged. "Old age, I suppose."

Live mice and roaches boldly wandered over everything. Half-eaten food was rotting in dishes and pans. The kitchen sink was full to overflowing. Filthy clothes were strewn all over. The floors were nasty with the excrement of animals and possibly humans. The stench made my eyes burn.

"Ms. Hagan," Buster said, "Where is your sister?"

"She took off a few days ago."

"Did she have a car?"

"No. She was walking."

"Aren't you concerned about her?"

"She'll be back."

"Do you know where she would've gone?"

"You have the most beautiful eyes, young man."

"Thank you, ma'am. Does your sister have a friend she would visit?"

"Are they real or contacts?"

Buster gave me a plaintive look.

"Deputy Mayhew, will you go out to the road and keep people from stopping? Extreme nosiness will start any time now."

Buster nearly ran from the room.

The place was so bad it was a wake-up slap in the face. Tamara Hagan was mentally ill in a big way. No telling what had happened to her sister, but Tamara needed urgent care so I went out and brought Mitch in.

He has a bedside manner that is legendary, and he remains calm at the most gruesome and chaotic of scenes. He stays focused on the job he has to do while treating his patients with love. *Wait a minute.* I never realized it before, but I think my friend Mitch channels the Chisos.

He spoke to Ms. Hagan in a soft, soothing voice. "Have you eaten today?"

She shook her head no and tears filled her eyes.

He touched her on the shoulder in the gentle way you would handle an injured child and asked to speak to the sheriff. She handed him the phone with no argument.

"Sheriff, this is Mitch. I'm going to take Ms. Hagan to the ambulance and check her out. She needs something to eat and drink, and I'm not sure what else. I'll hand you over to Margarita now." He paused. "You're welcome." He winked and handed me the phone.

I smiled at him and mouthed, *thank you, Mitch.* "Sheriff, we need… I don't know what we need. I've never seen anything like this. I think we need a team in Hazmat suits, and we'll need new uniforms when this is over."

Barney yelled, "I've got remains over here in this barrel."

Chapter 14

We determined the remains to be those of a large dog. It was sickening, but at least it wasn't Tamara Hagan's sister. When the sheriff called again, I gave him that information.

An approaching siren wailed in the distance and Barney said, "I bet that's the sheriff."

"He didn't mention coming."

"That's because he's the sheriff. He doesn't have to tell you diddley-squat."

That was true, but the comment renewed my anger with the big ol' lug.

After a while I went out for a breath of air and saw Sheriff Ben standing by the ambulance. He appeared to be conversing with Mitch, but I could only see him, not Mitch. He may have been trying to cajole Ms. Hagan into giving up the location of her sister, but I thought it was highly possible she didn't know it.

When he saw me watching, Sheriff Ben motioned me over. He stepped away from the ambulance. "Any sign of an elderly woman in there?"

"No sir."

"What is your take on this?"

"Ms. Hagan is mentally ill, so it's hard to know whether to believe her or not, but she says her sister wandered off. She thinks she'll wander back."

"Mitch is going to take her to the hospital for observation, and I'm going to send Buster with him. He's certified to drive the ambulance, right?"

"Yes. He'll be glad to get out of here."

"I thought it would be best for Mitch to stay with his patient because she can be unreasonable and panicky, according to him."

"When you see the house, you'll understand how ill she is."

He nodded in understanding. Then he said, "You look lovely today, Margarita, but you smell dead."

"Why, thank you, Sheriff Ben. I've never received a backhanded compliment of that magnitude before."

He laughed. "I see what you mean about needing a new uniform." There was a short pause. "Margarita, Vidalia Holder is dropping her lawsuit against us. She told the D.A. my deputies are like the Mafia. Care to enlighten me?"

"Not really."

"Tell me anyway."

I explained what happened in such a bare bones way that he was confused, which was the general idea.

"Maybe you can explain better later," he said.

"Yes, sir." Maybe he'd forget it.

"What happened this morning at Wynne's? Do you have any idea?"

I told him what little I knew.

"Barney indicated they were talking about you and it got out of hand between Buster and Wynne. Are you having trouble with Buster?"

"No sir. I hope you'll give him a second chance. But also please remind him that dating a fellow deputy is against the rules."

The sheriff's brow furrowed. "It seems like that would be common sense."

"He doesn't have enough experience yet to understand the reason for the rule, but he will."

"I'm going to have a stern talk with him, but if he's working out as a trainee, I hate to put someone else down here right now. We have that murder and now this mess. I know William Jackson will find a way to make me look bad over this. He'll call it more of the 'Terlingua lawlessness' that I condone."

"Sheriff, I want to look into his background. I don't think he's the squeaky-clean patriot-veteran-hero-justice fighter he claims to be."

The sheriff chuckled. "I know that's true, but first I want the Jennings murder solved. That's more important than my career."

If the voters of Brewster County could've heard that statement, every vote in the upcoming election would be for Sheriff Ben.

"I want you and Barney back on that today," he continued. "I've got Texas Search and Rescue coming with cadaver dogs, so we ought to be able to determine soon if the missing woman is anywhere around here."

"Should I get Barney and go?"

"Not so fast. You go take over for Buster and send him to my truck."

Pobrecito Buster. Poor Buster would have to endure one of those rambling, old man, "this is how we act" lectures. But then again, he needed to hear it.

Before the sheriff finished with Buster, Barney came out, saw what was going on, and sidled up to me. "What did you tell the sheriff about me?"

"Nothing."

"For real?"

"What would I say? That you're a big ol' sexist lug and I don't want to work with you anymore?"

"Jeez, I hope that's not true."

"The last part is not true."

"You used to be able to take a joke."

"That was before all your jokes became sexually harassing. Now I feel it's me against you and Buster and I'm losing."

"That's not true."

"On top of that, we have a brutal murder to solve, and I don't see that happening, do you? Everybody thinks I'm getting it on with the sheriff. His wife is hurt and angry. Hell, *he's* hurt and angry. The county commission treats him like he's a parasite instead of the best thing this county has going for it. Some asshole named Billy Jack is likely to be our next boss if we don't do something about it. Our raft is sinking, and you and Buster want to wisecrack about my body as if that's all there is about me that has value. I'm a fucking joke. I don't even know what I'm doing here anymore. And I've started cursing! That's on you. Also, a beautiful man came to my house last night and then he *ran*...he ran away because I'm crazy. I sure as hell don't need any shit from you."

My partner's mouth hung open. "Jeez, Ricos, I think you need a hug."

"Don't touch me. You need a hard kick in the butt with a steel-toed boot."

"How come you didn't tell the sheriff?"

"You're my longtime partner and that counts for something. And because you covered for me after Kevin died and I could barely get out of bed. And you covered for me when I drank and didn't ever tell the sheriff; and because you probably wouldn't tell him if I did something insulting to you."

"Thank you, Margarita."

"And the last reason is that I'm not perfect, either."

"Can I quote you on that?"

"No."

"So what beautiful man came to your house? Do I know him?"

"I doubt it. He's a Texas Ranger Zeke sent to say hi to me because he's working in Presidio County. I think I cured my father of trying to set me up with people."

Barney laughed. "I met him. He came to the office looking for you. He said he checked for you at the house and you weren't there. I told him you were probably out running."

"And?"

"He insisted I tell him where you ran."

"That's weird."

"I'm sure you haven't messed up as badly as you think."

"You're right. It's probably worse."

* * *

Barney and I smelled too awful to do interviews, so we stopped at a pullout, opened the doors and windows, and discussed a game plan on our murder. We agreed that our first move should be to re-check Bradley Jennings' home for any scrap of information that might be relevant.

"Do you think anybody will ever find that old gal's sister?" Barney asked.

"I doubt it. Look how long it took to find her father."

"Yes, but that was twenty years ago when she was younger and stronger and could move bodies around. Now she doesn't even have the strength to move dead animals out of her house."

"I think that had more to do with mental illness than lack of strength," I said.

"I wonder how she ended up here."

"My guess is that someone in her family, maybe her father, owned a little place on Terlingua Ranch and she got the chance to use it. People can live private lives here and do all kinds of things, both good and bad, that nobody knows about until the law or the government catches up with them."

"It's bad when the Social Security Administration busts your ass."

I laughed and agreed.

"Ricos, what you said earlier about being a fucking joke—that's not true. You know that, don't you?"

"I know it, but I don't know if you do."

"Of course I do. Sometimes I get carried away. I'm sorry. I do it with Julia too, and she kicks my ass, verbally speaking." Julia is Barney's wife.

"We're supposed to be a team. I need to know I'm an equal part of it. If I'm not, then I don't want to do this."

"Ricos without you there is no team. I'll do better. I swear it."

Since it was getting late, and we were getting nowhere and didn't smell any better as time went by, we finished the list of things to do that might get us somewhere and called it a day.

* * *

I whipped off my clothes on the porch. I just couldn't bring myself to carry the smell of death into my house. It was bad enough I had to take my body inside—and my hair. Ugh. If some creepy photographer was lurking around this was their big chance, but they'd have to be fast to catch me.

After the longest shower I ever enjoyed, I felt better, then dressed and sat on my porch to watch night claim the land from the day. The light, in its reluctance to leave, made an extravagant protest by creating long shadows, splashing showy colors all over the place, and finally, burning down the western sky in a fiery explosion. No matter how intense the protests, dark always wins the battle, for a while.

Chapter 15

The following morning I sat on my porch to watch the same process in reverse. Light was back, demanding its turn. The everyday tug-of-war between daylight and dark and good and evil was never-ending entertainment, the theme of many great literary works, and also the reason there are jobs in law enforcement.

Barney pulled up before I had finished even one cup of the coffee I rarely made for myself.

"You know it's Sunday, right?" I called from my comfortable position.

He unfurled himself from the truck and reached the porch with only a few strides because he has legs that allow that kind of progress.

He smiled. "Coffee?" was his greeting.

"Help yourself."

He came back with a mug and sat next to me. "By the way, I do know it's Sunday. Some people sleep late or take their loved ones out for a leisurely breakfast, but not us, Ricos."

"Crime fighters don't get no stinkin' weekends," I reminded him.

"On a positive note, spring has returned."

"Yes, Mr. I-Hate-Snow, it has."

"That's Deputy I-Hate-Snow to you."

"Right. Did you take the last of the coffee?"

"You told me to help myself. It's good coffee, by the way."

"Thank you. I know how to make it; I just don't drink it often because it keeps me awake."

"That's the point."

"I'll make more. If we're going to comb through a dead man's things, we need fortification."

* * *

The Jennings home was a sad, eerie place to spend a sparkling morning. The sun was warm, but a cool breeze drifted down from the Christmas Mountains. The air smelled of green growing things and fresh flowers: spring, in other words.

Many of Bradley's possessions had been removed, either by the killer or law enforcement, so we had little hope of finding something useful. Being champions of justice, we persevered. Every nook, cranny, closet, and all possible hidey-holes were investigated. As searches always go, we were on the last room, the living room, when we got something.

Barney lifted the cushions off the couch and felt along in the crevices. He dug in deep and pulled out a rumpled piece of paper and read it. "We have lift-off here, Batgirl."

"What is it?"

"It's a sappy love poem, but at the top is written 'I will always love you' and it's signed by John Cooper. Isn't John the name of Bradley's long lost love?"

"Yes! So his last name was Cooper. John Cooper. Why is that ringing a bell?"

"I have no idea, but let's think outside."

"Great idea."

Sitting on the stoop of Brad's house, I let my mind roam. You know where it went: up into the Chisos Mountains, where spring is especially spectacular and then it ran along the Rio Grande where new green and blooms had been in evidence for at least a month already. Then it skipped across the desert flats and colorful badlands, back over to where we sat near the base of the Christmas Mountains.

I jumped up. "I've got it. Oh my gosh, Barney! That strange old woman... Her last name is Cooper. She's Iva Cooper."

"Do you think she knows something?"

"She claims not to, but it's too coincidental. She sits up there on the hill where she can watch everything. It's creepy. What if John was her son or her brother? What if she moved here so she could spy on them?"

"Ricos, get a grip. John died before Brad moved here, remember?"

"There's a connection. I know it."

Barney waggled his nose around in the air. "Super Sleuth Ricos is on the trail."

"Shut up. Let's go see her."

Sheriff Ben had said she should be called in advance, but I thought not. She needed a surprise visit from The Law.

* * *

"This is a bad idea, Ricos," Barney said under his breath as we waited a long time at Ms. Cooper's door. We'd walked around the house twice to be sure she wasn't outside.

"Keep knocking. I know she's home."

"So now you have x-ray vision?"

"Yes. Didn't you know? Actually, it's a case of exceptional detecting."

He groaned. "Oh God, here we go."

"Her car is here, Pard."

"Oh."

"Stick with me."

"Yeah, and get shot."

Old Mr. Feldman crossed my mind.

After a few more minutes, Barney asked, "Can you think of an excuse for kicking in her door?"

"No, but I can think of some reasons why we shouldn't."

"Name one."

"Hello? Firearms."

"You think the old gal is armed?"

"She's a tough old Texas woman."

"Oh, true."

"Miss Cooper," I yelled, loud enough to awaken late sleepers in Mexican border towns. "She may be hard of hearing," I explained to Barney.

"Now *I* am." He started messing with his ear.

"Give it a rest."

Miss Cooper had one tree in her front yard and we went to sit under it.

After a short wait I said, "You know what? I think this is a job for Sheriff Ben. She's sweet on him."

"Does every older woman in Brewster County lust after our sheriff?"

"I think so."

"I hope I still have it goin' on like that when I'm old," my partner said.

"For that to be true, you'd have to have it goin' on now."

He slapped his head. "Goddamn it, Ricos. And you get mad at me for messing with you? This is some double standard shit we have goin' on here."

"Smart-ass insults and sexual harassment are not the same thing. I'll give you detailed lessons after we solve this murder."

"Oh, goody; I can't wait."

"Since you can't wait, here's your first lesson. How would you feel if I went to see a woman on Sheriff's Office business and we discussed your ass and chest and your other physical *attributes?*"

"Are you kidding? I'd be honored."

I stifled the urge to smack him. "That's because you aren't reduced every day to a sex object. People look at you and they don't question if you can do the job. They don't doubt your strength or your intelligence just because you have a nice butt or whatever. Nobody ever refers to you as 'that boy deputy' and I bet you've never heard, 'here comes Deputy Sweet Ass.'"

"True and I want to know who says that to you."

"That's not the point at all."

"I get it, Ricos."

"I just don't want you to be like them, Barney. Please be better than that."

"I'm trying, okay?"

"Bring a notebook to class because I don't want to have to repeat myself."

As a last resort, I called our dispatcher on the satellite phone. He reminded me that our sheriff was up much of the night overseeing the search for Tamara Hagan's sister. And no, she was not found, either alive or dead. Also, he suggested in a strong way that I not call our boss today.

"To bother the sheriff or not to bother the sheriff? That is the question."

"Don't go all Shakespeare on me, Ricos."

"He wants this murder solved yesterday, right? On the other hand, it's Sunday. His wife is hurt and angry. What would you do if your wife was hurt and angry?"

"I'd make passionate love to her all morning and take her out to a sumptuous breakfast and then make love to her some more."

"Exactly. I'm not calling."

"Then we'd better figure out how to get into that house."

162

We walked back over to the door, pounded on it, and Barney yelled, "If you don't open this door and speak with us right now, we're calling S.W.A.T. There won't be a door or window left in your house."

It worked like magic. Miss Cooper opened her door and blinked up at Barney. "What is all this fuss?"

Her expression was so innocent he looked over at me. "Deputy Ricos?"

"Miss Cooper, you remember me, don't you?"

"Yes, of course; come in, Deputies."

We followed her into her living room. I noticed right away that all the photos of her brother were gone. Had she been removing them while Barney and I waited? It was surreal to see all the empty spaces and bright places on the faded wall where the pictures had been.

"Miss Cooper, what happened to all the photographs of your brother?"

"I put them in storage."

"Why?"

"One can only grieve so long, Deputy. They were a constant reminder of my terrible loss."

"I'm sorry for your loss, but we need to see a photo of Bailey."

She made a wave-away gesture. "Whatever for?"

"Miss Cooper, you told me before you didn't know Brad Jennings well. Isn't that so?"

"That's true."

"Do you know someone named John Cooper?"

"No; I don't think so."

"What was your brother's full name?"

"What are you getting at?"

"I'd like to know your brother's full name."

"It was Bailey Cooper. He had no middle name."

"I don't believe you."

"Young lady, I don't know why I would lie about such a thing."

"I don't know either, but I suspect it's because you know more about the death of Bradley Jennings than you're willing to admit. I have to ask myself why that would be, and the only answer I get is that you're implicated."

She sniffed, insulted. "I'm going to report you to Sheriff Duncan."

"Fine," I said, "but if I were you, I wouldn't call him today."

Barney took over because I had lost it. "We still need a photo of Bailey Cooper."

"I don't have to give you one."

It was a standoff.

"Oh! I do have one." Miss Cooper went into her bedroom and returned with a baby picture of her brother.

"This is not helpful." My partner wasn't amused. "We need a clear photo of him as an adult."

"No can do," she snapped.

"We'll get a warrant," threatened Barney.

The old lady smiled. "Don't come back without one."

* * *

That evening, Jessie Williams, the bouncer from Slim Jimmie's in Odessa, called me. He had the name of the patron who had hassled Brad Jennings on the last night of his life. His name was Stan Hatch.

"I got his phone number," Jessie said. "Does it matter if I lied to get it?"

"No, but when I call him, he might figure it out."

"That's okay. I doubt if he'll give me any crap."

I doubted it too.

"Look. There's one more thing I should tell you. A few months ago, I asked Brad for his phone number."

"Okay, go on."

"I liked him. I didn't want to say that in front of the owner of the club because I'm not supposed to flirt with customers. I'm human though."

"I understand."

"There was something special about Brad. He was twenty-some years older than me but he seemed like a genuinely good man. There don't seem to be a lot of those who are still single."

No kidding.

"You won't tell my boss, will you?"

"No. I have no reason to tell him."

"That's good."

"Did you ever visit Brad or did he visit you?"

"No. I called him a few times, but he said the love of his life had died and he wasn't ready to date."

"Did that upset you?"

"I felt sorry for him, and for me, but I kept his number in case he'd be interested later."

Jessie Williams was big enough and strong enough to beat a man to death. That didn't mean he had, but I made a note to add his name to our murder board.

Chapter 16

The sheriff and I went back to Miss Cooper's on Monday. On the way, I made the mistake of referring to her as an "old woman." The sheriff informed me that she was "only" sixty-three. That was a surprise because she looked older. I explained that when I met her, I thought she was old enough to be his mother. He told me to just stop talking. Jeez, old people are so touchy.

The sheriff was certain a warrant would not be necessary. He was also sure that a woman of her age and sterling character had nothing to do with such a brutal murder. I thought making love all day Sunday had made the old guy loopy.

Miss Cooper opened the door for Sheriff Ben at first rap and her smile was sparkling, but maybe that was her extra-white dentures. They greeted each other in the manner of longtime friends. He even hugged her. Gag.

When her eyes moved over to me, her expression turned wintery. Great; I was becoming less and less popular in my county, across all ages and walks of life, proving that I do not discriminate.

Miss Cooper tucked her arm in the sheriff's and led him into the living room, chattering happily. I followed, firmly in my role of Invisible Woman.

"Would you like a glass of tea?" She addressed him and ignored me.

He accepted with typical manners and quiet charm, but he suggested that I might want a glass, too.

"Well, of course," she purred. "I didn't mean to leave you out."

Like hell. She brought me a glass but, in protest, I didn't drink it.

The old gal was so focused on the sheriff I wondered if she'd notice if I got up and looked around for a jar of Mr. Jennings' genitalia; besides, wasn't I invisible? If I couldn't mentally entertain myself, my job would be unbearable most days.

A solid thirty minutes of my life was wasted watching the sheriff work the old woman. It made me realize that to get cooperation I needed to be a handsome older man like our sheriff or a gigantic man like Barney. As if either was gonna happen in this lifetime.

Things got interesting when the sheriff turned serious and asked to see a photo of Iva Cooper's beloved brother. She claimed she had no photos of him as an adult. As he grew more demanding, she became spittin' angry with the star of her lawman fantasies. It was painful to watch. It was also painful to keep my mouth shut, but I pretended my lips were sown together.

At last we left, and as we got in his vehicle the sheriff said, "We'll need that warrant, Margarita," which meant I had to get it.

* * *

After work I took my troubles out for a run and tossed them to the wind. It was the least I could do for myself after enduring all that grossness with the sheriff and Iva Cooper, not to mention all the other gruesome things going on in my life. It was hard to understand old people, but then I didn't get young ones, either. I didn't seem to fit in anywhere, but running made me not care.

The fabulousness of where I live makes up for people and the terrible things they do. Running could even take away the sting-ing memory of the botched meeting between the handsome Texas Ranger and The Idiot. When I look at the mountains or even the hills and bumps and formations too funky to fit in a category, it's evident what is real and meaningful. In the day-to-day crap, it's difficult to keep my head on straight. Running is another thing.

I'd been home long enough to get a shower before my running afterglow was dimmed by the telephone. Victoria called, which is normally a good thing.

"Did you have to eat lunch with him in public?" she snapped.

"What are you talking about?"

"You and Sheriff Bad Boy had lunch together."

"You're not serious? It was lunch! Should we hide like cheaters sneaking around? I guess we should've eaten our lunch in bed."

"Now is not the time to be a smart-ass."

"When is the time? You should call back then."

"If I didn't love you, I'd hang up right now."

"Please don't. You're one of my only fingers."

"What?"

"I was thinking yesterday that I can count my Terlingua friends on three fingers. You're one of them."

"You are so crazy. If I have to be a finger, I'd rather be your thumb."

"My thumb is short and chubby."

"Okay, not your thumb."

"Why are we having this ridiculous conversation?"

"Because a lot of nosy, gossipy idiots saw you with the sheriff today and want to torture me with it."

"Did they mention that we were wearing our uniforms? We were having a working lunch in a public place and talking about solving a murder. And we never once touched or blew kisses at each other."

"That doesn't matter. You chose a place that's a hotbed of gossip."

"Where would we go in Brewster County that isn't a hotbed of gossip?"

"You have a point."

"Why are you so angry about it?"

"I'm sick and tired of hearing it. Why do people tell me? Hell, it's not even new news anymore."

"Vic, it's no news and never was; don't forget that. I'm not having, nor have I ever had, sex with the sheriff. If people tell you, it's probably because they think you'll tell me and I'll be hurt by it or I'll shape up and get my hands off the man. The sheriff and I were trying to solve a vicious murder. If people think that's sexy, then they're welcome to help us."

"If you'd come meet the man I've reserved for you, this book would slam shut."

"Oh Vic. Do you really want to introduce me to someone you like?"

"When you get to know this man, you'll thank me."

"Maybe so, but will he?"

She laughed.

"You laugh now, Vic, but you won't when he comes crying to you."

"Let me worry about that. Are you any closer to solving the murder?"

"Yes, I believe we are, but you know I can't tell you anything."

"I know. I'm glad you're getting closer. You rock, Deputy Ricos."

"I love you, Vic. Now go hug Morgan and forget what the dim-wits are telling you about me."

She laughed. "You mean like in high school?"

"Yep, exactly like that."

I managed to get my underwear on before I got a radio message to respond to an emergency at Doctores Fronterizos, my mother's clinic. My blissful runner's high went right out the window.

My uniform was on the front porch stinking. I had more, but

they were at the office. I found an old uniform shirt in the closet and wore it with jeans and my good leather boots, and tore out the door with my hair wet. So it goes for a woman on call.

The ambulance was parked at the clinic with its lights still flashing, which reminded me to turn mine off. I started to go inside the building, but I heard voices coming from the back of the EMS vehicle. Mom and Mitch were bent over someone I couldn't see. Neither one looked up when I entered.

"Come on in," my mom said over her shoulder, "and tell us if you know this young man. He has no I.D. on him."

Mitch pulled back a little so I could get a clear view of the patient. They were still assessing the man's injuries, so most of his clothes had been removed.

"I don't know him," I said. "It looks like someone tried to strangle him."

"Yes," Mom said. "That appears to be the case." A couple of beats passed and she added, "He's an extraordinarily good-looking young man."

"Yes, he is. Will you let me get a closer look at his neck?"

She stepped back so I could peer at the strangulation marks. In doing that I noticed something that surprised me. It was the tattoo of a blue bee high on his shoulder near the neck.

I took a breath. "Mom, I'm going to tell you this because of the health risk to you and Mitch. This young man works or used to work in the sex trade."

"What in the world makes you think that?"

"Do you see this tiny tattoo? It's a blue bee."

"Should that mean something to me?"

"It means he was a prostitute at a brothel in Ojinaga called The Blue Bee." Ojinaga is a Mexican border town across the Rio Grande from Presidio, Texas. It's located sixty-odd miles from Terlingua.

My mom's mouth dropped open. "And you know this from…" Her voice tapered off and she turned back to her patient.

I studied him instead of responding to her question.

"We're always careful," she said and glanced at Mitch. He was busy with the patient and trying to ignore us.

The young man's head was wrapped in a gauze bandage and blood had seeped through it. There was also a significant amount of blood on his shirt.

"What happened to his head?" I asked.

"He was shot, but the bullet only grazed him."

"So he was strangled and shot, yet he's still alive."

"Yes, but at this point, he's barely holding on," Mitch said.

"If he's from Ojinaga, how did he get here?" My mom wondered.

"I don't have any idea," I said. "How did he get to you?"

"He was found unconscious along highway 118, near one of the McFarley Ranch gates," my mother explained. "Isn't that the place that's so obnoxious about maintaining their privacy? They're hateful towards visitors."

"Yes; uninvited guests are considered trespassers and they prosecute them or try to."

Mitch interrupted to say to Mom, "His vitals don't look good."

She nodded and continued to work on their patient. "He needs to be in the hospital, but we can't get him stabilized enough to transport him." After a pause she continued, "The bullet didn't lodge in his head and that's good, but we don't think he was far from death to begin with. That's why he's doing so poorly now."

"It appears he was shot from behind," added Mitch. "My guess is he was running away and someone tried to stop him."

"You're sure there's no bullet?"

"I'm sure." My mom gave me a look and continued. "He's severely dehydrated from loss of blood and probably a lack of drinking water. His feet are full of blisters, as if he ran a long time."

"We're giving him fluids, and that should help," Mitch said.

"Who brought him in?"

"Mr. Sinclair picked him up on the highway."

"Why didn't he take him to Alpine?"

"I don't know. Maybe it was because he was headed this way and thought it'd be quicker to bring him to the clinic. He called 911 as soon as he had cell service and Mitch went to meet him. Mr. Sinclair's waiting in the clinic if you want to speak with him. Make it fast though, because you're driving us to town as soon as we get him stabilized." By "town" my mother meant Alpine.

Mr. Sinclair is a retired man who lives in Terlingua with his wife of many years. It was hard to believe he'd harm anyone, but nothing can be taken for granted. He never caused problems or made a spectacle of himself. The more I considered it, the less likely it seemed.

I greeted him. He smiled, stood, and removed his hat in the respectful way of a Texas gentleman.

"Please have a seat, Mr. Sinclair, and tell me what you know."

"I was comin' down 118 and I saw something lying by the road. I thought it was a bunch of rags someone had pitched out. I went back to clean it up. It aggravates me to no end the way people trash up our desert."

Mr. Sinclair was a man after my own heart. I think litterers should have to do jail time and clean-up work, but our lawmakers don't care what I think.

"Did he say anything to you?"

"Oh no; I thought he was dead he was so quiet. I felt for his pulse and he barely had one. I didn't know what to do because I had no cell service, so I put him on the backseat of my car and headed this way."

"After you saw that the pile of rags was a man, what was your first impression of him, besides the fact that he was hurt?"

He thought about it. "He'd been running from something. A piece of his clothing was caught on the fence, so I think he came over it. I also couldn't help but notice his looks. Even badly injured, he is a noticeably handsome man."

"Yes sir. He is. Are you familiar with the McFarley Ranch?"

"No ma'am, except people say it's vast and beautiful. I know they don't welcome visitors."

"And you found him near the ranch?"

He nodded. "Yes. It was their fence he came over."

"Thank you, Mr. Sinclair. Do you need a ride home?"

"No. I have my car. It's parked around on the other side of the building. They asked me to wait and talk to you."

"I appreciate it. May I take a look in your vehicle?"

"Yes, of course."

He had spread a blanket on the backseat, as I'd hoped. "May I take your blanket, Mr. Sinclair?"

"Yes. Of course you can."

"It might hold a clue about what happened or where he came from. It'll be returned to you after the crime lab looks at it."

"I understand. I hope you can get to the bottom of this."

"Thank you. I'll give it my best."

He smiled at me. "Then that should do it."

Aha. There was one person in my county who believed in me besides the obvious ones. My heart did a little happy dance and I went back to the ambulance.

Mitch was standing outside the vehicle and appeared to be waiting for me.

"We're about to transport."

"So he's better?"

"His vitals are improved enough for transport, but I can't promise anything. We're leaving as soon as Galveston gets here." Galveston is the usual driver and is also a medic. If he was going, that meant I didn't have to go after all.

"Your mom is coming with us," Mitch added.

"Margarita," my mother said, "I'm going to want the whole story on how you know about that tattoo."

"I figured, but I'll have to tell you later. Whatever terrible thing you're thinking, it wasn't that."

"I was only thinking that we should've used a tracking device on you when you were younger."

"I wouldn't be nearly as interesting if you had."

"Stop being such a smartass."

I didn't see how I could make that happen in this lifetime, so I hugged her and kissed her on the cheek. Poor mom.

Mitch spoke from behind me. "You'll find out who did this to him, won't you, Margarita?"

"I'll give it everything I have, Mitch."

"I'll take that as a yes."

* * *

I called Sheriff Ben and brought him up to speed. He was concerned and upset that a young man from Mexico had been found injured by the highway. He thought it did not bode well and I agreed. Unlike my mother, he accepted the fact that I knew of The Blue Bee and didn't demand answers to nosy questions.

After a while he left that subject and said, "After you see the judge about the warrant in the morning, I want you to go to the McFarley Ranch headquarters and inquire about the injured man."

I almost groaned. *Seriously? What about the other deputies?*

"Sheriff, wouldn't it be better to send Barney?"

"You're more likely to get cooperation from those tough old cowboys, don't you think?"

What? Why not send the largest deputy to intimidate them instead of sending the smallest one…to do what? Oh. I possessed the female genes.

Since I was speechless, he asked, "Do you have a problem?"

"No sir."

"I'm thinking they'll underestimate you. You're a master at using that to your advantage. Don't you agree?"

"Is anyone going with me?"

He took a deep breath. "Aren't you the woman who challenges me every time I try to send a man with you?"

Chapter 17

My eyes burned and my brain felt dead in my head as I waited outside the chambers of Judge Samuels, the grumpiest man in Texas. I was dressed in a clean uniform, but I didn't feel sharp enough to cut through pudding. It would give our judge an unfair advantage in an argument, but nothing could be done about it now.

My head was resting in my hands when a tall lawman rode in on a big paint stallion to save the day. Okay. He walked in and there was no horse, but he showed up. My boss strode down the empty hall, his boots making a clicking sound on the hardwood floor. He sat next to me, removed his hat, and hooked it over his knee. In his right hand he gripped a Styrofoam cup of wicked-smelling coffee. He took a sip of it and sighed. Lack of sleep showed on his face, too.

"Good morning, Margarita."

"Good morning, Sheriff Ben."

"I don't guess you got much sleep?"

"About four hours."

"Same here." He smiled. "I see the judge is making you wait."

"Yes, as always."

"Margarita, the injured man from Mexico was moved into a private room at dawn this morning."

"Oh, that's great."

"Yes. He's not coherent yet, but the hospital will call me when he is so we can talk to him."

"Don't you think you should send someone who speaks Spanish?"

"Why, I would never have thought of that." He paused. "In spite of what some folks think, I do know my job, Margarita."

"Yes sir, I know you do. That's why I want you to keep it."

He smiled. "I'll see you after a while."

"Aren't you going with me to plead our case to the judge?"

"No, not today." He stood and replaced his hat. "I can't stand the old coot."

My mouth opened.

He winked. "Carry on, Deputy Ricos."

After keeping me waiting twenty minutes, Judge Samuels opened the door to his chambers and peered out. His thick gray eyebrows furrowed in disapproval when he saw there was no one waiting but me. He barked, "Come in, you."

"Good morning, Judge." I tried to sound chipper and confident.

He wheeled around and went back to his desk. "Shut the door."

I closed it and sat on a chair in front of him.

He didn't look up from his paperwork. "What is it?"

"I need a warrant to search the home of Iva Cooper on Terlingua Ranch."

"For what reason?"

I explained the significance of the photographs of Ms. Cooper's brother and that she refused to cooperate. I had filled out the paperwork requesting a warrant and I laid it on his desk. He picked it up and read it with his trademark frown. That's his only expression besides sneers or smirks, the boring old man.

He cleared his throat. "How long have you and the sheriff been going at it like bunny rabbits?"

"What?" *Thank you, I'm awake now.*

"You heard me."

"That's not something that's happening. It's a rumor."

"That's not what I hear."

"Judge, you know hearing something doesn't make it true."

He smirked. "You'd better hope you don't kill the old guy."

I said nothing, but I wanted to kick his scrawny ass into the hall, down the stairs, out the door, down the sidewalk, and into the sheriff's office. Sheriff Ben could take a turn, followed by all the other judge-disgruntled lawmen in town.

"I can't issue a warrant based on coincidence and you sure as hell should know that by now. Two men happen to be named Cooper. So what? That's a common name, Deputy Ricos."

"I realize that Judge, but there has to be a connection. Why else would Miss Cooper refuse to let us see a photo of her brother?"

"Who knows? Maybe she doesn't think it's any of your business."

"But it's a murder investigation."

"That means nothing to her, most likely."

I tried to think of something brilliant to say that would make him see the light. I came up with zilch, except for pulling my weapon on him—bad idea.

Judge Samuels stole a spider-ish gawk at me. It was creepy and my gut clinched because it knew something was coming. The old codger winked. "We could discuss the merits of your warrant over lunch."

I gaped at him.

"Maybe you'd rather get a cup of coffee right now?"

"Judge Samuels, I need to get the warrant. I have a long list of things to do today and I don't have time for coffee or lunch, but thank you."

"Do you understand what I'm asking?"

Oh, gross.

"I think so, but I hope I'm wrong."

"We don't have to go to a motel." He made a room-encompassing motion with his hand. "Right here would work."

I was speechless.

"You show me a little cooperation and I'll return the favor."

"Judge, that's extortion." _I, of all people, would recognize it._

He slammed his hands on the desk with such force it frightened me. He stood and glared. "That's no way to speak to a judge, young lady."

I stood, too, because I felt the need to stand my ground. "You're asking me to exchange sexual favors for a warrant." Of course he knew what he was asking; I only blurted it because I couldn't believe it.

"Take it or leave it, sugar."

"That's not going to happen, and it's wrong of you to ask."

"I'll hold you in contempt!"

"Judge, please be reasonable. I have a right to say no."

"So do I. Now get out! Not _one word_ about this, you understand? Need I remind you that it's your word against mine? I can make your life miserable."

He already had.

I left his office, but I didn't know what to do. I felt like throwing up. I also wanted to go back and shoot him. Instead, I went to see Sheriff Ben. I swept right past his shocked secretary without a word and into his office.

He looked up from his desk in surprise. "What happened? Are you all right? You're white as a sheet." His concerned expression almost made me cry. "Please sit down, Margarita."

I took a chair and tried to tell him as succinctly as I could what had happened but I was ranting. Calm, I was not.

The sheriff ran his hands through his mass of hair. "Damn it, Margarita!" He stood and then sat again. "So that ol' bastard wants to trade you a warrant for sex? Who in the hell does he think he is? Has he lost his damn mind?" He stood again and started pacing. "He has. He's lost his mind. I want to go and cold cock that son-of-a-bitch."

That would've been fine with me.

"I'm going to call Josh Middleton right now." He picked up the phone. Josh is the Texas Ranger I mentioned before. He's stationed in Alpine.

"Wait, Sheriff. I don't think you should do that."

"Why not? The Texas Rangers go after corrupt officials."

"Yes, but it's Samuels' word against mine. It'll just draw more rumor and innuendo my way, which won't help you and your campaign."

"Forget that! I'm not going to stand by and see you treated this way."

"Thank you, Sheriff, but you need to think about you and this county. If 'Billy Jack' becomes the sheriff...well, I can't even imagine it. We'll all lose our jobs and the county will become corrupt."

"You don't think our judge just showed how corrupt he is?"

"Oh yes, I do. What I meant was that the county's law enforcement would become corrupt if Jackson gets in."

"What do you propose I do about Judge Samuels? Nothing?"

"Yes, for right now."

"No. I don't see how I can ignore this."

"I'm only asking you to think about it before you do anything. It's my word, the word of a young, female deputy from Terlingua, against the word of a much older, longtime, respected circuit court judge."

"Bullshit!"

"Yes it is bullshit, but you know I'm right."

"Margarita, if he ever touches you, I want you to hurt him."

"Don't worry!"

"What about your warrant?"

"He isn't going to give me one."

"You need more definitive proof that the names are linked. I'm sure you'll think of some way to get it."

"Sherrrriff!"

He laughed at my whiny response.

"What makes you assume I can do things with a snap of my fingers?"

"I have faith in you. For one thing, you like to use your brain."

"My brain feels like it's been in a blender."

"I know what you mean."

"Do you have any suggestions on getting *definitive proof?*"

"You should call Jennings' brother to see if he's ever heard of Bailey Cooper or Iva Cooper. Never mind. I'll put someone else on that today. You have other things you need to be doing."

"Right."

"Try not to worry too much, Margarita. Filthy Judge Pervert will get his. I'm going to plot his demise."

* * *

I went out to my truck in the parking lot. When I calmed down I called the sheriff. "After thinking about it, I don't want to go to the McFarley Ranch alone."

"That's good because Barney is going to meet you at the main entrance to the place in one hour."

"Don't you want to know why I'm afraid to go alone?"

"I have a fairly good idea, Margarita. A young man was running for his life from something or somebody on that ranch. I wouldn't go in alone, either."

"Really?"

"I'm old but I'm not senile!" The impassioned way he said it made me laugh.

* * *

Barney was waiting at the McFarley Ranch main gate. I waved, got out of my truck, locked it, and got into his truck.

"Did the sheriff tell you I was coming with you?"

"Isn't that obvious? I'm in your truck with no questions."

He gave me a sideways look. "I figured it would piss you off."

"I'm glad you're going. I didn't want to go alone."

He stared at me, dumbfounded. "For real?"

"Does this have to be a *thing*? Could we just go in, ask our questions, and come back out alive and unharmed?"

"So you were scared to go in alone?"

"Is that what the sheriff told you?"

"No. He just said he wanted me to go with you."

"Great; then let's go."

"Not so fast, Batgirl. Don't you think we should have a game plan?"

"My plan was to ask about the injured man and see what their reaction is."

"What if they don't want to talk?"

"Then we've seen what their reaction is."

"So that's your big plan?"

"Do you have a better one?"

"No."

"Then let's get this over with. I need to sleep sometime."

Barney started the truck and rolled the windows up. The road was dirt, and dust was a given. At the solar-powered gate, he spoke into an intercom and stated his business when requested to do so by an unfriendly voice. After a moment he was instructed to proceed slowly and with caution. The office was one mile ahead.

The gate swung open. I wondered what it would be like to own so much land that it was miles from one place to another. Also, whoever owned this ranch owned their own mountains, and their ownership was more than the heart and soul variety; it was the type that would hold up in court.

The road was rank with "no trespassing" signs. If they meant to make a visitor feel unwelcome, they succeeded. When we were half a mile from the headquarters, there was a large sign that read, "Do you believe in the hereafter? Keep coming. Find out for sure."

"Is that supposed to be funny?" Barney wondered.

"This place is cold and unfriendly."

"Do ya think?"

"Usually ranches have howdy signs once you get inside the main gate."

"This one is known for being snooty and secretive."

"And beautiful," I added because that was the other thing people mentioned about the McFarley Ranch. My eyes were on the mountains in the distance and the rolling hills of bluebonnets and pastures filled with yellow wildflowers.

"Have you noticed there are no cattle?"

"On a ranch this size, the cattle could be in pastures you can't see from here."

"That's true, Pard, or they might not have any cattle. Maybe they're dealing in something more lucrative."

"What's more lucrative than cattle?"

"Drugs, prostitutes, stolen property; it's hard to say."

"I sincerely hope you're wrong."

"I do, too."

The headquarters was well marked as such but there was no Texas Friendly. No sign read, "Welcome to McFarley Ranch" or "Welcome Friends" or any of the other types of greetings I'd seen on other ranches.

Barney parked the truck and we headed for the door.

"Deputies," a small, stocky man greeted us on the wood plank porch. "The sheriff advised me you were coming. I'm Dan McLeod, Ranch Manager." He gave a smile and a warm handshake. "Please come in. Can I get you something to drink?"

"No thanks," I said.

Barney shook his head. "We'll only take up a few minutes of your time."

McLeod led us into his office and invited us to sit.

"So what brings deputies to our ranch?"

Barney explained about the injured man and showed him a photo of him. I stayed quiet, watching McLeod's reaction. He was calm and cool and seemed surprised by the news.

"I don't believe he works here," McLeod said when he handed back the picture. "It's possible he was passing through with a group of undocumented folks. We still have some of that, but not like we did in the past. We try to discourage it."

That was interesting because we never said he was an immigrant. In the photo, the injured man looked as Anglo as Mr. McLeod.

"How do you discourage it?" I asked since he'd brought it up.

Barney shot me a look, but it was a valid question.

McLeod's eyes narrowed. "We have signs posted. We never offer jobs to anyone undocumented, and when we run across them, we escort them to an exit."

I let it drop for now and handed him a different photograph of the victim. "Please take a look at this to be sure you've never seen him."

He took it from me and studied it. "I'm sorry, but I've never seen him." He handed it back.

"Why don't you keep it and ask around about him?" I suggested.

"I'll do that. You know, it's possible he was never on this ranch. He was found by the highway, right?"

"Yes."

"Someone could have shoved him out of a vehicle or just pulled in and left him there. He could've gotten there a dozen ways."

"That's true," Barney agreed, "but we thought he came over the fence because a piece of his clothing was caught on it."

"There're other ways to explain that," McLeod insisted. "The thing I'm sure of is that nobody on this ranch would've shot this young man. That's just not the kind of thing that happens here. We live by the old cowboy code and shooting people is not acceptable no matter what."

* * *

"What do you think, Ricos?"

"I don't know what to think. Something could be going on that McLeod isn't aware of, but that seems unlikely since it's his business to know what's happening on the ranch."

"Isn't it weird that he thought he'd be an undocumented immigrant?"

"Yes. If they're hiring a lot of them, that explains their secrecy, doesn't it?"

"Yes, but their secrecy could also be about something else outside the law."

"It's possible he didn't come through the ranch. He could've been running along 118 and was picked up by the people or person he'd escaped from. They might have shot him when he tried to get away again. What do you think?"

"I tended towards believing McLeod until he started talking about the cowboy code. It seems like he dragged that out of another era to impress us."

"Barney, cowboy code is not a thing of the past. It might seem old-fashioned and I guess it is, but cowboys live by it. Or they're supposed to."

"Jeez, Ricos."

"What?"

"I didn't know you were so up on the cowboys."

"Seriously?"

"Oh." Barney looked sheepish. "Kevin."

Kevin was my husband. He died in a bull riding accident what now seemed like a lifetime ago.

"It wasn't as much Kevin as some of his friends, but yes, Kevin. Also, I grew up with a papi who was a rancher in his heart and still is. I've been on my share of ranches in Texas and in Mexico."

"I never thought of Kevin as a cowboy. A bull rider yes, I know he was that, but a cowboy, no."

"Even though he didn't ever ride the range or work with cattle the way cowboys do, the term would still apply. Rodeo participants are referred to as cowboys. Kevin had rodeo in his veins, along with horses."

"Explain this cowboy code to me."

"I don't know if I can tell you all of it."

"Tell me what you remember."

"A cowboy must never shoot first, hit a man smaller than him, or take unfair advantage. He rides for his brand. He always tells the truth. He works hard. He never goes back on his word. He must treat children, the elderly, and animals gently."

"Not women?"

"Women are covered by the respect part. A cowboy respects women, his parents, and the law. He must help someone in distress. There's more but it's not coming to me right now. Barney, we live by the cowboy code; we just don't call it that."

"Well, yippee ki-yi-yi."

"Whatever."

"I don't ride for a brand."

"Yes you do. It's called the Brewster County Sheriff's Office."

"I guess you're right. I never thought of it that way."

"All the things cowboys are supposed to do, we're supposed to do, too."

"Who can I hit if I can't hit someone smaller than me?"

"I think the point is that we don't hit or shoot first. If somebody starts trouble, that's a different story."

We stopped along the fence line where Mr. Sinclair found the victim. A couple of deputies had already combed the area for clues, but two more pairs of eyes couldn't hurt. Besides, we wanted to see it for ourselves.

When Barney wasn't watching I scaled the fence and spoke to him from the other side of it.

"What in the hell are you doing, Ricos?" was his response.

"I'm looking for blood."

"Whatever you find will be inadmissible because you're trespassing." He was leaning against a NO TRESSPASSING sign as he spoke.

"I know that. I just want to see if there's a trail of blood or tracks."

"You'd better hope nobody catches you."

"I don't see any clouds of dust coming this way, do you?"

"No, but we've had a lot of moisture recently."

After a few minutes I said, "Barney, come look at this."

"No."

"There's a trail of blood and running footprints." I followed it far enough to be convinced that he'd come from the ranch, not from the road. "It's hard to follow because the drops are faint and not close together. He wasn't bleeding much by the time he'd made it this far, but he was still bleeding. I'd like to see where this trail would take me."

"To the county jail, I bet."

"You're hilarious." I climbed back over the fence. "He definitely came across this ranch. Maybe McLeod never knew it, but the blood trail doesn't lie."

"We need to get a warrant."

I explained to my partner why that was problematic.

"Son of a bitch!" was his heated comment when I finished recounting my close encounter of the sex-crazed kind.

We got back into the truck and headed to Alpine to talk to the sheriff. I'd pick up my vehicle on our way back to Terlingua.

"Ricos, I want to ask you about something, but I don't need a truckload of attitude. It's a simple question."

I gave him a great big smile of encouragement. "Ask, Pard, and I'll give you a ten-second warning before the trucks arrive."

He gave me a look of exasperation but forged on. "How do you know about tattoos on prostitutes from a brothel in Ojinaga?"

"I know because I grew up here."

"Have you ever paid for sex?"

"Really, Barney? That's where you want to go with this conversation?"

"It's a valid question."

"It's completely out of line and none of your business."

Barney threw up his hands. "Here comes truck numero uno."

"Sorry. I forgot to warn you."

"Truce. Forget I asked."

"Okay. I will."

After that exchange, Barney and I were quiet, for us. I wondered if he really thought I'd paid a prostitute for sex or if he was just messing with me. That was his specialty. My snap reaction to his question would make him wonder for real. It was one more thing in his arsenal of ways to torture his partner.

I thought about the injured man, testing various scenarios in my head. Just because there's a code doesn't mean everyone follows it. Maybe he had worked on the ranch and witnessed something that put him in danger. But a former prostitute as a ranch hand was hard to imagine. "People change; tattoos don't," my mother loved to remind me whenever I mentioned getting one.

"Barney! Go back!"

"What the hell, Ricos?" He screeched to the side of the highway.

"Didn't you see that turtle?"

"See the *what?*"

"A little turtle was trying to cross the road. Now he's afraid to move because of vehicles whizzing past. We should move him to safety."

Barney was looking at me with his mouth open. "So now we rescue turtles?"

"We rescue any creature that needs our help. Hurry up or someone will run him over and crush him."

"Ricos, how many turtles do you suppose cross this highway during the year?"

"I have no idea."

"There are lots of them, I bet. I'm sure many of them don't make it. What's so special about this one turtle?"

"He crossed our path. When someone or something gets right in front of us, we have to help, even if we're only going to save one."

"Is that your theory of law enforcement?"

"It's my theory of life, but yes, it covers law enforcement as well. We're never going to stop all bad people or save everyone who needs saving, but we have to try."

"Even turtles?"

"Yes. And get that smirk off your face. That little turtle is a resident of Brewster County, isn't he?"

"True."

Barney stopped the truck in the middle of the highway and I got out and moved the turtle to the tall grass. I headed him towards Calamity Creek and commanded him to go there and stay off the highway, but he was a turtle and would do what he wanted.

When I got back in the truck, Barney said, "He's just going to cross again."

"That's up to him. We did what we could."

A few miles passed. Barney kept glancing over at me.

"What is it?"

"You have a soft, gooey center, don't you, Deputy Ricos?"

"Could we let that be our little secret?"

Chapter 18

I stripped off my clothes, slipped into an over-sized t-shirt, and flopped into a rocking chair on my porch. My plan had been to soak up the peace of the evening, but Judge Samuels and the day's events robbed me.

After a short run and a long shower, I decided to go by Papi's store to see if he'd heard anything. I needed something I could construe as a clue that would lead me to the killer of Bradley Jennings. It was a long shot, but I wanted to see my papi anyway and he often hears useful things.

My visit to Papi would give me a clue all right, but about another body.

* * *

My father needed a break, so after we hugged and had the *Que Paso?* talk, I told him I'd watch the store so he could go home to eat. He promised to bring me hot burritos, so it was a fair trade.

While he was gone, an old Mexican man limped into the store asking for agua. He looked as though he was about to fall over, so I pulled a chair out of the office for him, took a bottle of water from one of the fridges, and handed it over. After he emptied it, he raised his hat to me with a shaky hand and introduced himself as Pedro Valdez. I shook his hand and gave him my name.

"You're Miguel's daughter."

"Yes."

"Is he here?"

When I said he'd gone to eat, he asked, "Are you still working with the sheriff?"

"Yes. I'm a deputy."

"I need to tell you something."

My skin prickled. This was not going to be good news.

He confirmed my suspicion. "There's a dead man in a cave over on the McFarley Ranch."

"Do you know who he is?"

"No."

"Did you report this to anyone?"

"No, señorita, I'm reporting it to you." I'm called señorita so often I've given up explaining why I'm a señora. A young woman who has been married is still a señora, even if her husband died.

The old man removed his tattered cowboy sombrero, pushed his dark hair back, and then replaced the hat. The man was old and his moustache gray, but he had the jet black hair of a younger man. "Listen, I don't have working papers, so I don't look for people to talk to. I hope you aren't going to call the Border Patrol."

"No. I'm not going to do that."

"I'm trying to get back to Mexico."

"Where have you been?"

"I was working up around Odessa."

"What brought you to the McFarley Ranch?"

"I was walking back from Fort Stockton. I got a ride that far, but he was afraid to bring me all the way to the river. I decided to go to the headquarters to see if they would hire me. They've never cared about papers."

"Please tell me what happened."

"Do you know the McFarley Ranch?"

"No. I know it's huge and a secretive sort of place, but that's all I know."

He nodded. "Night before last, there was a rainstorm. I ducked into a cave for shelter because the wind and lightning were fierce. Something smelled wrong but when the wind calmed down, I realized it was the odor of death. As soon as the rain quit, I took my bedroll outside to sleep."

"What happened to your things?"

He pointed to the door. "I left them outside."

"Oh. Please continue."

"Once it was light enough, I went in to see what was making that smell. It was a small man in a cowboy hat, probably a Mexican man. He might've been crossing the ranch, too. It made me feel afraid."

"Did you ever see anyone else?"

"No. I never even saw stock. It seems they're not using that part of the ranch."

"Could you tell if the man was shot? Was there blood or any other indication of foul play?"

"Oh, no, I couldn't see clearly enough, and I didn't want to touch him. Will you report the body to the sheriff?"

"Yes, of course I will."

I waited on customers and in-between that, Pedro told me about his family and explained that he'd known my papi since he (Papi) was a little kid.

My dad came back and brought me five hot, fat, bean and cheese burritos. He forgets I'm not a strapping male ranch hand. I gave most of my dinner to Señor Valdez, who needed it much worse than I did.

I offered to take him to the Rio Grande, but first he had to tell Papi his story. While they had a typical, old man, we'll-get-to-the-point-eventually conversation, I called the dispatcher who said he'd have Sheriff Ben return my call.

"This is looking bad for the McFarley Ranch," the sheriff said when he called, "but I suppose someone passing through could've crawled into that cave and died. No matter what happened to him, I can't imagine they would object to us going in after the body. Why don't you take Buster and go talk to McLeod again in the morning? I'll give him a heads-up that you're returning."

"Okay, Sheriff."

"Would you rather I send Barney with you?"

"Buster will be fine."

"Get some sleep tonight, Margarita."

"I plan to."

Chapter 19

"You've been here twice in less than twenty-four hours, Deputy Ricos," stated McLeod at the door of the McFarley Ranch office. "This must be a record." His greeting was sour in spite of his bright smile and warm handshake. He welcomed Buster with equal warmth, or lack of it, and insisted we have coffee. Then he invited us to sit while he made a fresh pot.

McLeod disappeared into an adjacent room and while he was gone, a tall cowboy came in. "Oh." Our presence surprised him. "Pardon me. I didn't know Dan had visitors."

"It's okay; come in," I said. "He's making coffee."

"Come on in, Clay," yelled McLeod from the next room. Then he came to the door. "Deputies, meet Clay Ferguson, our lead cowboy."

Clay's spurs jangled as he walked across the room towards us. He shook our hands and McLeod talked him into joining us for coffee.

I repeated what I'd been told by Pedro Valdez, only leaving out Pedro's name and his admission of being an undocumented worker.

"Don't you think it's just some wetback that crawled in there and died of a heart attack or something?" asked Clay.

I tried to stay calm and not show how offended I was by his racist statement. "A human being died in your cave or else was placed there after his death. I never said he was a Mexican man, only that he was small."

"And we're supposed to do what?" That was Clay again. I really didn't like him.

"You don't need to do anything. We're here to get permission from Mr. McLeod to remove the body. No matter who it is, he should be brought from the cave and his family notified."

"And we need to determine cause of death," Buster added.

"No," interjected McLeod, "if there's a body in one of our caves, we'll take care of it."

"Meaning what?" Buster asked. That earned him a harsh look from both men and a couple of points from me.

"It could be one of our men," Clay suggested, avoiding the question.

"Are you missing a cowboy?" I asked.

"It's hard to say. They come and go."

"That's not an answer," stated Buster. "Do you have a cowboy missing or not?" My trainee made me proud.

"No," McLeod answered. "We do not."

"Where is the supposed cave?" Clay asked.

"A full report was faxed to this office by the sheriff this morning. We're here to get permission to go to the location and bring out the body."

"You two?" McLeod made it clear he believed we were incapable of it.

"I don't know who the sheriff will assign," I said.

After more dinking around and wasting our time, McLeod said, "I can't give you permission to come onto this ranch. The owner disapproves of outsiders coming in and snooping around. It's an invasion of privacy."

"Two or three law enforcement professionals will come and remove the body." I couldn't believe he wasn't going to cooperate. "There won't be any snooping. The Sheriff's Office is only interested in removing a dead man from your land."

"So you say," was Clay's snide comment.

"We've already told you we'll take care of it," McLeod added. "If foul play was involved, we'll notify the sheriff."

"There may have to be an autopsy in order to be sure about the cause of death. That's not a determination you're qualified to make," pointed out Buster.

"And you are?"

"Possibly not; that's why we order autopsies."

"I can't allow you to come onto this land. You'll need the owner's permission or a warrant," added Dan McLeod in a tone full of finality.

On the way out he was all smiles and engaged Buster in a conversation about the ranch's famous line of Polled Hereford cattle. Uninterested, I walked out to the truck to wait. In other words, I allowed us to be separated and it was stupid. Clay Ferguson followed me and proved I'd made a mistake. I heard the sound of spurs clinking behind me and realized there was about to be a problem.

"Wait up, honey," Clay called, but I kept walking.

He ran, knocked me against the truck, and pinned me. "I said to wait."

It hurt and was humiliating. "You're assaulting an officer of the law."

"If you want to see assault, bring your sweet ass back here again," he breathed against my neck.

"Now you're threatening me? I should arrest you."

"You should, but you won't. It's my word against yours."

Damn, if that wasn't becoming a tiresome problem.

When Clay stepped back and released me, I walloped him in the groin with my boot. He never saw it coming and went down with a groan and obscene cursing.

When he quieted down, I said, "It's your word against mine."

He spit boring insults of the usual variety. Then he tried to threaten me, but it sounded more like whining and made me want to laugh.

Buster walked up and saw Clay writhing on the ground. It didn't take him three seconds to put two and two together. "Is everything all right, Deputy Ricos?"

"We're through here, Deputy Mayhew. Let's go."

* * *

Judge Samuels looked up in surprise when the sheriff, Buster, and I walked in without an appointment. For a couple of seconds, I felt sure he thought I'd told my companions what he did and that we'd come to kick his ass. I wished.

"We need a warrant for the McFarley Ranch," stated Sheriff Ben with more attitude than I'd ever seen from him. It was clear he wouldn't be taking any crap.

"You'd better have a damned good reason," countered the perv with his usual crummy attitude.

"We do. Deputy Ricos?" The sheriff turned it over to me.

I pretended to be speaking with another judge, a good, reasonable man who would listen with the intention of helping. I explained what Pedro Valdez had reported to me last night and that Barney and I had been to the ranch yesterday to inquire about an injured man found at their fence line. Then I explained why Buster and I had returned to the ranch.

He made me explain every detail, which was not hard. In spite of what he may have thought, I knew what I was doing.

Buster glared at the judge the whole time. He had thought getting a warrant would be simple, so I'd brought him up to speed about my encounter with the nasty pervert during our drive from the McFarley Ranch to Alpine. He was horrified, but I still didn't think he understood what it was like to be a young woman in law enforcement in Brewster County.

As he mulled it over, the judge mumbled, as if talking to himself, "Daniel McFarley is my brother-in-law."

"That shouldn't make any difference," blurted Buster, "you're supposed to follow the law and apply it to everyone equally."

I almost clapped. *Go, Buster!*

The judge's eyes narrowed, forcing his bushy eyebrows into a brawl above his nose. "Young man, I want you to be quiet. I don't need a teenager to tell me how to do my job."

"I'm a twenty-one-year-old deputy," Buster replied, standing tall and proud.

Sheriff Ben put his hand on Buster's shoulder and gave it an affectionate squeeze. Our boss has a way of delivering a clear message without using a word.

"I don't believe you need a warrant," the judge continued. "Mr. McLeod said he'd bring out the body and he will. He's a man of his word."

"But he has employees, and if one of them had something to do with the death of the man in the cave, valuable evidence could be removed," explained Sheriff Ben.

"What makes you think they aren't removing it now?"

"We don't know that they aren't. However, I think there are lots of possibilities here. The man may have died of natural causes. If he was murdered, perhaps the killer is smart enough not to go back to the body. If that body disappears, a full-scale search of the ranch will happen because I'll call in the FBI if necessary."

Samuels scoffed. "You don't have the authority to do that."

"Are you really going to argue with me about my authority while a body melts into the ground?" Everything about the sheriff's stance said *Bring it on.* He looked ready to do battle.

The judge regarded him with shifty eyes. Then he turned to me. My insides did a flip-flop. "What makes you think anyone on that ranch had anything to do with the man in the cave…or the injured man, for that matter?"

"I was shoved against my vehicle and threatened with harm if I dare return."

"By whom?"

"It was an employee of the ranch."

The judge was about to blow a gasket so the sheriff stepped in. "When anyone threatens an officer of the law—"

"I know what that means!" Judge Samuels was furious. When he calmed down he addressed me again. "Do you swear you were assaulted and threatened by someone on the McFarley Ranch?"

"Yes; I swear it."

"In that case I'll give you a warrant, with limitations."

"What limitations?" the sheriff wanted to know.

"You'll have to go in on horseback because Daniel doesn't allow anyone to drive vehicles on his ranch unless he knows them and they understand his rules."

"What about a helicopter?" I asked.

That earned me a severe scowl. "Absolutely not!" he yelled.

I thought he needed a psychiatrist and medication for starters.

"Okay," the sheriff stepped in again. "I figured we'd have to use horses."

I thought the judge just wanted to make it difficult. "But a helicopter would be so much faster and—"

"Do not speak," Judge Samuels roared at me. Then he addressed the sheriff. "This warrant is limited to the cave, the body, and the southwest quadrant of the ranch. You're to go in, get the body, and bring it out to the highway. Once you're off the ranch, it doesn't matter what you do. A vehicle can meet you."

"Yes, of course."

"The faster this happens, the better for everyone. I'll talk to Daniel about keeping his staff away from the area until you're through with it."

"That works," said Sheriff Ben. "Thank you, Judge."

That should've been the end of it, but the perv had to get in a dig. "Deputy Ricos, do you understand the terms of the warrant?"

"What makes you think I'm go—"

My boss touched my arm and gave a tiny negative shake of his head.

"Yes, it's clear," I said.

"Good."

I glanced at the sheriff and back to the judge. "I won't be going anyway." I couldn't hold back. "The trip would be too hard for a *girl.*"

The sheriff pulled me out of the room.

* * *

Later that afternoon, Sheriff Ben called and spoke with Barney a long time. I didn't pay them any attention because I was watching my hill. It was wildflowers going for world domination out there.

Barney yelled, "He wants to speak with you."

I picked up my desk phone. "Hello, Sheriff."

"Margarita, Barney pointed out that you're a better horseman than he is."

"Well…"

"How do you feel about riding in to bring out the body in the cave?"

"Yes, of course I'll go."

"You don't think it'll be too hard for a *girl?*"

I knew he was only messing with me, but my retort was, "If you want the job done right and efficiently, you should send two girls."

He laughed. "I wish I had two."

"Sheriff, who are you sending with me?"

"A Texas Ranger is coming from Midland."

"Not Josh?"

"No; he's out of town on another case."

"Where do I meet him?"

"I want you to meet him at the southwestern gate of the ranch. Do you know where that is?"

"Yes sir."

"Can you be there and ready to go at six in the morning?"

"Sure. What do I need to bring?"

"Bring overnight gear because the cave is a long way in. The Ranger will have the food, water, and tents. When you find the body, you guys will be taking what evidence you can from it. That could take a while." He paused. "Margarita, are you sure you want to go? By now the body will be gruesome."

"I'm sure it will."

"Maybe it's not proper to send a man and a woman together."

"Seriously?"

"You don't have any qualms about it?"

"No. We're both professionals, aren't we?"

"Yes, of course."

"You're not sending me into the wilds with a man like Judge Samuels, are you?"

He laughed. "Of course not." Then, deadly serious, "Lord, I hope not."

"Sheriff, I can protect myself. I'm tough. I'm armed; I've got this."

"I know you do."

"What about the Jennings murder? Somebody needs to work on that while I'm gone."

"How will I ever manage this office while you're away?"

"I'm sorry, Sheriff. Sometimes I say what's in my head without filtering it. Well, you already know that."

"Barney and Buster will be working hard. Barney is going to take his own run at the judge for a warrant."

"I sure would like to be there for that."

He laughed. "Same here."

He gave me more instructions and then signed off with his usual, "Carry on."

Chapter 20

The headlights of my truck swept across three horses and a man packing gear onto the largest of them. He waved without looking into the blinding lights. I switched them off, lifted my pack out of the vehicle, and then locked it.

"Good morning," I greeted him. The sun wasn't up but the stars were dazzling, and I had no trouble making my way to the Texas Ranger from Midland.

He turned from the horse to greet me. "Good morning. Would you like coffee?"

I could *not* believe it. I was riding to the cave with Len Camacho, my would-be long lost brother. No way. How could this be happening?

"So, we meet again." His manner was calm and matter-of-fact. If he was disappointed his assistant was me, his face didn't show it.

"Yes." I felt sorry for the poor guy.

"You don't seem very enthusiastic about it."

"It's early."

"You didn't say if you wanted coffee."

"Yes, please. I'd love some." If I had to spend twenty-four hours or even twenty-four minutes with him, I needed to be awake so I wouldn't repeat my idiot act.

"I saddled the smaller horse for you. I hope that's all right."

"That's fine. Thank you."

"His name is Silver."

"Like the Lone Ranger's horse? Shouldn't you ride him?"

"I forgot my mask. I could never ride him without the mask." He took a sip of coffee. "Aren't you a bit young to know *The Lone Ranger?*"

"Saturday morning re-runs," I explained. "You're not much older than I am."

He laughed and displayed his attractive, aggravating dimple. "Yeah, me too, and I liked Roy Rogers."

"I liked all those old cowboy shows, and the more action the better."

"Yep, me too."

I drank coffee, which was delicious considering it was black, and tried to keep my mouth shut.

Sergeant Camacho added my things to the load of the large pack mare. I offered to help but he waved me away and said he was almost finished. I had a feeling he was holding his tongue the same way I was. Maybe he was nervous to go into the backcountry with me. It wouldn't be the first time a man questioned my abilities. If he'd judge me by those instead of my social skills, this would go fine. If not, well...

My companion opened the gate with a combination the sheriff gave him and we headed into our adventure. Sunrise was achingly beautiful. It would've been easy to believe we were there for fun instead of work. The sun came up slowly, as if hesitant to make an appearance, and its soft light made the puffy clouds glow peach and pink. The mountains flamed rose, red, and then looked golden. A hillside covered with bluebonnets shined a deep purple, almost black. For a few breathtaking minutes the air was as golden as the mountains.

Dawn gave way to morning. Birds began to chatter and sing out their hearts as they flitted from place to place, busy and joyous.

"Wow!" Len exclaimed. "This is amazing country. If you'd described a Big Bend sunrise to me before I came to this area, I would've called you a liar."

"I know. There are a lot of things here you have to see to believe."

He nodded in agreement.

"I was surprised to see you this morning because I thought you were working a murder in Presidio County."

"I was."

"Did you figure it out?"

"No."

"I'm sorry. I know how that feels."

"I think that murder might be related to the attack on the young man you believe might've come across this ranch."

"Why do you think the cases are related?"

"I suspect both of them are victims of human traffickers."

I sucked in a sharp breath.

"My specialty is that particular crime, which is why I was put on the Presidio murder and why I was assigned to help you remove this body. My boss suspects the McFarley Ranch is involved somehow, whether knowingly or unknowingly. Something strange is happening here."

His statement gave me goosebumps.

"You understand that I'm telling you this in confidentiality, don't you?"

"Yes; of course."

"I wish I could give you all the details, but I can't, not yet."

"I understand."

"Men and boys are also victims of traffickers. Or he could've been a victimizer who got crossways with another victimizer. These guys kill each other all the time. That would be great, except new assholes always take their places."

"Yes; there's never a lack of criminals."

"At least it gives us job security."

"That's true, but it's a sad statement of human nature."

"How right you are."

We rode along in silence a while. Looking at the ranch, it was difficult to believe anything bad could be happening there. Rugged cliffs stood in the distance, begging to be explored. Unused pastures were overflowing with wildflowers and blooming native grasses, and the new leaves on mesquite and cottonwood trees made green dots across the vast landscape. Arroyos were clearly outlined by riotous new growth along their banks. Silence ruled the land and was not interrupted except for birds and the occasional rustle of a cool breeze.

When we came to a water tank, Len suggested we rest and eat a snack. As soon as he said it, I realized how hungry I was. We tied the horses to a spindly cottonwood, allowing them plenty of moving room so they could graze and drink water.

Len took a thermos out of a saddlebag and two cold bottles of water out of a different one. He set those down and then handed me four wrapped burritos and a bag full of fruit. We chose the not-damp side of the tank and sat down in the dirt to eat. The opposite side was grassier but wet because of a slowly leaking crack in the side of the structure.

As the sun climbed higher in the sky the day warmed, and we had to remove our heavy jackets.

The burritos were made with potatoes, onions, cheese, and jalapeños. They were delicious and I asked Len where he'd gotten them. I thought he'd left Alpine too early to have bought them at the town's best places for burritos.

"I made them at the sheriff's house this morning. He let me stay there because it's hard to pack a decent trip from a tiny motel room refrigerator and without a stove. I really like your sheriff."

"I do too. I think he's the best type of man."

"Which is?"

"He's a man of his word, a moral man who always does what he thinks is right. He adores his wife and tries to make her happy." That was just the beginning of the list but I didn't want to sound all goofy over the sheriff.

"I got the impression they're off-the-charts happy, so I think she treats him the same way he treats her."

"I think so, too." I was relieved to hear that Marianne was happy again.

"There's a lesson in that for the rest of us," Len observed.

"That's true."

"Have you ever been married, Margarita?"

"Yes, but my husband died a few years ago."

"I'm sorry." He sighed. "That must have been rough."

"Yes; it still is sometimes."

"I'm going through an ugly divorce."

"Oh, I know that's hard, too."

"It is." He looked off at the mountains or into the distance anyway. Sadness seemed to settle on him.

"I apologize for starting this line of conversation. I asked about the burritos because they're fantastic, but I didn't mean to wander so far off the subject."

"I'm glad you like the burritos."

I handed him my second one. "Don't you want this? One is plenty for me, and I see you brought fruit."

"Help yourself." He took the burrito and set the bag of fruit between us.

I took a small bunch of green grapes and a banana.

"Have you done a lot of forensics gathering?" Len asked.

"No, I haven't done much. Will that be a problem?"

"I don't see why it should." After a pause he said, "We're fortunate the nights have been so cold. The corpse might not be as bad as we're thinking."

Any corpse was awful, but I knew what he meant.

We leaned against the wall of the stock tank and drank the last of the coffee and then water. The nightmare experience of our initial meeting never came up. I was never going to mention it. Len didn't seem to hold it against me, but the man was a professional. He was stuck with me and was trying to make the best of it.

* * *

We took a right fork in the road, which put us onto an overgrown cattle path. We were headed towards a ridge of rocky red outcroppings and tortured formations, following Pedro's map. Len had a GPS unit but we'd already determined that Dan McLeod had given him incorrect coordinates. We decided to go with the old man's map because, of the two men, he had no reason to lie.

"Let's gallop!" Len called from his position in back of me.

I halted my horse. "What about the pack mare?"

He came up next to me. "She knows how to gallop."

"I mean won't the stuff fall off?"

"Give me some credit." He made an exaggerated pout. "I know how to rig a pack animal. This is not my first escape from the barn."

I laughed. "Sorry. If I'd packed her, everything would fall off in a run."

"Let's put my skill to the test. You go first, Texas Gal will follow you with her load, and Chingadera and I will bring up the rear."

"You have a horse called Chingadera?" *Chingadera* is Spanish and, I think, specifically a Mexican Spanish word. It means fucker, the way that word is used instead of saying "thing." As in "bring that *chingadera* over here."

"That's what she's called. Hey—it wasn't my idea."

"I wonder what she did to end up with that name."

"Well, ma'am," he drawled, "I reckon she was a tough one to tame."

"Right, Lennie Bob, I reckon so."

He laughed and then yelled, "Let's go!"

We took off, galloping through rippling stands of the grasses and weeds that had overtaken the path. In places, the narrow cut was paved with teensy yellow blossoms for a few hundred yards, and then tall greenery took over again. The air was fresh and the vistas long-distance. It was a most fantastic day to be alive, but I felt sad when our reason for being there crossed my mind.

* * *

During a lunch of cheese, crackers, nuts, fruit, and cookies, Len looked at me and said, "I want to say something about the night I came to your house."

My heart sank into my boots. "Couldn't we forget about that?"

"I feel I owe you an explanation."

"I think that's the other way around."

"No, Deputy Ricos, I take full responsibility."

"But surely—"

"Please," he interrupted, "let me get this out. I lied to you."

Oh my god, Beautiful Dimpled Man was my brother after all. I always wanted one, but not a brother who caused random erotic thoughts to pop into my mind every time I looked at him.

"So you *are* my brother?"

His face blazed crimson. But he laughed. "Will you please give up on that? I'm not your brother. We could pretend if you want."

I wasn't sure what I wanted, but that wasn't it. I didn't trust myself to say anything.

"I lied about Zeke sending me to say hello. He specifically told me to stay away from you."

"Why would he do that?"

"He cares about you and I have the reputation of being a ladies' man."

"I see."

"No, you don't see." He took a breath. "I'm not a ladies' man, but I let the guys I work with think whatever they want. They believe my wife left me because I messed around with other women during my travels… I have to travel a lot. In truth, she messed around while I was gone, but I didn't want to tell them that. It's not anyone's business, but you know how the people you work with are."

"Yes, I do." Did I ever…

"She broke my heart into tiny pieces and then rubbed my face in the smelly mess she'd made. She moved away six months ago and I haven't taken a woman out, let alone carried on in the sordid manner these guys think."

"I'm sorry she did that."

"Please don't feel sorry for me, no matter how sorry you think I am. You see, there's more."

"Can you tell me, or is it secret?"

He burst out laughing. "I'm trying to tell you, you impatient little woman."

I smiled at that and he continued. "Zeke took you to Dallas and you were all he talked about for weeks. He is so proud of you."

"I know; I'm proud of him, too."

"I saw some pics of you on his desk. I thought, *so this is Zeke's daughter?* I asked about you and Zeke got hostile. You see, he knew I was coming to Terlingua. I know this'll sound lame as hell, but the more he tried to warn me away from you, the more determined I was to meet you." Len flushed red. "I'm not a ladies' man, but I am a determined one."

"I see."

"No, you still don't. I used my position of Texas Ranger to find out from your partners where you run and then I went to those places. I was only going to look at you at first to see if you were like your photos. When you saw me with the camera, I was checking you out, pure and simple, exactly like the cad everyone thinks I am. When you met me at the door and asked if I was your brother I just about fell apart. No, Ms. Ricos, your brother, I'm not." He sighed. "Thank God."

Since I didn't say anything right away, he added, "In Alpine, I heard that you and the sheriff were having an affair, but he set me straight on that."

I nodded but still didn't speak.

"I almost fell over when Sheriff Duncan said he thought Margarita Ricos would be his best deputy for this job, and he wanted you to have the experience." Len took a deep breath. "What I want to say is that I came to your door to ask you to dinner, but things got out of hand, as you know. I practically ran out of your home because I thought about Zeke and what he would do to me."

"You're not seriously afraid of Zeke?"

"Yes; I know he would hurt me."

"That's crazy. Zeke is a middle-aged man. You're much younger than he is."

"Have you seen how that man is built?"

"Yes, but I don't think he would start a physical fight. He's mature."

"He's the father of a beautiful daughter. Need I say more?"

"I'm a grown woman, not a little girl, and I make my own decisions. Zeke doesn't get to control what I do and he knows that."

"My biggest worry is for my career. Like everyone, I want to advance. I won't be able to do that if I make an enemy out of a man of Zeke's stature and reputation." He sighed and leaned back against a desert willow that was blooming for all it was worth above our heads. "Please say something, Margarita; it's your turn."

I leaned over and kissed him where his reclusive dimple resided.

He touched his fingers to the spot. "What does that mean?"

"It means I'm glad you're not my brother."

"Yeah?"

"Yes."

"You realize I'm a professional and nothing can happen between us because we're working?"

"Don't get too carried away with yourself, Sergeant Camacho. It was only a kiss on the cheek."

"I was hoping you were going for my lips and missed."

"If I went for your lips, I wouldn't miss."

* * *

We ambled along, coming closer to the ridge, until we saw a stock tank with a fading roadrunner painted on the side of it. Above it, the windmill was a peeling red color. Pedro had said it wasn't working, which was true. These things meant it had to be the right tank. According to the old man, there would be an obvious trail through the ridge soon after that tank. He had said it was the easiest pass, worn smooth by years of stock, wildlife, and cowboy usage.

The view from the top was a 360-degree panorama that was the definition of magnificent: high-desert pasture land; layers of reddish mountains; countless ridges and canyons; wildflowers galore; and hazy, dreamlike mountains, so far away as to seem like a mirage. The scene stopped us in our tracks.

I pointed out the multi-spired, higher ridge that held the cave where a dead man waited. It was not far, but too far to reach before dark.

"Ay, hombre," Len said in a reverent sigh. "We should camp here."

"I know what you mean, but that's a bad idea."

"Why?"

"There's no room for the horses and nothing for them to eat and no water."

"I brought grain, and we could stake them below."

"The wind is likely to blow hard up here and there's no way to secure our tents. It will be freezing. Also, we won't be able to hear if a predator attacks the horses."

"Say what? You mean like mountain lions?"

"Yes and even bears. This is the southwest quadrant and it's wild land. Look at the pastures. They're not being used and haven't been in a long time. The desert is reclaiming them."

"Okay, but we need to camp before long."

"Len, do you see that road in the distance?" It was now behind us, and I pointed to it. "It goes through a pass in those hills to the right."

"I see it."

"It's the only road that isn't overgrown with weeds."

"Meaning…"

"It's being used. No part of this quadrant is being used and yet that road is. I think someone is using it to go from one side of the ranch to the other on a regular basis. Maybe the ranch management knows about it and maybe they don't. Either way, that road tells a story."

"Damned if you aren't right."

"It could tell a story different than human trafficking, but it could also be that."

"You sure do have a great eye for details."

"Thank you."

"We still need to camp soon."

"I agree. Let's get off this ridge and head for that copse of cottonwood trees."

"You think there'll be water?"

"I suspect it because of the trees. There's probably a natural spring."

"You're not a city slicker, are you Deputy Ricos?"

I laughed. "What was your first clue?"

* * *

We had no one's permission to make a campfire but we made one anyway. First of all, who would see it? Secondly, it would discourage wild creatures. Thirdly, the night air was chilly and the temperature was going down. Lastly, nobody had said we couldn't. And, as Len said, "Who camps without a fire?"

I set up my tent and his while he made the fire and got supper underway. Our overnight shelters were separated by a respectable distance but close enough to not feel alone. I moved his sleeping bag and gear to his tent and put mine into my tent. I cleaned up and changed into warmer clothes.

"What's for dinner?" I asked when I had finished my chores.

"Crab-stuffed lobster, champagne, and steak."

"Wow. I'm impressed, but I don't eat meat."

"I know. Your sheriff told me that. You're a little weird, like Zeke."

"Yep."

"I didn't bring any meat on this trip out of respect for you and the fact that meat needs to be kept cold. That's possible to do, but why bother if I'm the only one eating it?"

"You're quite noble."

"Thank you. For dinner we have corn, Ranch-Style beans, camp potatoes with onions and tomato, and crusty French bread. For dessert, a chocolate Dutch oven cake will be baked in your honor. I hope you like chocolate."

"I love chocolate."

"I didn't bring champagne because Zeke mentioned one time that you don't drink."

"Do I have any secrets you don't know?"

"My guess is that you have many, but I'll let you reveal them to me as you see fit. I don't care if you don't eat meat or drink champagne."

"What do you care about?"

"Are you a good person? Would you play fair with a man's heart? Can you ride, rope, and wrangle, and be trusted? I don't know. I care about a lot of things. I like a woman who can make me laugh."

I turned as red as the Big Bend sky at sunset.

"Of course, we know you can really set me off. *Are you my brother?*" He took a deep breath. "I'm about to get hysterical again just thinking about it. Say something not funny!"

"Why don't you tell me about human trafficking?"

"Damn it, Margarita; that's it. That's the un-funniest thing I know."

* * *

The night was as beautiful as the day had been. We'd watched it fall with the same awe we'd felt that morning as the day slid into place. Then there was nothing to do but watch the stars.

Len had declined to tell me about trafficking because he was busy making dinner and because he thought it was a subject better discussed in the daylight hours. That made sense. It was something I wanted to know…and didn't.

The campfire died to glowing coals and even more stars were revealed.

"What is it with your stars?" Len asked.

"What do you mean?"

"There are more stars here than anywhere else."

"That's because the sky has no competition from city lights or any lights."

"I think stars are being seduced from their assigned positions all over the world by this sexy, sexy sky."

"That's the best explanation I ever heard."

"There were already millions of twinkles; now there are billions. What gives?"

"I love your poetic explanation of our stars, but there only appear to be more because the fire has died and with it, the last of the light competition."

He frowned. "You explain it your way and I'll explain it mine."

"I'd expect a criminal investigator to lean towards facts more than poetry."

"In my work, I do, but I'm not working right now, am I?"

"Touché."

Besides stars, the fragrance of baking chocolate cake filled the night. By the time it was ready, we were hungry again.

Len jumped up from the cozy fire. "Your cake is ready, madame."

He frosted it with canned chocolate fudge icing that melted right into the hot cake. Then he served two huge pieces in paper bowls. It was extra-delicious the way food outdoors tends to be.

We sat by the fire a little longer, mesmerized by the sky and night sounds. Neither of us wanted to say goodnight.

"I told you what I suspect about the man in the cave," Len said. "What do you think?"

"At first I thought it was another case of 'who cares about a dead Mexican?' but then I was threatened by the head cowboy."

"Sheriff Duncan mentioned that. What did the cowboy say exactly?"

"He shoved me against my vehicle. When I informed him he was assaulting an officer of the law, he said if I wanted to see assault, I should bring my sweet ass back there."

"Then what happened?"

"What makes you think something else happened?"

"I can't believe you would've taken that shit."

"When he stepped back, I kicked him hard in the crotch. He went down like a typical crybaby bully."

"Do you know how much that hurts?"

"I have a pretty good idea. Maybe he'll think twice before he shoves another woman into her truck."

"I don't think the sheriff knows that part of the story."

"He doesn't, and you'd better not tell him."

"You can bet I won't."

Chapter 21

We got up before dawn in order to get a head start. Yesterday had felt like a vacation; today felt full of terrible things waiting to be discovered.

Len made cowboy coffee on a revived campfire while I took down the tents. In the process, I lost track of one of my hair clips. I looked everywhere but didn't find it.

"Len, have you seen a hair clip?"

"I don't have a use for hair clips."

"Right, but have you seen it?"

"You're talking about one of those hair do-das, right?" He made a circular motion with his hand above his hair.

I laughed. "Yes. I never heard it called a do-da, but okay."

"Is it real valuable?"

"No. It's just a regular do-da. It's made of lightweight wood."

Len's gaze moved from me to the fire. "Made of wood, you say?"

"Oh no you didn't; not my do-da."

"I don't know, but maybe I did. Let your hair fly free, Deputy Do-Da."

"Very funny, Lennie Bob. Lucky for you I have others."

"Here, I offer coffee in a spirit of reconciliation."

"Thanks." It tasted awful but, in a spirit of reconciliation, I didn't complain.

Len ran his hand into my hair at the back of my head, lifting it off my neck. He played there a second, and then he pulled my head towards him as if for a kiss, but it was only for a disappointment.

He brought out fruit, leftover French bread, and oatmeal bars for breakfast. His eyes moved from that assortment over to the Dutch oven. "There's also cake."

Without a word, we picked up spoons and went to work on it without bothering to use bowls.

* * *

"People from all over the world want to come to the United States," Len was saying, "but I'm sure you know that."

"Yes. I'm well aware of it."

"In many cases, they pay for safe passage and when they get here, they're put right into the hands of traffickers, or I should say different traffickers. These assholes do all kinds of things with them. Some end up domestic slaves. Some work at hard labor or in factories, or they're sold as sex slaves.

"In most cases, they're told they have to work off their 'debt.' Of course they have no debt, but these people are powerless once they're here. They're in a strange place and are surrounded by new sights and languages they don't understand. The traffickers use fear and cruel treatment to keep them in line."

"It makes me sick."

"Yes, it does me, too. There are days I think of quitting and getting a job doing something else."

"Who would blame you?"

"Right now there are more human slaves than at any time in previous history. It's a global crisis that the so-called news agencies are mostly ignoring."

"Is any progress being made?"

"Very little. It's too lucrative, and every grade of criminal is getting involved, from cartels to street hoodlums. If you ever want to help, Margarita, opportunities abound in the field."

"I don't think my heart could take it. This job makes me cry enough as it is."

"I understand; it's wearing me down."

"Maybe you should stay with the Rangers, but take a break, do something else for a while."

"Like what? Chase murderers or rapists or child abusers?"

"As long as we're in law enforcement, we're going to keep seeing the worst side of humanity," I said.

"Yes; humans are disappointing."

We arrived at the cave and all talk ceased. The odor of decomposition was strong enough to make us gag, and we were still outside. Len shot me a look that said he didn't want to go in either, which made me feel less guilty about my sudden loss of courage.

And why had I eaten so much cake?

Len dug around in a saddlebag and brought out two pairs of white, disposable coveralls. "Put this on over your clothes. It'll protect them, but you'll probably still want to burn everything you're wearing when this is over."

No lie.

Len took a camera, a large flashlight, a saddlebag that held his evidence gathering kit, and a small jar of Vick's Vapor Rub from the gear secured on Texas Gal. He hung the camera around his neck, and then stuffed several pairs of crime scene gloves into a pocket in his coveralls.

I petted the mare, loving her along the sides of her face, and tried to console myself with the fact that this job would end. We'd bring out the body, take it to the highway, and then I could go home, burn my clothes, and possibly, my hair.

"We'll need these," Len said, referring to the gloves, "but we're only going to have a look-see right now. I'll take some photos, and then we'll come back for the kit and other things we'll need." He handed me the Vick's. "If you stuff some of this into your nose, the smell won't be as bad."

I did as he suggested, gathered the remnants of my courage, and followed him in. It was dim, eerie, and ay Dios, I wanted to run. Even with a nose full of Vick's the odor was unmistakable. We let our eyes adjust while Len fiddled with the camera.

Mystery Man was lying in a crumpled heap against one wall.

"The vic was dumped, so my first impression is foul play." Len spoke into a small recorder in his shirt pocket. He went on to describe the cave and the location of the body within it. He'd already identified himself, but at that point he identified me.

"Will you hold this light on the body while I photograph it?"

While he did that I stared at the crumpled, leaking ruin of a man and tried to still my mind, but I had this thought: If you ever believe, as I sometimes do, that your body is so fine and strong, and you feel invincible and all that, then observe the effects of death. You'll see firsthand how quickly the bodies we're so fond of melt back into the natural world. They go fast. The body I enjoyed so much and was so proud of would be unrecognizable in a week. It was sobering.

"You can come with me and breathe a while or stay here," Len said.

I chose to go with him and breathe.

Once we were outside again, Len asked, "Where were you? You went away for a while."

"My brain escaped for a few minutes."

"I hope you can get it to come back," he said with a dimpled grin, "because I need your help."

"I'm back. Just tell me what to do."

"We're going to move the body onto this sheet and then we're going to bring it out into the light of day. You'll guard it from insects, wild beasts, and stray cowboys while I gather whatever I can from inside the cave. Then we'll get as much forensic evidence as possible from Mystery Man's corpse. To say this'll be unpleasant is an understatement, like saying—"

"Let's just do it. I know it's going to be hell."

"But you're with me?"

"I'm with you. I don't like gathering evidence, but I love to solve a mystery."

"Ah…" He sighed. "You're my kind of woman."

"You might want to think that through."

He laughed. "Let's hit it."

"You want me to sing?"

"Sure; our guy won't care."

"You might."

We put on gloves and tied surgical masks over our faces. At the entrance, Len turned to me. "From this point, everything we say will be recorded."

"In that case, I'll hold back on the singing."

"You can sing to me later."

That was the last of the banter. We spread out the sheet and I waited while Len gave a running commentary of everything he observed. He described the cowboy hat, what we could see of the man's clothes, and gave a detailed description of the corpse that made my stomach begin a tortuous crawl up my throat.

When Len lifted the upper half of Mystery Man and I lifted the legs, I witnessed the most sickening sound I've ever heard. It was the two body halves trying to come apart, resulting in a wet slurping noise.

"Keep going. That's it. We're almost there." Len encouraged me because I think he knew how badly I wanted to bolt. Somehow the odor had worsened.

We wrestled the body onto the sheet and carried it outside. I willed myself not to think about the pool of fluids left behind or how the rotting thing would look in the bright light of day.

Outside, I pulled the mask down from my face and took deep breaths while I looked up at the ridge. It was topped by huge chunks of bald, red-brown rock, a color called *colorado* in Spanish. It reminded me, in a vague way, of Cactus Hill. All I needed was something calm and steady to hang on to. The Chisos Mountains.

Len moved next to me. "Don't let any of those little rascals get away." He nodded towards the covered body. Maggots. He was talking about the tiny maggots that were wriggling along the edges of the sheet and crawling out from under it.

I looked up at him with an open mouth. He laughed and handed me a bag and large tweezers. "I wish you could see your face."

"I don't want to touch those things."

"You're not going to touch them. That's the reason we have tweezers. You just pick them up gently and put them in the bag. I'll be back in no time."

"What about those beetle-looking thingies?"

"We'll need those too," Len said. "We need anything that tries to crawl, roll, run, walk, slither, dance, or hop away."

"I want to be cremated."

"Well…" Len appeared to consider it. "Okay, but I'm busy right now."

That got a laugh out of me in spite of the creepy-crawlies.

He winked and disappeared into the cave. Then it was just me, a dead person, and things I don't want to describe. It didn't take long for flies to come from wherever they hang out when they're not being a nuisance.

So there I was in the backcountry, a young woman of reasonable looks and intelligence, picking up slimy creatures that lived off decomposing things. At the same time I was swatting away flying insects that were determined to get their fair share. I willed myself to think about the Chisos and pictured them standing serene and unconcerned with death and dying. Life comes and it goes. The Chisos had seen a lot of that drama and didn't take it personally.

Also during that ordeal, an old Scottish prayer from my childhood came to mind:

From ghoulies and ghosties

And long-leggedy beasties

And things that go bump in the night,

Good Lord, deliver us!

No kidding.

* * *

Len brought out evidence bags, but to tell the truth, I tried not to look at what they contained. One saddlebag held cold packs, and it was into that one he put the things I managed to avoid.

He walked over as he removed his gloves. "How's it going here, Do-Da?"

I indicated the recorder but he grinned. "It's off."

"In that case, this job blows."

"Ya think?"

"But I guess it's better than what you were doing."

"You got that right."

"Were you able to get much?"

"Yes. Would you like a rundown?"

"Not right now."

He picked up the plastic bag of revolting thingies. "Wow. You've got a whole little community here."

"Yes. I recognize some of them as my neighbors."

He laughed at that. "While my hands are clean, I'm going to

bring the last of the cold water. Do you want anything to eat?"

"No, thank you."

"Yeah; maybe later is better." He took the bag of horrors and put it with the other bags and brought back the water. "Ditch those gloves and come with me a minute."

I put the gloves into the trash bag and followed because he was headed away from the cave, the corpse, and the crawlies. He sat underneath a stunted juniper tree and I plopped down beside him.

"What about the insects, wild beasts, and stray cowboys?" I asked.

"We won't be long, and we can see the body from here. I just thought we should enjoy our last cold water unaccompanied by the smell of death."

"Good move. I like your style."

"I know how to treat a woman. Bring her into the wilderness to hunt for a body and then force her to pick up the squiggling by-products of death."

"Stop it. You're making me weak in the knees."

"I wish."

* * *

We put on clean gloves and Len pulled back the sheet from Mystery Man. In the cave he'd been face down and crumpled. Now he was on his back and somewhat elongated by the effects of decomposition. We estimated his height at 5'7", taking that into account. His face was darkish and disfigured by bloating.

Len began talking into the recorder again. After a few minutes we cut away the clothes. It always seems like the last bit of dignity is taken from the deceased when we do that, but to investigate effectively we have to. The first thing we learned was that Mystery Man was a woman.

Len rose from his bent position. "Son of a bitch."

Yes, I thought, but I stayed silent.

"Damn it, Margarita," he whined.

"What is it, Len?"

"We have a woman here."

"Yes."

"So why is there a dead woman here?"

I shrugged. I was willing myself not to throw up.

"I'm sorry," he continued. "I'm having a bit of a breakdown. I feel like crying because of this poor dead woman, and I feel like laughing because you're here."

"Thank you. I think."

"We can stare at this tragedy all day but that won't help her."

"We need to collect evidence and get it to a lab pronto so we can figure out who did this to her."

"Right. Let's get on it."

After detailed instruction from Len, I picked fibers and debris out of her dark hair while maggots and wormy things crawled through it and in and out of all openings. It was grosser than gross, but I have to admit I was absorbed by the work. The desire for justice is a powerful motivator, not to mention solving a mystery.

I worked silently; Len gave his observations and findings into the recorder. He was taking swabs and I don't know what else because I didn't look. I didn't hear most of what he said because I concentrated on the job while various thoughts drifted in and out of my mind. I wondered, among many other things, about Bradley Jennings and was anxious to know if Barney had gotten the warrant to search Miss Cooper's house. Had Tamara Hagan's sister been located? When all else failed, I tried to put my head back in the Chisos but that didn't work.

As I moved down the body from the head, I noticed something. "Len, look at this."

He peered at it. "It looks like a tattoo."

"I think it's a blue bee."

"Is that significant to you?"

"She works, or did, at a brothel in Ojinaga called The Blue Bee. The prostitutes who work there have a blue bee tattooed somewhere on their bodies, usually at the base of their neck."

"How do you know?"

"Does that matter?"

"I don't know."

"I've never worked in a brothel, if that's what you're thinking."

He gave an exasperated huff. "That possibility never *once* crossed my mind."

"Good."

"Can't you tell me how you know?"

"I grew up here, which includes the other side of the river as much as this side. I have friends in Mexico and that's how I learned about The Bee. One time I was at a party and I met a prostitute from there."

"Listen to me, Margarita. If you know someone at the Blue Bee, maybe she could identify this woman. Oh my god! Maybe she could also identify my Presidio victim." Len paced around in excitement. "Holy shit! This could be a huge break!"

"Len, I don't know anybody from The Bee. I met someone once a long time ago. Does your other victim have a blue bee tattoo?"

"I think so. She has a tattoo and it's blue. In my ignorance, I thought it was a tiny flower. I barely glanced at it. I have to call the medical examiner right now!"

"Len, we'll have to radio the sheriff and ask him to call for you because our cell phones won't work here."

"If we get up high, will they?"

"No."

"That's what the sheriff said. Why is that?"

"The mountains interfere with the signals. There aren't enough towers and the ones we have aren't powerful enough. I don't know all the reasons; I just know they don't work."

I explained that if he radioed the sheriff, he needed to word his conversation so he didn't give away too much information to the county at large. For example, instead of saying he needed to know if the tattoo was a blue bee, he should ask the sheriff to find out what the tattoo is. Len changed his mind. He thought it'd be better not to mention any tattoos on the air in case the wrong people were listening.

I radioed the sheriff to say everything was fine and going according to schedule. His comment was the usual. "Carry on." Easy for him to say.

* * *

After we got everything we could from the body, we rolled her up in the sheet so nothing would be lost and then put her into a body bag. Len moved some of our gear to our other horses in order to make room on Texas Gal.

We removed our gloves, masks, and coveralls and put them into a trash bag. Then we checked to be sure we hadn't left any sign of our presence, mounted the horses, and rode away from there.

We talked about it and decided not to camp. We needed to bathe and didn't think a stock tank would cut it. Len was anxious to call the M.E. about the details of the tattoo. I wanted to know about the Cooper warrant. Not camping would mean riding through the night in the dark, but we already knew that wouldn't be difficult because of the stars.

Len rode up close beside me. "You're sure you don't know the name of someone who works at The Blue Bee?"

"I'm sure."

"Have you ever been there?"

"No. Women are discouraged from going there. Len, the victim who was found at the ranch gate also had a tat of a blue bee. Did the sheriff mention that?"

"No, he didn't. What the hell?" Len ran a hand over his jaw as he contemplated the possible implications. "Maybe it's not trafficking after all."

"Prostitutes from Ojinaga don't seem right for trafficking victims, but the McFarley Ranch is connected somehow to The Blue Bee."

"I think you're right, but I have no idea what is going on."

"I don't know either, but I think the place to start is at the brothel, don't you? If you go there and show the photos, someone will recognize these victims. That will give you the link."

Len nodded.

"If the McFarley Ranch is involved in human trafficking, how do you think that would be?" I asked. "Are they doing the trafficking or passing people through or allowing someone else to move them through the ranch?"

"It could be either thing, but I lean to the latter. The McFarley name is well-known and respected in these parts, so it's hard to believe old man McFarley would be involved, but it could be some of his hands. Or it could be his son. It's also possible the ranch is buying people as employees. Basically, they're slaves and they're abused in all the ways you'd expect."

"Len, how was your Presidio victim killed?"

"She was strangled."

"Was she raped?"

"Yes, she was either raped or had extremely rough sex. But since I believe she was trafficked, it was rape. Now stop sneaking these questions by me. I'm powerless to say no to you." A few beats passed and he added, "You, however, aren't powerless to tell me no."

"Len, I'm not holding anything back."

"You know how it is when you interview someone and you get a feeling there's something more, something they aren't telling?"

"Yes."

"I feel that from you."

"I really don't know anything, Len. I think you're picking up on my residual teenage guilt."

"For?"

"In order to go to the party where I met the pro, I lied to my parents. Once I was there, I was in over my head but it wasn't like I could call them to the rescue."

"Yeah. I get that."

"I wasn't supposed to go to 'wild' parties in Ojinaga—or any-where—but I was at the age where I went out of my way to break my parents' rules."

"We all lie to our parents, I think."

"My parents taught me right from wrong, most of the time by example. With the exception of my papi going on and on about drugs and the damage they do on every level to good people. I could write a 'just say no' manual based on Papi's rants."

He laughed. "I had a papi like that, too."

"I thought we'd be drinking beer and smoking cigarettes—both forbidden. I also thought I'd be dancing with other kids more or less my age. Imagine how I felt when I realized I'd taken myself to a drug-and-sex-fest with people much older and wilder. There were other teens there, but we were in the minority."

"Where you hurt?"

"No. When it got to the level of alarming, I slipped away. Len, it can't be a coincidence that one man and possibly two women with Blue Bee tattoos are connected to this ranch."

"I agree."

"Seeing the bee tattoos makes me suspicious that they're holding drug-and-sex-fests that are getting out of hand. Do you think it could be something as simple as that?"

"Yes, it could be that. Sometimes the simple, 'easy' answer is the most obvious one. Has anyone questioned the young man in the hospital?"

"I don't know because I'm here in the back country with Lennie Bob."

"Oh, yeah, good point."

We rode along in silence until he said, "I still think this is about trafficking. Even if they're throwing wild parties, why use prostitutes from Mexico?"

"They may make them disappear so nobody talks about what they're doing on this ranch. Also, they never have to pay them."

"Exactly."

"That's sickening."

"Yup."

"You could ask the sheriff for my help on this case. More help, I mean."

"I'll suggest it. Because this dead woman was found in Brewster County it's your Sheriff's Office case, too."

"You're just sweet-talking me."

"That's true, Do-Da. You saw right through me."

"I'm smarter than I seem. Fortunately."

Chapter 22

On the way back, before it got dark, we came across and then followed the well-traveled road that appeared to cut across the ranch. We ended up at an unmarked locked gate on Highway 118 that looked like part of the fence. I argued for following the road back in the other direction, but Len grumbled that it wasn't covered by our warrant. Also, we were losing time, he pointed out; the corpse was decaying as we "messed around."

I argued that knowing about this road could be important, but I lost the battle. Texas Rangers are sticklers for warrants, and I'm supposed to be.

Len and I rode the whole night, except for periodic rests to snack and drink water. We were exhausted from tense work and lack of sleep, yet energized by the seriousness of our mission and the breathtaking beauty of nighttime in Big Bend.

After sunrise Saturday morning, we arrived at the highway and had to wait for the hearse to take Mystery Woman to the crime lab. We were also waiting for a trailer to come for the horses. We loaded our things into our trucks and then we waited. I felt there were volumes to say but…

"Listen," Len said, "I do a lot of undercover work and I'm out of town all the time. You shouldn't get involved with a man who does the gruesome things I do."

"What is this about?"

"I alluded to the fact that we might have a relationship after this trip is over, but in so many ways, this trip will never be over for me. This shit is what I do. We break up one ring of traffickers but there is always another. I just don't think I'd be a good man for you."

"Is this about Zeke?"

"No."

"It sounds like you're breaking up with me, and all we did was ride in together to bring out a dead body. We shared an unspeakable job, a few laughs, and a chocolate cake. That's not what I consider a hot affair. Also, I'd like to point out that you're pissing me off. Who says I want to have a relationship with some Lennie Bob Texas Ranger from Midland?"

He stared at me with his mouth open.

"Also, you threw my do-da into the fire."

He snapped his fingers. "Damn! I knew that would come back to bite me."

"If you want to break up, that's fine, but when you burn a girl's hair do-da, I think the least you could do is take her to dinner."

"Is that what you think?"

"Did I stutter?"

"No. I'm receiving you loud and clear, Deputy Ricos."

No. He wasn't.

* * *

Len had to take the evidence to his crime lab and speak to his boss in Midland, but he said he'd be back. No mention of dinner and not even a handshake. I'd shared more animated good-byes with suspects.

He'd been right all along. The stars, as all-out fabulous as they were all night, were not aligned in our favor.

I drove home, took a long shower, and considered whether to wash or throw away my clothes. I threw them in the machine and started it. Then I checked in with the sheriff, but he said, "Go to sleep and call me later."

I fell into bed.

When I awakened, the room and everything in it glowed red, faded to gold, and then to shadows. I was confused, but then I realized I'd slept until sunset. I was dragged out of bed by pounding on my front door and Barney yelling, "Ricos!"

I pulled on a bathrobe and went to let him in.

"Great hair," he commented as he came in followed by Buster.

"Thank you. I went to bed with it wet in order to get this effect."

"It must be great to lie around all day," Buster joked. The big ol' lug was having a bad influence on the new guy.

"What brings my fellow deputies to my house?"

"Aren't you glad to see us, Ricos? We thought you were never coming back."

"Of course I'm happy to see you, but I was only gone two days, Barn."

"Yeah, but it seemed longer."

"If you'll wait a few minutes, I'll get dressed."

I saw a wisecrack forming behind Barney's straight face, but he swallowed it and asked, "Want me to make coffee?"

"Sure, that would be nice."

When I came back to the living room, the brewing coffee smelled wonderful. My partners were wandering around peering at my things.

"Are you guys looking for something?"

"Yes," Buster answered in a serious voice, "Mr. Jennings' genitals."

"Believe it or not, I don't have them. I thought you'd have located them by now. What have you two been doing?"

"That's what we came to tell you."

"Did you solve the murder?"

"Not yet." Buster sighed and sat down.

"What's going on?"

"I got the warrant," Barney blurted as if he couldn't wait another second.

"That's great! How did you do it?"

"I pointed out to the judge the ways in which our warrant was a reasonable and legal request. He denied me, of course."

"That's his M.O."

"At that point I stood up and looked down at him. You know I can be a little bit intimidating."

"Right."

"I told him I knew what he suggested to you. He fell all over himself explaining that you'd misunderstood him. When he saw I wasn't buying it he claimed that, in truth, you came on to him, just an oversexed young female deputy, you know."

"That lying old freak. Then what?"

"I said *I bet you don't know that Margarita's father is a Texas Ranger. One phone call is all it would take.* That's all I had to say, Ricos. I got the warrant."

"Way to go, Barney!"

"Why didn't you use the dad card when you were there?"

"Who wants to involve their father in stuff like this? I'd rather handle it myself without running to Daddy."

"Ricos, I'm sorry, but Zeke just bailed us out without knowing anything about any of this."

"Yeah, it's kind of amazing the things his name can do."

Barney laughed. "I'm gonna start telling people my dad is a Texas Ranger."

"Work it."

"All's fair in love and law enforcement," Buster quipped.

"Did you serve the warrant?"

"Jeez, have a little faith. Of course we served it. Miss Cooper showed us photos of her grown brother. He's not John Cooper and doesn't look anything like him."

"Crap. That's another dead end. Wait. How do you know she showed you her brother and not some other man?"

"I don't know that. What makes you suspect her so strongly?"

"I guess it's her general weirdness and reluctance to cooperate. Also, from an age and physical standpoint, she seems the least likely. So I was thinking how typical it would be if the least likely person did it."

"Ricos, you've got to stop reading so many mystery novels."

"Buster, you saw those pics of Bailey Cooper all over her living room. She was obsessed with him, right?"

"That's true. She was so starry-eyed and goofy when she spoke about him that we thought maybe they had a sex thing going on at one time."

"Maybe you two shouldn't work together. You go see some sweet old gal and the next thing we know you've got her in bed with her brother?"

"You had to be there," I said. "Buster's not kidding. She was over the top. It's peculiar that suddenly the photos are gone…every single one."

"Ricos, 'peculiar' doesn't even start to describe so many of the people here."

"Don't I know it!" Buster exclaimed, making us laugh.

After that I served the coffee and told them what I could about the body in the cave, which meant I couldn't tell them much.

"What was Camacho like to work with?" Barney wanted to know.

"He was competent and professional. He's knowledgeable about crime scene investigation, everything you'd expect from a Texas Ranger."

"Did you learn anything?"

"Yes, a few things, one being that I don't like gathering evidence off a body that's been dead at least four days."

"Well duh. Is Camacho a cowboy type?"

"He was comfortable with horses if that's what you mean. Why do you ask?"

Barney shrugged. "Just curious. You said he was the 'beautiful man' who came to your door."

"He's beautiful all right, but he's too arrogant."

"So you're sweet on him?"

"Are you listening? No."

"Uh-huh."

"Take it or leave it; that's the truth. Could Brad Jennings' brother shed any light on the John Cooper-Bailey Cooper dilemma?"

"He says Brad was in love with and lived with John Cooper many years, such a long time that John used 'Jennings' as his last name. Dr. Jennings never heard of a Bailey Cooper."

"That's disappointing."

"Yes, but it just means we have to dig deeper."

"Has anyone spoken with the injured man?"

"No. He escaped."

"He left the hospital?"

"That's what 'escaped' means, Ricos."

I gave him a look. "How did he get past the deputy?"

Barney's expression was priceless. "It was Lonnie Davidson."

"It's no wonder the sheriff didn't want to talk about this earlier."

"Yeah, he's pissed," Buster said. "He says you think he's a pro from Mexico."

"He might be."

"Based on his tattoo?"

"Yes."

"Do you think he's gay?"

"What does that have to do with anything?"

"Men pay him for sex, right?"

"Yes. Most likely, men and women pay him. He could be gay or straight but that doesn't have any bearing on the fact that he's a witness and he's gone."

"I don't understand." Buster looked perturbed.

"I think you're failing to hear the part about 'pay,' Buster," Barney said. "He gets paid to have sex with whoever wants to pay."

"I wonder if he makes a lot of money."

"Are you considering your career options, or what?"

"I can't see that being a deputy is all that big a deal," Buster whined.

It made us laugh and we agreed with him, to a point, but I said, "Just think about the fact that his services are sold to people he doesn't get to see first. Once the deal is made, he's in."

"Yuck."

"Yes, those are my thoughts exactly." I waited a beat and added, "We sure need to talk to him about what happened. Did anybody look for him?"

"Yes, but he wasn't found. He could be hiding in Alpine, I guess. Most likely he's gone back home."

"I left my card on the bedside table at the hospital, so maybe he'll call me."

"I don't think you should hold your breath on that, Ricos."

I changed the subject. "Was Tamara Hagan's sister located while I was gone?"

"No. That's still a puzzle. Tamara is in the county jail, but the

Social Security Administration is charging her with fraud, so the feds might move her before long."

"We never interviewed her about the Jennings murder. Do you think she could have done it?" I asked.

"Well sure," Barney said. "She's as likely as anyone else. Someone had an extreme reaction and I can see her having one."

"But his genitals weren't found in her house," Buster pointed out, "and she had practically everything else you can imagine."

"Maybe they're in a jar in a storage locker," Barney suggested.

"The only storage unit she has is a small one and nothing like that was found," Buster said. "Maybe she fed them to her dogs."

"So what you two are telling me is that we are right where we were when I left two days ago to go to the cave."

"Pretty much," Barney admitted.

* * *

I was settling down to read when I heard a loud thud on my porch. It was Wynne knocking things around in the dark. He stumbled into my house when I opened the door. His face was bleeding and both eyes were puffy, but one was swelling shut. He peered at me out of the other one and held his midsection as though his stomach was going to fall out.

"I'm okay," he groaned.

"You are not. Why are you here and not at EMS or the clinic?"

"Talk to you."

"Wynne, I'm going to call Mitch."

"Don't make a big deal."

"You need medical attention."

"It was only an ass-whoopin'. You know first aid."

"Who beat you up?"

"McCann Brothers."

"What in the world?" The three brothers, Tommy Mac, Billy Jon, and Mitty, were on the weird side, but we'd never had trouble with them. Strangely, or maybe not, they lived way the heck out on Terlingua Ranch, and when I say way out there I mean like at the drop-off point of the planet.

"Tommy Mac McCann took that pic of you and the sheriff."

"What? But why?"

"I'll explain." He groaned and sank into himself with pain.

"Just rest a minute. I'm getting my first aid kit and a cold pack."

"Can't you hold my head in your lap?"

"If I do that I can't fix you up."

"If you held me, it would fix me up."

When he said that, I knew he was going to be fine, same ol' aggravating Wynne. I brought the things I needed and began to doctor him. He shut his eyes and his mouth and allowed me to do it. Afterwards I had him lie on the sofa while I got him a glass of water.

"Better," he said when he finished drinking.

"I have Tylenol in my kit if you want it."

"Do you have any better drugs? Never mind; I know you don't."

"My mom could give you stronger pain meds. Do you want me to call her?"

"No. I'll be fine. I have stuff at home."

"Do you feel like telling me what happened?"

"I went to the Bad Rabbit Café to meet a friend. Tommy Mac was there swilling beer." The Bad Rabbit is the restaurant on Terlingua Ranch. "My friend didn't come, so Tommy Mac invited me to join him. I ate a burger and had a few beers with him. He mentioned that he saw you when you and Buster came to the café a while back. He asked me if I'd ever gone out with you."

"And what did you say?"

"I told him we went to dinner one time, but that we're friends. We don't always agree, but we're friends, right?"

"Sometimes I wonder, but yes, we're friends."

"He asked me if I thought you'd go out with him. I seriously doubt it, but I told him he would have to call you and ask. Then he showed me that photo of you and the sheriff. We went out to his Jeep to get more beer and he said something that made me think he knew about it. So I asked him if he did it and he admitted it. He did it for five hundred dollars."

"Did he say who paid him?"

"Nah, he wouldn't, so I pushed him up against his Jeep and demanded to know who gave him money for doin' that. His brothers came up in that old Chevy they drive and saw what was happening. They blocked my truck and piled out. They didn't even ask what was goin' on. They jumped me and you see what they did to me."

"I'm sorry you were injured, but pushing people up against their vehicles is a bad way to start a conversation."

"I know. It just pissed me off so bad that he took a picture like that of you."

"Yet you wanted one."

Wynne reddened. "Well…"

"Thank you for trying to get answers and for letting me know who took the photo. I'll talk to Tommy Mac."

"He ain't gonna tell you."

"Maybe I'll have the sheriff work on him."

"That's a better idea. Margarita, he's one of those Terlingua Defenders."

There was a group of would-be warriors, sworn to protect the integrity of the U.S., which boiled down to strutting and bragging about their weapons. "My gun is bigger than your gun." As long as they didn't hassle people or hurt anyone, Sheriff Ben was content just to keep his eye on them.

"I'll let him know, Wynne. Thanks."

Chapter 23

Welcome to another ruined Sunday. Sheriff Ben showed no mercy or respect for my sanity or personal life. Looking on the bright side, it was a knock-your-socks-off March day.

My boss picked me up early because, "I'm sick and tired of this bullshit and we're going to get to the bottom of it right now."

I agreed, but jeez.

He smiled when I got into his truck. "Good morning! I brought two thermoses of coffee and a few breakfast burritos from Alicia's."

Food from Alicia's improved my outlook for the day. Also, Marianne had made the coffee. It was tasty and strong but not walk-out-the-door-on-its-own-strong like the sheriff makes.

He remarked about the beauty of spring mornings, or any mornings, in the south of his county. Then he added, "This scenery is so awe-inspiring. It jump-starts your day, doesn't it?"

"Yes sir. I love it."

It was a glittering morning with a baby blue sky hanging above it. Mountains in Mexico were peeking at Texas. They always do but we don't always catch them in the act. The air was so clean I thought we could see all the way to the Pacific Ocean if we climbed high enough. Colors were soft and understated. Sometimes the sun hit a deep cut slicing down the side of a mountain, an arroyo still wet from the recent rain; it would shine like diamonds were embedded in the dirt.

"It occurs to me," the sheriff said, "that we should try harder to find out what happened to the young man who left the hospital. That should take priority over this, I think. What if he was taken away against his will?"

"Isn't that unlikely since a deputy was there?"

He sighed. "I don't know what to think. It seems like every possible thing is going wrong since I decided to keep my position as sheriff. Now I let someone we had under our protection get away from us. I'll be a laughingstock."

"Sheriff, I think we should tackle one thing at a time. Let's see what the McCann brothers know and then we'll go to Ojinaga."

"You think he'll be there?"

"Yes. That's what I expect."

"And you know how to find him?"

"No, but I can ask about him."

"Do you know that his tox screen showed high levels of cocaine and meth?"

"No. I didn't know that."

"I certainly would like to know his story."

"Same here. Sheriff, a rape kit was done on him, right?"

"Yes. It didn't appear he'd been sexually abused, but he'd been strangled. Those two things often go together."

"He didn't look like a drug addict," I said.

"That's true, and maybe he's not addicted."

"He could have been overdosed."

In a change of subject, the sheriff said, "I had a long phone conversation yesterday with Captain Alan Nelson. He heads up Texas Rangers Company E in Midland. He's Lennon Camacho's boss."

How irritating that the mention of Len's name made me blush. I hadn't done anything but kiss him on the dimple. *Good grief.* The sheriff's eyes flitted from the road to the scenery, so I don't think he noticed.

"Camacho told his boss the bee tattoo is a significant lead and he's impressed you knew about that. Camacho also told him you were willing to go to Ojinaga."

"Yes sir. Do you want me to go?"

"I'm not sending you."

"Why is that?"

"I think the Texas Rangers should handle it."

"But why, Sheriff?

"The subject of you going to Ojinaga is closed. A Texas Ranger is going."

Great.

"It's good luck for this investigation that you know about the tattoos."

"That remains to be seen. It's possible nobody at The Blue Bee will talk. Whatever is going on most likely involves the brothel. It's run by criminals."

"I understand that. It's one more reason not to send you."

"I could slip over there, locate the injured man, and see what he says."

"For the love of Pete, Margarita! It appears someone is abducting young people from Ojinaga. It would be irresponsible of me to send you right now."

"But Sheriff, I don't have a blue bee tattoo. Also, I—"

"The subject of you going to Ojinaga is closed, Deputy Ricos."

Fine. I never wanted to go there again anyway.

* * *

The McCann brothers live in a jaw-dropper of a location, but getting there is tricky and takes a long time. The road is steep and not maintained with regularity due to its location. It winds and twists over the land like a snake in its death throes. At times it was nothing but a scratch in the dirt along the side of a boulder-littered mountain. At other times the truck listed so hard I thought it would topple over the edge.

We passed bald-faced rock formations the size of football stadiums and powered our way through rough-and-tumble arroyos. The still-wet gravel and sand sucked at the tires. "Wild and untamed" took on new meaning here at the end of the earth. I lost count of how many times one of us exclaimed, "Wow!"

At one point I said, "Sheriff, Wynne says Tommy Mac McCann is one of the Terlingua Defenders you've been watching. Did you know that?"

"All three of the brothers are armed and standing ready."

"I find that terrifying."

"Good. You should. Did Wynne say anything else?"

"No. Not about that."

"Do you think he's involved in that group?"

"I don't know, Sheriff. I don't think so. He's armed, but he doesn't strut around or talk about 'illegal aliens' or 'wetbacks,' and he's never mentioned a fear of the government coming for his guns."

"I want you to keep in mind at all times that in a situation, in their eyes, you *are* the government. Buster didn't want to work here and those guys are one of the reasons. If they ever perceive they're in a stand-off with 'the government' they'd think nothing of eliminating all of us." This was an old rant, stated differently.

"I'll keep that in mind."

"You'd better."

* * *

The brothers' house isn't much. It looks slapped together with this and that and afterthoughts, but the views make up for what the structure lacks. I nearly fell on my face because I was gawking at the spire-topped mountains instead of watching where I was going. The path to the house is steep, rocky, and uneven, everything you'd expect from three men who don't want to have visitors.

Even though we were in Sheriff Ben's big BCSO truck and dressed in our uniforms, Billy Jon met us at the door with a shotgun. I was getting tired of that form of greeting. I glanced at Sheriff Ben; he didn't like it either.

Billy Jon was a short man compared to my boss and had a long, thick beard that made me wonder how many small creatures could burrow into it at one time. Add to that rotting teeth and brown eyes that looked gigantic because of his glasses. "Nobody called the law," he snarled.

"That's true sir, but the law has come calling for you," the sheriff said in his good-natured way. "Put the weapon down."

"Get off my property."

"I'm Ben Duncan, the sheriff of Brewster County." His tone was friendly but his smile had faded.

"I don't give a shit if you're King Tut."

"Hey, Billy Jon, we need to see Tommy Mac," I interrupted before the men got into it. "Is he here?" Enough of my life was being lost to inane crap.

"Hey Margarita, how's it going?"

"Great. How've you been?"

"Fine, 'cept I have the goddamned law at my door."

"Would you get Tommy Mac for me please?" I gave him a big smile.

"Sure. Wait a minute." He turned and went back in the house.

"Nicely done," the sheriff said under his breath.

I grinned at him.

It took a long time for Tommy Mac to make it to the door. If I had to guess, I'd say he had a painful hangover. He wore the same clothes he'd worn yesterday, judging by the blood and dirt stains. At least one night had been spent in them. He was a rumpled mess with bed hair and a three-day stubble.

"Now listen," he began in a contrite manner.

"You listen," growled the sheriff. "I want to know how you came to think it would be all right to drag my reputation and Margarita's into the dirt. Was it entertaining for you? Do you think it's funny to make my innocent wife cry all night? Can you even imagine the mess and heartache you've caused?"

The sheriff clenched and unclenched his fists. His body language said he was poised to beat the snot out of Tommy Mac McCann. It would've been great to see that, and I was all for helping him. Although the odds were against us, frustration and righteous outrage fueled our side. Tommy Mac had Billy Jon with his shotgun and another brother sneaking around hoping for trouble. Remembering Wynne's busted-up face dampened my enthusiasm for a brawl.

"May we come in, Tommy Mac?"

"Sit out here." He indicated a rusty metal table and chairs under a stunning example of an ancient mesquite tree. "Whatcha want?"

"I want to know who paid you to take my photo with the sheriff," I said.

"Can't say."

"You'd better say or you're going to jail," threatened the sheriff.

"You can't take me to jail for what I done."

"Think again."

"Is that true, Margarita?" he whined. His breath smelled like a week of all-night drinking and a while since the last toothbrushing.

"Yes, Tommy Mac. You're in deep."

"All I did was to take a picture of you and the sheriff. It's not my fault that guy made your shirt come off. I don't know how he did that."

"Which guy do you mean, Tommy Mac?" the sheriff asked, losing patience.

"He paid me cash."

"But you know his name," I said because I sensed that he did.

"I'm not supposed to tell nobody."

"Stand up," the sheriff ordered.

"Why?"

"I'm going to cuff you and take you to jail."

"It was Derrick Chaney," Tommy Mac blurted.

"Who the hell is Derrick Chaney?" the sheriff thundered. "Do you know that name, Margarita?"

"No sir. I've never heard it."

"He's not from here," Tommy Mac volunteered. "The picture was for somebody else."

"He didn't say who?"

"Naw, he only said the guy needed a picture."

"How much were you paid?"

"I spent the money!"

"I don't want the money," the sheriff explained through gritted teeth. "I want the man who paid you. Tell me exactly what he said."

"He asked if I knew Margarita."

"And you said?"

"I said sure."

"Then what?"

"He said he'd pay me five hundred for a clear photo of her and you."

"How did you know I would be at her house on that day?"

"I called your office and your secretary said you were in Terlingua, so I took a chance. I was there a different day, but you never came. It was only Margarita."

That did it. I needed a large, mean dog or at least a loud one.

"What else?"

"He said a man in Alpine needed to prove that something was goin' on between you and Margarita. He said you were fucking her." He turned to me. "Is that true, Margarita?"

"That's not true."

"That's good."

"He said 'a man in Alpine' needed the photo?"

"Yes sir, Sheriff."

"What does Derrick Chaney look like?" asked my boss.

"He's not as tall as you, but he's bulked-up and probably weighs more. He's got longish brown hair."

"Keep talking."

"He has a lot of tats."

"On his arms or where?"

"All over. Well, the parts I could see."

"Which parts would those be?"

"His neck and arms—it's not like I saw him nekked."

"How old is he?"

"How am I supposed to know that?"

"Take a wild guess."

"Middle-forties."

Sheriff Ben looked up at the mountain looming over the house, a mammoth thing covered in a frenzied bloom of wildflowers poking up between giant boulders. "Do you enjoy living here, Mr. McCann?"

"Yep, I sure do."

"You'd like to stay?"

"What are you gettin' at?"

"Have you told me the truth about everything?"

"Yes, of course."

"Want to add anything?"

"I got nothin' to add."

"Would you bet your freedom on that?"

"Huh?"

"If I find out you held back one scrap of anything, it will be a long time before you see these mountains again. I can charge you with all kinds of crimes and keep you tied up for years, waiting in jail. Do you understand what I'm saying to you?"

"Shit, man. When did you become such a big asshole?"

"You decided to show a lack of respect for my wife, my deputy, and me. That tends to bring out the asshole in me. You don't want to go to war with the Brewster County Sheriff's Office, Mr. McCann."

"No, I don't. Look, Sheriff, I didn't know what they was gonna do with that picture. I swear it. I just wanted the money."

"Okay. We'll leave it like this then. Do you have a phone?"

"I have a satellite phone."

"Good. Call my office if you hear anything else or think of something you haven't told us. Can you do that?"

"Yes sir."

Tommy Mac stopped us as we were leaving. "There's one more thing. It's about the Brad Jennings murder."

"What is it?"

"It's about the aliens." He looked back and forth between us.

"What sort of aliens?"

"You know—*aliens*. I think aliens killed Brad Jennings."

"Explain that."

"We've had lots of those big, flattish clouds that hide their space-ships so they can come in close."

I've never seen a look like that on the sheriff's face. I had to bite my lip hard to keep from laughing.

"Why would aliens want to kill a peaceable man like Mr. Jennings?" Sheriff Ben asked without laughing or snorting. I couldn't have done it.

"They don't care who they kill. Nobody understands why they do what they do or why they come here."

The sheriff was speechless. He turned to me but I had nothin'.

"You found the body, right?" Tommy Mac asked.

"Yes."

"Maybe it wasn't aliens then. They would've taken it, I think. Did the body have any strange marks or burns or anything?"

"No; there was nothing like that."

Tommy Mac shrugged. "It was just a thought—something to think about."

"Yes, it certainly is." The sheriff offered his hand. "Thank you for your help. In the future, if someone asks you to take a photo of someone else without their knowledge, will you please decline to do it?"

"Yes sir. You can believe I will." He turned to me. "I'm awful sorry about all this, Margarita. I'm gonna call you one day and I'll make it up to you."

"Okay." *I'm not gonna answer.* "See you later, Tommy Mac."

We got into the truck and the sheriff started it and pulled away. I was trying not to laugh and started choking. We got a half-mile from the McCann place and my boss lost it. He had to stop the truck to wipe his eyes. Every time he looked at me he started again. "Oh my god, Margarita." He bent over the steering wheel, shaking with laughter. "Oh my god. I can't quit."

After we recovered, we took a reverse trip through the same land-before-time scenery, but everything appeared to be different. Needle-like spires jutted up at the sky from the mountain ahead of us.

"Were those there before?" the sheriff wondered.

The sun had changed position and a few clouds had drifted in. It was their usual fun and games, messing around and making a spectacle of our scenery.

"Don't look now," Sheriff Ben said, "but there's one of those clouds like the ones the aliens favor. It's rising up over the mountains to the left of us."

* * *

"The county commission approved my budget request for a new deputy," the sheriff said after we recovered from our laughing fit.

"That's great."

"I asked around and it seems as though Conway Bradford led a push to move it through. I called to thank him and he didn't seem too thrilled. He said I should speak with you. What is that about?"

"After the commissioners meeting I had a talk with Conway. I told him I thought it was wrong to treat you the way they do."

"Thank you for that. Conway made it sound like you'd done something wrong or underhanded."

"I pointed out to him that he should shape up and represent his constituency. They would expect him to approve the funding you need for your Office."

"Thank you, Margarita. I appreciate your support."

"You're welcome."

In a few more miles we were back on the main ranch road. The vistas remain drop-dead gorgeous in all directions, but the road is easier to navigate.

"Who do you think is behind Derrick Chaney?" the sheriff asked.

"I think it's William Jackson, don't you?"

"Yes; I think the same thing."

"Who else has an interest in making you look bad, Sheriff?"

"There's nobody else that I'm aware of."

"The timing says it's him. My guess is that Chaney works for Jackson. I bet he's an ex-con who needs a job or else Jackson has some other kind of hold on him. For all you know, Jackson met up with him in prison. Have you ever looked into his background? Who's to say Billy Jack doesn't have a prison record?"

"You have a busy imagination, don't you, Margarita?"

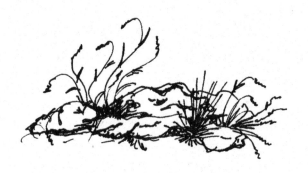

Chapter 24

On Monday morning I was in my office trying to get my head back on the Brad Jennings murder case. Barney and Buster were interviewing substitute teachers to see if they had any out-of-school connection to the victim or information that could be relevant. It was doubtful, but since we had nada piled on top of nada, we had to speak with everyone who knew the deceased.

My father Zeke called. After the "how are you, honey?" talk, he got to the point of his call. "Is it true you rode into the backcountry with Lennon Camacho?"

"It was a large ranch, but yes; why do you ask?"

"What were you doing?"

"We didn't go for fun, if that's what you're wondering. We brought a dead body from a cave on the McFarley Ranch. Why do you ask about him?"

"I told that scoundrel to stay away from you."

"Why would you tell anyone that?"

"He has a questionable reputation."

"It wasn't his choice to work with me. He was assigned by his boss and I was assigned by mine."

"What did he do?"

"He did his job. He's a professional and so am I. What's going on?"

"I don't trust him."

"I can look out for myself. Will you please remember that I'm not a little girl?"

"I want to be a good father to you."

"Zeke, relax. If I need you to stomp somebody, I'll call."

"One day you'll understand that a man who is worth your tears won't make you cry."

"Now you're pulling random advice out of your hat. Nobody is making me cry."

"Len Camacho will. It's his M.O."

"Leave it alone Zeke, or my father is going to make me cry."

He laughed and cut the advice-giving.

"Len Camacho was a gentleman and I enjoyed working with him. I learned some things about forensics gathering."

"Revolting, isn't it?"

"Yes, but I knew that."

"What are you working on now?"

"I'm trying to figure out where to go from here on the murder of a local man."

"Good luck, sweetheart. I'll talk to you later."

"Bye, Zeke."

Fathers are as aggravating as other men—just in a different way.

The next treat in store for me was Danny Finch. He is a forty-something-year-old who lives in Terlingua. When I heard the door open I went into the front.

"Hey, Danny."

"Hi." He peered at me in a way that made me think he needed glasses. "It's strange you didn't interview me about the Jennings murder."

"We didn't interview you because you don't live anywhere near there or have a connection to Mr. Jennings. We've been asking people who know something to come forward ever since the murder."

"I guess you don't know about my gift. That's why I'm here."

"Have a seat and tell me what you know." I sat at Barney's desk.

"You haven't figured it out yet, have you?"

"No."

"If you want I could go over to Brad's house with you."

"How will that help solve the murder?"

"I'm psychic. I can see through the veil into the next plane."

I waited for a punch line but the man was serious.

"If you'll take me there, I'll try to contact Brad. He'll tell me who killed him."

What to say, what to say? Holy crap!

I decided to pass the buck to where it stops anyway: Sheriff Ben. "I wish you'd call the sheriff, Danny. As far as he's concerned, we're through with the crime scene. I can't go back there unless he authorizes it." When you're freaked out, lying can seem like the only way out.

"Can I call him from here?"

"Sure."

"Can you give me the number?"

I dialed it for him, but I didn't get to hear what he said because a call came in on another line. I took it in my office. It was someone calling to back up Tommy Mac McCann's "Brad was killed by aliens" theory. I didn't know which was harder to believe, the theory itself or that Tommy Mac had a close friend who shared it.

When I walked back out to Barney's desk, Danny said, "He's going to call you."

I could just imagine.

It didn't even take a full minute. "Margarita, first we had the 'murdering aliens' theory. Now we have a psychic. Are you messing with me?"

"No sir."

"I have the impression Danny Finch wants to get you alone at that house. Do *not* let that happen."

"Don't worry."

"He gave me a bunch of reasons why you shouldn't take Barney. He says you're a woman and Jennings is more likely to speak if it's just you and him, him being the sensitive psychic. Now I'm determined you'll take Barney or you're not going. Not Buster—I want Barney to go."

"Yes sir. I get it."

"I'd like to tell Mr. Finch to kiss my butt, but there's one reason why I don't. He may have committed the murder or knows who did. It will be interesting to see what he comes up with. It could be telling. That's why I want you and Barney to do this. It could be a waste of your time, but it might not be."

"I understand."

"I'd like to know when you're going, so please notify me."

"I will."

"What'll be the next theory, Nazis? Disgruntled Apache ghosts?"

"It's hard to tell in Terlingua, Sheriff."

"Carry on."

To Danny I said, "I can't leave the office until Barney and Buster return. I'll call you when they do and we'll work out a time."

"I told the sheriff it'd be more effective if you and I go alone because—"

"Two deputies have to go, Danny. It's protocol." It was another harmless lie, told in the interest of getting him out of there with the least possible amount of arguing.

When Danny left I called Stan Hatch, the man who had hassled Brad Jennings on the night he decided not to go into Slim Jimmie's. Talk about a long shot. The number Jessie had given me was for a cell phone, so I didn't know if I was calling him at home or at work. He answered; that was the good news.

After I explained who I was, there was stunned silence.

"Mr. Hatch, are you able to talk in private for a few minutes?"

"Yes. I'm in my office."

"Where do you work?"

He gave me the name of a bank in Midland and said he was a vice president and head of the loan department. Then I explained why I was calling.

"I remember the incident," he admitted, "but I didn't even know that man's name. I acted like a jerk, I know that. The bouncer got in my face about it, but I didn't mean anything. I'd had too much to drink and I got mouthy."

"Have you had any contact with Brad Jennings besides that night?"

"No. I never have. Why are you asking about him? He can't be suing me? I didn't do anything except make a snide comment that I regret."

"Mr. Jennings was murdered later that night."

"That's terrible, but...but you don't think I did it?"

"No sir. I'm interviewing all the people who might have seen anything. Did you notice anyone watching Brad Jennings? Did someone follow him to his car?"

"No. I...my friend came and we went inside. I can't even tell you if Jennings came into the club or not."

"Will you call me if you think of anything?"

"Yes, of course."

I gave him my number and that was that—another dead end. Maybe he was lying, but I had no reason to think so, nothing to go on, and nothing to tie him to Brad Jennings except a wisecrack outside a bar. It was a long stretch from a snarky comment to a brutal murder and mutilation.

* * *

Barney was not pleased about going back to the Jennings home and especially for the reason we were going. "Are you kidding me, Ricos, a psychic?"

Buster volunteered to go, but the sheriff had specified Barney and I understood why. "El Grandote" is formidable. People are unlikely to pull crap in his presence. He has more experience than Buster and is not flustered by Terlinguans and their surprises. Also, Sheriff Ben knew what had never been voiced: if he had to, the big ol' lug would kill anybody who tried to hurt me.

Danny Finch agreed to meet us at the Jennings home, so we were free to talk on the way to the place. Barney related that the substitute teachers didn't know Mr. Jennings well. None of them had tried to date him and seemed clueless about where he lived. Their names were added to the murder board anyway.

The suspect list was still growing. I'd added the bouncer, Jessie Williams, snarky Stan Hatch, and now the physic, Danny Finch. The only name that had come off since we started was Brad's brother because he had an airtight alibi.

"What's your take on this psychic, Ricos?"

"He's a kook. I think he's harmless, but Sheriff Ben thinks otherwise."

"Is that why I have to go with you?"

"Yes. He thinks it's possible Finch murdered Brad or knows who did. I think he just wants to help in his own unique way."

"So you believe he can see through the veil?"

"No, but I think he believes he can. It'll be interesting to see what he says."

* * *

It took Danny a while to settle down. He said it was upsetting to "see" all the blood. By now, everyone in Terlingua knew Brad had been bludgeoned, so the fact that he saw blood wasn't surprising. If he'd mentioned the missing genitals, that would've been impressive…and it would've moved him to the top of our suspect list.

At Danny's request, we brought three chairs from the kitchen table into the bedroom where Brad died. The psychic sat and shut his eyes.

Barney gave an exaggerated eye-roll and mouthed, "I see dead people."

I grinned at him but I was trying to keep an open mind. I know there are those who can "see" more than the rest of us, but I didn't think Danny Finch was one of them. Also, I wasn't sure how I felt about communicating with the dead. I found the possibility both intriguing and ghoulish.

Danny's placid voice snapped me back. "There's a man standing behind the house. He's a long way behind it." He spoke as if in a trance, with his eyes closed. "He's blurry, but they're all like that at first."

I got another eye roll from my partner.

"No. Wait. He's doing something."

"Can you tell what?" I asked in an attempt to move this along.

"He's flying a drone, one of those small ones. I think he's spying on Brad."

My partner and I exchanged a look.

When Danny didn't say anything else, Barney asked, "What does he look like?"

"He's average in size and weight and has brown hair. I'd guess mid-forties. He's dressed in a dark pullover and sweatpants."

"Do you recognize him?"

"I don't think I know him. Just give me a minute. I'll try to contact Brad."

If Danny was faking, it was a pretty good act. His expression was intense and he was concentrating so hard beads of sweat popped out on his forehead. It was also possible he was guilty and trying to cast blame on someone else. The drone reference was interesting and pointed to a man we knew.

"I need your help Brad," Danny said after at least five minutes passed. He spoke in a soft voice, encouraging the dead man to cooperate. He used various entreaties that meant the same thing.

After another five minutes, Danny said, "Brad isn't here."

That would've been my guess from the start.

"Before you open your eyes," Barney said, "can you tell us more about the man with the drone?"

"I sense he's come to spy on Brad, but he doesn't live on the Ranch. He lives near the Ghost Town, I think."

I indicated to Barney that he should let it go. I knew who Danny had fingered. It was even possible he'd done it.

When Danny opened his eyes, he said to my partner, "If you could leave for a few minutes, Brad might come."

"How do you figure that?"

"You don't believe it's possible to contact the dead and you give off a strong vibe to that effect. Margarita might believe it or not, but I think at least she's open to the possibility. Also, her presence is gentler, less overpowering."

Barney stood. "Okay. I'll go." He made it to the door, but he came back and addressed Danny. "One wrong move and 'gentle' Margarita goes from zero to bust-your-balls in one second flat."

"So I've heard."

"Believe it."

Jeez.

* * *

"So we're clear," my partner said, "I didn't leave you alone with him. I was standing nearby."

"Thank you. I knew that."

"Didn't you get a creepy vibe from him?"

"Yes, but I get it from a few of Terlingua's men."

"I know. He has a hankering for a female deputy but at the same time, he's trying to contact the dead."

"That makes him creepier than most, but 'hankering'? Have you been watching old cowboy movies or what?"

"Hankering is a perfectly acceptable modern-day verb."

"I've never heard you use it before."

"Well, excuse me for having a varied vocabulary. Try to keep up, Ricos."

"Okay. I'll try."

"I assume you know the man with the drone since you were motioning me to knock off the questions."

"Yes. He's talking about Shaw McAfee."

"What's Shaw doing with a drone?"

"How would I know? He says it's for photography, but a few people have complained because they think he's spying."

"How come you've never told me this?"

"It's not important. I answered a complaint once when you were doing bailiff duty in Alpine and another time when you were taking a few days off."

"Do you think Shaw did it?"

"He's as likely as anyone else. Shaw is intolerant of people who are not like him. He's a 'Terlingua Defender' but he takes it a step farther. He stops short of full-on Aryan Brotherhood-type stuff, but not far."

"Meaning he would kill a gay man."

"Meaning it's not out of the realm of possibilities."

"We should talk to him."

"Let's go."

"Maybe Buster and I should go. Shaw has a thing for you."

"I can ignore that if you can. Also, you and Buster got in trouble the last time you went to see a man who has a 'thing' about me."

"Are you going to hold that against me the rest of your life?"

"I don't know."

"When will you know?"

"Someday; you'll get the memo."

"Great."

"What do you think is going on in this place?"

"Meaning?"

"We have no real evidence, and almost anyone could be guilty," I said.

"What if Brad made a sexual advance to Shaw McAfee?"

"What would make Brad do that since he wasn't ready for a relationship?"

"Maybe that was something he said to keep women away."

"But he had a gay man pursuing him and he told him the same thing. Why would he make a pass at a known bigot like Shaw McAfee? Why take that kind of risk? It doesn't make sense."

"True, but you and I know people don't always make sense."

* * *

Shaw McAfee is mid-to-late-forties in age. He's an average-looking guy with brown hair and brown eyes that always look away after a few seconds, as though he's guilty of something. He probably is but of what, I can't say. He's another male who believes he should have my job, but I doubt if that makes him feel guilty. He believes he's entitled to it, like Wynne. Also like Wynne, he's never studied law enforcement and has no training, but he's convinced he would make a better deputy. This is based on his Army experience and the fact that he's a man.

Shaw threw open his front door with a big smile that faded fast. "If it's about the drone, it wasn't me. Mine isn't working right now."

"Then you won't mind if I look at it," Barney said as he stepped in uninvited. He does what he wants because he's huge. I followed him because I could.

"You can't just barge into my house!" Shaw was right, and yet there we were.

"Sorry; I assumed you'd invite us to come in," Barney claimed.

Shaw looked to me, but I shrugged and tried to seem innocent.

He turned back to my partner. "What do you want?"

"Your drone," Barney said.

"You can't come in here demanding to see my things. It's illegal. You need to get a search warrant."

Barney glanced at me, so I stepped up. "Are you hiding something, Shaw?"

"What do you think I'm hiding?"

"Did you kill Bradley Jennings?"

He looked shocked. "What? What makes you ask me something like that?"

"It's a yes or no question. If you didn't kill him, then you shouldn't care if Barney looks at your drone."

"What does my drone have to do with Brad's murder?"

"Did you know Brad?" I persisted.

"He seemed nice enough, but I can't say I knew him. He was a teacher, right?"

"Yes."

"Why are you busting in here asking if I killed Brad?"

"A witness said you were flying your drone near Brad's house. He thought you were spying on him."

"What witness?" Shaw looked back and forth between us. "I've never been to Brad's house. I'm not even sure where it is."

"Do you know where Iva Cooper lives?"

"Yes."

"Have you ever flown your drone near there?" asked Barney.

"No. That old busybody would've reported me and complained about it."

"What is the purpose of your drone?" Barney continued.

"It's for fun. I do some aerial photography with it. I meet with other guys sometimes and we have dogfights. Aerial fights," he was quick to clarify.

"Do you ever use it for spying?" Barney asked.

"It depends on what you mean by spying. I've used it to see if a friend's car was in his drive, that sort of thing."

"I meant spying on women, looking in windows—"

"Of course not! Even if I wanted to do that, it's not like it can sneak up on people. You can hear the drone coming. What in the hell are you implying?"

"We're not implying anything," I said. "We're asking questions. Someone suggested that you'd been spying on Brad Jennings."

"I want to know who said that."

"It's confidential."

"But I deserve to defend myself."

"Yes," I agreed, "and that's why we're asking you about it instead of hauling you in to Alpine."

Shaw looked back and forth between us and then his eyes settled on Barney. "*If* I could spy on people I'd spy on women, not men. Why would I spy on a teacher?"

"Maybe you suspected him of something."

"Such as what?"

"Did you suspect him of something?"

"I never gave him any thought. I only ran across him at community functions a couple of times and at the café once or twice."

"Did you ever try to recruit him into your group?"

Barney was out of line and wasting time. Those guys don't admit they're a "group" around anyone who doesn't display beliefs that mesh with theirs. Being deputies keeps us out of that little club.

Shaw responded as if he hadn't understood. "Did Brad have a drone? I don't think he had one."

Barney's eyes narrowed. "That's not the group I mean."

"Well, if you mean the guys who hang out at the café, Brad showed no interest in us. But he was friendly. I think he was a little on the shy side."

"I'm referring to your other group—the one you don't talk about to us. Did you approach Brad about that?"

Shaw's expression turned murderous. "Hell, no. He was a teacher, man."

Barney let it go.

I took a different tack. "Shaw, do you know how Brad died?"

"He was beaten to death. That's what I heard, but I don't know if that's true. You know how the gossip is around here."

"Do you have any more questions, Barney?" I gave him a look meant to discourage him from saying another word.

He took the hint. "No."

"I know who told you it was me," Shaw said. "It was Danny Finch, wasn't it?"

"I can't say."

"No problem; I know it was him. He hates me."

"Why is that?"

"I laugh at his psychic 'gift.' I know I shouldn't but he's such a fake. Sometimes I fly my drone over there just to piss him off."

"Maybe you should stop doing that," I suggested. Wouldn't that be a given, like not shoving people against their trucks?

We almost made it out of there but at the last minute, Barney turned back to Shaw. "Do you ever spy on Margarita with your drone?"

He reddened. "No. I don't."

"Do you spy on her some other way?"

"I don't spy on her or anybody else."

Barney shrugged and got into the truck.

Shaw took me by the arm. "I thought it was my age keeping you from me, but I see that wasn't it at all."

"What do you mean?"

"The sheriff is older than I am and—"

"Listen to me. Nothing is going on between the sheriff and me. If you saw the photo, then look again. It was Photoshopped. If you know anything about that, I hope you would tell me."

"I don't know anything concrete. There's just a bunch of talk."

"Will you keep your ear to the ground for me?"

"Of course, but I'd like to do a lot more than that for you. What I want—"

"Thank you, Shaw. I've got to get going."

"Sure. We'll talk later."

I got in the truck. As we pulled away, Barney said, "What do you think?"

"Why were you antagonizing him? That didn't get us anywhere."

"It sure as hell did. I don't think he killed Brad Jennings, do you?"

"No."

"I thought if he got angry he might reveal something without meaning to. I don't think he knows anything."

"I agree. His reactions were those of an innocent man unless he's one heck of an actor."

"I'd like to kick Danny Finch's ass for wasting our time."

"I know, but that won't move this investigation along."

"What will? That's what we should be doing. What if Danny did it and he's just trying to pin it on Shaw?"

"My gut says no, that's not it. I think Danny was using us to get back at Shaw. That makes me angry too, but let's not waste any more time."

"How does your gut feel about lunch?"

Chapter 25

After lunch we went to the Post Office. An Express Mail packet from Dr. Ted Jennings was waiting for us. I tore into it, hoping it would have a clue we could follow to nab Brad's killer. A note from the doc was brief and to the point:

"Dear Deputies,

I went through Brad's storage unit and this is everything I could find in regards to John's name. When John died, Brad put his private things in storage with his own belongings. I hope what I'm sending will help.

Thank you for using your discretion in disclosing private information about my brother. I appreciate it more than you know.

My best to you,

Ted Jennings"

A photograph of Brad and John fell out into my lap. It was like the one Buster and I had found in the trash, but it had their names scrawled on the back, along with "fishing in the Gulf." The photo alone was significant, but there was more.

At the office, I cleared my desk and emptied the envelope onto it. There were a few photographs of the men at different ages, always together and holding hands or with their arms wrapped around each other. They had exchanged rings and those were there. At first I was surprised that Ted sent them, but then I saw why. They were inscribed with loving words, like most wedding rings. John had given Brad a ring with this inscription: "I love you more every day," and it was signed "John Bailey Cooper." Bingo!

The envelope also held love letters that brought tears to my eyes. John's driver's license was there and the birth certificates and college degrees of both men. The name John Bailey Cooper was used on everything official.

Iva Cooper was lying and now I could prove it.

I was ecstatic at the find but sad at the secret love story the mementos told. How awful to be so in love and have to hide it. How long are decent human beings going to allow backward thinkers to withhold inalienable rights from some of us because of who we love?

Barney came in and sat in my chair with a view. I wanted to cry and rant, not talk to him, but I told him what I'd learned.

"Now this is getting interesting," was his comment, "but I still don't think that old lady killed Brad."

"It doesn't matter what you think, does it?"

"No, but how would she get the upper hand with a man so much younger?"

"You're underestimating women, as usual. It would surprise you what a woman can do if she feels the need to, even an old woman. The point is that John Bailey Cooper is John Cooper is Bailey Cooper. Iva Cooper has been lying. Why lie?"

"Lying doesn't mean she murdered anybody."

"Maybe she didn't kill Brad but she knows something, and she doesn't want us to know it."

"It could be that she's ashamed her beloved brother was gay."

"That's what I think, but there's more."

"How are we going to get the truth out of her?"

"I don't know. Leave me alone so I can think about it."

Barney gave me a look and returned to his desk. I moved to the comfortable chair, looking for solace and something, anything, that made sense. Cactus Hill always delivers. Its usual magnificence was enhanced by stunning wildflowers and new green growth. Everything was washed clean by the recent rain and snow. The afternoon sun made the colors soft, like a painting. Or it could have been a scene out of a romantic poet's imagination.

My friends Vic and Morgan refused to play the secret love game, but at great personal cost to them and their families. Vic had had people in her face ever since it became obvious she was different from other little girls. She'd been shoved around as a child and also as an adult. People had threatened her. They made nasty comments behind her back and to her face. She couldn't work for the school because a bigot ran it. Now we had a new bigot, but Vic still couldn't do the thing she would've loved most which is to work with kids. She loves them and they know it and they love her in return.

What I needed was to drink until I could no longer feel my face or else go kill somebody. *Chisos, Margarita.* My mantra hadn't crossed my mind since the day I picked squirmy things off a dead body in the middle of nowhere. It seemed to have lost its magic.

My mantra might have quit working but the sheriff hadn't. He called, and his calm voice talked me down from the figurative ledge.

"Lennon Camacho asked his boss to call me," he said, "so I could let you know that the tattoo on the Presidio County murder victim was not a blue bee. It was a tiny blue flower. Does that mean anything to you?"

"No, Sheriff."

"He hoped you might know something."

"I happen to know about one tattoo. That doesn't make me an expert on tats. Maybe he should talk to tattoo artists."

"Do you know the artists in the area?"

"No, and there's not much chance the tat was done in the U.S. If his victim was trafficked, as Len thinks, then it was probably done in her country of origin. If she came from Ojinaga, there are several artists there."

"I'll pass the word along." Ten second pause. "Margarita, do you think the injured man came here with the woman you brought from the cave?"

"That's possible. Does Lennon Camacho's boss still think the McFarley Ranch is involved?"

"I don't know. They don't tell me much. They're investigating and I guess we'll know more when they deign to inform us."

"Do you know if they had any luck at The Blue Bee?"

"No. I haven't heard anything about that, either. But I do have some reports from the crime lab."

"Let me get the others and put you on the speakerphone."

"Don't bother. Bradley Jennings' killer didn't leave us much. However, she did make one mistake."

She?

"The blood on the bathroom mirror was the victim's, as we thought, but it also contained DNA that didn't match his. It was from skin cells."

"Someone touched it with their finger?"

"A woman kissed the mirror with her lips. The lipstick was obscured by the dripping blood, but it was there. They've not come up with a match, though."

It was the usual great news/bad news.

I went back to perusing my hill and checking my gun.

* * *

I left work early and went for the long run I desperately needed. My weapon stayed home in a drawer. The people of my community would have more respect for running if they understood its power. So far, it had kept me from killing any of them.

I consider the steep, uneven road to the top of my bluff a challenge. My legs and lungs are strong, but the climb reminds me I'm not as tough as I like to think. Still, I got to the top without stopping. *Take* that *you stupid road.* I collapsed onto the ground, huffing and puffing. Standing across the miles, Cimarron glimmered in all its glory. Whenever I see it, I feel like waving.

Once I'd recovered my breath, I headed across the mesa to check on Craig. He has a porch that wraps around his unfinished house. Any spot you choose, the view will bliss you out. Sit and be amazed.

Craig and Marine were hanging out on the national park side. Sunset hadn't begun to paint the Chisos Mountains, but they were earthshaking anyway. Like the rest of the landscape, they'd been washed, and they gleamed like they meant it in the soft afternoon sunlight.

I greeted my friend with a hug and gave his kitty a head scratch. Craig was friendly, but he gave me a questioning look. I'm sure he wondered what I was doing.

I took a seat in the other chair. "Are you going dressed like that?"

Craig shrugged. "Where do you think I'm going?"

"Tonight's the night."

He turned to gape at me. "What is wrong with you?"

"Aren't we going to look for a wife?"

He laughed but quickly returned to his stone-faced expression. "If I wanted a wife, I'd have a wife. Why have you come to aggravate me when Marine and I are sitting here in peace not bothering anybody?"

"I couldn't resist messing with you."

"Women," he grumped.

"Didn't your momma ever tell you that girls tease you 'cause they like you?"

He answered me with a harrumph, but he was making an effort not to laugh.

"In truth, I came up here to think," I said.

"Then stop running your mouth."

He had a point. I hugged him and went back to the Cimarron side of my bluff. I lay stomach-down at the edge and studied my mountain. Cimarron is the answer to a riddle: What appears to be constantly different yet remains unchanged?

Here is another riddle, but more difficult: Who murdered a peaceful, well-liked man and left behind no useful clue? The answer would be a person with nerves of steel who knew the house, knew Brad's comings and goings, and knew they'd have time to clean up. The killer would be someone eaten up with outrage. Brad's murder had been planned, I thought, and possibly for a long time. His killer was someone who hated Brad Jennings for a reason almost no one in Terlingua would know.

Buddy Holly interrupted my musing with the same ol', same ol' about fighting the law. The way he told it, the law had won. That wasn't adding up in our current situation, and it was starting to get old.

"What's up, Barney?"

"Ricos, where in the hell are you?"

"What do you need?"

"The sheriff called. He wants us in Alpine."

"Why don't you go and take Buster along?"

"He wants all of us. Someone confessed to the murder of Bradley Jennings."

Chapter 26

Our sheriff looked clean and crisp and sharp standing at his desk, but the strain on his face made him seem old. "Mitty McCann says he killed Jennings," he said when we walked in.

No way.

"Did he say why?" Barney asked in an incredulous tone.

"He says he and Brad were drinking beer and they got into it over a woman. He followed Jennings home and killed him in an argument."

"That makes no sense," I blurted. "Why would Brad fight with anyone over a woman?"

Barney stated the obvious. "Mitty doesn't know Brad was gay."

"According to everything we've learned," Buster added, "Brad was not much of a drinker."

I nodded in agreement. "Plus, there's drinking and there's the McCann brothers level of drinking. For Brad to get drunk with weird and sneaky Mitty McCann…no, that didn't happen."

"That's what I think," agreed the sheriff.

"Also," I added, "there's a timeline problem. Brad went to a bar in Odessa that night so he couldn't have been drinking with Mitty."

"That's true," the sheriff said, "and he knows only that Brad was bludgeoned, which everybody knows. I asked Mitty to tell me everything and he has no idea about the rest of the details and can't even describe the weapon. His answer to that was, 'I grabbed the closest heavy thing.' I don't buy it."

"What do you think is going on?" Barney asked.

"Before I say anything more," the sheriff said, "I want the three of you to take a look at him. I put him in the interrogation room a few minutes ago because his attorney is coming."

It was hard to imagine the McCann brothers hiring an attorney, but maybe they were going to need one. Something was off with that bunch. More off than usual.

We observed Mitty through the one-way glass. He is the least social of the brothers, another thing that made it hard to believe he'd been drinking with Jennings. Mitty is a silent lurker, not a party-in-public guy. In the case of trouble, he might make a silent and even deadly attack, but that would most likely be in defense of one or all of his brothers.

Setting his odd appearance aside (eyes too close together, head like a fuzzy peach, long hairs thick as a forest sticking out of his ears), Mitty had been battered. One of his strangely-placed eyes was swollen shut and his face was splotchy with bruising. There was a cut on his lip and dried blood on his shirt. It brought to mind the beating Wynne had taken from the McCann brothers.

Barney voiced what we all saw. "Somebody's been whaling on him."

Sheriff Ben nodded.

"Did he say who?"

"No. He wouldn't say." The sheriff turned to me. "Margarita, I want you and Buster to go in and question him about his beating or the confession. It doesn't matter which. Barney and I will stay here to observe."

I had questions, but I kept them to myself. The expression on the sheriff's face made me think he was maintaining control of his temper by sheer will.

Mitty looked up in surprise when Buster and I entered the room.

"Howdy, Mitty," I said, "have you met Deputy Mayhew?"

After I introduced the two I asked, "What happened to you?"

"I got beat up."

"I need names, places, anything you can tell me. Who did this to you?"

He shrugged.

I tried another tack. "Sheriff Duncan told us you confessed to the cold-blooded murder of Brad Jennings. I can't believe that, Mitty."

"I never said it was cold-blooded."

"Did you kill Mr. Jennings or not?"

"I'm waitin' for my attorney 'fore I say more."

"Mitty, I don't think you even knew the man, yet you signed a confession to his murder. That makes me wonder."

"Shut up. I did too know him."

"Tell me something about him—anything—that not everybody in Terlingua would know."

"I'm not talking to you, Margarita."

"Will you talk to me?" Buster asked.

"Not if you're one of *them*. You can go to hell!" He waved his hand in a way that encompassed everybody everywhere.

"One of what, Mitty?" I challenged. "Law enforcement? The human race? What are you saying? I've never treated you poorly, nor has Buster."

"I ain't talkin' to no more law."

"Why?"

He was puffed up with anger. "You don't think I could kill somebody?"

"I know you could, but I don't believe you killed Brad Jennings. You claim you got into it over a woman. I'd like to know what woman."

"It wasn't you and it therefore don't concern you."

"Yes it does. I'm supposed to figure out who killed Mr. Jennings and you haven't given me any reason to think it was you."

"You can stop your figurin' it 'cause I signed that I done it."

"Why would you admit to something you didn't do? Are you covering for one of your brothers or is it somebody else?"

At that point his attorney arrived. The brothers had chosen William Young, a fairly good guy as far as I could tell by his actions in court and his reputation. He was young and as he liked to say, "They don't call me Young for nothin."

Will spoke with his client and then left him in the room so he could have a word with us. "He claims you," and he indicated all of us, "beat a confession out of him. He wants to retract his statement."

"What?" Barney jumped out of his chair with the surprise of it.

The sheriff glanced at me and in that instant I thought I knew what this was about.

Then our boss said, more calmly than I could have, "My deputies left Terlingua less than two hours ago. They have a dated gas receipt that puts them at a store there when McCann was in here confessing. If someone beat a confession out of him, that would have been me. I don't see how he can make that fly since my secretary saw him come in and he was already a mess."

Will started to walk back to his client, but the sheriff wasn't through. He held out his hands to the attorney. "Look at these, Will. Look at my clothes. Nothing about me backs up Mitty's story. You'd better go back in there and tell your client that wrongly accusing me or my deputies will bring hell down on his head."

Poor Will went back to try to reason with his client.

We went into the sheriff's office and sat when he commanded it. "What in the world?" He asked in a sigh.

Since his gaze turned to me, I told him what I thought. "I think the same man who paid for the photo of you and me together is behind this. It's another ploy to make the Sheriff's Office look bad, to make you look bad as a sheriff. The Photoshopped picture didn't fly the way they'd hoped, so they're trying something new."

It seemed obvious to me, but everyone's mouth was open.

"We all know," I continued, "that we don't beat confessions out of suspects, but this is something people can sink their teeth into. That photo was a mild distraction compared to what this will be. They want to believe the worst, and the truth? Who cares about that? Of course you can prove in court that you didn't beat anybody, but that'll take too long. Sheriff, we need to go after this guy."

"But we don't even know who he is!"

"That doesn't matter because William Jackson is behind him."

"We have no proof of that."

"I can get proof of it."

"How?"

"I don't know. I need to work it out."

"Margarita, never start an investigation assuming you already know the guilty party. You know that. If this is something else, the whole thing could blow up in our faces."

"Yes. I know that. But do you think there's another explanation?"

"No."

"Well then?"

He gave me a look that made me change my wording. "Okay, let me say it this way. We'll find out who is out to destroy your reputation. We have no assumptions. It could be anyone. How's that?"

"That's better."

"Who is this 'we'?" Barney wanted to know.

* * *

Mitty McCann retracted his confession but not his accusation of abuse. We were back to where we started with the Jennings murder but in every other way, things were worse. Mitty was hanging the Sheriff's Office out to dry at the worst possible time. Since Mitty wouldn't know that, it screamed of Derrick Chaney's involvement.

It didn't matter to Mitty that the three deputies he was accusing had an airtight, time-stamped alibi. It didn't matter that the sheriff's secretary had witnessed his condition when he entered the building.

"I advised him against proceeding," Will Young said before he left.

You can't reason with a man being paid to lie. That was my take on it and the only thing that made sense.

"Then I have to release Mitty," the sheriff said.

Will didn't wait around for that to happen. He bowed out fast saying he would file the necessary motions in the morning.

The sheriff said, "I want each of you to write your statement about this, please. Be detailed. Do you know how to write a statement, Buster?"

"Yes sir." He glanced at me because we'd gone over it a few times.

I gave him a smile of encouragement.

After the sheriff read our statements, we took photos of his hands, clothes, and face and then ours. He said he'd get a statement from his secretary in the morning.

"This will come before Judge Samuels before it goes anywhere," Sheriff Ben said. "I'll stall it as long as I can."

Being a lecherous old man was just the start of what was wrong about Judge Samuels, and it wasn't the worse thing. He didn't care for our sheriff, his deputies, or anyone in law enforcement unless there was something they could do for him. He would have the power to nip it in the bud, but nobody held out any hope for that.

As we were leaving, Sheriff Ben turned to me. "You know that I think solving the Jennings murder is the most important thing."

"Yes sir."

"Take tomorrow and see what you can find out about William Jackson and Derrick Chaney. If we can connect them to this, it's over for Jackson."

"Are you saying I only have one day?" I was incredulous.

"Do you have a problem with that, Deputy Ricos?"

Well, heck yes. How would I do anything in one day? "No sir."

"I think you should use an unmarked car. Do you want to take one from here?"

"I'll use my Mustang."

"I've been meaning to talk to you about that. I want you to slow down."

I smiled.

"I'm not kidding. You'll end up with a ticket or in a wreck. You can't uphold the law in this county and then break it every chance you get."

Yada, yada, yada. He didn't seem to expect me to address his concerns and moved on to his other hapless victims. "Barney, you and Buster need to interview all the females who visited Brad Jennings in his home and ask them to volunteer a mouth swab for DNA purposes. Explain that we're trying to eliminate them from our suspect list."

They nodded at him in understanding, but I cringed to think of that hell. I tried to keep my face a blank.

Sheriff Ben touched my shoulder on the way out. "You have

one day, Margarita. Make it count. The next day you're back on the Jennings case."

Why didn't he just shoot me?

* * *

My one day started when we returned to Terlingua. The guys went home but I went into my office and turned on the laptop. Then I turned off the light and sat in my comfortable chair while the computer warmed to the idea of working late.

The sliver of moon, along with the stars, cast a silvery light on the scene I adored. I let my attention stay there a while and tried to think about nothing.

If I get to have another life, and I seriously doubt it, I hope I come back as a yucca on my hill. It would be great not to have to explain myself every time I turn around. Yuccas don't have to turn around. Nor do they take orders...or tolerate any bullshit. As a yucca, my view would be superb all day and night. My comrades would be giant hulking boulders, rocks and pebbles of every size, small trees, shrubs, tall grasses, and wildflowers almost always.

If I were a yucca on my hill, some future deputy would watch me as she tried to make sense of her life. I hope she has better luck. Maybe she'll be the one in charge, kicking ass and taking names. I hope she's the sheriff.

Yuccas don't get lectures about speeding. Never getting to speed made the prospect of yuccahood less appealing.

Sheriff Margarita Ricos. Hm.

I fell asleep with my butt in the chair, my boots on the desk, and facing the window. The computer was warm and ready to roll but had nowhere to go.

Chapter 27

When I jolted awake, I had the sinking feeling I'd lost my One Day and a vague terror I was the sheriff. I took a deep breath and looked around. I was not the sheriff. It was 4:00 AM on Tuesday, plenty of time left to do the impossible.

No way would I ever be elected sheriff in Brewster County. I was barely tolerated as it was.

I made coffee, washed my face, and reminded the computer there was work to do. It came back from snoozing the same way I do. What? Where am I?

I put enough cream and sugar in my coffee to make it a bad choice in every way. A big slug of Irish whiskey would've rounded it out but alas, I had to limp on without a crutch.

Here's the thing about searching for people. Everyone has a trail, good and bad alike. I didn't find William Jackson or Derrick Chaney in the Texas prison system, but I also didn't find a normal trail for either of them.

I found a few men with the name "Derrick Chaney" but the predominating one had been accused of rape in another state. He was in prison, and he was black. I found no trace of the white man who had been described to me. So Derrick Chaney was not his real name. No surprise there.

William Jackson worked a few years as a policeman in a tiny Texas town, then as a prison guard. For the last three years, his trail had almost disappeared. So he was not who he claimed to be either. *I told you so, Sheriff Ben.*

Most articles about Jackson included Amanda Mullen, our county judge. There was the place to start.

* * *

I showered, packed a few things—it was hard to say what I'd

need—and hit the road about the same time as dawn began its glow in the east.

I ignored my boss's direct order about speeding and arrived at the Sheriff's Office before the sheriff's secretary. He was there, of course. It was bound to be a big day for him.

"Good morning, Sheriff," I chirped as if I'd slept all night.

He looked up and his expression was priceless.

"Close your mouth, Sheriff Ben."

"I was just...I...I've never seen you in a dress, Deputy Ricos."

Jeez. "I can't sneak around dressed as a deputy, can I?"

"I guess not."

My dress was short, purple with tiny black stripes, and shirt-waist in style. It was killer. The skinny brown leather belt matched my kick-ass shoes. I didn't think the sheriff understood how cutting-edge fashionable I was.

"I just want to run something past you, Sheriff."

"Have a seat. Would you like coffee?"

"Thank you, but I've had enough coffee for this week."

"Tell me what you have in mind."

"I'm going to schmooze with Judge Mullen." At the look on his face I added, "I'll never mention that I know about you-know-what. You can trust me, Sheriff."

"I know that. I guess it was just a shock when you mentioned her. I think I have a touch of PTSD from that incident."

I laughed at that.

"Do you get a lot of propositions from men?" Talk about out of the blue.

"Sheriff, what does that have to do with anything?"

"I just think it'd be hard to be a young woman in law enforce-ment."

"It is, but I don't understand how this relates to Judge Mullen."

"It doesn't. My mind is wandering all over this morning. When you walked in wearing that dress, I just thought…I thought…"

"What, Sheriff Ben?"

"I thought *Deputy Ricos is a woman.*"

I laughed. "I always thought you knew that."

"I'm sorry; I'm not even making sense to myself. I guess what I mean to say is that I never think of you as a girly 'dresses' type. I hope this doesn't make you angry."

"Sheriff Ben, there're a lot of things about me you don't know. You don't need to know. There's a part of me that's pure girly-girl. I love sexy shoes as much as I love guns, probably more. I like being a deputy, but I also like many other things. I think we're all more than what we do in our jobs. You're the sheriff of Brewster County, but I know you're a lot more than that."

"Yes, Margarita, that's true. Thank you."

"Now that my part-time girliness is established, can I run my plan past you?"

"Yes, please do."

"I'm going to ask Judge Mullen how I can find William Jackson. My reason will be that I want to talk to him about the sheriff's race and see how I can help. If she calls you to say I'm working against you, you'll know what I'm doing. I just want to talk to the man. After I get a feel for him, I may ask about Chaney. I have to play that part by ear."

"That sounds good."

"I might need more than one day."

"That's true, but you have one."

"Why, Sheriff Ben? This is important."

"I already told you this once. Listen carefully, and please take this to heart. Getting justice for Brad Jennings is more important in the scheme of things than being re-elected sheriff. I'm old enough to retire. I just don't want to."

"Your deputies don't want you to. The people of Brewster County might not know it yet, but they don't want you to, either. So in the scheme things, keeping you the sheriff heads my list. Let me ask you this. Would 'Billy Jack' give a rip about the brutal slaying of a quiet gay man from South Brewster County?"

"I don't know."

"I think not. Also, none of the deputies you have now will be able to stay. He'll want his own crew. What will I do then, Sheriff?"

"You have a bright future anywhere you go, but I understand your point." He thought about it, sizing up the situation. "I might be able to give you two days."

Ah-hah.

"Call me if you need me," he added.

"I will. There's one more thing. I don't think I should use my Mustang after all. I need something less attention-grabbing."

"I agree." He walked to the front and took keys from a locked board. "Try this little white thing out there. It's not very fast."

"That's okay. Some people think I shouldn't speed."

"Yes. All the Highway Patrolmen in the state would agree. I don't want you to hurt yourself or others. Do you need anything else from me?"

"I don't think so."

"Carry on."

I was at the door of his office when he called, "Margarita?"

"Yes sir?"

"Can you run in those shoes?"

"I hope I won't need to. I'll take them off if it comes down to it."

He smiled and waved me on.

I was heading out of the building as two of my fellow deputies were coming in. They gave me the same open-mouthed look I'd just seen on the sheriff.

"What's wrong? Haven't you ever seen a woman in a dress before?"

"Is that *you,* Margarita?" Lonnie Richardson wanted to know. He turned to his companion. "She's a *girl!*"

Jokers, everywhere I turn. I hate men.

* * *

Amanda Mullen, though not a man, is another joker. She stumbled all over herself and eventually said, "I didn't recognize you out of uniform."

I didn't know what to say. *You're as big an idiot as Lonnie Richardson* didn't seem right. I needed her cooperation.

"Ms. Mullen, can you tell me how to reach William Jackson? Does he have an office?"

"Yes, he does." She gave me the address but added, "I happen to know he's not there right now. May I ask why you need to see him?"

"I want to ask him some questions about his campaign."

"I see." She looked at her watch. "He's drinking coffee at the Bread and Breakfast. He'll be talking to people about his bid for sheriff, so I'm sure your questions will be welcome."

I stood. "That's perfect then."

"I thought you were a staunch supporter of Sheriff Duncan. Did being romantically involved with him change your mind?"

"I'm not involved with him except as his deputy. I think you know that."

"The scuttlebutt is that you are."

I wanted to say something dripping with sarcasm about her failed attempt to seduce Sheriff Ben, but I held my tongue. "You're correct that I'm his supporter."

"All right. Well, so am I. But I think Jackson will be the better sheriff."

She was lying. She was backing Jackson for some other reason. I was fairly sure it was the usual: money. But what were they planning?

* * *

I didn't know if Jackson knew who I was or not, but I had to assume he did. I thought he was the man who had overseen the removal of my shirt in the infamous photo that hadn't done the damage he'd hoped.

I approached him the way you would any poisonous reptile in a black hat with a beadwork band. I needed my Beretta but it didn't go with my dress. Jeez. I'd have to rethink the whole girly thing, but not right now.

He stood when I strutted right up to his table and said, "Hello, Mr. Jackson."

"Well, hello." He held out his hand. "I'm William Jackson, but my friends call me Billy Jack."

I smiled at him. "I'm Margarita Ricos." *My friends call me Batgirl.*

My name surprised him. So he hadn't recognized me. He looked around the table at the men sitting there and said, "You'll excuse me for a few minutes? I need to speak with this young lady."

They indicated in various ways that they would soldier on in his absence. Their talk resumed as we walked away. I wondered if I had done them a favor.

Billy Jack moved me to a table as far to the back as he could get. Any farther and we'd have been in the kitchen. The sweet, cinnamon-y scent of baking goodies assaulted my nose, but it was my empty stomach than whined about it.

"Would you like coffee?" Jackson asked.

"I'd rather have orange juice, please."

"What about something to eat? I was about to order breakfast."

Jackson and the waitress looked surprised when I ordered a large bowl of oatmeal with a double order of toast. What? The toast is fantastic in that place. Maybe it seemed like a lot of food, but my body was incinerating calories at the rate of an iron smelter. It does that when I'm so nervous I can barely function.

I looked back and forth between them. "Am I missing something?"

"No," responded the waitress. "I thought I'd misunderstood at first."

When she'd gone, Jackson whispered, "I think she was wondering where you're going to put all that food."

"I'm a runner." That didn't have much to do with it but it was all I could offer him. Of course, he already knew the running part.

"Are you married, Mr. Jackson?"

"No. Why do you ask?"

"No reason. I only wondered."

"Are you making yourself available?" He asked it laughingly, so I only said, "No" instead of "oh, hell no."

He smiled and got down to business. "How can I help you, Ms. Ricos?"

"I'd like to know why you think you'll be a better sheriff than Ben Duncan. Please don't give me that crap about the lawlessness in Terlingua and the sheriff squandering his budget because I know firsthand what a crock that is."

That took him aback but he recovered quickly. "I think your loyalty to your sheriff is commendable, and I hope you'll give me the same loyalty if I'm elected."

"Do you plan to keep the current deputies?"

"Yes, of course. As long as I have their full support and cooperation, I think Sheriff Duncan has put together a fine staff." He went on to explain why he was the better of the two men. It was standard political posturing and even if he'd had my vote, he would've now lost it.

Our food came, which rescued me in more ways than one.

He perused the dishes set in front of me. "I think you have a hollow leg."

I laughed. "Maybe that explains it."

We ate and our talk was pleasant in the way of strangers who are trying to get along. The train clattered into the station across the street. The whistle bleats until you want to scream *okay, we get it. The train is here!* I love it though.

Jackson complained about the noise while I said nothing. To tell him how much I like trains would be like letting him in on something personal. Not happenin'.

For a little while things went back to a normal noise level and then the whistle blared. Again, we got the message before the engineer stopped sending it.

"I guess he wants to be sure the people in El Paso know he's leaving Alpine," I commented as the train rattled and banged out of town, headed west.

That caused Billy Jack to laugh, but it was short-lived because the next words out of my mouth were, "Do you know a man named Derrick Chaney?"

He nearly choked on his bacon. "No. Is he someone I should know?"

"He paid a Terlingua man to take a photo of me with Sheriff Duncan. It was an innocent meeting, but Derrick Chaney Photoshopped the t-shirt off my back. It makes our meeting look like something it wasn't. Haven't you seen it?"

He started to lie but decided against it. His head shook "no" but he said, "Yes. I've seen it. I wondered what that was about."

"Please don't insult my intelligence."

"What do you mean?"

"I asked myself who would want to destroy the sheriff's reputation and the only answer I get is William Jackson. I think you paid Derrick Chaney to arrange with a Terlingua nitwit to take that photo."

He set down his fork. "Wow. That is some story."

I rested my case. People, especially guilty people, can't stand silence.

When I didn't respond, he asked, "Why would I do something like that?"

"You want to win. People aren't buying your rant about the sheriff being old and outdated, so you thought you'd try to level the playing field. What you don't understand is that his relationship with his wife is legendary. They adore each other. Even if I wanted to break them up, how would I?"

"You're an attractive young woman. He's a man."

"Wow. You are really missing the point. And you don't know the sheriff. Or me."

"Look. I'm being wrongly accused. I don't know Derrick Chaney. Isn't that the bottom line here?"

"Yes. If you say you don't know him, then I can't make you say you do."

"Well, then."

"A man who would make a good sheriff should own up to what he's done."

He reddened in anger. "You're talking to the wrong man, honey."

I can't stand a person who can say "honey" and make me feel like I need a shower. I ran over the Mitty McCann problem in my head and decided *what the hell?* I'd already made another enemy in Brewster County so what did I have to lose? And I only had two days to figure this out.

"Mr. Jackson, the photo is not the most serious thing."

"Oh?"

"No. Since you're feigning ignorance, I'll explain. We had a brutal murder in South Brewster County, as you know. We've been working hard to solve it. Yesterday a man confessed."

"That's wonderful."

"It's not. You see, he didn't do it."

"What makes you think that?"

"He can't give the details that weren't made public. I'm sure you know it's protocol in a murder case to hold back some of the details."

Jackson nodded as if he were an old pro at solving murders. I'd believe he committed one before I ever believed he'd solved one.

"He says he was out drinking with the victim and they got into it over a woman. That doesn't fit. The victim wasn't a drinker, I doubt if he knew Mitty McCann, and he wasn't in Brewster County until late on the night of his murder."

"You seem to know a lot about your victim."

"I've been working this case since we discovered his body. Understanding the victim is one way to get to the killer. So there's no doubt that the man who confessed is innocent."

"That doesn't make any sense."

"Some people can't resist money, and they'll do things they shouldn't to get it."

"Which means?"

"Someone paid Mitty McCann to confess. But that's not the worse part."

"Oh?"

"He now claims a confession was beaten out of him and he retracted his statement. Unlike the photo that didn't cut it, this will hurt Sheriff Duncan. It hurts all of us in law enforcement because there are a few officers who mistreat suspects. We don't. Our sheriff would never stand still for that in a million years. If the three accused deputies were bullies, we wouldn't be working for him."

Jackson was doing an innocent act, but color was creeping up his neck to his face. I'd be lucky if he didn't go for my throat. And there I sat without Bad Beretta... And in a fashionable dress.

"What does this big, fancy story have to do with me?"

"You're the man who wants to be sheriff. You're the man with the money. You're the man paying Derrick Chaney to do your dirty work."

"You'd better shut your mouth, little lady. You have no idea what you're saying. I'll slap a lawsuit on you so fast you won't know what hit you."

There. He might as well have worn a sign around his neck, "It was me."

"I don't know anyone named Derrick Chaney," he hissed at me. "You're out of your damn mind."

"Maybe so." I stood. "Thank you for breakfast. If you run across a man named Derrick Chaney, will you let me know?"

"Of course I will." He was all smiles again and offered his hand.

I had to take it. "Adiós, Mr. Jackson." I thought if I counted one, two, three, he'd be on his phone, but I didn't look back.

I stood on the street a minute and then walked east on Holland Avenue, opposite the direction of my boring little white car. I rounded the block, walked west a block on Holland, and got into the car. No way would he see me unless he was standing on the street and he wasn't.

I wondered how long it would be before he went to Chaney or Chaney came to him. I opened the glove compartment and pulled out a holster that held Bad Beretta. I ran my hands over my trusty pal while my heart rate slowed to something near normal. Then I laid it in my lap. I watched people coming and going, moving about their day with no inkling of what was at stake.

I was hungry again. Waiting is hard.

Chapter 28

An hour passed, but it seemed longer. Billy Jack came onto the sidewalk. He stretched, settled his expensive hat on his bald head, and looked up at the sky. It was blue and cloudless except for a puffy wisp hanging above "A" Mountain. Did he have the slightest clue how extraordinarily beautiful the largest county in Texas is? When he opened his eyes, what did he see?

Jackson headed towards the street, but a man stopped him. They shook hands and slapped each other on the back. How did a man with a six-month history know so many people in Alpine? Amanda Mullen was the answer.

At last our would-be hero, Billy Jack the Second, left the sidewalk and got in his truck. I started the car.

Thanks to Netflix, I watched the movie "Billy Jack" after the sheriff told me about it. It was corny in the way of old, vigilante, one-hero-makes-a-big-difference movies. That aside, Billy Jack the movie character was a Vietnam veteran and "half-breed" Navajo. He dressed in a black t-shirt, blue jeans, a denim jacket, and a black hat with a beadwork band. He took a stand against the unjust treatment of his people. He kicked ass. What was there not to love about him? Among other things, he fearlessly faced a corrupt county official. No way to miss that irony.

I followed Jackson to the outskirts of town, to a picnic area/rest stop on Highway 118. It was a lovely location, heavily treed and full of big boulders. It was meant to be a place to take a break, not a hot spot for the nefarious.

It wasn't as though I could pull in there unnoticed, so I stopped beside the highway. Trees were in my way. I live in a land of few trees and uninterrupted vistas. When I need a clear line of sight, I get trees. Irony was the theme of the day.

I assumed Jackson was meeting with Chaney, but assumptions don't work in law enforcement. I took out my bag and changed from sexy shoes to running shoes. I stuck my hair under a dark ball cap. I had no choice but to change out of my dress. *I bet some women get to wear nice clothes all day,* I whined to myself. My deputy side thought I should shut up and dress right the first time.

On the off chance I'd be spotted, I couldn't look like the woman Jackson had just seen. I had blue jeans with me, but I had to get out of the car to put them on. There was no traffic noise coming from either direction so I made a quick change. On the upside, I was getting good at that. But I doubted I'd win an award.

I grabbed binoculars and headed across the road. I scrambled up on a boulder that was warm from the sun, welcoming in its quiet way. I thought again of being a yucca. I was surrounded by them. I closed my eyes a second but when I opened them, I was still a woman.

Jackson and another man were standing by Jackson's truck. The unknown subject was bulky, not as tall as his buddy, with longish brown hair. Guessing, he was mid-forties in age. I couldn't tell about the tats because he was wearing a jacket. If he wasn't Derrick Chaney, that would be too much coincidence.

I looked away for a minute, to the top of a rise that was covered with junipers, native grasses, and a few boulders. My thoughts went up there and when they came back, Chaney, I presumed, was getting into his truck. It was a beat-up-looking Ford that was green and an old model. I ran back to the little nondescript car. My heart was pounding with exertion and excitement.

Jackson pulled out, headed in the direction of Alpine. I ducked my capped head and studied my phone with intensity. He flew past and kept going. Then the unknown subject, assumed to be Chaney, entered the highway going the other way. What to do?

When the green truck was nothing but taillights in the distance, I followed. We were headed towards Terlingua.

* * *

It's beyond me how anyone can be among the south county mountains, or even within viewing distance of them, and maintain evil in their hearts. Maybe their general darkness clouds their eyesight. These were a few of a thousand thoughts I had as I tailed a cool truck with a villain driving. At least the air was clear and brisk and the views were spectacular and then some.

Was Chaney going to my home base to eliminate Tommy Mac McCann for talking to the law? Or was it Mitty he was after? Was he coming after me?

It was none of the above, or at least not yet. He stopped at a locked gate, put in a combination, and then headed into the McFarley Ranch. Holy crap!

I tried to think of a plausible reason to follow Chaney, but the gate had closed. Even if it had been standing open, I couldn't go in. He might recognize me in spite of the fact that I was wearing a shirt. Since I couldn't follow, I headed back to Alpine.

* * *

"Margarita!" the sheriff jumped up, sending his chair crashing into the wall.

"Sheriff!"

He laughed and sat again. "I was worried because I let you get away from here without putting a radio or sat phone in your car."

"I have my cell phone."

"Then why haven't you called me?"

"How could I call? I was chatting up Amanda Mullen and then I had breakfast with Jackson."

"Then?"

"I followed Billy Jack."

"Please give me every detail."

I did, and at the end of the recounting I added, "It can't be a coincidence that Chaney has the combination to the gate at the McFarley Ranch."

"You don't know if that was Chaney, Margarita."

"Who else would it be? This is connected, Sheriff. The man we had in the hospital, the dead woman in the cave, and Jackson's run for sheriff. Jackson wants to be the sheriff because he and Chaney and Amanda Mullen and the McFarley Ranch are up to something illegal; it's something that is getting people killed."

"Slow down, Margarita; I'm trying to process this."

I could barely sit still.

"You were down in the land of no cell service, so you would've needed an alternate way to call for help."

"That's all you've got to say? That I might have needed your help? Sheriff, did you hear what I said about Jackson and Chaney?"

"I heard you. I was just making my point about the radio."

I groaned. Sheriff Ben was like my papi. I can tell Papi a breathless, edge-of-the seat story for fifteen minutes and he'll say, "Were you wearing your coat?"

"I need to think about this," the sheriff said.

Why was he being so slow? Did he not understand the urgency here?

Sheriff Ben picked up his hat. "Let's get some lunch and think about this."

Lunch? Who could think about eating while they were still doing who-knew-what at the McFarley Ranch?

On the other hand, I was hungry.

Chapter 29

The sheriff invited Marianne to join us, but she'd already made plans for lunch.

I thought it best if we didn't go anywhere together, but he was impatient with me. "For the love of Pete, Margarita, we work together and we have to eat. Marianne knows what we're doing."

Someday I would ask him about this "Pete," but perhaps not today.

"I'm not worried about Marianne," I said. "I'm worried about everybody else."

"I only care about my wife."

Person after person came up to our table, so I couldn't have asked about Pete even if I wanted to.

"There's nothing going on here, people," I said under my breath when there was a short lull.

"It's not that, Margarita. I'm the sheriff of this county and everybody knows me or thinks they do. This is part of my job."

I was eating lunch with a celebrity. It was like standing next to Cimarron Mountain and trying to feel important.

* * *

As we were getting into the sheriff's truck, he said, "I need to talk to you about the rest of the crime lab results on the Jennings murder." That was a surprise. He waited until I had shut the door before he continued. "They faxed me another report this morning."

"Does it help us?"

"Yes. What I'm going to tell you is sensitive information."

I had a sinking feeling. "I understand."

"There was semen found on Jennings."

"There was?"

"Yes. In his mouth."

"Why do you look so upset? Was there no match?"

"There was."

"Are you going to tell me whose it is?"

"Give me a chance. You're so impatient."

You're so slow. "You're making me nervous with this stalling."

"The semen belongs to Donovan Vincent."

I felt like throwing up lunch. Vincent is a prominent business-man in Brewster County. He is wealthy and powerfully-connected, but I know him as a kind and generous man. Surely he wouldn't have killed Brad Jennings. He and my mom had been friends a long time. He held me as a baby! He'd made generous gifts to her non-profit clinic, and she says without his help to get it off the ground, her dream might never have happened.

"Margarita, are you all right?"

"I'm just shocked—that it would be him, I mean."

"We can't jump to conclusions on this," he said, but then he added, "I had the same reaction. I blurted, *are you sure?* to the lab guy who called me. That didn't win me any friends up there."

I stayed silent, hoping with my whole heart that my mom's friend hadn't committed that brutal murder. No. It couldn't be.

"Donovan was married many years to a woman," the sheriff con-tinued. "Who knew he was gay? Did you know that, Margarita?"

"No sir. I had no idea and he might not be."

"But his semen was—"

"I don't think that necessarily means he's gay. Some people go both ways."

"Really?" He looked so exasperated it made me laugh.

"I'm trying to keep you up-to-date, Sheriff Ben."

"You do realize the going-both-ways thing has been around a long time, don't you?"

"Yes sir; I do know that."

"I'm not as out-of-date as you think."

"I know that also, sir."

"I want you with me when I go interview Vincent. You know him, right?"

"Yes; I do. I thought I did. When do you want to go?"

"How about doing it right now?"

"But this is one of my only two days. How will I find out what's going on with Billy Jack and that Chaney creep if you keep giving me other things to do?"

"I'm sorry, but this takes precedence."

"I know; I just needed to whine a little."

"Are you over it?"

"Pretty much."

"Good. Do you have a uniform with you?"

"No sir."

"How about wearing that dress you wore this morning?"

"Are you sure?"

"I think you should let your girly girl out of the closet, Deputy Ricos."

* * *

We made a surprise attack on the Alpine office of Donovan Vincent. He was standing at his secretary's desk, so he couldn't claim not to be there. When he saw us, I had the feeling he'd been expecting us to come. I thought his expression was relief more than anything else. When good people do bad things they need to talk about it, but at the same time they don't want to.

There was none of the "What is this about?" bullcrap we are accustomed to. Mr. Vincent said, "Come on back to my office" after he hugged me and shook the sheriff's hand.

Sheriff Ben got us started by asking, "Don, why haven't you already spoken to us about your relationship with Bradley Jennings?"

"I can only imagine what you're thinking."

"First of all," the sheriff said, "it doesn't matter what we think. Secondly, we are not here to judge you. We want to find out who killed Mr. Jennings and that is all we want. The fact that you had a relationship and didn't come forward is suspicious. It puts you in a very bad light, Don."

When he didn't say anything, the sheriff added, "I pray you'll tell me you had nothing to do with it."

"Of course I didn't murder him!"

"We're waiting to hear what you have to say."

Don's hands were folded together on his desk. He stared at them without looking up. "I cared for Brad. He was a wonderful human being in every possible way. I would never have hurt him no matter what."

"You were with him on the night of his death."

He nodded. "He was distraught. He came to see me because he'd tried to go to a club in Odessa. You probably already know about that."

"What do you know about his visit to the club?" I asked.

"Nothing, except that he couldn't go in and it upset him. Also, he was stopped by a state trooper. That upsets anyone, but Brad was wearing women's things."

"Did the trooper treat him poorly?" I asked.

"No. He was kind. He could see how distraught Brad was and according to Brad, he tried to help him."

"He'd been telling everyone he wasn't ready for a relationship," the sheriff said. "Was that because he was having one with you?"

"No."

"Please elaborate."

"That night was the first time we did anything sexual, but I'd been attracted to Brad for a number of months. He put me off the way he did everyone else. And that wasn't something he just said; it was true he wasn't ready."

"What happened that night?"

"I tried to be a comfort and one thing led to another."

"Did you go to his home?"

Vincent stared at his hands. "No. He came to me at my place here in town."

"When was the last time you were in his house in Terlingua?"

"It's been a couple of weeks at least, maybe more."

"What was the reason for your visit?"

"I needed to go to Terlingua to look at some land. When I called Brad to say I was coming that way, he invited me to his home for dinner."

"Was everything all right with him?"

"Oh yes. He was getting along fine. He spoke mostly of his students and the school. Brad had a passion for teaching. Also, he loved Terlingua—its history, the scenery, and even the unconventional people."

"Do you have any idea who killed him?"

He hesitated a few seconds, and then he answered, "No."

"Mr. Vincent, is there something you aren't telling us?" I asked because I thought there was. I glanced over at the sheriff and would've bet he was thinking the same thing.

"No. I wouldn't do that. I want you to find out who killed Brad."

"Any little thing might help us do that," the sheriff said. "Please don't hold back even if you have an idea that seems wild."

Vincent's look was pure sadness, and he shook his head. "I know nothing."

"Did you ever know John Cooper?"

"John Cooper? Oh, you mean Brad's... No, I've only seen his photos. John Cooper is the man Brad couldn't get over."

"Did he speak about him?"

"Not often, but when he did, it was with much emotion."

"One thing we've wondered about," I said, "is whether someone killed Brad because they discovered he was gay."

"I hope that isn't true," Vincent said with tears in his eyes.

"That is what we hope as well," Sheriff Ben said. "Did Brad mention anyone making a pass at him or anything like that?"

"No, but he wouldn't necessarily have told me about that."

"Did he ever mention someone being angry with him or was there someone he didn't trust?"

"If there was, he didn't mention it to me."

Sheriff Ben stood and handed his card to Mr. Vincent. "Please call if you think of anything, no matter how trivial you may think it is." Then he offered his hand and they shook while Vincent promised he would.

"Does what you know have to be made public?" Vincent asked.

"Of course not," the sheriff responded, "Unless you murdered him."

"I didn't," he said softly.

I gave Don Vincent my card, but I doubted I would hear from him. Wealthy, powerful men call the sheriff, not a deputy.

* * *

After we got back in his truck, Sheriff Ben said, "See? That didn't take long."

I had the perfect witty comeback, but this was the sheriff, not Barney, so I had to be satisfied with giving him a look.

He plowed ahead. "What does Donovan Vincent know that he's not telling?"

"I don't know, but there's something."

"It might be something irrelevant that embarrasses him."

"Or he's trying to preserve his reputation as a straight guy."

"That's sad," the sheriff said. "Our society needs to accept people as they are and not how we assume they should be."

"I agree."

"We'll take another run at him later. So." He sucked in a deep breath. "You're all dressed up. I don't look too bad for an old guy. Whose day should we ruin now?"

"Billy Jack's," I responded.

He laughed. "You are surely my most stubborn deputy."

"If you don't want me to bust your nemesis, I could go home, put my feet up, and watch the entire last year's season of *Justified*."

"I'd rather you take your hard head and use it against my enemies. I do believe that in this case, it would be justified."

* * *

I took my hard head over to the county clerk's office to check their records. What I wanted was a list of the owners of the McFarley Ranch. It was no surprise to learn that it was owned by a corporation. I decided not to follow that trail yet. It would be lengthy and shadowy, and I didn't have much time. For my immediate purposes it didn't matter. Billy Jack would be in there somewhere but under what name was anybody's guess.

I was standing on the courthouse steps thinking about what to do next when I received a text from Manny Ricos, my cousin in high school. *Rita, I forgot something important about Mr. J,* it read.

Hey Manny! What? I responded.

Can you come by my house?

In Alpine now.

Later.

Can I send Barney?

Sure. Bye.

I called Barney but, before I could say anything, I had to hear his rant about getting mouth swabs from the women on our suspect list. "Not one of them wanted to cooperate," he griped, "except Flora Smith. She was great about it. Guess what?"

I could've guessed what, but he didn't let me guess. "Old Lady Jablonski and that old bag Iva Cooper refused. We'll need a court order for them."

"Hang 'em at first light!"

"This is not funny, Ricos."

"What about Vidalia Holder?"

"Buster convinced her to come in. He might be worth keeping on, Ricos. The older ladies love him."

"Poor Buster."

"Are you having any luck?"

"Not any worth mentioning."

"We heard you had lunch with the sheriff."

"Wow. News travels fast."

"You'd better believe it. Also, we know you ate breakfast with

William Jackson and you were wearing a dress."

"Did that blabbermouth tell you what I ate?"

"None of the blabbermouths care about what you eat, Ricos."

"Is there anything you don't already know about my day?"

"Other than breakfast, lunch, and Deputy Ricos in a dress, that's all I got."

"Do you know that Manny Ricos texted me?"

"Naw, I missed that."

"He thought of something he wants to tell us about Jennings. Will you please go by his house after school?"

"Sure; when are you coming back?"

"Tomorrow night or when I figure out what Jackson is doing, whichever comes first."

* * *

I refused to be teased and intimidated out of my beautiful dress and sexy shoes. Some people needed to grow up. My deputy side rolled her eyes and thought I should get on with the mission.

I went back to Amanda Mullen's office. She was not thrilled to hear I was there, but at least she didn't ask her secretary to turn me away.

"Did you locate Billy Jack?" she asked as I walked into her office.

"Yes, thanks."

"Do you feel better about his run for sheriff?"

"Yes, but I need to know the name of the man who works for him."

She gave me a blank look so I described Chaney and added, "I saw them together this morning."

"You may be talking about Bo Middleton."

"Is that who I described?"

"Yes."

"Are you familiar with the name Derrick Chaney?"

"No," she said, but she blushed so I figured she was lying.

"Where can I find Mr. Middleton?"

"You could inquire about him at Mr. Jackson's office."

"I will. Thanks."

I waited a few seconds in the hall by the door to the county judge's outer office.

"Julie," she yelled to her secretary. "Get BJ on the phone."

I assumed "BJ" was Billy Jack, smiled to myself, and moved on.

* * *

An old green truck I recognized as "Bo Middleton's" was parked in front of Jackson's office building. If I stormed in and busted the two of them together, what would that gain me? Besides, I wasn't dressed for storming. Waiting was not gaining me anything, either. I needed to go for a run and think about it, but my girly-girl getup wouldn't allow it.

The radio in the little nondescript car was tuned to the local country station. A man with a nice voice sang: "In the corner of my mind stands a jukebox. It's playing all my favorite memories. One by one they take me back to the days when you were mine, and I can't stop this jukebox in my mind." I couldn't think of the name of the group, but I liked the somewhat-corny old song.

I'd be grateful if a jukebox was all I had in my mind. In my corners I had men. One of them, lanky and blond, had been my husband. He was smart, sexy, and I was crazy about him. He was addicted to danger and it cost him his life.

The other man was also smart and sexy, with turquoise eyes a woman could fall into. He met his bloody death on the plaza in

Ojinaga. While he lived, his smile had melted my heart. If only he hadn't been so much like the moon: breathtaking, but I could only see one side of him.

These and other random thoughts popped in and out of my mind as I waited to see what was going to happen next.

Clint Black happened next, and then Merle Haggard with an old one from back in the day. The national news followed him but I tuned it out. I had enough negativity going on in my life. At some point I realized the music had returned, and a woman was claiming to be a redneck girl and proud of it. I clicked her off. Sometimes country music is good for what ails you, and it can be great for dancing and getting drunk, but sometimes it'll make you gag.

Derrick Chaney aka Bo Middleton aka his Birth Name came bounding down the short set of steps at the front of the building. I slid down in the seat. He stopped at his truck and glanced around but he missed me. Sheriff Ben was right about the white car. It was perfect.

Chaney was on the move with me tailing. He stopped at the bank drive-through while I waited on the street. Then he filled his truck using a credit card. I would have loved to know the name on that card, but it was most likely "William Jackson."

At last we headed west on Avenue E which becomes Highway 90 as you leave town. He picked up speed and I let a couple of vehicles get between us. It appeared we were going to Marfa, but that was wrong. We breezed through the little town and turned left on Highway 67 towards Presidio. What in the world?

I followed the bright green truck out of Marfa, through the Chinati Mountains, past the silver-mining ghost town of Shafter, all the way to Presidio. It's a scenic drive I usually enjoy (just more of the mind-blowing mountains of West Texas), but I prefer not to be tailing an asshole when I do it.

Although Ojinaga was a place I had not intended to visit again, it was where we were headed. Ahead of me were the Rio Grande and the International Bridge that connects Texas to Mexico.

Chaney drove on across, but I was forced to stop. I had to leave the car in the lot at the Customs and Border Protection office. I couldn't take my Beretta or the county vehicle into Mexico.

I thought about calling the sheriff, but what if he ordered me to return? I took a taxi into Ojinaga instead.

Chapter 30

I asked the taxi driver to drop me at the Motel Claudia because the prices there are reasonable. My room was plain to the point of severe, but it was clean. I set down my bag of next to nothing. I'd only brought what I already had with me when I started out that morning to spy on Billy Jack and Chaney.

I changed from my killer dress to jeans and set out to have a look at The Blue Bee. My body begged for a run, but what it got was more of a fast walk because of the jeans. A bench at a bus stop sat across from the place, so I took a seat to get my breath and think about my next move. With any luck I'd see Chaney, but that was not to be.

The Blue Bee started as a men's bar and grew up to be a brothel. If you don't know Mexico, you might not know that all bars used to be for men only. That is still true in some tiny pueblos, but in most of the larger ones you can find "Ladies' Bars." The name says they welcome women, and they're cleaner and tend to have dance floors and music.

At one time men's bars seemed enticing because of being off-limits. Tell me I can't go somewhere and I want to go. Double that if the only reason I can't go is because I'm female.

My papi killed my curiosity early-on by describing the bars. If I wanted to see men belch, slap and grab each other, and tell filthy jokes, I could hang out in the break room at the Brewster County Sheriff's Office in Alpine.

Not long ago, brothels, houses of prostitution, and sex shows were corralled in a part of Ojinaga gringos called Boys' Town. It was a red light district. Always seedy, the seediness had worsened over the last few years, and many places closed. As that happened, a few men's bars stepped up to fill the void. The Blue Bee is one of those.

When I think of Mexico, brothels and men's bars don't come to mind. Rather, I think of its best assets: music, food, tequila, and its gracious people.

A fine example of Mexico's Asset Numero Uno slid in next to me and smiled. He looked like a businessman and carried a briefcase. *"Buenas tardes."*

I returned the smile and the greeting.

He remarked on the beauty of the day, exclaiming that the weather was *"muy delicioso."* It was delicious all right.

We chatted, and in my imagination he asked me to go dancing. A bus came in reality and he hopped on it with a grin and a wave.

I told myself to get a grip, but it was not easy to sit in front of a men's bar and not think about men.

* * *

It was growing dark and I was unarmed in a bad part of town. When a man approached and asked if I worked "in there" I thought I should either call a taxi or go in and ask about the victims I felt sure were connected to the brothel. I didn't want to go in, but I also didn't want to end up as an "unidentified female" in a vacant lot.

My backside hadn't made it all the way into the room before a man behind a bar motioned me to come to him in a most urgent way. He was a short, stocky, attractive bad boy with scars on his face from a short boxing career. He wore his dark hair long on one side, but the other side of his head was shaved and decorated with an impressive tattoo of a colorful fighting cock.

His nickname is "El Gallo" but I don't know if the tattoo is because of the name or if it's the other way around. I know the man from dances, parties I shouldn't have attended, and other Ojinaga gatherings. His name is Hector and he runs The Blue Bee for whichever gangster currently owns it. They come and they go, but Hector remains.

"You can't be here," he hissed.

I pulled out the photos. "I need to ask you about—"

"If you want work, I'll need you to go in my office and strip down."

"The hell I will."

He laughed. "I guess you're not a pro."

"You're right. I'm looking for this man." I showed him the photo of the injured man found on Highway 118, the one who did the disappearing act.

Hector gaped at it. "What the hell did you do to him!?"

"I didn't hurt him, but someone did. Is he here?"

"His name is Ignacio and he works here."

"May I see him?"

"Will you pay?"

"Yes."

"Do you want him for sex?"

"If I pay, it shouldn't matter to you what I do with him."

"Women don't come in here. He goes to them. You've got some kind of balls on you coming in here. If I put my hand in your pants, what would I find?"

"If you put your hand in my pants, you'd find yourself with a broken jaw."

He stared at my face and his eyes narrowed. "Oh, I remember you now. You're Margarita-with-an-attitude."

I laughed. "Yes."

"You're a hell of a dancer though."

"Thanks. Listen; I really need to speak with Ignacio."

"I understand, but you can't be in here."

"You wouldn't put me out on the street, would you Hector?"

He looked me up and down. "You could make good money here, Margarita. It'd be more than whatever lame job you have now."

"That might be true, but I'll keep my lame job, thank you."

"You can't be here unless you work here."

"Could I please talk to Ignacio?"

"He's with a customer."

"May I have a soda while I wait?"

"You can't wait in here. And you can't drink a soda here. It's not decent and you'll make these guys nervous."

"Seeing a woman drink a soda makes men nervous?"

"OUT!"

That's the polite version of how I came to be standing on the sidewalk by the door of the place. The light of the sign spilled onto me and made me feel safer than standing in the dark, but who was I kidding? I was a woman under a red light with a blinking blue bee; I may as well have been walking the street in a miniskirt.

For five minutes I seethed about men and their messed-up double standards, but then I got bored and called Sheriff Ben. He was glad to hear from me. I admitted I was in Mexico and why, but I kept our conversation short. I couldn't tell him I'd been in a brothel or that I was now standing under their sign. So my answers were vague, probably not a surprise to our sheriff by now.

I explained my reason for following Chaney, which was that Chaney plus Jackson plus an injured man plus a dead woman plus the McFarley Ranch equaled serious crime. I had some of the puzzle pieces but no idea how they fit together until I had a few more. He grudgingly agreed.

"I'd tell you to carry on, but I'd rather you come home," he said towards the end of our conversation.

"I'll be back tomorrow."

His final words were, "Please stay in touch. Don't make me come looking for you in a foreign country, Margarita."

I ventured back into the forbidden zone and strode right up to the bar without looking around. My mandar (special man-sensing radar) felt eyes on me, but I was in a brothel, where I didn't belong for tons of reasons.

Hector looked up and his mouth opened. "You have to be the most hardheaded woman on the planet."

"I've been accused of that."

"Well? Get out!"

"Hector, you have got to get your priorities straightened around."

"In what way do you mean?"

"You think it would be okay for me to prostitute myself, but it's not okay to quietly drink a soda in here."

Hector leaned across the bar. "This. Is. A. Brothel. It's for men. Only. Why is that so hard for you to understand?"

"If you would let women come in, I bet you'd have a lot more men in here drinking, and you'd make way more money."

He threw up his hands. "Well, fuck me!"

His facial expression made me laugh. Then he scowled and the cursing increased in intensity. He scrawled something on a piece of paper and handed it to me. "Ignacio is at home. He can't work because he was injured. This is his address."

"You said he was with a client."

"That was before I decided to tell you the truth."

"Thank you." I wanted to show him the photo of the deceased woman, but I thought I'd pressed my luck enough for one day.

Hector grumbled all the way to the door and held it for me. "You want out the front or would you rather leave naked from the backdoor to my office?"

"I'll go out the front. You're a sweetheart, Hector."

"Stay out of brothels, Margarita," he called as I headed down the street.

I waved without turning around. Then I power-walked away from there.

* * *

Ignacio's apartment was dark and no one answered my pounding. I walked a few blocks, ducked into a café, and ordered hot tea and an empanada. Empanadas are similar to fried pies, but they're baked and have less sugar and more fruit stuffing. It was delicious so I ordered a second one. A woman has to have some kind of vices.

I asked about Ignacio but got a shrug from the waiter. He knew him but hadn't seen him. He suggested the plaza, of course. "Everyone goes to the plaza."

I had been coerced into Ojinaga by circumstance, but I was *not* going to the plaza to be forced to relive one of the worst times of my life. No way.

After my short break, I decided to go to the plaza. My mother calls it "putting on the big girl panties" but I call them my "law enforcement panties." Who cares what they're called? It's about doing what you have to; I'd known all along I would have to. But it would've been wrong to give in without a fight.

I whined to myself all the way there, which wasn't long because it wasn't far. The plaza was hopping because it was the plaza. It used to be a place I enjoyed being, from when I was a small child. A man I loved had been gunned down there, which changed my attitude towards it. All the sights, sounds, and smells had been so intoxicating. They still were, but I wasn't ready to admit that.

I looked around and there were so many men I couldn't tell if Ignacio was there or not. Lively mariachis were playing so I sat near them, closed my eyes, and let the music take me back to a time of innocence. Nothing bad ever happened there then because I was with my parents. The first time I can remember dancing it was with my papi at the plaza.

After a while I bought a bottle of water and a bag of still-warm popcorn. It was buttered, salted, and sprinkled with chili powder. It tasted scrumptious, and was spicy enough to raise a woman's core temperature, just like the men of Mexico.

Chapter 31

My cell phone woke me earlier than I wanted to be conscious.

"Are you alone?" was Barney's greeting.

"I think so."

"Maybe you should have a look around."

"You should stop playing my mother and tell me why you called."

"Your cousin gave us a lead."

"That's great. What did he say?"

"Jennings found out that some of the kids are messing around with meth and he went ballistic, according to Manny."

"That's bad."

"Well duh… Manny thinks it led to his murder."

"That is entirely possible."

"Manny seems like a kid who uses his head."

"He is."

"He thinks Mr. Jennings made an enemy of whoever supplied the kids with the drug and that's who killed him."

"Did he say who it was?"

"He doesn't know, but he gave me the names of a few kids who do. It'll be tricky getting them to talk. I think you should do it."

"I'm busy right now. I think you should call the sheriff and make a game plan that doesn't include me. What about Buster? He's closer to their age."

"He has no experience with this sort of thing."

"He has a good head and an innate sense about how and what to ask."

"Are you throwing me over for the green-eyed boy?"

"I wouldn't throw you over for anybody."

"I think you're starting to like me again, Ricos."

"Don't push your luck."

"Did you locate Running Man?"

"No. The guy who manages the brothel said he couldn't work because he was injured. He gave me his home address, but he wasn't there last night."

"Ricos, did you go in a brothel?"

"I had to. What other chance do I have of finding him?"

"Does Sheriff Ben know what you're doing?"

"Not to the letter, and you'd better not tell him. He doesn't need to know every detail. He wants results and I'm not leaving here until I have some."

"You might not leave there ever if you hang out in seedy places."

"The Blue Bee is not dangerous, Barney. Women aren't welcome, but they don't put us to death for walking in."

"You hope."

"A Mexican brothel is safer than a dive in the U.S."

"How do you figure?"

"Because not every man has a gun and is aching for a reason to use it."

"Oh. You do have a point there." He took a breath. "What are you going to do today?"

"I'm going to call my attorney friend Franco Orozco. If it's happening in Ojinaga he knows about it or can find out. Do you remember him?"

"Sure. We met him when we were looking for Jimmy Taggert. He's that gay lawyer who lives with good-looking what's-his-name. "

"Rudy."

"Right…Rudy. Do you think they're still together?"

"Yes, I know they are. They got married."

"In Mexico?"

"Sí."

"Is it legal there?"

"Yes. Isn't that weird? Mexico is far ahead of us on some things and behind us on others. Two people of the same sex can get married, but a woman in a bar freaks out everybody."

He laughed. "Did everybody freak out when you went in?"

"Yes, according to the bartender they did. He wanted me to go to work there, but he wouldn't serve me a soda."

"Ah, México."

"Ah, men."

* * *

Franco and I met for breakfast in a café near his office. It's a hole-in-the-wall, but the coffee is "American style" and served with cream. The food is so excellent I can't bear to think about it when I'm stuck in the United States.

I ordered chilaquiles, a food dreamed into existence by a goddess. It's a side dish often served with eggs, made from corn tortillas and red chili sauce similar to what's used on enchiladas. Chilaquiles can also be made with a green chili sauce, but I'm partial to the red.

I asked the waiter to skip the eggs and bring double the chilaquiles with a side of refried beans.

He looked at me as though I'd lost it. Maybe I had, but I know how to eat.

"Just bring her what she wants," Franco instructed our flustered server.

My friend is one of those gay men who make a straight girl's heart ache. But more important than the way he looks is that he's a good man.

"How is Rudy?" I asked, and his beautiful face lit up.

After we caught up with each other's lives in short-story form, I pulled out my photo of the injured Ignacio. "Do you know this man?"

He nodded. "His name is Chavarría. Ignacio Chavarría. You know I try to help the people others won't help, don't you?"

"Yes I sure do know that about you. Is he a client?"

"Yes, in a manner of speaking he is. Do you know what happened to him, Margarita?"

"I don't know any of the details, but he was found injured on Highway 118, not far from Terlingua."

"Oh. So he was near you?"

"Yes."

"He doesn't know where he was. He was drugged and woke up on what he assumes was a ranch in Texas."

"Was he trafficked?"

"It wasn't trafficking, or not in the usual sense. He had agreed to attend a party as entertainment, but he didn't know what he was getting into."

"Will you tell me what happened?"

"It would be better if he explained it to you."

"I've been trying to find him with no luck."

"He's frightened that he'll be hunted down because of what he knows. Let me see if I can talk him into seeing you."

"Please tell him I'll do everything I can to get justice for him."

"I will, but he has no faith in uniforms."

"I'm not wearing one."

"True, but you are 'the law.' He lived most of his life homeless and was abused by everybody, even the police. He knows all lawmen aren't bad, but he's slow to trust anyone. It will help that you're a woman."

I snapped my fingers. "I knew that would be an asset sooner or later."

Franco smiled. "I'd think that would be an asset all the time."

"It's not. Are there many women in law enforcement here?"

"No."

"That's part of the problem."

"Do you know that Ignacio is a prostitute?"

"Yes."

Franco looked surprised.

"Is he gay?" I asked.

"No. Well, that's a difficult question. Sex to him is not like it is to you and me. It's something he does for money with anybody who pays. But I think his preference is women. Does it matter?"

"No. I'm just curious about him."

"He's messed up, Margarita, but he's a human being with the rights of all other human beings. I know you believe that."

"Yes, I do or I wouldn't be in law enforcement."

"The things that happened to him in your country violated those rights."

"I know. That's why I'm here. I have another photo to show you, but it will be more difficult to see. The young woman in it is dead."

"Show it to me and get it over with."

I handed it to him. He said, "Ignacio told me she was killed, but I wasn't sure he knew that for a fact since he was given a large quantity of drugs. This is Luisa Losoya, and she worked at the same brothel as Ignacio. Where did you find her?"

"It's a long story, but she was dumped in a cave on a large ranch. Ignacio was found at one of their gates, so I thought the two were connected. Also, they both have a tattoo of a blue bee."

Franco was wide-eyed. "How do you even know about that?"

"I know a lot of things. I grew up around here. Sometimes I went places I wasn't supposed to go and met people I wasn't supposed to know."

He laughed. "Yeah, didn't we all?"

At that point, he tried to call Ignacio. There was no answer.

"Does he have a cell phone?" I asked.

"Yes."

"Will you text him and explain who I am and why I'm here? Also, please give him my cell number."

He did that. Within a few seconds, Ignacio returned a text in reply.

"You're smart for a policía," Franco commented.

"True," I agreed with a grin.

Franco wrote out an address and handed it to me. "He's been hiding out here off and on. Please proceed with caution, mi amiga. There's no telling what kind of place this is."

* * *

I went back to my motel via several clothing shops. Ojinaga has any clothes a woman could want, and oh, the shoes. I bought two pairs so hot they burned a hole in the bag on the way to my room. It was a shame I couldn't wear them where I was going, although I had no idea where I was going.

When I got into the taxi and told the young driver where I needed to go, he said, "Will you repeat that address?"

I did that and he was blunt. "No señorita. That's not right.

Someone has given you an incorrect address."

"Is it a brothel?"

"*Es un lugar donde se vende crack cocaína dura.*" It was a crack house.

I had a horrible sinking feeling.

"Some people never come out of there," he added.

"I understand, but I still need to go there."

"Señorita, it has become more of a place addicts go for *metanfetamina* than anything." He was talking about meth. *Holy hell.*

I knew the place would be bad, but there are degrees of badness. *I can't go in there,* was my gut reaction when I saw it. At one time it was a residence, but it now looked like the victim of a bombing. It stood in the shadow of a taller building, which made it appear even more sinister. The yard was so littered it seemed to be sprouting garbage instead of weeds.

The driver turned around in the seat. His eyes were wide and his tone pleading. "Señorita, I think you shouldn't go in. Please don't do this. You might be injured. You could be killed."

"I'm just going in to get somebody and coming back out." At the look on his face I added, "Should I call the police?"

"No. Your friend will be in trouble and you also, by association."

"Yes, I know how that goes." Guilt by association was another of my life's pervasive themes. Well, crap.

My driver scratched his head in thought. "If you must go in, you can't go like that."

"What do you mean?"

"You're too clean, too wholesome. They'll eat you alive."

"So I need to be dirty?"

"Yes, and desperate; you should look like an addict."

"I don't have time to get sores on my face and lose my teeth!"

"You misunderstand me, señorita. Used clothes would do the trick, and to dirty your hair and face. Then you have to fidget."

"How do you know?"

"I know because I see them."

"What is your name?"

"My name is Joaquin. I'm at your service, señorita."

"Thank you, Joaquin. My name is Margarita. I don't have time to find used clothes. I'll do better as myself anyway."

He didn't like it and issued a long, impassioned string of curses that was also half prayer.

"Listen, Joaquin."

He looked up expectantly.

"If I pay you double, will you wait here ten minutes?" At the look on his face, I changed my offer. "I'll pay you fifty dollars in American money."

He agreed to wait.

I got out of the taxi while I still had the courage to do it. If my papi knew I was going into this place…well, there was plenty he didn't know. What was one more thing?

The smell hit me before the visual. I've smelled some bad things but in some ways this was worse than putrefaction. These people were presumably still alive. My skin crawled. Then I opened the screen door.

In one large room that was littered with everything you can imagine, there were people of various ages passed out on the floor, smoking cigarettes, drinking tequila, snorting cocaine, talking, shouting, throwing up, slow dancing, mashing up little rocks of meth, snorting it, and pissing their pants. That was what I saw in seconds one, two, and three. In seconds four and five, I stepped across the threshold.

A hulking man grabbed me by the arm. "What do you want?"

I tried to keep the tremor out of my voice. "I'm looking for a friend. His name is Ignacio Chavarría. Do you know him?"

"Who wants to know?" The man looked like a dark-skinned version of Mr. Clean if you take away the clean.

"Is he here?"

"He might be, might not be."

"Please tell me the truth."

"Are you looking to buy?"

"No."

"*¡Vámonos!*" He grabbed me by both arms to throw me out.

I jerked away from him. "I'm not going anywhere without Señor Chavarría."

"Leave her alone," growled a younger, smaller guy sitting against the wall. He was so stoned he couldn't focus, but I gave him credit for trying.

Mr. Clean-minus-the-clean said, "Ignacio works at The Blue Bee."

"I was told he would be here."

"He had to leave."

"He was hiding from bad people. Do you know about that?"

"Oh sure, but I don't know who you are, your name I mean."

I didn't want to tell him.

After a few seconds, he seemed to forget he'd asked. "Ignacio was here an hour ago, but he had to leave." He grabbed his crotch. "People to fuck, you know."

"So he's at The Blue Bee?"

"That's what I said."

"Thank you." I backed towards the door. I didn't know if Ignacio had left, but things had gotten too real to stick around and search the place.

"Listen," Mr. Not Clean said in a spirit of friendly cooperation, "you can do me and I'll give you a couple of hits for free."

Free, my butt. That would be exorbitant. But never mind; that was one more thing not happening in this lifetime.

When my heel touched the threshold, I whirled and ran as hard as I could. Sometimes it pays not to wear sexy shoes.

I threw myself into the taxi yelling, "Go, go, go!"

Joaquin had already started the vehicle. We screeched from the curb into the street. "I guess your friend wasn't there," my new pal commented.

"He's gone over to The Blue Bee."

"That's a brothel. Señorita, I beg you. Don't go there. Men go for women who—"

"I know what a brothel is. Please take me to the plaza."

He heaved a sigh and crossed himself. *"Gracias a Dios."*

Chapter 32

As I sat taking in the sun-dappled cobblestones and quiet peacefulness of the plaza, I realized how much it's like the Rio Grande. For millions of years, the Rio flowed down from the mountains and on to the sea, doing its thing, not bothering anybody. Then a bunch of men came along squabbling over this and that, and they got the bright idea to make the river a border. "Don't touch my side!"

My point is that the Rio Grande doesn't know any of this. Human craziness, heartlessness, and ridiculousness are rampant on its banks, but it flows along without a care. The plaza is like that, too. What happened there could never be undone, but I could let it go in the same way the plaza had let go of it. With that thought, I gave myself permission to enjoy Mexico again.

My thoughts rambled all over, the way my thoughts tend to do. I was thinking about Mexico's Rio Conchos and the canyons it carved through the mountains, when I received a text. It was from a number that was not in my phone.

Where are you now? It read.

Who is this?

Ignacio

I'm at plaza. Will you join me?

No. Not there. Will you come to Restaurante Herrera?

On Chihuahua Hwy?

Sí.

Now?

Por favor.

Be there soon.

I took a taxi to the restaurant, went in, and was handed an envelope by a teen I knew to be Jose Herrera, Jr. My papi loves to eat at their restaurant, which is how I came to know the whole family.

I sat at a table for two, but when I read the note, realized I wouldn't be staying. It read: *I'm sorry. I thought I saw that man go by on the highway. I'm a nervous wreck. If you'll tell Sr. Orozco where you're staying, I'll call him and then I'll come to you. Thank you, Ms. Ricos.* He signed it, *Ignacio.* It was in English.

When I called Franco from the taxi, I mentioned that surprise. He said, "I failed to mention that Ignacio speaks, reads, and writes English. He's an American citizen. Do you think that's to his benefit?"

"I don't know. Either way, a crime was committed against him. I don't think it matters where he's from."

I gave Franco the info he needed, and he promised to pass it on.

* * *

Ignacio burst into the room when I opened the door. He was even more handsome conscious. Wow.

"I know you think I'm a coward," he exclaimed in English, "but I've been through hell." He still had fading, yellowish bruising around his neck and a small bandage on one side of his head where it had been shaved around the bullet injury.

"I'm Ignacio Chavarría." He offered his hand.

I took it. "I'm Margarita Ricos."

My stark room lacked places to sit, so I perched on the end of the bed. Ignacio plopped onto the hard, dowdy loveseat and improved its look one hundred percent.

"Ignacio, I don't think you're a coward. You're brave and strong to have survived what you did. I want you to tell me about it."

"That's why I'm here."

"May I record our conversation?"

"I'm a prostitute. Doesn't that bother you?"

"No. I'm a deputy sheriff in Texas. Does that bother you?"

He laughed. "No."

"Let's don't judge each other."

"Okay. That's good." He smiled. "You can record what I say. It's all true."

I got the recorder going and he blurted, "This guy offered me three thousand dollars for a weekend. I just…I just thought I could get ahead a little."

"Please start at the beginning. Who was this man? How did he find you? What kind of weekend? Tell me everything and try not to forget anything."

Ignacio put his head in his hands and when he didn't lift it, I realized he was crying.

I jumped off the bed and sat next to him. "Please don't cry. Everything is going to be all right."

He sobbed. "Are you angry?"

"No. I'm sorry if I sounded short. I'm too impatient sometimes."

"I'm so frightened. You weren't there. They were going to kill me, and they still plan to. And now I've put you in danger."

"Let's work on this together and then neither of us will be in danger."

"I wish I could believe that."

"Let me prove it to you. But first, I need to know everything you can tell me. Who was the man and how did he find you?"

Ignacio wiped his face. "I'm sorry to cry. It was awful."

"I know. I'm so sorry this happened to you."

"We knew each other through The Blue Bee."

"Because…?"

"He's one of those so-called hetero guys that 'enjoy something different from time to time.' He was okay, treated me fine. He was nothing to me but he never forgot me, it seems. He convinced Hector to call me, but I'm sure he had to pay him."

I nodded. No doubt.

"Hector gets his cut but, in fairness, he'd never have set me up with this deal if he'd had any idea what was going on."

"What was going on?"

"It was supposed to be a big party, and it was, but it got out of hand because of drugs. They started playing games, but then they brought out coke and meth. I can't mess around with that shit anymore."

"You were forced to take them?"

"Yes, but how do you know that?"

"They tested your blood at the hospital."

"The drugs weren't the worst of it." He stopped talking and looked away.

"What happened?"

"Can I speak frankly with you?"

"Yes, please do. I need to know the whole truth."

"A couple of guys were choking us. You know… It's supposed to intensify orgasm. It was just messing around at first, but then it wasn't funny. Or fun. They were doing meth and everything got more out of hand as the evening went along. Things turned mean. Have you ever done meth?"

"No. I never have."

"That shit will make you crazy."

"That's one reason I've never messed with it. Also, I like my teeth."

"Yes. I feel the same way."

"So they brought out meth and they became mean," I prompted him.

"Violent."

"Did you know where you were?"

"No, but after I got away from the house, I thought it was a ranch."

"You were found on the highway near a ranch gate. Do you remember that?"

"I don't remember a highway."

"You were in bad shape so I'm not surprised."

"The guy who hired me said he had a big spread near Alpine, and he and his associates were throwing a party for some important customers."

"Did the man give you his name?"

"Yes, but he never uses his real name."

"What name did he give you?"

"He calls himself Sam Houston, like I'm an idiot."

"He wouldn't be the first Texan named for Sam, but I know what you mean."

"He assumes I'm uneducated even though he knows I speak English. But nobody asks for me because I'm able to speak two languages." He smiled a sad smile.

"Please describe 'Sam' in as much detail as you can."

"He's in his forties. His hair is longish and brown. Every time I've seen him it was clean and tied back in a ponytail. My guess is he's two or three inches shorter than six feet."

"Okay. What else?"

"He's muscular—bulked up. I think he works out a lot. He has tattoos of dragons and naked women and fancy designs. There's one in his groin area. 'Big Daddy' is how it reads but he's only average.

For a man who thinks of himself as a big daddy, he has performance anxiety you wouldn't believe. He likes to—"

"You're giving me too much information. I don't plan to see him naked. I just need to know how to recognize him when I see him."

"Of course. Sorry."

"I think you're describing a man who is also known as Derrick Chaney. That's probably not his real name, either."

"You know him?"

"No, but I've been trying to prove that he and the man he works for are not who they want people to think they are."

"They're sons-of-bitches, and they murdered Luisa."

"Luisa went with you to the party?"

"Yes. They offered the job to both of us."

"You saw them kill her?"

"No, but I saw Sam and another guy move her body. That was when I realized they were going to kill both of us because of everything we knew."

"How did you get away?"

"I was in bed with Sam. When he went into the bathroom, I crawled out the window. I didn't even know where I was, but I couldn't stay there."

"How did you get shot?"

"Sam came after me on an ATV. I was following a dirt road because I figured it would go somewhere, but I guess it was stupid because it made me easy to find."

"That was smart. Otherwise you might have gotten lost and died there."

"He shot at me but I had the advantage of darkness. The bullet only grazed me. I hid behind some boulders. I could see Sam because of the headlights. I hit him as hard as I could with a rock. He jumped off and staggered around and I took off. I stayed near the road but not on it, and he never caught up to me again. But now he's here and I know he's going to kill me."

"You've seen him?"

"Yes. There's no doubt."

"When was the last time you saw him?"

"It was right after I got back here. But he returned yesterday. I didn't see him, but he came into the Bee looking for me. Hector told him I hadn't come back from the U.S., but I doubt if he believed him."

"Yesterday I followed Sam here."

"How did you know he would come to Ojinaga?"

"I didn't, but I was tailing him because I know he's up to something."

"Has he done other bad things?"

"Yes. I believe so. What else can you tell me? What about the other people at the party? Did you hear any names?"

"I don't remember. I don't think anybody was using their real names."

"Do you think they're selling meth or just using it?"

"They're making it!"

"They're cooking meth on the ranch? You're sure?"

"Oh my God, you aren't paying attention! They want me dead because I know about it. I saw it!"

"Okay. Try to stay calm."

He collapsed onto the loveseat. "I'm sorry."

"It's all right, Ignacio. I understand how upset you must be."

"Unless you've had some bald bastard's fancy hatband around your neck, I really don't think you do."

"Did the bald bastard have a name?" I thought it was "Billy Jack," but it would be unprofessional to put the name in a witness's head.

"Yes, he has one, but I don't know it. I thought I was going to die." He leaned his head against the loveseat and sighed.

"Let's take a break. I could call the desk to bring us sodas."

He waved the idea away. "No thanks. I want to get this over with."

"I need to show you a photo, but it's not pleasant. According to Señor Orozco, it's Luisa."

"You found her body?"

"I helped bring it from a cave."

Tears stood in his eyes. "Please don't show me a photo of a dead person. Please don't. I'm freaked out enough." He bolted off the loveseat and began to pace. "Oh, fuck. Fuck. Fuck. Fuck." He went to the window, pulled back the curtain, and looked out onto the street.

"Get away from the window!"

He jumped back and began pacing again. "You're saying they left Luisa in a *cave?* Those heartless sons-a-bitches!" He stopped and stared at me. "Are you going to get these bastards?"

"Yes."

He plopped down next to me. "How do you know?"

"I know because I'm not going to quit until I get them."

"Nobody will give a shit about a dead Mexican prostitute."

"How about having a little faith? Murder is against the law."

"We're disposable and you know it."

"Nobody is disposable to me and or to my sheriff, or I wouldn't be here. Stop trying to depress me. I need to be able to think, and I need your help."

"I'll look at that photo if you still want me to."

"I'm sorry you have to look at it, but I need to know for sure if it's Luisa."

He took it from me and looked at it in stages. Sometimes I forget that most people don't see dead bodies. Of course it's ten times worse when you knew the person and cared about them.

Ignacio handed the photo back to me. "It's her." He began to cry again.

"I'm so sorry."

"She was only eighteen."

"How old are you?"

"I'm twenty-two."

"Does Luisa have family?"

"No. I guess I was her family. She went to work at The Bee and I was trying to get her out of there. That's no kind of life."

* * *

Hector looked up when I walked in that afternoon and I wish you could have seen the look on his face. He threw up his hands. "I do *not* believe this!"

"Don't flip out, Hector. I've come to tell you something important."

"Do you have a thing for me or what?"

"No."

"You sure? 'Cause I got the cure right here."

"As seductive as your hospitality is and all, it's not about that. I need to speak with you in private."

"Will you get naked?"

"Please be serious."

"I am serious."

"This is important and affects your business."

"Miguel!" he yelled, and a man came from the back. "Watch the bar while I speak with the señorita."

He nodded and took over for Hector. We went into the office. I was prepared to defend myself, but my rough companion turned into a gentleman. Well, that is if you don't hold his bad boy language against him.

"What the fuck is going on?"

"I'm here on behalf of Ignacio. I've put him into a safe house."

"What the fuck does that mean?"

"He's in a secret place where he'll be safe until I can locate the people who want him dead."

"You're fucking with my head!"

"No. I'm not."

"Well, fuck me! Is he in Ojinaga?"

"He's in Mexico."

"Does anybody else know where the fuck he is?"

"Yes. The police know. If you need to talk to him you can go through them, but they aren't going to tell you where he is."

"Ha ha! The police! Ha ha!" He didn't intend to go to them any more than I intended to get naked in his office.

"He won't be gone long, Hector."

"What the hell am I supposed to do until you release him? Huh?" He glared at me. "I have a great idea; you can fill in for him."

"We both know that isn't going to happen."

"What if I keep you here against your will?"

"Is that how you want this to go?" I have a scary glare, too.

He backed off. "No. I knew it was a 'no' when you wouldn't get naked with me."

I laughed and got out of there.

* * *

"I'm back in the USA, Sheriff Ben." I had just gotten into the white car.

"Thank God. How did it go?"

"I found out what I came to find out."

"That's excellent."

"You aren't going to believe it."

"I have some news you aren't going to believe, either."

"Is it good news?"

"Yes; for a change, it is."

"Should I come to your office?"

"Posthaste."

"Does that mean I should speed?"

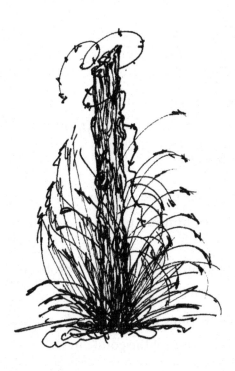

Chapter 33

Sheriff Ben's great news was, "We have a new judge."

"What happened?"

"Samuels resigned."

"That's excellent. Do Barney and Buster know?"

"Not yet."

"Do you think the new judge will be more cooperative with us?"

"I don't see how he could be worse than the last one."

"Have you met him?"

"Yes; now let's talk about that later. I have one more piece of news and then I want to hear what you've learned. The murder of the Presidio woman turned out not to be a case of human trafficking."

"Who murdered her?"

"Her boyfriend killed her while she was visiting from Mexico."

"How awful. How did you find out?"

"Lennon Camacho called to inform me, but he asked me to pass the information on to you."

"Thanks."

"He asked for your phone number."

"You didn't give him my personal cell phone number, did you?"

The sheriff reddened. "Yes. Is there a problem?"

My face flamed in a dead giveaway. "No, sheriff."

"I shouldn't have done that. I'm sorry."

"It's all right. He's one of the good guys."

"Oh, there's one more thing you should know. Tamara Hagan's sister has been located. She's in New Mexico visiting with a friend and has been for a month. I guess Ms. Hagan forgot she was going."

"That's not surprising given her mental state."

"She's undergoing a competency evaluation as we speak."

"I think she's going to fail that."

"I believe you're correct. Now, I want you to tell me everything you learned in Mexico."

I told him how I'd located Ignacio by going to my friend Franco. The sheriff had heard me speak of him before, so he knew who I was talking about. I left out the parts about the brothel and Hector and the crack house and Mr. Not-so-Clean. After that I played the recording of Ignacio's testimony. I had to play it again because the sheriff was so stunned. Then we listened a third time.

At first Sheriff Ben just stared at me. Did he say, *Thank you, Margarita* or *You were right all along, Margarita* or *Way to go?* No. He said, "We don't have proof of anything. We have the word of a prostitute who uses drugs. I can't see how this changes anything."

I couldn't believe it.

He held up a hand. "Don't be angry. I know you went to a lot of trouble to get this information. It's not that I don't believe the young man. The problem is that what I believe is useless. We need proof."

"We could get a warrant and bust them for the drugs at least."

"We can't get a warrant based on this."

"They're making meth and Ignacio saw it!"

"A drug-crazed Mexican prostitute claims they are."

"He doesn't use drugs, Sheriff. They were forced on him at the party. They shot him! They killed his friend Luisa Losoya."

"Losoya was found dead on the McFarley Ranch, but that doesn't prove they killed her. It's suspicious, but we have no proof. We have to have solid proof."

"Ignacio is a living witness. He speaks English, Sheriff. He's not some scabby, in-and-out-of-reality meth addict. Also, he's an American citizen."

"How did he end up in Mexico?"

"That doesn't matter! What matters is that he saw what's happening and they tried to kill him because of it. He described Chaney. I had just followed Chaney to Ojinaga. Before that, I followed him to the McFarley Ranch. We know Chaney and Jackson are connected, and they're doing something shady. How many coincidences do you think there can be involving one man? I thought you didn't accept coincidence in law enforcement work." I was about to cry from the frustration of it.

"Okay, let's say we could get a warrant. Don't you think they've already moved their lab by now? If someone saw them and lived to tell about it, they would've done that first thing."

It took every scrap of my resolve to not sob and scream. I knew one thing. I *promised* myself one thing. As soon as I could get away from the sheriff I was going to drink myself into a coma.

As I sat there listening to my boss doing nothing, the disheartened words of Ignacio came to mind: "Oh, fuck. Fuck. Fuck. Fuck."

* * *

It was a toss-up. Should I try to get "proof" or go to a bar? The bar was winning until I got a phone call I never expected.

"Margarita, I want to talk to you." It was Donovan Vincent. "Please come now if you can. I'm at my house. I need to tell you everything."

* * *

Mr. Vincent was tearful when he came to the door. Also, he was drinking bourbon. It smelled like everything I ever wanted for just one second. He offered me one and, strangely enough, I didn't want it. I put off taking the first drink in the only way that ever works for me: by thinking *I can do that later if I really want to.* Later would become tomorrow, tomorrow would turn into next week, and so on. I knew in my gut it needed to be never.

"I've done something terrible," Don said when we sat in his study. "It's a long story."

"That's all right. I have as much time as you need."

"You precious girl." He gazed at me with a goofy, adoring look. "It pains me to change your opinion of me, but this is too heavy a burden to carry any longer."

I was afraid he was going to confess to the murder of Brad Jennings, but that wasn't it.

"For a year or so, I've been attending wild parties."

My heart took a leap into my throat.

He continued. "I was surprised to be invited, but I was because I…I move in the same circle as these people."

"I understand."

"We're successful people with money, and we tell ourselves we deserve to cut loose now and then. We drink expensive liquor, eat expensive foods, and experiment with various drugs. And prostitutes. Prostitutes are there. Women and men. Are you getting the picture?"

"Yes sir." I was about to launch myself into space with the sheer energy of squelched anticipation. *Just say the name. Say the name.*

"It was all fun and games until last week or maybe a bit longer than a week."

"What happened?"

"Everything was the same as usual, but someone suggested trying meth. I didn't want to because I've heard too much about it. Supposedly the sex is great, but it can be addictive from the start. Did you know that?"

"Yes. I know that."

"I refused, but it was no big deal to anybody. The big deal happened later in the party when things got twisted. Somebody suggested choking the...the prostitutes...to improve the sex or whatever. They used a hatband on one and a scarf on the other. I complained that it was too dangerous, but they laughed at me. Both prostitutes were gagging and I couldn't see how it could be any fun for them."

"What happened then?"

"I left. I left, but I understand one of them died that night. It was the young woman. That's what was rumored to me, but I'm not sure if it's true." He hesitated and then pressed on. "You know how it is in a small town. After a while, I heard that you and a Texas Ranger had gone onto the ranch to bring out the dead body of an unidentified female. Is that true?"

"Yes."

"Then you know I'm talking about the McFarley Ranch."

I reminded myself to breathe. "Yes. It was the McFarley Ranch. Someone had dumped her body in a cave on a remote section of the ranch."

"I'm so sorry, Margarita. I'm sorry I ever agreed to go to those parties."

I didn't say anything because it wasn't my place to forgive him. I thought he would be sorry about it for the rest of his life.

"There's more," he said, "and it's about Brad. I think someone from the ranch killed him or had him killed. He found out about the meth and he went to them."

"How did he find out?"

"One of his students told him. The boy was afraid for his friends. He somehow discovered how they got it and the trail led, by a winding route, to the McFarley Ranch. It was naïve of Brad to go there, but he was hell on wheels when it came to his kids."

Holy crap.

"Mr. Vincent, I should ask the sheriff to come here. He needs to hear this."

"I know. I almost called Ben myself, but I was too ashamed. I don't know why I thought it would be easier to tell you. Maybe it's because he's closer to my age. I can't stand to see his disapproving look."

I knew the look.

"Go ahead and call him," he said. "Let's get it over with."

* * *

The sheriff and I were back in his office. Donovan Vincent had repeated his story to Sheriff Ben and made a list of names. This will be no surprise by now, but Billy Jack was on it. Amanda Mullen and her husband were on it. And oh-my-god, Judge Samuels was on it. A man Don called Everett Spelding was on it, but the person he described was Derrick Chaney/Sam Houston/Bo Middleton. "Spelding arranged the prostitutes." "He arranged everything." "He was the go-to guy."

When prodded by the sheriff, Mr. Vincent admitted he'd been threatened by Spelding. If he told what had happened, he would be exposed and his reputation ruined. People would know he'd used prostitutes and that he preferred men. They thought that would keep him in line.

"Sheriff, do you know what aggravates me the most?"

He gave me a questioning look.

"*Now* you want a warrant. *Now* the whole fantastical story is believable. You're taking the word of Donovan Vincent because he's a wealthy, respected man you know. To you, Ignacio is just a drugged whore. I'm having a hard time reconciling this with the man I know as you, Sheriff Ben."

He was red in the face but I figured, what was the worst that could happen? He could fire me. That was no sweat for a girl like me; I had a standing job offer at The Blue Bee. The thought made me want to laugh and throw up at the same time.

"It probably seems like a double standard to you, but—"

"It *is* a double standard. Don't try to call it something else." I glared at him. "I want you to come with me and meet Ignacio."

"I saw Ignacio."

"You didn't see him conscious, Sheriff. He has a believable presence. Maybe you don't approve of his work, but at least he's who he is. He's not some creep hiding behind his money pretending to be something he's not."

"Everybody has vices, Margarita."

"Yes, and if you're wealthy you get away with them."

"Nobody is getting away with anything."

"No, they're not now because a rich white guy is willing to testify."

"You're being unfair."

"You should think about it, Sheriff." Then I thought I should shut it before I lost my job. I'd never make it at The Bee. At least the old guy was finally moving on this and some justice would be done.

As we parted, the sheriff said, "Be here in the morning at 10:00 and we'll get the warrants. You can meet the new judge."

"Did you have something to do with Judge Samuels' resignation?"

"When you tell me the truth about your Ojinaga trip, I'll tell you the whole story about the judge."

"What makes you think I haven't told you the truth?"

"You were there too long. You either have a boyfriend in Mexico, or you put a lot of work into getting what you got. I know it wasn't as simple as the way you tell it. I wasn't born yesterday, Margarita. Also, I've worked with you enough to know that you leave things out."

Busted.

* * *

Texas weather is schizophrenic. Just because it's warmish one day doesn't mean the next day will follow suit. It was cold again and a strong wind buffeted my Mustang all the way home.

I sat on my porch anyway and stared at Cimarron Mountain in the dark. Maybe I needed a vacation. In some exotic place. Where it was warm. With a beach. And a lot of men. Men who could dance. Men who couldn't talk. Instead of a bunch of yada, yada, yada, there would be kissing and they would be damn good at it. Yeah.

My phone rang and when I saw it was the sheriff, I almost didn't answer.

"Hello Sheriff," I made myself say instead of *what the hell do you want?*

"Margarita, I was thinking about what you said. In thinking about it, I realized how much work you have done on this. I never thanked you for that and so I called to thank you."

"You're welcome, sir."

"I was cross and short with you when you returned from Ojinaga. The truth is I'm in trouble and I can't think about anything else."

"What sort of trouble?"

"Deep trouble. I punched Judge Samuels, Margarita. I walloped him so hard it knocked him down. I'm sure to receive some sort of disciplinary action."

"I can't believe it." *But yay!* "How did it happen?"

"I met with him about the way he treated you. I know what you said, but it's unacceptable on every level. I knew I couldn't live with myself another day if I didn't do something. I asked him to resign, and I told him the fact that he'd said something so out of line to you was proof he needed to retire."

"What did he say?"

"I won't repeat those words to you, but he accused me of being jealous and of having my hands on you...and other things. Then he said you took your clothes off in his chambers and begged him and well, I lost it."

"Thank you for defending me."

"I don't care if I lose my job. It was worth it. Now it'll be more than his word against yours."

"Thank you. I don't know what else to say."

"We'll talk more tomorrow. Good night."

"Good night, Sheriff Ben."

Men. They're full of surprises.

Chapter 34

Before I left for Alpine, I got my run in. It felt so good I was tearful about it. As I sucked in the frigid air, it cleared my mind; I felt awake and alive. The dark and cold didn't bother me because I was dressed for it. I ran hard to the top of the sandstone bluffs near my house, where I feel like Queen of Everything and Cimarron looms next to me, the longstanding keeper of my dreams.

I raised my arms high above my head in a joyous salute to the bright sky, to the coal-colored shapes of mountains, to the miles of desert below me, to Mexico and the Rio Grande to my right, and Big Bend National Park to my left and in front of me, and to Texas everywhere I looked.

"Good morning, my loves!" I yelled. The canyons and ridges on Cimarron bounced my voice back in an echoed greeting of their own.

"Good morning!" a man answered from below me. "I love you, too!"

I forget people live in Tres Outlaws Canyon at the bottom of the bluffs. A car started. Then the guy who'd made me smile drove away.

I sat at the edge of the sandstone monoliths and thought about the crimes of the privileged. Men could hire prostitutes but turn up their noses at them as human beings. I didn't get it and was trying hard to understand. The cold seeping through my sweatpants didn't want me to get it, or not right then. I had to get moving before I understood anything—if I ever would.

As I jogged down the steep path to the dirt road that led home, the sun began its slow rise behind the eastern mountains. Just the thought of it shining above the land warmed me from head to toe.

I mulled over what I did understand. It was this: Bradley Jennings, Ignacio Chavarría, and Louisa Losoya deserved justice. Whether they would get it or not was up to the court. My job was to bring evidence to the judge.

* * *

It was disheartening that our new judge was another old man. He had a great smile, though. He was a Latino named Enrique Torres but was called "Henry," except of course, by deputies and others of low rank. The entire time we were there he didn't snarl, curse, yell, or ask me to get naked. So I took that as a good sign. Maybe Henry and I would get along fine.

Donovan Vincent came with us to give his testimony to the judge. Based on what we told Judge Torres and what Vincent said, he gave us a search warrant for the entire McFarley Ranch. He was "considering" warrants for the homes and persons of all the party participants named on "the list." Those warrants would be issued depending upon the outcome of the ranch search.

The sheriff and I had a private huddle. We thought those warrants should come first so physical evidence wouldn't be destroyed. The sheriff pressed the judge and instead of yelling, he said, "Give me ten minutes to think about it."

We spent the ten minutes in the hallway outside his chambers. I don't know about the sheriff, but I was making fervent pleas to the God of Lawmen Everywhere. *Please make him do the right thing. I've worked my butt off. You need to help us.*

Who knows if anyone or anything was listening, but Judge Torres issued the warrants. He decided we were correct; evidence would be destroyed if we waited. He held back the ranch warrant pending the outcome of those.

Donovan Vincent was accompanied home by a deputy who would stay with him until the sheriff called him off. This was so Vincent couldn't alert anyone about what was coming. Sometimes people give things away without meaning to. I thought the sheriff was sharper than I gave him credit for.

Amanda Mullin, her husband, and all the other suspects were brought in separately, but all at the same time and by surprise attack. This took every deputy the sheriff had at his command, including Barney and Buster. It also took the help of Texas Ranger Josh Middleton and another Ranger who was "just standing around," according to our sheriff. Of course it was Beautiful Dimpled Man because… I don't know why. Perhaps the God of Lawmen Everywhere was just showing off her wicked sense of humor. Naturally, I saw him. He smiled and winked, and my face blazed.

The sheriff assigned officers to each culprit and we headed out. A few of us had partners. Barney and Buster went together to get Chaney because the sheriff thought he'd be armed and dangerous. The two Texas Rangers went after our former judge together even though he'd been weakened by a "hard fall." A meth addiction had been the old grump's downfall and the possible reason for his outlandish behavior. Since it increased the chances of him being violent, two tough hombres went to bring him in.

Sheriff Ben decided to go for Billy Jack himself and thought I should go with him so there would be no "hard falls." I laughed at that because our sheriff is not a violent man—unless he is cornered or pushed. I also reminded him that no matter how you cut it, this would be a hard fall for the would-be hero of Brewster County.

"Damned right," he growled.

We discussed a sort of game plan, but we both knew we'd be playing it by ear because nothing goes as planned when the law comes for the accused.

Billy Jack was in his office on the phone. We blew past his open-mouthed secretary without a word to her. He gaped at us, and then said into the phone, "I'll have to get back to you on that."

Jackson was wearing his "Billy Jack" costume, except for the hat.

It was sitting on his desk *with the hatband.* The sheriff ordered him to stand and turn around.

"Why would I do that?" the still-arrogant man asked with so much insolence it was hard not to smack him.

"Because I'm the sheriff of Brewster County, and I'm arresting you for murder, Mr. Jackson."

"Murder?" he bellowed. "I haven't murdered anybody!"

"And for the reckless endangerment of the life of Ignacio Chavarría," the sheriff added, unperturbed by Jackson's song and dance.

"I don't even know who that is."

"He remembers you," I said, causing the sheriff to miss a beat and frown.

He continued, "You're also under arrest for the manufacture and distribution of methamphetamines. That part, we'll leave to the DEA and the Texas Rangers."

"You don't have proof of anything."

His comment was met with silence. That works faster than anything on people accused of something.

Jackson kept sputtering about his innocence and demanded to know on what grounds he was being accused, and yada, yada, yada. There was a telling gleam of sweat on his bald head and he had the wild-eyed look of a cornered animal. We were wary because cornered animals and people are dangerous.

Sheriff Ben was about to lead Jackson from behind his desk when Derrick Chaney of many-other-names fame strolled into the room as if he owned the world. For a split second, what was happening failed to compute in his brain. When it registered, he pivoted and ran.

"Stop!" the sheriff and I yelled in unison with zero effect.

I took off after Chaney. He made it out the front door before I jumped on his back. It was a slick move but I lost my Beretta. That was bad, and it didn't bring him crashing down in quite the way I imagined. I only slowed him.

It might have looked like a comedy sketch to somebody watching, but it was deadly serious. He was a sturdy sort but I was as determined as he was built like a bull. I pounded his head, yanked his ears, and tried to poke him in the eyes. He would've thrown me in a short time but two things happened: Barney and Buster. They seemed to come out of thin air with their pistols drawn.

"Hands up right now," Barney roared in the intimidating voice of a six-and-a half-foot man.

Chaney glanced around but he saw the futility of fighting us. He had a huge armed deputy facing him, a less large but serious-looking one with a pistol he was aiming to use, and a little one beating him about the head and shoulders. His hands came up slowly, and I slid off his back and picked up my weapon.

"Thanks," I said to my partners, and I was sincere about it. I was minutes away from being injured by a desperado.

"We were following him," Buster explained without needing to.

Sheriff Ben yelled from the door, motioned us inside, and disappeared again.

"Let's go," Barney ordered. He cuffed and guided Chaney up the three steps and into the building. When the big ol' lug "guides" a person, they move along whether they want to or not.

Inside, Jackson was ranting about making a deal. Everything was Chaney's fault. As soon as he heard it, Chaney screamed, "Liar!" and tried to run at him, but Barney had a firm grip and all his effort was wasted.

My partner looked over at me and winked. I wanted to hug him.

* * *

In a nutshell, the two men blamed and condemned each other and told us even more than we knew going in. All of the guilty confessed, more or less, to what they'd been a part of. Most had attorneys, but they gave it up anyway, against the legal advice they were paying for. There were a whole lot of people in Brewster County with heavy consciences, making for a remarkable day in law enforcement.

The thing that cratered Jackson was his "Billy Jack" hatband. I asked to see it. He wanted to know why.

"I need it for the crime lab. Ignacio Chavarría's skin cells will be on it and will prove that you tried to strangle him with it."

"We have a warrant," the sheriff reminded him, "and can take it from you."

Jackson blanched, but he wasn't ready to give up. "A Mexican prostitute's word will never hold up in court over mine."

"You might want to think that through." I let him listen to the tape at this part:

"It's all right, Ignacio. I understand how upset you must be."

"Unless you've had some bald bastard's fancy hatband around your neck, I really don't think you do."

"Did the bald bastard have a name?"

"Yes, he has one, but I don't know it. I thought I was going to die."

"You were the only bald bastard at the party," I said.

He handed me the hatband and blurted a full confession.

Thank you, God of Lawmen Everywhere.

* * *

I left my Mustang in the Sheriff's Office lot and rode home with Barney and Buster. We were high on seeing justice coming for people who deserved it. The only thing dampening our party was the Bradley Jennings murder. That killer was still in the wind, so to speak.

At the end of the day, we thought Donovan Vincent was wrong. The culprits at the McFarley Ranch had not killed Jennings. Their reaction was the kind of surprise that's hard to fake. And they were angry that one of their "reps" had spilled the beans to anyone, and "especially a teacher, for the love of Christ." Jackson and Chaney had a screaming match about Chaney's poor choice of personnel. It was humorous and tragic at the same time.

In addition to a still-unsolved murder, we had kids messing around with meth. One thing at a time, I reminded myself.

We had more work to do but, as Barney pointed out, "We have to enjoy success when we experience it because there will always be terrible things going on."

As with the little turtle crossing the road, we could only help with some of them. Living with that is not easy, which is why nobody parties like law enforcement.

It was the wee hours of the morning when we got back to Terlingua, so nothing was open. We decided to party later because my house had no liquor, Buster's was too small, and Barney's was full of his sleeping family.

When the guys let me out at my Sheriff's Office truck, I said, "Come for breakfast tomorrow. I mean later today. Around noon. After we eat, we'll go arrest the murderer of Brad Jennings."

"Ricos get a grip. How in the hell will we figure that out at breakfast?"

"Just come. I'll make waffles and explain what I think."

"Oh no," Buster groaned, making us laugh.

"I'm coming for the waffles," Barney said.

As the door closed, I heard Buster say, "Maybe she's putting magic in them."

If only.

Chapter 33

Bright sunlight awakened me at nine and a cool, clear day was calling my name. I gathered what I needed to make waffles, made a mug of blueberry-flavored tea, and sat on my porch to savor it. The world was brilliant, the sky blue, and the clouds missing. The mountains were present and accounted for, lying around in their desert, showing off.

All I know about the weather is that in Texas it answers to no one. A warming trend was underway again. In March it tends to do a cold again-warm again thing until it relents and the thermostat goes to "broil," usually sometime in May. Of course that is subject to change, any and every day and through every season.

Cimarron Mountain made me wish I could paint. It's made up of a hundred shades of brown no human could reproduce anyway— from red-brown to serious brown, and all shades in-between. It all depends on the light, the atmosphere, the clouds or lack of them, the time of day, and its mood. No two days are alike.

I knew who had killed Brad Jennings and why. In some ways, I had known it all along, but I'd let other people talk me out of it. Heck, I'd almost talked myself out of it. About the time I was ready to give my thoughts to the sheriff, McCann made his false confession and I roared off after Jackson and Chaney.

Dena Jablonski had admitted to the sheriff that she kissed the bathroom mirror. In tears, she told him she was in love with Brad, but he had no feelings like that for her. In fact, he seemed to dislike her. *Imagine that,* I had responded, *a gay man disliking a snarling bigot like Jablonski. Will wonders never cease?*

That the mirror was later dripping with blood was a fact not known by Ms. J. She was also another suspect who appeared to have no clue about the missing genitals.

Before my breakfast guests arrived, I called the safe house in Mexico and asked the person in charge to have Ignacio call me. As a precaution, they kept all cell phones so that fatal mistakes weren't made by the people they were trying to protect. The woman said she would take him his phone and ask him to call.

I also told her the threats against Ignacio had been removed. She gasped as if I'd admitted to killing them.

Before five minutes passed, Ignacio called. "Is it true, Margarita?"

"It's true. Sam Houston is in jail and so is the bald bastard."

He whooped. His next words, "Will they stay there?"

"There is a chance they'll get bail, but killing you will not be on their minds. What would it accomplish now? They'll wear ankle monitors that tell where they are, so they won't be able to go to Mexico. Ultimately they'll go to prison, along with the other people who participated in the party and the choking of you and Luisa."

"Thank you, Margarita. Thank you so much. I don't know what else to say."

"You're welcome. When the time comes for the trial, I hope you'll be willing to come and testify in person. I'll come and get you."

"Okay."

"The recording is great, but being there in person to give details and answer questions will make it a slam dunk."

"Of course I'll come. Should I wear a suit? I look respectable in a suit."

"Yes, that'd be perfect, but I bet you look great in everything."

"You should see me in nothing. Sorry. That was overboard. I forget that you're not..." Three second pause. "Margarita, seriously, if you ever want to have sex of the kind that's all about you and what *you* want, you know where to find me. It will be free for you any time you say. That's pretty much all I've got to offer you."

"Thank you, Ignacio."

"I wish you everything good."

"Thank you. I wish the same to you."

"Don't forget my offer."

"I won't." How would I? Who doesn't want sex like that?

* * *

"We should do this more often," Buster said with his mouth full of waffle.

"We could, but I don't want to be the only cook," I said.

"I make the world's best blueberry pancakes," Barney claimed. "We could meet at my house next time."

"That sounds good," I said. "What do you make, Buster?"

"A mess."

It was all jokes and laughter until Barney said: "Ricos, out with it. Tell us what's on your mind."

"You know, we can arrest somebody because we suspect them of murder and hold them 72 hours before charging them. So I was thinking—"

"We need some kind of proof," Barney interrupted.

"We only need to have legitimate suspicion. To quote something I remember from the law enforcement academy, 'An arrest requires articulable probable cause to believe a crime has occurred and that the person arrested committed the crime.' We have that in a big way."

"I hope you aren't going to say—"

"Iva Cooper," I said.

"Yep! That's the name." Barney frowned. "No way did she do it."

"Please have the courtesy to hear me out, Pard."

"Well, if you're gonna be so polite about it..."

"Brad Jennings was bludgeoned to death and his genitals were hacked off. You have to think about that, Barney. That says he offended someone with them. What other reason is there to do that?"

"I can't think of one."

"It's one thing to be angry with a person, but to cut off the offending parts is a telling act. Miss Cooper is the only puzzle piece who was offended in that way. If it had been the druggies of the McFarley Ranch, they might have beaten him to death, but his penis didn't offend them."

"Okay, we're following," Barney said, "I think."

"If one of the macho men from Terlingua had found out Brad was gay and killed him... I know that wasn't it. Brad would've had to make an overt pass at one of them and he wasn't making passes at anyone. He was heartbroken.

"Also, he wasn't stupid. He hid his homosexuality from Prying Eyes Jablonski. He was good at hiding it to the point that most of the single ladies of Terlingua were still after him at the time he died."

"Go on," Barney said.

"To understand, you have to look at the Brad/Bailey relationship from Miss Cooper's point of view. A gay man took her beloved Bailey away from her. She might have also killed a woman who did that. It's hard to say and doesn't matter. The fact that Bailey fell in love with a man was a double whammy."

"If what you say is true, Ricos, how are we going to prove it was her?"

"She's going to tell us."

"Are we going to beat it out of her or what?"

"No. Of course not."

"How then?"

"She's a sad, lonely old woman. She's at the end of her life and all she had was Bailey. Once Bailey was gone, she was left alone with her simmering outrage at Brad. How dare he?

"By the time she stomped down off her hill, the anger was eating her alive. She was close to blinded by it, and then, there stood Brad in a dress. Can you imagine how reprehensible that would be to her? 'What balls this queer has!' So she beat him to a pulp and took those balls. Am I upsetting you, Buster?" He had paled.

"No. No, it's just…it's weird to hear you talk this way."

"I'm sorry, but I'm speaking what I think is the truth in the only way I know how to say it."

"Let's assume all you've said is true, and it does kind of make sense," Barney conceded, "we still have the problem of proof."

"Iva is going to admit it to me."

"Why would she?"

"I'm going to give her the opportunity to gloat."

Barney threw up his huge hands. "Holy shit! And you think that'll work?"

"I know it will. She's a nosy old busybody who loves to talk. She's lonely. She's had no one to tell and by now she's about to burst."

"What if your plan doesn't work?" Buster asked.

"Do you have a better one?"

"I don't have anything."

"Then how about having a little bit of faith in your partner?"

He shrugged. "Okay. Let's see whatcha got."

"Barney?"

"I'm in. The sheriff might yell until we're deaf, but at least he can't say we sit on our asses."

"He's in a pretty good mood with Jackson off the ballot," I pointed out. "We should do this before somebody else challenges him."

"Let's do it then and see what happens."

* * *

On the way to Miss Cooper's house, I laid out my game plan. I thought my partners should wait in the vehicle and let me go in alone. They agreed to that until we were sitting in front of her house.

"Oh God, Ricos. Are you sure?"

"All three of us together will be too intimidating. Besides, let me do the woman-to-woman thing."

"Doesn't she dislike you?"

"Yes, but she's going to see a different side of me today."

"If she killed Brad Jennings, she's a cold-blooded, brutal murderer. What if she goes for your throat or shoots you?"

"She has no reason to kill me. It took a long time of resenting her brother's lover before she came to killing him. Most of the time she's a sad, lonely old woman."

"You hope."

"I'm betting on it."

"How will we know if you need us?"

"I'll scream it on the radio. Also, she's going to know you guys are waiting for me. I'm going to point you out, so be sure to wave at her when I do."

Barney let out a long breath. "Lawdhavemercy. Let's just do this thing."

I went to the door and knocked.

Miss Cooper did not seem excited to see me.

"Good afternoon, Miss Cooper. Do you remember me? I'm Deputy Ricos."

"I've told you everything I know."

"That's not true, so please don't insult my intelligence. Do you see my fellow deputies out there in the truck?" I pointed them out and they waved just as I'd asked. I almost laughed.

"What about them?"

"They want to storm in here, handcuff you, and take you to jail."

"Whatever for?"

"May I come in?"

"The door's open."

I stepped in and shut it. My heart was flopping like a blown-out tire at high speed.

"I suppose you want to sit, or are you going to cuff me?"

I sat. For the record, all of the photos were back, for whatever that was worth.

"Miss Cooper, I'm forced by law to record our conversation, so I want you to say you understand that." That was not true, but I could use a recorded admission of guilt to get a search warrant. I hoped.

"That's fine. I have nothing important to say to you."

"I want to tell you I understand how difficult it must have been seeing your bright, handsome brother fall in love with a gay man."

"You don't know anything about Bailey."

"I know a lot about him. I've read his love letters to Brad. He was a romantic, your Bailey."

Miss Cooper looked devastated.

"I also have the wedding rings the two men exchanged."

She looked ready to blow, but all she said was, "What does this have to do with me?"

"Your attitude caused them to leave you out of their life, didn't it?"

"That pervert made Bailey queer!"

"You got even with him, didn't you?"

"He didn't like it when I moved onto this hill above him. I made him nervous."

"He knew you wanted to kill him, didn't he?"

"I did want to. I wanted to kill him from the first time I saw them together. But I don't kill people, Miss Deputy Whoever. I only thought about it."

"Yes, you thought about it. Then you broke into Brad's house while he was at school and you discovered the dresses and shoes and other feminine things in sizes that would fit a man, not a woman."

"I house sat for him."

"You never did. Brad would never have asked you."

She shrugged.

"Brad had a lot of friends and he had women bringing him food, and here you sat all alone with no one to care about you. Brad even took Bailey from you."

Miss Cooper jumped up. "He did! That pervert ruined my life and Bailey's."

"He loved Bailey and Bailey loved him and that made you crazy. Do you want to know what I think happened?"

"I don't give a rat's rear end what you think."

"I think you'd seethed until you were boiling over. You went to confront Brad, but he wasn't home."

"I wanted him to give me Bailey's things."

"You waited for him. I bet you were sitting in the dark living room. He came in during the wee hours of the morning, wearing a dress, and you lost it. You followed him into his bedroom and grabbed the first thing you saw and hit him with it. It only stunned him, but he went down and you didn't quit. Your smoldering resentment over all those years kept you beating and beating on him until he was dead."

She plastered her hands over her ears. "Shut up!"

"Then you removed Brad's clothing, jewelry, his shoes, everything. You cut off his penis because seeing it offended you."

"Shut up! Shut up!"

"You burned everything out back for two reasons."

"Shut your damn trap!"

"Number one, the clothes he was wearing were bloody. Two, you didn't want anyone to know Brad had those things. Before the night was over, you burned or removed everything like that from his house because you knew the law would come. You thought Brad's feminine things would reflect poorly on your brother."

"It was Bailey's house, too!"

"Yes, but when Bailey died, everything of his went to Brad."

"That was wrong."

"That was what Bailey wanted."

At that point, the old gal reared back and let her crazy out. "I have his goddamned penis! All right? Are you satisfied? If you want it, I'll give it to you. It's in a bag inside a box in the freezer. If you're born with a penis, you should not wear dresses. It's common decency."

While she went to the freezer, I went to the front door and motioned my partners inside. To her I said, "Miss Cooper, you'd better grab a jacket."

"What for?"

"Deputy George and Deputy Mayhew are going to handcuff you and recite your rights."

"You're going to arrest me even though I have a reasonable explanation?"

"Yes ma'am," Barney said.

"Miss Cooper, why did you write 'sorry' on the bathroom